10630976

In the Shadow
of the
Peacock

GRACE EDWARDS-YEARWOOD

In the Shadow of the Peacock

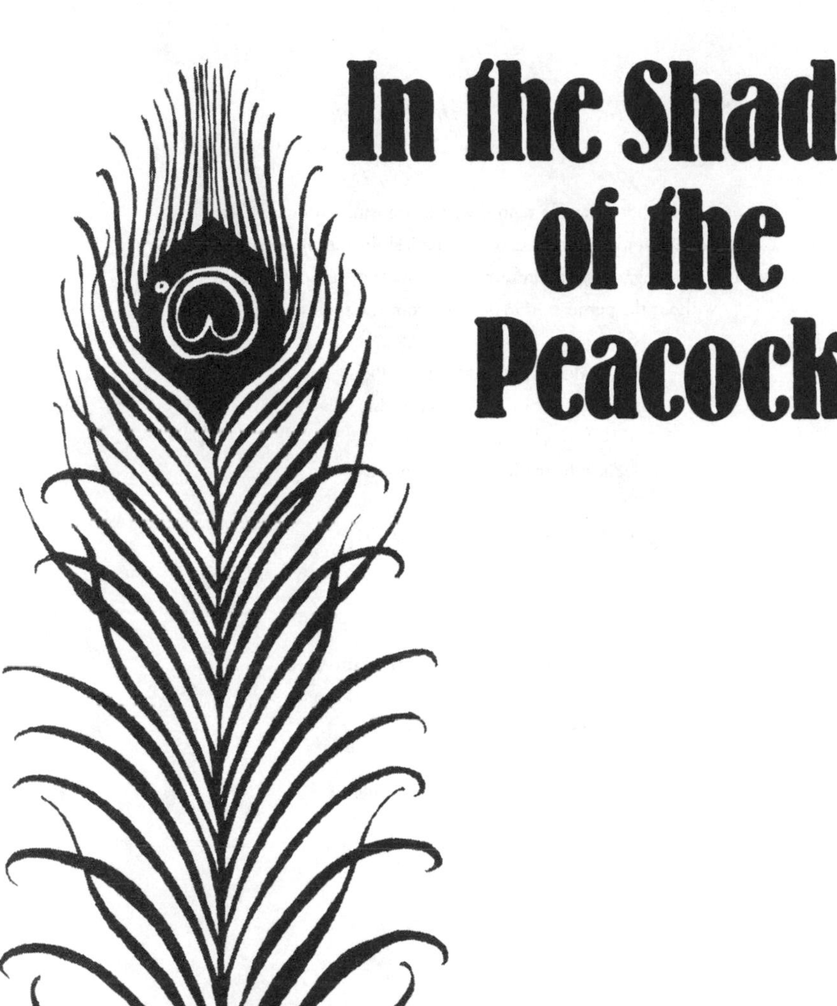

THE HARLEM WRITERS GUILD PRESS
Literary Excellence Since 1950
San Jose New York Lincoln Shanghai

In the Shadow of the Peacock

THE HARLEM WRITERS GUILD PRESS
an imprint of iUniverse.com, Inc.

For information please contact:
iUniverse.com, Inc.
620 North 48th Street, Suite 201
Lincoln, NE 68504-3467
www.iuniverse.com

Originally published by McGraw Hill

ISBN: 0-595-12940-4

Printed in the United States of America

To my daughter, Perri,
and to the members of the
Harlem Writers Guild.

ACKNOWLEDGMENTS

I want to thank the members of the Harlem Writers' Guild, particularly Bill Williams-Forde, Louise Meriwether, Walter Dean Myers, and Donis Ford, for their support and encouragement. I also thank my five brothers for giving me the rhythm of my language.

In the Shadow of the Peacock

Prologue

Harlem 1943

Frieda heard the sound and ignored it. When she heard it again, she opened the window and leaned out. The noise had come from the direction of the avenue and was faint, barely distinguishable from the other, ordinary, night summer sounds. She strained for a better view but, as usual, was blocked by the fire escape.

She listened intently for the sound of a motorcade. Perhaps it was another Negro Freedom rally organized by Paul Robeson, or it might be Mayor LaGuardia again, touring Harlem as he had done a few weeks ago with the Liberian president. But those motorcades always came up Seventh Avenue and this sound, this noise, was different.

Directly below, she noticed that the loungers had given up top positions on the stoop, and strollers, in frozen attitudes, appeared to be listening for some extraordinary signal. Across the street, flowered, striped, and gauzy curtains were torn aside and windows were suddenly filled with wide-eyed, frightened faces.

She thought of climbing outside but wondered what Noel would say if he came in and found her on the fire escape in her condition. The thought was broken again by the sound, no longer an undercurrent but elevated high on the hot night wind.

It was heavy and pulsating, a roar rolling before the measured tread of an army on the march. It poured up the avenue, preceding the mob by several minutes. It engulfed the strollers and loungers, sucked them in and swelled the dimensions of the sound and the mob.

Fragments:

"Whut?? Whut happened, man?"

"Cop kill a Gee-Eye...outside the Braddock!"

"Naw!!"

"If I'm lyin', I'm flyin'."

It happened in Chicago, Texas, and Alabama, where a colored man in uniform, momentarily confused by the heady breath of patriotism, might forget himself and then pay for the lapse. But this was New York. Harlem. Where there was safety in collective anger.

"Mmm...uhm! Cats gon' raise some hell tonight, betcha that!!"

At first the bricks connected only with the streetlights and glass rained down in darkness. All but invisible, the mob, a solid sea of blackness, surged up the wide avenue. Their familiar badges of mops and brooms now transformed into torches that winked dangerously in the blackness. Then came the sound of heavy glass. Storefront glass. Pawnshop glass.

Frieda listened, thought of Noel, and left the window where she had crouched.

"Don't let nuthin' happen to him...don't let him be in the middle of this, whatever it is..."

She had abandoned prayer as comfort years ago, but her mouth moved anyway as she made her way down the stairs. At the bottom of the landing, she paused, breathing heavily, and realized that she had not run this fast in a long time. She sat on the third step from the bottom, feeling her breath leave and enter, leave and enter in fitful bursts, burning her nostrils and drying her mouth.

...calm...calm...quiet...don't...don't get too excited...not now, not now...

The lobby door swung open and she recognized Sam and Dan as they slipped out of the darkness of the street into the dim hallway. They moved toward the steps, huge, handsome young men burdened with the weight of several large cartons. Despite their size, they had the quick, quiet grace of street cats. They stopped when they saw her.

"Frieda! Outside ain't no place for you. Not tonight anyway!"

Sam turned to his twin. "Where this girl think she goin'?"

"He's right, Frieda. Things is jumpin' off out there..." said Dan as he surveyed the dim hallway for a place to stash his take. It was going to be a long night and he didn't plan to make more than one trip up four flights, no matter how much he stole.

The only available space was the shallow alcove behind the stairs. Anything placed there would be visible from the lobby, easy pickings for any common thief who had no respect for another person's hard labor.

"Hell with it," he sighed, turning again to Frieda. "Looka here now, you can't go outside. Not in your condition..." Frieda instinctively put her hand to her swollen stomach.

"Dan...I didn't mean...what's goin' on...you seen Noel?"

"Ain't seen nobody 'cept wall-to-wall busted heads. The bulls is swingin' and we swingin' right back..."

"But why? What happened...?"

"Gee-Eye took a bullet," said Dan as he started up the stairs, "right here on his own turf. Didn't even git overseas and he a casualty. And they don't be dealin' no purple hearts for the Braddock."

Frieda was surprised. The Braddock restaurant had always been a lively, crowded place where people waited hours to taste Miss Beryl's West Indian cooking, but there had never been any trouble.

"Listen," said Dan, pausing as he passed her, "don't go out there. Them people'll run right over you, pregnant or not. You won't stand a chance..."

"Besides," said Sam, "we goin' back out. Give us a list. We'll git anything you want...."

Frieda, silent, stared toward the door with wide eyes, trying, all at once, to absorb what she had just heard, and listening for some new sound.

"Girl, stop worryin'. Noel, he all right. Now look, you place your order while the gittin's good. We deliver. No money down and no monthly payments. Not even a slight installation charge.

You name it, you got it—basins, bowls, basinettes, bottles, brooms, everything and anything for the pretty little mama..."

His sales pitch was interrupted by a howling scream outside which caused the three of them to recoil.

A woman was running, crying. "Help me git 'im to the hospital. His hand is nearly off!! Help me...!!"

"Who tol' 'im to put his fist through the goddamn window in the first place," someone yelled back. "Everybody else usin' garbage cans and this nigger wanna play King Kong. Oughtta bleed to death on gee-pee. Come on...but dammit, don't bleed all over my car!!"

The screaming continued down the block in a long, unbroken wail. Sam shook his head and started up the stairs after his brother. At the top, he leaned over the railing. "Don't you worry 'bout Noel. He all right. You just sit tight. Things is too hot out there. Just sit tight."

As soon as their footsteps faded, Frieda opened the door. The streets had gone from wartime brownout to total darkness. Only the lights from the hallways sliced the night at measured intervals. Broken glass covered every inch of sidewalk, and runners, heading for the avenue, performed strange arabesques as they slid and skated in and out of the dim yellow pools.

She left the stoop. Where was she going? Suppose Noel came from another direction....no...he always came this way...from the avenue...I know...I know...

She stayed near the buildings, clinging to the handrails as she crept along. The roar by now had become so sustained that she felt it had always been there, as part of the background. Except for the futile howl of a burglar alarm and an occasional scream louder than the rest, the noise reminded her of the waterfall back home in the south.

She remembered a night like this. A different kind of mob running wild. Heavy, sweating faces staring down the barrel of a shotgun. Retreating, retreating...

She shook her head....calm...calm...once I see Noel...calm...calm...

At the corner, two men carrying a huge orange sofa blocked her way. "You be careful out here, little girl..." They maneuvered their cargo around her with a series of grunts and groans and were gone. A woman followed in their wake with a portable sewing machine balanced delicately on her head. Graceful as a ballerina, she stepped lightly over the shards of glass and disappeared in the dark.

Eighth Avenue was devastated. Windows were smashed and locks and gates were bent into intricate curlicues. Broken furniture spilled from discarded cartons, and headless mannequins, stripped of clothing, lay amid the debris, their stark plaster limbs spread at impossibly obscene angles.

Frieda crept past Johnson's meat market and Clark's grocery store, two places where she shopped every chance she got because the mysteriously abundant displays of food reassured her and she didn't have to think about the war and shortages and red and blue ration stamps. Now, both places, side by side, appeared to have been sucked out by a giant vacuum. Even the refrigeration systems had been destroyed.

...how could this happen...they say somebody shot a soldier... what did he do...is he dead...what could've happened to cause all this...

She concentrated on the devastation to keep from thinking about Noel, but that was impossible. Somehow the two were intermixed. She felt cold standing there trying to think and not think.

The siren clanging above the roar distracted her and she saw, four blocks away, the faint glow as it spread in the dark, small at first, then seconds later, leaping in long orange tongues up the side of the building from the store below, bursting windows and buckling frames.

Frieda could hear the screams from where she stood. The tide, which had been flowing away from the wreckage, stopped in wonder. "Who the hell set that fire?? Don't they know there's people upstairs over that store? Who set the fire??"

The question shot out of the darkness, and the tide reversed itself. People began to run toward the building, careless of the glassy pavement, as the screams of the trapped rose above the roar.

Frieda was overcome with confusion, and the terror which had crept up her back by inches now immobilized her.

"What's goin' on?? What's goin' on??"

There was no answer as the mob pressed in. That is, she heard no distinct answer. Only the hollow scream that rolled out of the darkness as she was swept like flotsam into the tide that enveloped her.

A few blocks away, the "A" train pulled into the 145th Street station and Noel was asleep as usual. He slept with his head thrown back, but the rest of his six-foot frame was curled into itself protectively.

Al glanced at him. He did not understand how Noel could have accustomed himself so quickly to the fast pace of the city and, worst of all, the grinding noise of the subway.

Damn, he thought, dude in the city less than a year and he cattin' like he born here. Probably sleep right on through a Jap attack…

He poked Noel lightly with his elbow. "Rise and shine, man. This is it."

Noel was awake, instantly alert although his eyes retained a sleepy, languid look. He rose from his seat and suppressed an urge to stretch. Several women in the crowded car looked up from knitting and newspapers and put a smile on the edge of their lips just in case he glanced their way. But Noel was too tired to notice. He yawned and waited impatiently for the train to stop.

"Tell me somethin'" Al said, "what you gonna do when I catch my digit and quit this job? You liable to ride all the way up to the yards some nights…"

"You can hit the number all you want to," Noel replied, "but you ain't quittin' this job. This the most and steadiest money you seen in your life."

"That's only 'cause of the war," Al said as they made their way to the door with the crowd, "only 'cause of the war. And how long can it last? Six months? A year at most? Sam got a B-24 rollin' off the assembly line every hour. What them Japs got? They just a dot in some ocean nobody never heard of. How long can they last? This war could be over tomorrow, then what? Where we gonna be? Worse off than ever, that's where.…They singin' that stuff 'bout 'praise the lord, pass the ammunition and we'll stay free' don't mean us, you know."

They headed for the exit, both feeling the weight of the twelve-hour, six-day work shift. Noel only half listened as Al spoke. He was too tired to argue.

He thought: That's what happens when a man been catchin' hell too long. He never forget it. Then again, he ain't supposed to...keep 'im prepared for whatever comes up...but hell, he ain't the only one seen a bad time...

He knew what was coming and with effort tried to rechannel his thoughts. He had promised himself, once he and Frieda had gotten safely away, that he would live only in the now and think only of the future. But sometimes, in that hour of the night when the mind exercises the least control over the body, Noel would waken out of a deep sleep, bolt upright in the bed, arms and legs twitching frightfully as he saw the flames, smelled the terrible odor, and tried to close his ears to the screaming that never stopped.

Sometimes, Frieda would wake him. And they would wrap themselves into each other, silently, and remain like that until dawn.

...I'm tired, he thought, I'm just tired, that's all. Got enough grit on me to weigh a ton. Nobody'd believe that Navy Yard could be so dirty. They don't show that on them posters. A slip of the lip might sink a ship. Pitch in for democracy. Shit. They hired the women, old men, even the crippled folks, then they hire us. Give us the dirtiest jobs left over and swear to God they doin' us a favor. Ah, hell with 'em. Right now, the first thing I'm gonna do when I git home is hit the tub. Nice...warm...let Frieda rub my back a little.

But it wasn't his back that was bothering him. He relaxed, slackening his pace as he imagined the touch of her hands, soft and gentle, on his back, neck, and shoulders and, finally, sliding between his thighs in the warm, soapy water.

...sure be glad when the baby finally git here, awh, Jesus...

"Hey Noel! Man, you sailin' 'long like you in a trance," said Al, "bet you didn't hear a word I said. If I'd a known the dream was that good, I'd a left you on the train. Didn't mean to disturb you."

"Naw, man, naw. It ain't like that. Just thinking..." said Noel. He did not remember coming through the turnstile or passing the change booth. They had come to the stairs, and he was surprised to find the exit blocked, jammed with people.

"What's goin' on?" yelled Al, "come on, let's move. I'm tired and wanna git home..."

Al was short and powerfully built and had a scar near his ear which he had never spoken of to Noel. They had both arrived in the city on the same bus a little less than a year ago and wound up working on the same job and living in the same building.

Noel seemed quiet and easygoing, and it puzzled Al when he noticed that Noel never smiled and never talked about home, wherever that was. But, on reflection, he realized that he himself said very little.

"Come on," Al yelled again, "what's goin' on up there?"

"We trottin' fast as we can," someone shot back, "keep your drawers on, for chrissakes."

Outside, on the avenue, they stared in open-mouthed surprise.

"What the hell happened?"

"Look like the japs got us..."

"Man, where in hell alla these people come from...?"

"...and lookit all that smoke..."

They heard the story on the run—in distorted, disjointed chapters.

"...they say she wasn't nuthin' but a trick..."

"So what? That don't give no wop cop no right to be beatin' on her..."

"Braddock'll never be the same..."

"Sho' won't. They done crisped the joint..."

"...poor Miss Beryl...work so hard..."

"Heard the Gee-Eye come from uptown. Ex-Jolly Stomper..."

"Good God amighty. No wonder he so bad..."

"Took that cop's billy an' made 'im eat it. Them uptown cats 'bout the baddes' things on two feet..."

"He still alive? Heard he took three bullets..."

"In Sydenham, they say..."

"Naw, took the cop to Sydenham. The Gee-Eye up at Harlem..."

"Hell...make it to Harlem breathin', he make it all the way. They say 'what come in, if it's still squawkin', guaranteed it'll go out walkin'."

The crowd flowed in all directions, its members imagining in the dark confusion that anyone or anything flowing against them was a mortal enemy. The thick, wet smell and taste of blood was in the air and on the tongue.

"Hell gon' pay tonight..."

Al and Noel were out of breath when they approached the burning building. The heat radiated out and over the scene. Fire engines and yards of tangled hose cluttered the area. The crowd, uncontrolled by the few police still present, milled around the blaze. The flames had reached the third floor, and one by one the windows bulged from the intense heat, burst outward, and sprayed shards of hot glass on the crowd below. The people retreated momentarily, regrouped, and surged in again.

Noel pulled at Al's sleeve. "I'm cuttin' out man...wanna see 'bout Frieda."

He turned and nearly fell over the small boy standing directly behind him.

"Jim-Boy!"

"Please, Mistuh Noel..." The rest was lost in the uproar.

Noel crouched down, gathering the child in his arms. "Whut you doin' out here in all this mess??"

For answer, the boy clung to Noel so tightly that Noel could feel, almost hear, the wild beating of the child's heart.

Jim-Boy and Noel had a special friendship, begun last summer, when Noel had retrieved a ball thrown wild. "Better be careful with that traffic, sonny," Noel said, "them cars don't stop on a dime, you know..."

"—name ain't Sonny, it's Jonrobert but Granma call me Jim-Boy..."

"Well, it don't matter who calls you what, you go after that ball and traffic catch you the wrong way, you won't have no name at all, understand?"

Every evening after that, Jim-Boy sat on the stoop and waited, his small, round face dark and expressionless except for the lemon-yellow mark above his eyelid. When Noel appeared, Jim-Boy smiled, waved, and disappeared into the house. The house was now on fire.

"Where's your mama?"

"She down south, but Grandma...she...she..."

"Where's your grandma—"

The boy was pointing to the top floor. "—in'er wheelchair..."

Noel could not bring himself to look at the building. He concentrated on the boy's shaking finger instead and fought the urge to run, to push Jim-Boy away from him and run, screaming, from this nightmare.

...here it is all over again, he thought. All over again. He wanted to rock back on his heels and laugh and shout and demand of God how something like this could happen twice in the lifetime of one man.

But the crowd milled around him, pressing him in the awkward crouching position. He felt the boy's heart beating against his own and, unbidden, the nightmare memory flashed in, obliterating present sight and sound. He heard his father's cry, strange and strangled behind the sheet of flame.

...curse all you...curse all your...children's children...and the cursing dissolving into a screaming, gurgling sound, then nothing save the crackling flames. And he, unobserved, creeping upon that scene too late, not knowing it was his own father until one of the mob laughed.

...this'll teach 'im...this'll teach 'im. Wavin' that shotgun... Now. We gotta git that no count nigger gal..."

That no count nigger gal. Frieda.

The yellow flames tore at the body against the tree, until the man no longer looked like a man and even the tree turned a dull crimson in the dark.

...daddy...daddy...daddy...He had shut his eyes to keep from screaming, and the flames leaped orange against his closed lids.

...daddy...daddy...daddy...

"Noel!! For God's sake, you okay? You gonna squeeze the life outta that kid!" Al's hand shook him, and Noel blinked Jim-Boy back into focus.

"Your grandma—she in there and you ain't said nuthin'...?"

"But I did, I did...oh!...I tol' 'em..." The child pointed to the firemen and his voice, drained by fright, sank to a whisper.

Noel felt the constriction in his own voice and spoke rapidly. "Now listen, boy. You sure nobody got her out..."

"She's still there, Mistuh Noel, I know she is..."

"Top floor?"

"Top floor...near the roof. Sometimes I go play on the roof but Grandma don't like it. She like for me to be in the street where she can watch me...but the roof..."

"How you git down—"

"Over the roof...I tol' you—"

Al followed Noel as he pushed his way through the crowd.

"What you gonna do, man? You can't do nuthin'...come back!"

Noel reached the core of the crowd, and a fireman working the pump yelled, "Keep outta the way!"

"There's a woman up there!" Noel shouted, "on the top floor!"

"No there ain't," another fireman replied. "They're all out. Out stealin'..."

The firemen's laughter was heavy and their movements, though coordinated from years of routine, were extremely slow. Noel was perplexed. Then he realized that they were all drunk. Without another thought, he left the crowd, skipped over the scattered hose, and raced into the adjoining building.

"Where you goin', you crazy nigger??" yelled another fireman at Noel's retreating figure.

Al, who had been behind Noel, grabbed the man by his throat and lifted him off the ground. "Who you callin' nigger, motherfucker?"

His arm shot out like a piston and the fireman went down under the blows. The crowd had heard the word, and the roar reached a deafening level as the people surged forward. The remaining firemen grabbed hatchets, pikes, and picks and crowded together in a tight circle to defend themselves. The few policemen at the scene joined the firemen.

"Get back! Back, or we open fire!"

The order came from a red-faced sergeant, frightened into sobriety and frightened beyond reason.

Inside was black with smoke. Noel reached the third floor, smashed a rear window, and leaned out. On the fifth floor, he tripped over some debris and lost his footing. He went down and continued on his hands and knees until he reached the roof.

The two buildings were separated by a brick hedgelike barrier three feet high. He swung his legs over and the tar stuck to his shoes as he moved.

"Stairway's out," he said aloud to himself, surprised by the calm in his voice. "She watched him on the street, so she gotta be in the front..."

The smoke was thick and smelled of old rugs. He could not see in front of him but knew that he had reached the edge when he felt the sharp rise under his foot. The railing leading down the fire escape was warm. As he descended, the metal felt hotter. The entire right side of the building was now enveloped, and the heat hit Noel in the face like a hammer, taking his breath away.

He was suddenly fatigued and thought of turning back, when a loud roar went up from the crowd below. They had seen him and, not knowing his mission, shouted for him to come down.

Al looked up with tears in his eyes. "Noel!! You damn fool! Noooeelll..."

The name buzzed in circles.

"Noel..."

"Who...?"

"Some damn fool name Noel..."

It reached the ears of a pregnant girl who had been caught in the crowd.

She began to scream and claw her way to the front. Two big men, who stood head and shoulders above the rest, spotted her and plowed forward, shouting her name.

Inside the burning building, the heat was not half as intense as it had been outside, but the smoke was worse. Noel crawled only a few inches before he touched the wheel of the overturned chair. The woman lay beside it.

"Lady..." He barely whispered. He wondered what he would do if she were dead. Bring her out anyway. Leave her. He could move faster if he left her. He wondered if he could leave another body burning. Smell the smell again. And who was to blame now. Last time, it was different.

"Lady," he called again.

With great effort, he placed his hand on her chest. His fingers touched a double-strand rope of pearls, rising up and down in slow, laborious rhythm. He found her shoulders and began to pull her toward the window. From the ease with which she moved, he knew that she didn't weigh more than a hundred pounds.

Out on the fire escape, he saw that he was right. She hung in his arms like a frail gray doll, eyes closed, breath coming in shallow, irregular impulses.

The ladder had grown hotter, and he wrapped the hem of the woman's dress around his hands before climbing up. On the roof, his shoes sank deeper into the tar and he noticed that it had begun to bubble in some places.

He made it to the second floor of the adjoining building before the flames spread laterally and engulfed the stairwell above him. The intensity of the heat staggered him so that the old woman nearly slipped from his grasp. He clawed at her shoulders and drew her up again.

A terrible crackling roar filled his ears, and he began to run blindly down the last flight of stairs. He did not know where he was. He felt the heat behind and around him. A tight band squeezed against his chest, emptying his lungs.

Suddenly, he felt the flow of air. Through the smoke and tears, he could make out a doorway and the street beyond. It was only a glimpse before he was blinded again by the smoke. He moved forward by sheer force of will.

A keen eye in the crowd noticed that the sergeant's arm was shaking.

"Hey sucker, whyn't you rest that piece?"

"Mebbe he need a little help..."

"He gonna need a lotta help..."

"Get back, I'm telling you!!"

"...*been* gittin' back, motherfucker. All our lives, matta fact..."

The crowd, bold, pressed nearer. The white man was in their territory now. Familiar ground and strange circumstance. His uniform, soaked and stained, smelled of a mouth-drying, gut-turning, ball-shrinking fear. The smell floated out and touched those in the crowd nearest him and they were amazed. It was no different from the way they had felt every minute of every day of their lives as they floundered in unfamiliar, dangerous, downtown territory, their only protection being a flimsy waiter's apron or doorman's uniform.

The shouts and threats melted into thick, ominous silence. Everyone was waiting, but no one saw the bottle sail out of the darkness until it actually hit the sergeant in the eye. He got off a single, wild shot before he went down; the crowd, hungry in its hatred, seized the moment and closed in screaming.

"Git 'em, git 'em, giii..."

The roar reached a pitch too high to hear.

Switchblades and straight razors flashed open as axes and picks swung in wide, furious arcs. Fighters grappled and grunted and slipped in their own blood. Two firemen grabbed a high-powered hose and focused, scatter-shot fashion, on anything that moved.

The tremendous force of the water hit Noel as he staggered from the building, the flames at his back. The force struck him, catapulting him back into the heart of the inferno where the wall collapsed on him and his frail burden.

Frieda fell to the ground screaming. The twins leaped over her, tore the two men from the hose and tossed them, like sticks of kindling, into the flames. They watched as the flames licked at the rubber slickers, the bodies inside performing grotesque gyrations, snapping and jerking like dancers in a film gone awry.

"We oughtta fry all these motherfuckers..."

"Later...we gotta git this girl to a hospital quick."

Halfway from the scene, halfway to the hospital, the twins stopped. Frieda had made no outcry—she was beyond that—but there was a sudden convulsion. They laid her down in the shattered street, but before they could summon help, they heard a crying so faint they might have imagined it.

The twins looked at each other.

"How could she—how could anybody—bring a kid into this—this goddamn mess," Sam cried.

Dan turned away from him to kneel beside Frieda. He did not want to see his brother's tears. "She didn't know, man. She just didn't know it was gonna turn out this way..."

PART ONE

1

Two months later, the curfew ended and the tramp of the military died away. Old men lounged on stoops and watched the tight cadres of little boys in welfare knickers and high-top sneakers perform the fancy footwork of the Negro MPs. They marched with style and precision and called time to the tune of the day:

Jody got yo' gal and gon'
ah hemp...ho...ha...hem...
sweetest thing you ever known...
ah hemp...ho...ha...hem...
got her one night all alone
fixed her so she moved and moaned
now she quit the coop and gon'
leavin' you to grieve and groan...
ah...hemp...ho...

The thin falsetto flowed in their wake as they double-timed down the block, leaving the men only half listening. Most of the old men were preoccupied with the loss of the seventeen pawnshops and forty liquor stores in the thirty-block area and speculated as to its impact on the local economy. They were thinking how strange it was for so many men in the area to be called so suddenly by the draft board. And they wondered how it was that for every dozen or so who took the subway down to Whitehall, only one or two were given the nickel carfare to return.

Within two months of the disturbance, a thousand greetings had been received. Streets, stoops, basements, and bars were swept clean by fiat, leaving sad old men, precocious young boys, and angry women.

Al and Sam and Dan went down with one group. Al was given the nickel carfare and did not see the twins again for two years.

The women and old men gathered for comfort where folks were known to do the most talking: The women drifted into Tootsie's "Twist 'n Snap Beauty Saloon," where the air was thick with gossip and fried dixie peach. The men congregated in Bubba's Barber Shop to listen to orators, smooth as water-washed pebbles, alter history with mile-long lies. And the young boys, eager initiates, eased into the empty spaces at the Peacock Bar. They bent their elbows and nodded sagely as the Inkspots crooned on the ornate jukebox. Then they crawled home around midnight, to retch in secret silence and, the following day, rap cool about this new definition of manhood.

Everyone spoke—not of the Big War, where Negro men served as cooks and mechanics in some remote arena—but of personal battles right down the block. Casualties were multiplied or divided depending on liar and listener. And they all remembered Frieda whether they knew her or not.

"Girl's baby born right here on the sidewalk. Seen it myself," said Jimmy, a regular who haunted Bubba's but who had never indulged in the luxury or necessity of a haircut.

"Now how in hell you see so much with all the lights out?" asked Bean, whose visits Bubba also tried hard to discourage. Bean had once given himself a homemade conk job, and now Bubba felt his bald presence was bad for business.

"Never mind," Jimmy said, "I seen it. I was home mindin' my own business when I heard this baby cryin' right under my window—"

"Under your what? As I recollect correctly, you and me was out together. In the window of Wilson's Liquor Store to be exact. And the only cryin' I heard come from them bottles, hard as you was squeezin' 'em."

"Well, I heard somethin'...I heard the mama..."

"Now I know you lyin' and ain't heard a damn thing. The mama didn't come to herself for a solid two months and ain't nobody heard a peep outta her before then. If it wasn't for Al takin' care of things, that girl woulda been shipped out to Pilgrim and never heard of again. She didn't know nuthin'. Didn't know Sam and Dan had got drafted. Good thing Al was around..."

"Yeah, that Al...evil lookin' cat with that slice on his ear... what's his story anyway..."

"Ain't got no story that I know of, but his ear...that's what kept 'im out...ear ain't no good..."

"Ain't what I heard. Heard he don't take tea for the fever—don't take no shit from nobody—and told them damn folks just like that. They tested his head and—"

"Well, ain't his ear in his head?"

"You see, that's why nobody can't talk to you. Always got to be comin' up with some technical bullshit."

"Well, bullshit or not, he went to that hospital, looked them white folks dead in the eye, and said he was Frieda's brother. And what they know? They so smart with all their records and things, they still don't know nuthin'. In the end, we all look alike. He got in, worked his flimflam floogie, and walked that girl right on outta there..."

"Yeah, but she still kinda off though..."

"Hell, you'd be too if you seen somebody fry. That stuff take time. You just don't jump back overnight. Takes time."

2

America remembered Pearl Harbor at Hiroshima and the war ended. Sam came home with a bad leg and a purple heart, and Dan returned with a collection of faded photographs of women from Paris to Anzio. The separation pay evaporated in a week-long party, and the twins joined the thousands of other ex-GIs looking for work. They subsisted on 52/20 ($20 a week for 52 weeks), while President Truman and the Marshall Plan reshaped Europe.

Al, long before, had quit the Navy Yard for the Post Office, where the pay was low but the job was secure. He had read the signals and made the switch before the war ended. During one of the office's regular poker games, he spoke to the foreman, casually mentioning that his cousin had a purple heart. The foreman, impressed, got a letter from his club, sent Sam and Dan downtown, and within a week they were stacking mail.

They were assigned to the loading dock, moving parcels that the other workers refused to lift, but it was a job. Better than no job at all. Now they could afford to keep up the lifestyles they had acquired courtesy of Uncle Sam, namely, gambling and women.

While the battle raged, Sam made a bundle on the boards and Dan raised hell in bed. Sam was temporarily laid up when shrapnel caught him in the middle of a crap game.

The players said nothing. After all, they were supposed to have been *in* the kitchen, not behind it.

Despite his wounds, Sam managed to pull three other crapshooters to safety. He accepted the medal in the silence of a hospital room, furious at the inconvenience, but grateful that all of his working parts were intact.

Dan, on the other hand, was amazed that his dark good looks and tight curly hair could cause European woman to act so strange and serious, threatening to kill themselves or, worse, kill him if he ever left. No colored girl had ever acted that way. If they didn't like what he was putting down, they told him to straighten up and fly right or else.

When the war ended, they were both glad to return home. They bragged about the Red Ball Express and the Negro flyers of the 99th Fighter Squadron, but privately they pushed back the echoes of the wholesale, senseless violence that had raged around them: of patrols and platoons, battalions and divisions, smashed and mixed into the mud of a landscape they would never have seen had it not been for the war.

They had come home. They congratulated themselves and set about learning to feel good again about familiar things, like Thursday nights, when they invaded the Savoy and jitterbugged with agile kitchen mechanics, and Fridays and Saturdays, when they stormed Rockland Palace and the Golden Gate ballroom and set the crowd back with more displays of fancy footwork. At Park Palace, they drank and sang and danced calypso to the frenetic beat of Duke of Iron and reveled in the sweat that opened their pores. It was new and fresh and flushed away the remnants of the unnameable fear that had weighed against them in the blazing air of Europe.

They calmed down by degrees and finally settled into the jazzy darkness of Minton's to ponder the message of Al Hibbler and Thelonious Monk.

In between, they watched Frieda as she finally began to move about, though she was still not saying much to anyone. They praised and encouraged her when she took the baby, Celia, to the park. Sometimes, she stayed a whole hour. They watched and were silent when the distant wail of a fire siren brought her running, wide-eyed and breathless, back to the safety of her apartment. They remained silent, too, as they watched her watch the child fearfully and jealously. No neighbor could touch Celia or inquire after her health. A sudden sneeze brought out extrathick sweaters and quilts regardless of season, and huge doses of cod liver oil, emulsions, and tonics.

They saw something else but waited to speak to Al.

They were seated around his kitchen table playing an infrequent game of poker. Dan shuffled, Al cut, and Dan began to deal. The cards spilled from his fingers and slid easily across the tiny formica tabletop. The three men picked them up and Sam said, "What's wrong with the kid's leg?"

Al concentrated on the hand he had been dealt and let a moment pass before he answered.

"...you know, when I brought 'em home from the hospital, I was so busy tryin' to keep head above water, I didn't notice nuthin' in particular about her. I mean it was enough just tryin' to feed her and git them diapers pinned on straight..."

He placed a card faceup on the table and held the rest like a tight fan near his chest.

"Then," he said softly, "there was all that medicine. For Frieda, I mean. Man, there was bottles and bottles and pills and capsules that look like it was doin' more bad than good. You know, like maybe they was experimentin' to see which ones worked and which ones didn't, and didn't give a damn one way or the other. So I threw all that shit away and started talkin' to her...just talkin'...she didn't answer at first. Just sat and stared. Meanwhile, I'm steady changin' diapers. I guess I never noticed nuthin' else 'til a card come from the clinic sayin' the kid was overdue for some shots, so I took her. The doctor looked at her leg and rolled some fancy name off his tongue—congenital somethin'—I can't pronounce it to this day, but sure enough, I look close and one leg did seem a little thinner... so all I wanted to know then was if she was gonna walk...

"He called in another doctor and they both said yes, so I went back to concentratin' on Frieda, figurin' that once the kid started walkin' and runnin', you know, the leg would fill out by itself. I mean it wasn't bent or shriveled or nuthin' like that, just thin...

"Well, finally, one day I put the kid in Frieda's lap—Frieda had started to come 'round by then—and the first words out her mouth was 'git me some warm oil so I can rub my baby's leg.'

"Man, what a day that was...what a day...seein' her holdin' that kid, talkin'...finally talkin' to it..."

He put his cards down and was silent. All three listened to the night sounds drifting through the window on a current of heavy summer air. Somewhere, Billy Eckstine was offering a "Cottage for Sale."

Sam cleared his throat and threw in his hand. "Man, hell with these cards. Let's breeze on down to the Apollo. Erskine Hawkins there and this his last week. I don't wanna miss 'im."

January 1947

Frieda lay the *Amsterdam News* flat on the dining table and scanned the advertised specials. She sighed, then added several items to her grocery list.

"...rationin' might be over but these prices risin' so high, you still can't buy what you want to...nine cents for Silvercup... pretty soon, only the millionaires'll be able to eat."

On the opposite page, a large ad announced the grand opening of Sugar Ray Robinson's restaurant. Frieda's attention wandered as she imagined all the well-dressed women in page-boys and furs and the men in their sharp zoot suits dropping in to greet the champ and then perhaps heading over to Small's Paradise or the Baby Grand.

She wondered what their lives were like because each time they turned up on the front pages, they were always smiling, and posing with one foot on the running board of a big Packard or DeSoto.

She idly turned the pages. The dance halls with their big bands competed for the crowd in three pages of advertisements. The music kept the crowds coming, and the crowds kept the musicians going. She read the ad for Minton's, where Sam and Dan hung out listening to that music that had everybody all excited. Even Al had wanted to take her downtown to hear it. Jazz at the Philharmonic. But she had only smiled and shaken her head. She could not travel downtown. Not by subway. Not by bus. Not even in a Packard or a DeSoto had one been available to her. So she had smiled and said no, she would not understand the music.

And Al, knowing that the new music, to her, was as much a mystery as the old sound, looked beyond her parted mouth and said, well, okay. Some other time maybe.

She folded the paper and settled in the dining room chair....one of these nights when I can't sleep, I'll listen to that new man, Symphony Sid...he's playin' all that stuff...I get tired of blues... nuthin' but blues...

But she listened to the blues anyway, not realizing how comfortable the sounds made her feel. They became a part of her, making her feel less alone in her sorrow.

...Al is right...I should try to get out more...go for a walk down Seventh Avenue...a walk can't hurt nobody...put Celia in the carriage and just go...

These fantasies lasted sometimes for hours; then she would revive and turn her attention to the baby who was the core, the center, the matrix of her constricted world.

If the child was asleep, Frieda sat in the shadow of the crib and watched in silence the odd and free twists and turns, the stretching and yawning, and sometimes a hint of a smile on the otherwise tight little mouth. When the small hands opened and closed, she wanted to grasp the fingers and compare them to what she remembered of Noel's hands. But she remained where she was, barely moving a muscle, trying not to disturb the dull ache uncoiling in her chest.

3

1952

"Good God, look at that child run." Mrs. Austin nudged Mrs. Cole, then leaned forward, shading her eyes.

"Poor girl, always runnin'. She run to school and run home, always runnin'..."

The two neighbors watched as Celia headed toward them, arms flying. They moved to one side of the stoop, crowding each other comfortably in the manner of professional hangouts. Their main occupation between noon and four was the numbers—the lead, the middle, and the last. The rest of their time was spent comparing dream books and unraveling the riddle of Ching Chow's buttons. Mrs. Austin maintained a respectful silence as the girl bolted past them into the house; then she nudged Mrs. Cole again.

"Ain't that somethin' her mama still walkin' her to school. Right up the block and her mama still walkin' her...eight years old too."

Mrs. Cole, vaguely annoyed, shook her head. It was nearly time for the last digit and she needed to concentrate. On the early advice of Mrs. Austin, she had blown the lead, and then Ching Chow had misled her on the bolito. Now here was this crazy woman's child to further complicate her life. She had other things to think about—like how many groceries she'd be able to buy if she had caught the bolito. Maybe Jerry on the corner could extend her credit for another week. Mentally, she juggled the shopping list and became more annoyed.

Mrs. Austin was still talking about Celia.

"...and you remember how her mama used to practically carry her 'til she was five? Remember that?"

"Was it five? Oh yeah, I remember." Mrs. Cole sighed and made a mental note to play a five on the back. She wished Mrs. Austin would be quiet so that she could concentrate.

The two women felt the warm flow of air as the lobby door opened behind them. Not wanting to appear inquisitive, they fought the urge to turn around. They stood straight as sentries, necks aching, waiting to see who would pass them on the way out.

When Al and Frieda finally walked by with Celia, the two women were nearly exhausted but revived quickly enough to exchange greetings. As soon as they passed, Mrs. Austin remarked, "She lookin' a bit peaky..."

"...yeah...where you think they headin'..."

"...under the bridge to get some more fabric probably. Now that she startin' to sew—"

"Why he got to take her everywhere? Even to the store..."

"What you mean 'everywhere.' She hardly go out at all. If it wasn't for that dressmakin', she be stuck up in that house all the time and wouldn't see a soul."

"Mmm, uhm...no wonder she lookin' peaky."

"How come your mama gotta walk you to school?"

Celia did not answer but moved a little faster to put some distance between her and the pack. She walked fast, passing the icy man and the vanilla sno-cone she had dreamt all day of buying, passing Mr. Powell's candy store and the alternative two-cent hootens (small, unwrapped chocolate bars), passing fast, counting the cracks in the sidewalk.

They don't mean me, she thought. Mother stopped almost two months ago. They must have noticed. Surely they don't mean me.

"Hey you! How come your mama gotta walk you...?"

She pretended not to hear when someone else said, "...cause her legs so funny, her mama be there to catch her 'case she fall..."

Her mother was rarely seen, that is, she did no hanging out, lingering, or loitering. She appeared, suddenly and wraithlike, startling the noisy hangouts, smiled a quick greeting, and was gone.

And Celia was quiet in class, speaking only to give the right answers. Beyond that, mother and daughter represented unknown quantities.

And mysteries that could not be handled were greatly resented. But now, here was Celia's pencil-sized left leg with a drooping sock that never stayed up. This was real.

"Heeyyy...limp-aaayyy!!"

The malformed leg objectified their resentment, and the greeting became their rallying cry.

So she had started running, thinking that by moving fast, no one would see what held her up. She ran in and out of the house, up and down the stairs, to the library, to the store, with open mouth and heaving chest. She was thin to the point of emaciation, and her brown face with its pinched nose and tight lips did not seem appropriate for the owl-like eyes.

She ran everywhere until the running was no longer novel, and one day it stopped abruptly when a foot snaked out from the pack and tripped her.

She limped away in frozen silence, pretending that it was an accident, that it didn't even happen. She was halfway down the block when Tessie caught up with her.

"Don't pay them no mind, girl. If you wanna carry on like a bat outta hell, ain't nobody's business but your own!"

Celia held her books to her chest and continued to limp along. She was grateful for the concern, as most people are after a public embarrassment, but she wished that this big, boisterous girl now walking beside her were a little less vocal about it.

Tessie lived on the top floor in Celia's building and played her record player so loudly that Celia could barely concentrate on her homework. She was only two years older than Celia but already had begun to fill out at an accelerated rate.

It was a few seconds before Celia saw the handkerchief that Tessie held out.

"Here, girl. Wipe them bloody legs else somebody'll think you got your period by accident."

Celia had no idea what a period was but knew it had to be bad if it was caused by an accident. She snatched the offering, whispered a nervous thank you, and ran into the house.

Frieda was in the dining room hemming a yellow plaid dress, and Celia knew without looking at the garment that the lady for whom it was intended weighed at least two hundred pounds.

Celia watched as her mother concentrated on the yellow plaid; then she asked, without preamble, "What's a period?"

Frieda did not look up but continued to draw the needle in a straight line, rapid and precise. She could have hemmed the dress blindfolded, but she did not look up.

Mother and daughter remained silent as the thread became shorter and finally ended in a knot so small that, like the stitching, it was nearly invisible.

"Where did you hear about that?" Frieda asked.

Celia hesitated. The silence had been longer than she expected and now her mother's voice sounded strange, as if she had some unpleasant, private information that she wanted to hold onto as long as possible.

"Where did you hear it?" she asked again.

"From Tessie. Today. On the way home from school..."

She answered slowly, vaguely aware that she had exposed her new friend to some ill-defined danger. She looked up and found her mother staring as if seeing her for the first time.

"Does your stomach hurt?"

Her voice was like a smooth stream moving over a rocky river bed.

"My knees hurt," Celia answered, wondering what her stomach had to do with her knees. "They started bleeding when I fell down and Tessie said—"

Frieda dropped the plaid dress. "Your knees! What...happened to you?"

She moved from the table and stood over her. "What happened... to you...I knew it...I never should've let...I knew you weren't strong enough..."

"Mama...it's only my knees...I tripped over someone...I was running..."

Celia had visions of her mother again taking her to and from school and a hard knot began to form in her stomach. "It doesn't hurt anymore—"

But Frieda wasn't listening. "Here. Sit down...let me see..."

She held Celia's leg near the table lamp, examining it closely.

"It's only my knees," Celia said again softly. She saw that her mother's hands were shaking slightly and that her eyes held a faraway look as she stared at the blood-caked knees. When she spoke, she sounded tired.

"You go and take a bath. A nice warm one right away. You don't want that knee to get infected..."

The bathroom door closed, and Frieda listened hard to hear the sound of water running. Then she leaned back in the chair, barely able to breathe. She stared at the door for some minutes, resisting the urge to open it, to make certain that her child was not floating facedown in the bath water or sprawled unconscious on the cold tile floor.

She was on the verge of calling out when she heard Celia's voice filter unevenly beyond the door in an attempt to follow a tune coming from Tessie's record player.

"—tomorrow night. Will you remember what you said tonight..." She heard it dragged out, low and heavy, in imitation of the whiskey-voiced singer and his mournful, steel-stringed guitar.

Frieda listened, breathless.... Tessie is eleven years old...a child... and playing those fast records. She shook her head. Tessie knew of periods...what else did she know...

All at once, she needed something to combat the breathlessness and quiet the erratic rhythm in her chest. She opened the small bar near the table. Her movements were mechanical and she was surprised, when she raised the glass, to see that she had filled it to the rim. The first sip, tasting bad as usual, went down slowly. The second, as usual, she never remembered.

She rose and moved toward the bedroom. Her gait was unsteady—not from drink, but from a peculiar unclarity of purpose.

She groped blindly at the bottom of the clothes closet, under stiff, pressed sheets, rolls of tar paper, and yards of assorted pieces of fabric which, she kept telling herself, would someday make a splendid quilt, and finally extracted a folder in which had been gathered all the articles ever written about the riot, and another, older clipping from a distant, southern paper.

She concentrated on a particular passage until the lines blurred; then she closed the folder and placed it in the closet. She plumped up the pillow in the sagging chair near the window, sat down, and for the next twenty minutes, calculated the score: one policeman and two firemen. She always felt better after she thought about it.

She remembered the other, older news clipping, mailed to them from a surprised and cautious relative. She had not looked at it since Noel placed it there and refused to look now because it would only enlarge the pain she carried in her chest.

But, she wondered again, had she said anything, accused anyone, in all those days she had lain, barely conscious, in the hospital? Did she speak at all? Did anyone listen and wonder where she had run from and why?

She felt the rhythm in her chest again. It seemed to push

against the rib cage in spasms, sharp and tight. She held her breath, trying to regain control.

Where she and Noel had run from no longer mattered since she knew she could never go back. But it was home and it still informed her thinking.

The people there called it the "low country," although it wasn't really low. The larger area, dotted with bays, inlets, swamps, and forests, stretched along the Atlantic coastal plains before beginning its gradual rise from southeast to northwest. She had been born in the southeast part, where the soil was black and loamy.

She remembered how easily it had yielded to the slight pressure of her young, bare feet. In odd moments, she had practiced walking backward in the shadow of the lush pecan trees just to see her footprints appear and disappear in the soft earth, brown and black in the shifting pattern of the leaves. She remembered asking her father where the soil had gotten its color from.

"River silt," he had said, "makes the best soil in the world..."

And she wondered, if she walked in the soil long enough, would it change the soles of her feet from ash white to the warm nutmeg color of her legs.

"God made you the way you are," her mother interjected, "and ain't much nobody can do about that..."

But since Frieda had never actually seen the god her mother continually and patiently called on, she said nothing and continued to walk in the soft soil, sinking ankle deep in spots, hoping if not for nutmeg, then at least cinnamon.

When the transformation failed to occur, she meant to inquire further but other concerns intruded:

One was the boy Noel. He had spotted her, after a sudden storm, strolling ankle deep in the thick mud.

"You act like you like that...ain't you got nuthin' better to do?"

And she had shrunk from the authority of his fifteen years, but not before telling him, "I got plenty to do, plenty..."

She had run off, as fast as the mud would allow, struggling to stay a step ahead of his laughter, and suffering the humiliation only a ten-year-old could feel.

That night, she prayed to a god that she did not believe in, but she was desperate and had to cover all possibilities. Noel was the boy she loved, and he had caught her actually enjoying herself in the mud, just like a pig.

"...maybe, Lord, you could just make him forget the mud and... or maybe, You could...he could just think about me and forget about the...feet...or maybe..."

Sleep rescued her from her confusion.

The days that followed were bad, but not because of Noel. In fact, she had not had time for the luxury of despair.

For months, talk in the northwest part had been about crop destruction, but it seemed to hit the southeast almost overnight and boll weevils crawled and nested where cotton should have been. Now, only the bright leaf tobacco stood between the people and starvation. Every man, woman, and child she knew picked, cut, graded, and bundled the pungent leaves, but their best efforts, at times, were not enough.

The town grew smaller as whole families filled cardboard suitcases and moved away. Up north, they said, where the streets were paved with gold. The others waved goodbye, wishing them well, with upturned hands, the palms of which were stained a deep tobacco brown.

Before Frieda could reconcile the irony of brown palms with ash-white feet, her mother had secured a job for her in one of the several big houses that defined the perimeter of the county.

Frieda went to work, walking miles of narrow road shadowed with old cypress and Spanish moss. On rare occasions, her father hitched the wagon and drove her, but most of the time she walked.

In the predawn coolness, she entertained herself by counting the red oaks that stood like sentinals along the road, curly leaves changing with the seasons.

She knew she had reached the three-quarter mark when she passed the wrought iron gates where curved driveways led to sculptured lawns—where one magnificent house dominated acres of land and reflected the sun in a hundred windows.

The house she had gone to work in was not nearly as grand as the owners pretended.

She could tell from the texture of the sheets she washed that the family had a long way to go before they'd see any curving drives. The linen was cheap and thin, and Frieda had to handle the sheets carefully or bear the blame when they came apart.

She laughed about it in the evenings when she came home. "Sheets so thin, they dry before you even get to hang 'em out..."

Sometimes, Noel would be waiting to walk her halfway home. In the gathering darkness, she could feel the strength of his presence and all the fatigue she had felt during the day would ease away.

She worked three years, on and off, and watched with growing alarm as the linens reached the shredding stage. To compound her problems, the son of the family watched her.

She saw Noel's mouth tighten and become a thin, drawn line as she spoke of this, but her mother said quietly, "Keep a hot pot of water boilin', girl...and don't turn your back. When they pay you next week, you ain't goin' back..."

The water was boiling, but she had forgotten about her back and the boy had come up behind her as she bent over the washtub, her fingers slippery and smelling of lye soap. But she had smelled him above the lye because he must have cut through the pigsty to sneak around to the back door.

"Why you runnin' from me?" His voice had a high, whining sound, as if he expected rejection and was angry beforehand.

She turned to face him, to explain that she worked for his family, and what he wanted was not part of her job. She stared into his colorless eyes and called him mister even though they were the same age.

He had grinned to hide his outrage.

"Smart nigger gal like you need her mouth cleaned out. Gimme that damn soap..."

She had dropped the soap and picked up the pot, the water trailing a scalding arc through the air before hitting him in the face.

She stood rooted to the spot in fear and wonder as his screams through distant rooms caused the fine hair at the nape of her neck to rise. She was amazed at the transforming power of heat and water and no less amazed at her ability to conclude that it would be safer to run to Noel's house, where his father could protect her with his shotgun.

They had come, looked down the barrel, and retreated.

But Noel knew she wasn't safe, so he took her to the next town, walking twenty miles in the gathering shadow of night, to stay with her mother's sister until things quieted down. He retraced the twenty miles, and by the time he had returned home, his father had been taken by the mob.

The older news clipping related how two men had drowned when their rowboat had tipped over. But Frieda knew that Noel had skirted the black woods, hid in ditches so muddy that he became part of the mud, and, smelling the mud in his pores, knew that no dog could track him. He became part of the night and broke from its blackness, swift and fatal as summer lightning. It had been so easy. The men had been drinking a little while night fishing. Noel came up silently under the boat, tipped it, and was gone.

"One of 'em nearly made it to shore," he said later, "but I held his face in the mud until the bubbles stopped."

That was all he ever said about it. But Frieda and her mother's sister watched in silence as he burned the shirt and coveralls he had worn and washed his hair and skin two and three times a day for the week they were there, trying to clear his nostrils of the thick swampy smell of the lake.

In the middle of the second night, Frieda lay awake, listening. Her aunt turned restlessly in the bed beside her, coughed once, then settled into a low, deep-throated snore. Across the room, she heard Noel's sounds, small, muffled murmurings that reminded her of the time a puppy next door had become entangled in a coil of rope: The harder it tried to free itself, the tighter the rope had become.

She left her aunt's bed and quietly crossed the room to where he lay. She eased herself in beside him and placed her mouth near his ear.

"Noel...Noel...Noo...el...listen...we...gonna have our tomorrow... you hear..."

He did not answer, but she knew he was awake because the fitful rocking had stopped and his breath, warm against her face, was deep and measured.

In the first few minutes, she had only wanted to press him to her, to squeeze with all her might the last drop of the swamp-smelling water from his pores. And he had only wanted to forget, but then, each knew that as long as they lived, that would never happen, and they would have to find a way to build their lives and love around it.

Noel spoke not a word, but his breathing had become so heavy that Frieda was afraid the sound would rise above her aunt's snoring. She tried to concentrate on everything at once, but soon gave up and pressed her mouth to his, losing herself to his strong hands and fierce undulating rhythm.

When he finally slept, it was on the bus heading north. While Noel dozed, Frieda avoided the curious gaze of a short, stocky man with a scar near his ear, sitting across from them.

Frieda woke with a start. How long had she been asleep? The room was nearly dark. Was Celia still in the tub? She felt panic as she moved from the chair and entered the living room. A light was coming from under Celia's closed door.

"Celia…?"

"Yes?"

Frieda eased the door open and saw Celia had been reading.

"Finished your homework?"

"Yes. I tried to wake you, but you looked tired so I let you sleep. My knee's fine…"

"You must stop running…why are you always in a rush…? Your leg is not strong, your leg—"

"I know…I know…but it doesn't hurt anymore…"

4

In school, in the crowded corridor, Tessie made a practice of calling loudly when Celia passed, drawing attention to them both. "Goin' to the Apollo tonight, girl. Can't miss them Clovers. And next week is Larry Darnell. That man is too fine…"

The conversation, directed at Celia, was meant for all as Tessie strolled down the hall. "Too fine," she sighed, enjoying the resentment and attention.

The other girls frowned and wondered because Tessie had only turned thirteen. The following term, when Tessie had trouble fastening her skirts, they watched and whispered: "Dreamt 'bout fish again last night," the more vocal of the gossips said, as if to confirm by divine attribution what they had suspected all along.

"She do look kinda plump. You sure it ain't from all those sweets she been eatin'...?"

"Well, some might call it sweet, but I heard my mama say you only gain that kinda weight from a special chocolate bar..."

"Maybe she shoulda tried the kind with no nuts..." And they smiled and waited.

Tessie, meanwhile, kept Celia entertained. "Girl, the Apollo's second balcony rocks with the Orioles, but you ain't seen nuthin' 'til you seen Johnny Ray at the Paramount..."

No one sounded or looked better than the Orioles when they took over the stage in their white suits and patent leather shoes and sang as if their hearts had been fractured, but going to the Paramount meant visiting pink-marbled powder rooms and walking up wide, curved stairs. Tessie spoke of thick carpets, ornate carved ceilings, wide seats, and popcorn that was as fresh as they said it was. She had cried for Johnny Ray, but she screamed for the Orioles until she lost her voice.

Home was where the Orioles were; where Sonny Til opened his arms wide and leaned back and made young girls cry when he asked, "What are you doing New Year's Eve?"

But the Paramount had class—an elusive downtown feeling—which Tessie wished she could feel at the Apollo. She tried to explain this to Celia but gave up when she saw her confusion. So she switched again to her favorite subject: Lady Day. Tessie sang her songs and even began to wear a small white paper corsage tucked in the side of her pompadour, so that it framed her face, just like Lady Day's corsage.

She also took to wearing an old cardigan every day and walked with her books held close to her midsection. Celia watched and said nothing. Tessie had never carried a book as long as she had known her.

School was quiet, a dead place, after Tessie left, but she carried her loudness with her to the street, stalking the block, daring anyone to look directly at her. She was proud and defiant and, in the end, went to the hospital alone.

The stoop watchers had a field day.

"Tessie's mama oughtta be run in," clucked Mrs. Canty.

"Run in?" smiled Mrs. Austin, "honey, you gotta find her first. She only come up for air on the first and the fifteenth, then wanna mug the mailman if he ain't got her check."

"Just as well when she don't git it, for all the good it do," observed Mrs. Cole. "God only knows what she do with it, but when the money blows, she goes..."

"Well I know one thing," Mrs. Canty added, "when they find out how young Tessie is, they gonna put her away and take that baby."

Celia caught this last fragment as she entered the lobby. She took the stairs two at a time and paused to catch her breath before entering the apartment.

How could she mention the gossip and all the strange names the women had used to describe Tessie's baby. She wanted to tell Frieda, but Tessie's name had been banned in the house since Celia had skinned her knee.

She closed herself in her room and thought of looking up the strange words in the dictionary: bastard, illegitimate. She knew what unwed meant, but so what. Her own father had died when she was born. Didn't that make her mother unwed again. Thinking about it made her head hurt, so she leaned out of the window and propped her chin on her folded arms. Someone was playing a tune by Nat King Cole. So low and soft that she could barely make it out. It was not Lady Day, so she turned her attention and studied the clotheslines. They hung from the windows, crisscrossing the yard with so many fine filaments of information: the long johns on Mrs. Mason's line meant that her seaman husband was home and the shades would be drawn for a few days. There were black lace stepins on Marcie's line, which meant that she was stepping out tonight.

After a while, the lines had conveyed all their information and

Celia was bored. There was no activity. Except for the occasional bark of a stray dog, there was no sound at all. Even Nat Cole had stopped. She thought of the music that had come from Tessie's record player, crying and stomping out the blues, filling the backyard and flowing into her consciousness so that she was able to sing a few of the songs better than Tessie.

...and now they're going to take her baby. How come...it's hers. She had it...who could take it...

Her head began to ache again. She left the window and walked to the dining room. Frieda watched her pick up a book from the table and reach for her sweater.

"Where are you going?"

"To the library. I got the wrong book."

Frieda looked at the clock.

"You be back in this house by five. I don't want you roamin' the street at all hours."

The hospital and the library faced each other across the wide avenue. The light changed and Celia moved with the crowd. She had never been on the other side of the avenue before, and now she slowed to a walk. The hospital loomed large before her, awesome even in its decrepitude.

She finally entered the lobby and loitered, almost dizzy with fright. Nurses, doctors, and other official-looking people rushed in blurs of white through mysterious doors as the public address system crackled with inaudible urgency.

Celia moved out of the path of an elderly man who wandered distractedly in a ragged circle, calling aloud for someone who, everyone knew, would never answer him again.

Finally, she held her mouth firm to steady her chattering teeth, moved close to a woman with two children, and followed them off the elevator directly into the maternity ward.

She saw Tessie at the end of a long row of narrow beds. The ward was noisy with visitors but Celia approached on tiptoe, as if she were at a wake. Passing the beds, she saw the same expression on the faces of all the women—uniform masks of fatigue and resignation. Tessie had it also when she looked up.

"Celia! What you doin' here?"

Her voice and body, bent by fatigue, seemed older as she moved from the bed. Her hair, always pressed and curled, was now in thick braids. The bright polish was gone from the fingers, and her face, clean of makeup, showed traces of darkening circles under her eyes.

Celia wanted to touch her and straighten out the too-big hospital gown that kept slipping off her shoulders. She wanted to hear Tessie laugh and talk about the Apollo and the latest records Dr. Jive was playing.

But something beyond her comprehension had happened, and Tessie had changed; Celia was embarrassed to look at her. Instead, she stood silently near the bed and concentrated on the high ceiling with its off-white, flaking paint and on the row upon row of narrow iron beds with the rusting, prisonlike bars, each enfolding its private burden.

And over all hung the odor. It reminded Celia of the lunchroom on Wednesdays, when the free passes were confiscated by the score because no child could get past the smell long enough to eat the rancid soup.

"...you hear me, Celia?"

"...what?"

"You come to see me or the ceiling?"

"Tessie...I came to—"

"Never mind. I'm glad you did...I'm glad..."

She fingered the edge of the bed sheet and looked away. Finally, she whispered, "I got a baby girl. I got a girl..."

"...oh, Tessie, how..."

"She's beautiful too, but Mac'll never see her..."

"Mac?"

Tessie did not answer immediately, and the name hung in the awkward silence.

Celia watched Tessie's face, the dark, round, baby-fat face with its high nose and full lips that she envied. But it was Tessie's eyes that had changed the most. They were black, haunted pools almost as wretched as Celia's mother's, and they made her ask again, "Who...who is Mac?"

For several minutes, the silence was filled with the loud laughter of the other visitors; then Tessie sighed, overwhelming them.

"I met 'im last year," she said in a low voice. She seemed relieved now and glad to talk.

"He thought I was seventeen, you know. We went a lotta places, then he joined up in the Marines 'cause he got laid off and couldn't get nuthin' else. When I found out I was gonna have a baby, he wanted to come home and get married. Instead they shipped him off down south..."

Her voice trailed off and Celia, not knowing what to say, waited in silence.

"He was all right, you know...sent me money every month 'til last month. Then three a my letters come back all at once with a stamp across the front..."

She fumbled in the pocket of the gown. "God, I wish I had a cigarette...anyway, that's the way they do you, you know, when you don't count. Just a stamp. One word. Deceased—"

Celia stared at her but said nothing. She remembered seeing Tessie with a slightly built, dark boy in uniform. After that, Tessie seemed to wrap herself in a cocoon only large enough for herself and her music.

"...he died in some kind a maneuvers," Tessie said, more to herself than to Celia. "...and all I got is some letters..."

Celia thought of Al and how he had argued against fighting in what he described as some stupid war that he didn't start.

"...black man ain't got a dime in that dollar, no sir," he had said. "We been in every war ever fought and what we git for it...a royal ass-kickin' every time. Them enemy prisoners was treated better...ain't we learnt nuthin' yet?"

He had put the question, years ago, to the pink-faced induction officer down at Whitehall. They had given him a psychiatric examination and subway fare back uptown.

Tessie sat on the edge of the bed looking so old that it frightened Celia.

...how come she's too young to keep the one thing that belongs to her...

"Tessie, why didn't you say something?"

"To who...?"

To me, Celia wanted to say. I was your friend. But she remembered her mother and kept quiet.

Tessie laughed suddenly. "Remember how I used to party a

lot? And how I used to brag. When I met Mac, things got different. Funny, once you find what you lookin' for, what you need, you don't have to say nuthin' to nobody no more..."

This was far beyond Celia's understanding, so she said, "What are you going to do?"

"I...I don't know yet...once I get outta here, I..."

Celia leaned closer to the bed and lowered her voice. "Listen. I have something to tell you...I have to be quick because my mother doesn't know I'm here..."

Tessie nodded. "I believe it. My mama don't know I'm here either..."

Her laughter was loud and dry and caused visitors and patients alike to turn and stare.

Celia was frightened and reached for her hand. "Tessie, listen to me. They're going to put you away. They're going to take your baby..."

Tessie straightened up. "Who said??"

Her eyes, narrowed, reminded Celia of a street cat. "Who said?" she repeated.

"I heard Mrs. Austin and Mrs. Canty talking, and you know they know everything. They say you're too young and the baby is going to be taken away..."

"No they ain't! I had it, didn't I? I dee-double dare anybody—" She stopped because she didn't know whom to dare. She pressed her hands to her head and stared hard out of the uncurtained window. Celia thought she was about to cry, but Tessie stood up abruptly and walked, shuffling in a bent-over fashion, to the metal nightstand in the center of the floor which she shared with three other women. She rummaged through the drawer and produced a scrap of paper.

"This my Aunt Carolyn's number. She in Brooklyn. Big in the church and ain't spoke to my mama in a dog's age. But you call her. Tell her what's gonna happen to me. They ain't gettin' my kid, Celia. She's all I got left..."

"...but Tessie!"

"I don't have no money, Celia. Not even a nickel for a phone call."

"If she hasn't spoken to you, how do you know she'll help?" Celia asked. For a fleeting second, she felt as if she were being drawn into something beyond her depth. She had lied to her mother, had sneaked into this awful place, and now this. All she had wanted to do was warn Tessie. She owed her that much.

Then she thought of nights when she had been unable to fall asleep without the music. She had lain in bed, listening through the open window, reaching for meaning in the deep, sad sounds that kept slipping just beyond her, not understanding half the words but knowing they had come from the bottom of someone who had been at the bottom.

She remembered her mother's reaction: "Can't that child play some happy music for a change. What's wrong with her anyway?"

Celia had not answered but saw, in her mother's eyes, that the music she complained about affected her strangely, sometimes causing her to put down her sewing or whatever it was she was doing and walk quickly to her room. Sometimes she sat for hours staring at nothing. Other times, she closed the door and stayed so long that Celia thought she had fallen asleep. What had she felt? Did Tessie, young as she was, now feel the same thing?

"...you gonna do it, Celia?"

"Suppose she asks me a lot of questions...?"

"Tell her the truth. That way we ain't gotta remember no lies."

"Suppose she won't come?"

"Then you gotta let me know fast, so I can think a somethin' else. They ain't gittin' my kid. I mean it..."

The following day, as Celia waited for the right person to sneak in with, she saw Tessie come out with a thin, middle-aged woman carrying a baby as if it were her own.

"Celia," Tessie cried, "everything's gonna be all right." She was smiling and looked better than she had looked in a long time, but Celia avoided the gaze of the grim woman and wondered if she had done the right thing in calling her.

"Aunt Carolyn, please let my friend see—"

The woman quickly uncovered the baby's face and just as quickly covered it again, as if Celia's breath might contaminate it.

"Ain't she cute?" Tessie beamed.

Celia did not know quite what to say. She was disappointed to see a small, red, wrinkled face when all the time Tessie had said that the baby was beautiful. She racked her brain but could think of nothing except the time when she had been in a similar predicament with Miss Judy.

She remembered bending politely over Miss Judy's brand new carriage, congratulating her on her brand new marriage—late as it was after five children—and lifting the brand new blankets to stare at the brand new baby, whose face had defied description.

She had simply stared, speechless, for a long minute. Finally, Miss Judy had said, "This one was my biggest baby..." Which was true. Except that fifty percent of the weight was concentrated in his ears.

Tessie's baby was not as bad as Miss Judy's. Nothing living could ever be, but Celia was still at a loss for words. Aunt Carolyn spoke for the first time, sparing Celia the embarrassment of equivocation.

"This wouldna happened if I had been around, but that no good sist—never mind. Praise God, I got here in time. God sent the word and I got here in time..."

Celia was surprised. It was her nickel which enabled Aunt Carolyn to receive the message. Why then, if the word had been conveyed by a higher authority, had the telephone taken her coin. She could have invested in a bag of peppermint balls and a fat sour pickle. She thought of asking Aunt Carolyn for an answer, but she was still locked into her sermon.

"Yes, Lord! Praise God, I'm gonna bring this child to God and Glory!!"

A small crowd began to take shape as passersby sensed drama in the making. Celia felt a thousand pairs of eyes on her.

The voice reached fever pitch before Tessie touched her Aunt's hand. "...Auntie..."

Aunt Carolyn stopped in midsentence and blinked as if seeing Tessie for the first time.

"Oh. Yes. Well, hurry and say goodbye. We can't stand here all day. We got to get home and feed this baby."

And the one friend that Celia had, disappeared into the noise and rush of the subway, leaving her to wonder which child the aunt intended to bring to glory.

5

The music left also. It was as if a deep chasm had formed in the courtyard overnight and all the sound, activity, bustle, and just plain noise of Tessie's presence had gathered itself up and fallen in.

Brooklyn. She had gone to a place called Brooklyn. Where was Brooklyn? she casually asked her mother.

"Over there," Frieda had replied vaguely. She might have been talking about France. When pressed as to where "over there" was, she said, "south of downtown."

Celia later found it on the map. It was part of New York, connected by bridges and trains and occasional news reports. But still—it was far enough away to engender a soundless desolation.

"Were you able to get that book you needed the other day?" Frieda asked. Celia mumbled something inaudible and headed for her room, leaving the sound of her mother's voice behind. She eased the door shut but opened it after a few minutes when the empty quiet began to close in. It was a quiet that not even the thought of her father, lately resurrected from the back of her mind, could dispel.

A record player, she thought idly. Maybe if I had a record player, things would be different. It wouldn't have to be big or fancy like Tessie's. Just a little one to…to…

She discarded the thought as quickly as it had come. She knew, as surely as she knew her name, that the record player was not the answer. Of course if would help. It would push back the quiet somewhat, but it wasn't the answer because that wasn't the problem.

She lay on the bed, feeling the stillness of the courtyard creep in. She squeezed her eyes shut until pain forced her to relax, but still she could not fathom an answer, a reason for her desolation. The quiet grew heavier, pressing against her, pushing her deeper into the bed. The coverlet crept up and around her throat, robbing her of breath.

In the doorway, an indistinct image of a tall man, vaguely handsome in the half-light, held out his hand. She strained to reach him, called out to him, but he turned to the window, his hands to his ears, as if to shut out a volume of sound that she herself was unable to hear. He concentrated on the sound, ignoring her as she struggled to free herself from the bedspread.

...I'm dying and he doesn't care, she thought in wonder. I'm dying and he's worrying about the music. What kind of father is that...?

You don't care, she cried, hoping he would hear her above the silent music. You don't care...you don't care...

Strong hands, disembodied by darkness, leaped over the coverlet. They probed near her throat and she was overcome with hysteria.

"No! No!"

"Celia...!" Frieda shook her awake, "You were screaming at the top of your lungs. What's wrong??"

"I don't...know. I don't..."

She sat on the edge of the bed, dizzy with fright. Frieda switched on the light and looked at her closely. "Maybe," she said quietly, "you should get started on your homework. Take your mind off things. If you had gotten that book, you would have been readin' instead of dreamin'."

"Book?" Celia asked. She blinked uncomprehendingly, and Frieda knew.

"You didn't go to the library? Where were you yesterday...off wanderin'...and after I told you...suppose somethin' happened... suppose..."

She clasped her hands to her chest, turned slowly, and left the room.

Celia sat huddled near the edge of the bed, listening for, and finally hearing, the slam of the door as Frieda left the apartment. She was, Celia knew, on her way upstairs to Al's place. She always went there when something went wrong.

...I was only four blocks away...only four blocks...I wasn't wandering. Mama is acting as if I had disappeared forever...

She wanted to lie down again but the shadows had gathered in the silent courtyard, frightening her more than ever.

Frieda waited impatiently for Al to open the door and was surprised to find Sam and Dan there. All three had been working the four to midnight shift for the last three months and had complained bitterly about the transfer. Today was Al's day off, but the twins should have been at work.

Frieda entered the kitchen and quietly took a seat, her anxiety over Celia's behavior compounded in the face of a new uneasiness.

"What's happened...?"

"Same old...same old," Dan replied.

"...no it ain't" interrupted Sam, "it ain't the same old bullshit no more. We put the brakes on that motherfucker last night..."

Frieda looked at him, watching his agitation increase with each word.

"You got fired," she said. It was a statement rather than a question.

"We got quit," Dan grinned.

Frieda looked from one to the other and then said. "You all quit...just walked out drylongso?"

"We walked for somethin' better," Al said as he sat at the table hunched over a pad. His pen moved rapidly, adding figures, crossing out lines, double-checking. He placed the pen across the pad and looked up.

"Okay...between us...we got...with payroll savin's...and what we put in that retirement fund...we got enough to buy out Old Man Best's movin' business on the corner. Truck and all."

"That's okay by me," Sam said, "but what about the fish-and-chip place we was talkin' about..."

Dan looked at him and wrinkled his nose. "I wasn't too anxious to be smellin' fishy on no Friday nights. Y'all know I got things to do."

"Awh, once you git into it, you ain't gonna know the difference..."

Al looked up and glanced at Frieda. "Y'all cool it. We got a lady in the house."

"Don't mind me," Frieda said, "the movin' store sounds like a good idea, but it's some hard work."

"All work is hard," Al said, "but least we'll make more money. There's a gold mine out there, but the man is just too old to haul it in..."

Frieda was glad that the tension was finally under control. She had seen it and felt it when they described the antagonism at the post office that threatened to boil over into murderous hatred; the hundred different subtle subterranean forms of petty harassment, consistent enough to let them know that they were not good enough, medal or no medal.

Somehow, the other workers never, ever, bothered Al, perhaps because they were able to read his history in his eyes or smell old blood spilled in rage. Whatever. When they were not playing poker, they left Al to himself.

Sam and Dan were a different story. When they were transferred to the shift, the legend of the medal seemed to ignite a smoldering fuse.

The other men cast surreptitious glances at the tight, curly hair and saw the catlike grace with which the twins handled the heavy sacks and cartons. They persuaded the new supervisor to deny overtime to Sam and Dan and increase their workload.

The harder they worked, the more work they got. They crawled home bone-tired, able to do little more than fall into bed.

"Man, they doin' it to us..."

"This what Lincoln got done in for? That Booth cat coulda saved himself a hell of a lotta trouble. They ain't killed slavery. They just relocated it..."

"Man, I wouldn't work this hard for my own self..."

So they checked out Old Man Best's Light Hauling Company, bought it, and changed the name to Groovy Movers ("You Aint Been Moved Til You Been Moved By Us").

In six months, they had more work than they could handle. It was still hard and they were still tired, but now the sweat was their own.

Al taught Celia to answer the phone and on Saturday mornings, while other children crowded the Odeon and Roosevelt theaters to cheer for Zorro or lined up to catch the freebie swimming lessons at the Bradhurst Pool, Celia rushed out right after breakfast in order to pick up the phone on the first ring.

The first two calls were from Frieda.

"Everything all right?"

"Everything's fine, mother."

"Okay, call me if you need me..."

The next half dozen calls were for estimates, packing barrels, and moving dates. As Al returned the phone to its cradle, it rang again and Frieda was on the line.

That evening, he spoke to her. "Celia's right downstairs, you know..."

He watched as she wrung her hands.

"Ain't nuthin' to worry about," he said again. Actually, he did not mind her calling because he enjoyed hearing her voice, but he could not afford to allow his feelings or her fear to impede business. "We lookin' after her, Frieda..."

He knew he was going to lose either way and could not understand his relief when she finally said, "I don't know...I don't know...I want my child where I can see her..."

Al continued to give Celia five dollars a week although she was no longer a part of Groovy Movers. It hurt him now more than ever to see her sad, pinched little face, when she had been so happy a short time ago.

"...good morning, hold on for Groovy Movers."

She had enjoyed saying that and then passing the phone to Sam or Dan or himself. The customers had loved it and when they complimented her, she had beamed with pride.

"Where you off to now?" Al asked, as she turned to go. He had been paying her for three weeks and knew that since she never went any further than the library, a small fortune in crumpled five-dollar bills was probably accumulating in some secret place. It wasn't healthy. He'd have to find time to take her to Coney Island or at least to the movies. It just wasn't healthy.

"I'm going to the library," she said. "I have to hurry. Mother said I have to be back by three..."

"You be careful." He watched her walk away and shook his head. Although he had no idea what he was going to say this time, he made up his mind to speak to Frieda when he got off later.

6

At two-thirty in the morning, Frieda woke suddenly and reached for the clock. In the darkness, the iridescent symbols glowed dully in the reflected light of the Peacock Bar.

"I only slept three hours..."

She sat up and swung her legs over the edge of the bed. Her toes curled involuntarily against the cold floor, but she made no effort to look for her slippers. Instead, she concentrated on the pattern of neon as it played against the brown tone of her thighs. Her legs turned orange, brown, orange, then brown again before she moved from the bed.

She stood, naked, in the shadow of the partly drawn drapes and watched the neon bathe the rumpled bedding: white, orange, white. Her head ached and her mouth held a stale, slightly metallic taste.

"...should have slept longer than this, considering..."

She drew her robe around her and padded, barefoot, to the bathroom in search of aspirin.

"...that wine was...too sweet...almost like soda...should have stopped at one glass, but Al...was talkin' so much foolishness..."

She put two tablets on her tongue, cupped her hands under the faucet and drank. The water made her teeth chatter.

Back in the bedroom, she drew the curtains aside and took her usual seat by the window. The light from the Peacock flickered, dimmed, and went out. Then the customers began drifting through the door.

Three women came out, the middle one supported by the other two. Their sounds carried on the stiff breeze and hit, like small pebbles, against the cold window.

"...he can't tell me how much to drink...who the hell he think he is...little shrimp actin' like little Caesar...got a good mind to go back and kick his little ass..."

"Well, the joint done closed...if you wanna kick ass, you got to come back tomorrow..."

"Just what I'm gonna do. I'm gonna do just...that. You remind me, now, you hear...always knew you was in my corner... we gonna do just that...you remind me..."

A cab stopped and absorbed the women and the threats, and the night was still again.

A minute later, a man came out. He peered at his watch and lit a cigarette. For several minutes, he gazed down the dark avenue; then he bent his head against the wind and hurried in the opposite direction, tall, thin, and alone.

There were a few more solitary stragglers. She watched them, shadowing them with tired eyes, wondering about their destinations, and thought of their bedrooms, warm, with soft lights and heavy blankets.

She suddenly thought of Noel, saw him in her mind's eye as he moved easily on long legs down the block, approaching the stoop, taking the stairs two at a time. A minute later, the scrape of the key against the lock in the dark hallway.

His soft voice. His mouth against her face. The weight of his hands in her hair. He was home.

She was filled with a profound sense of dislocation and turned from the window, no longer able to watch. She faced into the darkness of the room and whispered aloud:

"...you used to come back in my...dreams...now it's gettin' harder and harder...I don't understand...I'm still the same... what happened...do you think I'm mistreatin' Celia...I'm not...I hardly let her out of my sight...I don't know what more to do... suppose somethin' happens to her too..."

She drew the robe around her and closed her eyes against the empty room. "...I don't know what more to do...tell me...tell me."

She sank to her knees and clung to the edge of the bed. Her body curled into itself and she buried her head in the sheets.

"...you ain't comin' back...no more pretendin'...dreamin' that it mighta been a mistake...oh Noel, you ain't comin' back... what do I do??"

She knelt there, feeling extremely tired, but dared not climb back into bed for fear of the other dream, a recent, recurring nightmare in which she would fall into the water from a huge ship ringed with a thousand lights. She would flounder, screaming, in the shocking cold as the ship pulled away, alive with music and laughter, leaving her bobbing in its foamy wake. Soon, even the foam was gone, and there was nothing to connect her to anything, only a void, bottomless, vast and immeasurable, reverberating with the sound of her screams. And always she would wake confused and frightened, nearly knocking over the small table lamp in her haste to switch it on. She would lay there, feeling her legs shake under the covers. What did it mean? She had never even seen a big ship, except for pictures in the papers. And the music. It was a strange kind of waltzing sound, not like the music Al, Sam, and Dan talked about.

She stood up, moved around the bed, and reached for the phone.

...maybe I shouldn't be callin' him at this hour...he got a hard day ahead...

She pressed the receiver to her ear until it hurt. A ring and a half and she heard his voice, sleepy, angry, then alert.

"What's wrong? What's the matter?"

"Nuthin'...I had a bad dream, Al..."

She let the robe fall open as she spoke and looked down beyond her breasts to the slight curve of her stomach. "I had a bad dream...I'm sorry to bother you..."

"Ain't nuthin' to be sorry about...you been havin' them dreams a lot lately...feel like talkin'?"

His voice was mellow with sleep, and Frieda felt an edge of guilt. "You gotta get up early...you got a busy day...you said so yourself..."

"Hell, I'm wake now...come on up..."

She sat again at the tiny kitchen table where a few hours earlier she had listened as Al tried to talk about Celia. She had become angry and closed out the sound of him, drinking several glasses of wine in the process.

She sat now with eyes averted.

What on earth, he wondered, could have possessed her to leave her place dressed only in a robe.

She pulled the lapels closer as Al poured a second cup of coffee. He caught the slight movement out of the side of his eye and knew that she had nothing on beneath the robe. He tried not to look at her. He did not want to scare her away.

He watched the small muscle in her throat as she sipped from the cup. Her skin was like caramel and seemed almost wet in the glow of the overhead bulb. He shook his head....no wonder...no wonder…it was so hard…to match her up. Her skin is…she ain't like those women…

Fifty dollars. Sometimes as much as seventy-five dollars. But the skin was never the same. Sometimes the hips and waist came close and he'd pay and close his eyes and call her name, but when he opened them, praying for caramel, he looked upon coffee or cinnamon and he'd struggle into his clothing and leave without looking back.

Now she was sitting across the table from him in her caramel skin, and for some reason he was afraid to look at her.

…what the hell kinda dream was that to git her outta bed so fast…and with no clothes on…she don't sleep with nuthin' on…ain't that somethin'…ain't nuthin' on them big hips but a sheet…Lord…

His head pounded and he had to sit down.

"You all right, Al? I knew I never shoulda woke you…"

"I'm all right, I—"

"—what's wrong, then. Is it the business?"

He shook his head, not trusting himself to answer….there's only one kinda business I wanna take care of right now…

He stirred his coffee, still avoiding her gaze.

…now the logical thing to do would be to…hell, no, ain't nuthin' logical when your thing comes down…but that's how mistakes git made—people actin' too quick…damn, ain't all them years quick enough…suppose I make a wrong move…better than no move…suppose she just git up and leave…don't let her…how can I stop her…Lord…

"—Al, I'm talkin' to you…"

"What…?"

"How much sugar you gonna put in one cup?"

Al looked at his shaking hand as if it did not belong to him. "…oh…Lord…"

He dropped the spoon and put his hands to his head. Frieda was on her feet and by his side instantly. "Al, what is it? You so strong, it scares me when I see you like this…what's wrong?"

"Nuthin—"

He closed his eyes and leaned back. The shock of her fingers on his face made him jump. She was standing behind him as he sat at the table. "Relax. You just tired…" Her fingers skirted the nape of his neck, his shoulders, and behind his ears. "...relax... come on now..."

Without effort, he turned and pressed his face against her. He felt the soft mound of her stomach against his mouth and felt her move—not away—but in an incredible, side-to-side, swaying motion. He could not believe it and pressed in close to see if it was really happening. She leaned back, allowing the robe to fall open, and he breathed in her sweet thick scent.

He lifted her, his face still to her stomach, and made his way out of the kitchen. He passed through the living room and heard her whisper, "...here...right here..."

"What...?"

"Yes...here..."

The floor was hard and he was heavy, but that was the way it was and he wasn't going to argue. He had waited too many years. He would have loved her in the bathtub, against the stove, spread out on the dining table, even on top of the Empire State Building if he could have managed it. But here she was, on the living room floor. He was not going to argue.

In the half-dark, he lay beside her and, for a fraction of a second, listened to the small sounds she made.

"Listen," he whispered, "it's gonna be all right...everything's gonna be all right...I promise..."

She felt soft and smooth under him. He saw that her hips were not so large as her waist was tiny. She fit into the bend of his arms as perfectly as if she had been born there. He tasted the coffee on her tongue and breathed in the heavy, sweet oil of her hair. She was small, as if she had been closed forever, and he had to ease in, ease in. She moved back involuntarily and he tried again. He felt the sharp intake of her breath, but she brought her knees up and crossed her legs over him. Her trembling gave way and she lost herself to a smooth, rolling undulation. He placed his hands under her hips, palms wide, to pull her closer.

"I been waitin'...baby...I been waitin'..."

"Al..."

"Girl, I been waitin' for you...all...this...time..."

Her rhythm quickened and became wild and erratic. Suddenly, she stiffened and her head and shoulders pressed back, away from him.

"Al...oh...oh..."

He felt the sound start from deep within her and sweated to hold on. "...come on, baby..."

"...ahh, no..."

"...give it to me, baby, let go...let it go..." His mouth was near her ear, and he was about to beg, plead, cajole, threaten, do anything to release the tremendous pressure. He forgot about easing. He forgot everything, He felt an external force take hold of him and he lost control and pressed in, pressed in. All at once, she flung her arms outward. Her back arched and her legs tightened around him and he drove in hard and quick. He was amazed and frightened by the force of the rhythmic suction that drew the searing liquid from him. Her head turned from side to side so that her hair covered her face and he had to search, to feel for her mouth to kiss her.

"Baby...baby...baby..." he whispered the word over and over, grateful that he was able to use it so freely at last.

7

March 1959

A Raisin in the Sun opened on Broadway. It was the first play that Celia, and several others in her senior class, had ever seen.

They sat in the last two rows of the balcony, mesmerized by Claudia McNeil and Sidney Poitier. Celia cried and laughed, totally immersed in the unfolding drama, but mainly she cried for the hero. He reminded her of the time when she had captured a fly on her windowsill, trapping it beneath an empty jelly jar. For several minutes, she had watched it buzz frantically against the thick glass before it finally fell back, exhausted. It had lain on its back with its wings twitching, and she remembered wondering what the insect was thinking. Had it given up? Was it prepared to die? She remembered that she lifted the jar the merest fraction of an inch and the fly zipped out and hit the pane of the half-closed window twice with a pinging sound before it found the current of air on which it flew to safety.

She was amazed that the playwright was able to make her remember this.

Four days later, on March 15, as Groovy Movers prepared to complete the last run, the music on the truck radio was interrupted. Lester Young had just died, the deejay announced.

Al, Sam, and Dan listened in silence. The Prez had finally given in to the pressure and laid his pork pie brim and his horn aside. "Bop ain't never gonna be the same," Dan said.

It was as if everyone shared Dan's feeling and made a concerted effort to keep the Prez's spirit among them. For days, the sound of the famous horn floated in the air, and the rear courtyard filled with a cacophony of sound: "Love Me or Leave Me," "You Don't Know What Love Is," "Jumpin' with Symphony Sid."

Celia opened her window. This was the first time she'd heard so much music since Tessie had gone. She took out the little book in which she had begun to keep a journal:

...so much music...and someone had to die for me to really hear it. The sound is rich, haunting...almost like an epiphany. Why hadn't I paid attention while he was alive? No doubt, we're all asking ourselves the same thing. What was I thinking of? Now I feel like everyone else...cheated.

Four months and two days later, on July 17, Lady Day took off her gardenia. Everything had been drawn out of her, and she had probably been more tired than the Prez.

Celia took her notebook and sat by the window again but wrote nothing. The courtyard was quiet, and the silence weighed in soft and deceptive, like bricks settling in a deep and muddy place. Celia thought of Tessie and tried hard to imagine what records she might be playing as a requiem. She looked up at the patch of sky and wondered, idly, if stars really fell on Alabama the way Lady Day said.

PART TWO

8

June 1960

Frieda sat in the last row of the sweltering auditorium, refusing to acknowledge the heat as the other parents did. She watched them fan themselves furiously, imprinting their sweat on the graduation programs and perspiring all the more from the effort.

She serenely scanned the faces, recognized some from the block, and, when eyes met, inclined her head slightly. Al and the twins sat next to her but she remained silent, preferring to listen to the whispered fragments floating around her:

"...Timmie made it...didn't think I'd live to see the day..."

"You damn near didn't. Remember when—"

"Never mind. Lookit Valerie...vee-dee Valerie, the senior class nicknamed her. She git that little problem cleared up yet?"

"Must have...that robe lookin' mighty snug in front..."

"...and who all them flowers for? Somebody die?"

"They for James. He sure *woulda* died if he didn't show me some kinda diploma this year. When I was his age, I was already workin' five years..."

James lived across the courtyard, and many nights, especially if the windows were open, everyone could hear his father shouting in his crisp 'Bajan accent, heavy on the R's: "Boy, ef yer dern crack dem books, I gon' beat yer 'til yer black back bleeds..."

James sat now in the first row. His cap, tilted at forty-five degrees, hid the smile on his handsome face. Graduation meant, among other things, that his father was no longer in danger of biting his own tongue every time he opened his mouth.

Celia sat in the second row directly behind James, wondering how soon his cap would fall off. Watching it only added to the tension she had been denying all morning. She felt her curls were too tight and made her hair seem shorter than it was, and the brown organdy dress her mother had worked so hard on was now crushed under the heavy satin robe.

She glanced at the silver watch on her wrist, a gift from Al and the twins and elegant in its thinness. She fingered it nervously, aware that she was the only one that day to receive such an expensive gift. The undercurrent of rustling and restlessness dissolved into expectant silence and she looked up as Dr. Nolan stepped to the podium.

The principal scanned the crowd, tapped the mike, and began to speak almost immediately.

"Distinguished graduates, honored guests, ladies and gentlemen, since our multimillion-dollar air-conditioning system isn't functioning too well, I promise that this commencement will be quite short."

The sweating assembly gazed at the three ancient wall fans and the laughter turned to cheers and whistles, then subsided. Celia watched him and wondered if she should have gone to him for help.

...he probably wouldn't have done anything except agree with mother...

And, even as he began to speak, she broadened her anger to include him.

"—and you graduates know that you didn't arrive at this point without the love and support of family. You know that someone was always in your corner when the going got rough..."

His voice was soft and soothing, and Celia wanted to laugh. My corner, she thought, was so crowded, there was hardly any room for me...

She felt constricted in the heavy robe, as if the satin had closed her pores and turned the sweat inward, where it gathered and seemed to flow in a steady roaring rush to her brain.

She looked again at the watch, trying to concentrate on the tiny numbered chips that seemed to dance on its face. The watch was not a gift, but a reward, an assuagement of guilt. She had accepted it and, in doing so, accepted her defeat.

Frieda had rejected out of hand the idea of her going away to school. In classic fashion, she had closed her mind to the scholarship and the pleas, and Celia, in tears, had gone to Sam and Dan. They gave her a lecture.

"You gotta understand," said Sam, "your mama don't have nobody but you. You can't go roamin' around the country and not expect her to worry..."

"Roaming," she repeated, surprised at how well they all managed to use the same word. Hearing it made her feel as if they had met in secret council and conspired together to keep her prisoner.

"I'll be in one place. School. One *place*!"

She emphasized the word and the wonder of it. One place. Except for her expedition to the hospital to warn Tessie and her school outing to Broadway, she had remained in one place. She especially remembered the long listless summer afternoons sitting stiff and starched in the park with Frieda, watching others half her age glide by on roller skates and bicycles or tumble, chase, and lose games she never knew the names of. Rough, wild games that sent them home tired and covered with half the park's dirt, while she returned as stiff and starched as when she set out.

The library had been the only place she had been allowed to go, and even that had required an urgent note from her teacher explaining to Frieda the importance of reading and research. Once there, however, she managed to move beyond her homework into a paper world of intrigue and adventure. She devoured the classic and the mediocre without discrimination, and they became the foundation of a restless imagination, a free ticket of transport to anywhere but where she was.

She opened her eyes when the principal coughed. He paused, sipped from a glass of water, and continued. He had forgotten the fans and warmed to his subject, whatever it was, and the assembly hung on every word.

"...they say de facto slavery has ended, but we, as a people, have not been entirely emancipated. Now we must free ourselves from ourselves, our mental chains. We must free our minds of negativism, stop telling ourselves that we can't do this or shouldn't do that, because it's not time yet. We must not stand in the way of our own progress..."

He looked at the first ten rows, where the graduates sat.

"If the door is even slightly ajar, you must push your way in without hesitation. Open it up all the way. Never doubt your ability to succeed!"

He received a rousing ovation and Celia regretted that she hadn't paid attention to the entire speech.

...if he's talking like that, perhaps I should have gone to him. He might have made mother change her mind. There was my chance...

"—and once you've achieved your goal," he continued, "whatever it might be, don't forget those whose care and concern helped you over. Remember their sacrifice, and love them for it. You must—"

Celia's head ached. She rubbed her fingers against her ears, creating a hollow-seashell effect, which muffled the rest of the speech. ...love them for their sacrifices...who's going to love me for mine? Why couldn't she let me go. She wouldn't have been alone. Sam and Dan are here. And Al. He was the only one to agree with me, yet even he couldn't go against her...

"She's afraid," he had said, "she see all them things happenin' to those college kids in the south; Eisenhower sendin' in federal marshals, that young boy, Mack Parker, lynched for nuthin'. She see all these things and she's scared if somethin' happen to you—"

"Nothing's going to happen to me..."

"Maybe not, but there's other things..."

"...like what?"

"Well, like mostly stuff in her...head...her imagination git the best of her sometimes...she still talk about your leg sometimes..."

Celia stopped listening then, knowing that things imagined and things remembered were altogether two different things. But she had looked at Al carefully as they talked and saw the tough mask drop away. For a fraction of a second, she glimpsed profound sadness. And fear mixed with indefinable longing. She forgot her problem then, and watched his hands as he gestured helplessly.

She had wanted to take them in her own hands and rub and smooth away the callouses and all the old pain that lay beneath.

...what do you want, she had almost asked him. What, more than anything on earth, do you want...

But she had not taken his hands or asked him anything because asking would have been like opening a door to that windowless room where nameless things lurked in darkness, waiting. She saw in his eyes the fear that if she went away, her mother might slip back into the windowless room and remain beyond his reach forever.

The applause caught her unawares, and the uproar was deafening. The first chords of the piano sounded and she rose to her feet automatically. The graduates, with a controlled cadence, started soft and low; then the teachers and parents joined in, adding determination to the anthem's promise.

The girl next to Celia was crying and she glanced at her.

...why is *she* upset...I'm the one who should be crying...

She stole another look as the girl dabbed at the corner of each eye, careful not to disturb her makeup. She was as tall as Celia and looked as awkward, but she had the reputation for being the best dancer for blocks around and had been voted Miss Shing a Ling of 1960 by the senior class. She was also smart enough to receive the scholarship that Celia had been forced to turn down.

...why is she crying? In two months, she'll be going away to the school I should be going to...why is she crying... Celia closed her eyes finally and eased away from the sound of heavy hands clapping and palms meeting in the ancient, extraordinary, quarter-time rhythm. She closed them out to listen instead to her own song:

I never danced
the shing a ling
never learned to
shake that thing
never had a
boy to say
girl where you learn
to move that way
if I went to Toogaloo

I'd show those folks a
thing or two
I'd show those folks
a thing
or…

She opened her eyes in time to catch the last sentence of the last stanza. The procession had begun to move and she fell in step, gliding down the aisle behind Shing a Ling, who was marching as if she'd seen too many war movies.

She watched the girl strut, and it occurred to her that she would never see her again. Or this room.

Celia looked around frantically in an effort to commit to memory a picture of the broken and scarred seats, the stained curtains at each end of the small stage, the crisp American flag loaned from central board to be returned immediately after the ceremony. She gazed at the walls and ceilings and the flakes of dull green peeling paint and tried to memorize each configuration.

The three ancient and overworked fans creaked noisily in the heavy air as she tried to hold in mind the wilting heat of the day. She gave up finally when the tears came, and all the proud, anxious, weary, and beaming faces blurred into a kaleidoscope of black, brown, and beige.

9

In the other Harlem, east of Fifth Avenue, a council was convened. On the second floor of a billiard parlor, hoodlums in sharkskin suits, with Borsalino hats and big cigars, looked carefully at their profit margins and decided to declare war on their neighbor.

They had made some small inroads on the jazz scene, but now the time had come, the mobsters decided, to broaden their base. They opened up on all fronts, and central Harlem was buried under a gray heroin blanket.

The street gangs, whose time and function had already passed, and whose members had devolved into a loose confederation of social cliques, were the first to go. These young boys, pushing into manhood but still strolling with the telltale bop of adolescence—leaning slightly to the side, with fists curled hard, too cool to speak even when sailing past their own girlfriends—these were the first to go, disintegrating from impenetrable clique to individual terrorist. Their sole ambition now was to outdo Rip Van Winkle on a quarter cap of gray lady, and nod out of the nightmare that controlled them.

In the process of their disintegration, a whole community was held hostage. Old-timers longed for the minor public inconvenience of ducking for cover when zip guns blazed during intratribal struggles for territory. Gone were the minor hardships of paying lunch money tribute in order to attend school in recently captured territory. Times had changed, and Harlem suffered a massive assault. Storefront grilles and window gates altered the landscape. People spoke only to those they knew, and strangers were stared down hard when they asked for a match.

The graduating class dispersed into this landscape. Its members remembered the principal's advice and went in search of doors to open. They found corporate fortresses, guarded by stiff-coiffed receptionists who took their neatly written applications with dazzling smiles and empty promises to call.

So some decided to go on to college, hoping that four years and an additional piece of paper might make the difference. Others joined what they believed to be "the first peacetime army ever." And some others followed the narrow path of the terrorist and suffocated under the gray blanket.

Celia did not go job hunting. Instead, she absorbed Frieda's plan to attend school fourteen blocks away, but the impressive gothic structures that held other freshmen in awe only reinforced her resentment and frustration.

Even on days when other buildings reflected the sun's beneficence, the campus projected a foreboding aspect unbroken by the best efforts of the creeping ivy. She went through the ritual of registration wondering about Shing a Ling, and her resentment mounted with each wrong turn she took.

She resented the drafty interiors, the crowded classes, and the steamy social atmosphere of the cafeteria, yet when classes were over, she was in no rush to return home. She retreated instead to the school library—a building with cool, high-ceilinged rooms where the quiet, near darkness was softened by amber-shaded reading lamps. Long after her homework had been completed, she sat for hours, absorbed in the cool, soft silence.

She developed the habit of selecting a book at random, reading the first chapter, and then gradually allowing her mind to drift beyond the print: Morocco, Hyderabad, Istanbul. Traveling by jet. Oceangoing yachts. Today she was on the Orient Express, enveloped in the old-world opulence of the cabin-*lit.* The engine turned. She drew the gold-tinted brocade curtains. She was moving. The wheels were smooth, fast. Even the blurred image of her mother, running along the platform, peering frantically in the window, could not keep up. She was moving. Away. Away from the voice that trailed off to a hollow echo.

"Wake up," James said, as he slid into a seat beside her. "You readin' or you nappin'?"

Celia did not answer immediately. Privately, she hoped he would go away. James had continued in school because he had decided that classwork was preferable to real work. His father was still yelling in his clipped accent, but now James had learned to ignore him.

"How you doin'?" he whispered. Not waiting for an answer, he pressed a news clipping into her hand.

"Remember her?"

Celia looked closely. It showed a group of black students demonstrating at an obscure luncheonette. In the forefront was Mary Anderson—Shing a Ling—being led out in handcuffs.

"Ain't she somethin'? Ain't she somethin'?" James repeated. "I danced with her a couple of times." He was proud as a peacock and twice as vain. "Ain't she somethin'?"

"Yes, she is," Celia said, looking at him. It was as though, through the magic of dance, he had personally transfused the courage Mary Anderson needed to defy the system.

"Yep, she all right—could tell just from the way she moved that she didn't take no shit..."

On the way home, Celia bought a copy of the newspaper, intending to show Frieda. She tried to step fast and look sure, but by the time she arrived home, her neck hurt from holding it at an unnatural angle and she was out of breath. She buried the article in the bottom of the drawer next to the watch.

Near the end of night, sleep eluded her, and she lay in the half-dark studying the changing pattern of the brickwork beyond the window as dawn approached. The quiet was full of small sounds. She left the bed, retrieved the article, and looked closely at the picture in the dim light.

Shing a Ling's mouth was drawn tight with defiance and her eyes were wide with wonder. A nightstick pressed into the small of her back forced her to assume an awkward, spine-straight stance. Celia looked at the nightstick, and the last remnant of resentment, the anger she had displaced against Shing a Ling over the scholarship, drained away.

She clicked on the small light near the bed, found some notepaper, and wrote her a letter, apologizing, calling her by her given name. Before sealing the envelope, she folded a twenty-dollar bill—all she had—within the note.

To her surprise, Shing a Ling wrote back two weeks later:

Dear Celia,

I was very glad to hear from you and to know that you're not angry with me any more about the scholarship. Thank you for the money. It came right on time. We're going through so much down here and only half of it will ever reach the newspapers. I've been lucky so far—no beatings. Right now, the police seem to be leaving the women alone, but the brothers are catching it. As bad as it is, we're not discouraged. We have three-quarters of the students involved and more are joining. We receive some support from the instructors but the higher administration has to keep a low profile. This is, after all, a state-supported school and the governor can shut us down on the pretext of maintaining public order. But be that as it may, we're here to stay. Thanks again and keep in touch. I want to know what's happening up there in the city.

Sincerely,
Mary

Celia was surprised. Shing a Ling had been known for her wild dancing and wilder language. Now this letter seemed to have come from a different person. Somewhere along the way, she had acquired a sense of style and sophistication—and commitment.

Before Celia had a chance to reply, a second letter arrived from Mary. The state's attorney general was checking into the backgrounds of the students involved in the sit-ins and was pressing for their expulsions. The bail bond fund had to be diverted to fight this latest maneuver, so those arrested now were staying in jail longer.

Celia put the letter in her purse and, the next day, searched for James on campus. As usual, he was in the student lounge, deeply involved in a chess game.

"We've got to do something," she said, showing him the letters. "If she's arrested again, she may be in jail for months."

James read the letters and shook his head slowly. "You right. What you doin' after class?"

"Nothing. The library—"

"See you there. There's this group I wanna take you to..."

A dozen blocks from the campus, James led the way through what appeared to be an abandoned building. As Celia followed along the darkened hallway, she began to have second thoughts.

...All I wanted him to do was to show the letters to his father, and I would show them to mama and Al and the twins...between us we could have gotten over a hundred dollars to send...James is complicating things...

There were eight of them in a small room lit by a single overhead bulb. They sat on the floor lotus style and all wore the loose-fitting tops that Celia had been seeing on campus. The five men and three women all wore the new natural-style haircut.

"We don't have a name yet," James said as he introduced her, "but that can wait."

A small woman with an Arabic-sounding name that Celia could not pronounce moved over and Celia squeezed into the space on the floor. "Now," said James, pulling out the letters, "I want you all to take a look at this..."

The letters were passed around; then one of the men spoke,

"What has this to do with us? We got our agenda in place already."

"Yeah," a second one agreed, "how can we help her? The sister is hundreds of miles away, fightin' on a different front."

Celia said nothing as someone else added an opinion. They seemed to speak in the language of the military. They discussed the strategy of confrontation, passive resistance, and incitement. Celia felt silly about bringing up the idea of simply collecting a few dollars. These people were planning some sort of invasion.

"Look James," she said, getting to her feet, "mother's expecting me, so I'll have to be going...we can talk more about this later."

Outside, James handed her the letters as they walked down the hill. "They some serious people, Celia. They dead serious..."

"I suppose they are," said Celia, "but all I'm trying to do right now is raise a hundred dollars. That can go a long way. I don't want to plan a revolution, I just want to keep Shing a Ling out of jail..."

James was silent as they crossed the street. Then he said, "Who knows...it might take a revolution to keep her out..."

She left him at the corner and walked into the cool, semidark interior of Groovy Movers. Al was sitting at the desk. "What's goin' on? How's class?"

"Okay. Everything's okay. I received a letter from the girl who used my scholarship..."

"Yeh?" Al watched Celia closely. That had been a sore point with her for months, and he wasn't sure if she had gotten over it yet. "How she doin'," he asked cautiously.

Celia handed him the letters. "She's not doing too well. I'm trying to send her something...bail money..."

Al read the letters. "You kiddin'...well, I'll be damned...the girl got stuff..."

"Travel broadens," Celia observed. Then she whispered aloud, "I wondered what would have happened if I—"

Al interrupted her. "Forget it. Your mama would've been on the first bus down the minute somethin' jumped off. You better off up here, you better off." He reached into his pocket and handed her a fifty-dollar bill.

She took it, wondering if it was bail money for Mary or bribe money for her memory.

10

1961

"May 20: Attorney General Robert Kennedy sends 400 United States Marshals to Montgomery, Alabama, to investigate charges of brutality against the Freedom Riders."

At school, Celia read the latest dispatches and gritted her teeth. She maintained a steady flow of correspondence with Shing a Ling, who had been expelled and then reinstated and was now devoting all her spare time to a new organization called SNCC.

When Celia arrived home from school, she retrieved her weekly letter from the mailbox and headed up the stairs.

She became aware of a different sound as she climbed the stairs, old and sad and familiar. It echoed off the faded marble walls and flowed around her. The volume pounded and grated with each step, and she knew that Tessie had returned. Celia held her books to her, not daring to breathe. "I can't believe it. After all this time..."

The music drifted down the narrow stairwell, sadder than she had ever heard it.

She decided it would not be wise to drop her books off before going upstairs. If she heard the music, her mother had heard it also. Better to keep on going and explain later.

She climbed the extra flight and pounded hard on the door. The sound inside snapped off, and the unfamiliar clicking of high heels moved down the hall. The fragile door chain held, and through the narrow opening, the two women stared at each other in the brief silence of strangers.

Then Tessie laughed. "Damn, girl, you ain't changed one bit..."

She slipped the latch open and held the door wide, still laughing. "You ain't changed at all. Come on in..."

"I heard the music," Celia said as she entered the dim hallway, "but I wasn't sure if it was you..."

She followed her into the living room and stopped, suddenly at a loss for words. She stared at Tessie and remembered once long ago when they had both wondered what it was like to be pretty.

She was amazed now at the change. Tessie was tall, bust and hips as full as ever but her waist was now more defined. The dark brown hair was streaked with auburn, and her brows were thin arcs of black over cloudy eye shadow. She knew Tessie no longer wasted her time wondering what it was like to be pretty.

Celia looked at her and remembered the long private hours she herself had spent posing before an unsparing mirror, wondering about the distribution of things. While some girls had worried about the length and thickness of hair and nose, she had worried about the shape of her legs. And her face was so plain and unimaginative that she had not even considered the idea of makeup.

But, like an oasis emerging in the heart of a parched landscape, there had been her teachers, all of them, saying, "such a bright child, so quick, so smart..." And she had sucked these words in like water on a sponge and clung to them for sustenance, and finally she reached a point where being intelligent and capable was enough to make her feel good about herself. Now she looked at Tessie and began to wonder all over again.

She heard herself saying, "You really look great, Tessie..."

The phrase sounded foreign on her tongue, and she wondered how often she would have to use it. Perhaps not too often. Perhaps Tessie had come for a visit. Then she glanced at the pile of unopened cartons as Tessie spoke.

"I was gone awhile, but now I'm back..."

She watched Tessie light up a cigarette and put it out just as quickly. Her movements were light and birdlike.

"What happened?"

Tessie looked away and said in a low voice, "My baby...my baby... died..."

Celia felt as if someone had drawn the breath out of her. She sat down on the sofa and stared, unable to speak. Tessie sat on the arm of the chair, facing her.

"...one night...just like that..." She went on almost in a whisper, "I went back to check the covers on her and she wasn't breathin'... she was ice cold..."

She got up and began to move around, as if trying to move away from memory even as she spoke.

"Auntie's house was cold...we always had to have the oven goin' full blast. You know how those places are...wind come through like the wall wasn't even there. It was cold, but we took care of her. I can't understand what happened...."

Tessie's voice was barely audible and Celia had to strain to hear her.

"—I should've moved out right after it happened...come back here...but Auntie had been so tied up, you know...with the church and the baby and everything. I thought she would've snapped if I split. It was almost like it was her baby and I was her kid too. I mean she just took over and started raisin' us both. You should've seen the clothes she made. Pretty little things, pretty... but that place...you ain't felt cold 'til you been inside there..."

She lit another cigarette and was silent.

Celia was struggling with her own thoughts. Why hadn't she called Tessie. Why hadn't she made an effort to maintain a connection, a tie, anything instead of nursing the dull feeling of abandonment that had dogged her for months after Tessie had gone. If she had been able to forgive Shing a Ling and write to her, why hadn't she been able to do the same with Tessie?

Then she remembered that Shing a Ling was engaged in warfare, public warfare on a grand scale, while Tessie's battle had gone unrecorded. How could she have known?

And now, never having understood the mystery of birth, Celia was even less prepared for the phenomenon of death, and her mourning gave way to anger and confusion. She struggled to remain silent as Tessie spoke.

"And even after that, I guess I would've stayed 'cause Auntie'd been all right. Religious but all right. I mean she helped me through a tough time. But then...I don't know what happened. I think it mighta been some a them storefront sisters turned her 'round. Biggest bunch a hypocrits you ever saw. When they facin' you, first thing out their mouth is 'praise His name.' But behind your back, the next thing out their mouth is *your* name, and they steady draggin' it through the dirt.

"So Auntie gradually started in on me. Pullin' me to that two-by-four church every chance she got, had me standin' up there in some funny lookin' white dress while they screamin' and yellin' about sin and death and bullshit and poundin' their bibles and pointin' and more screamin' like it was my fault.

"I tried to hold out, hopin' Auntie would cool down, but she never did. When I couldn't take any more, I took a walk...cut it loose, the whole damn thing..."

Tessie began to pace again but after a minute stopped to gaze out at the courtyard. Celia looked at her silhouette framed against the curtainless window and shook her head....what can I say to her... children are supposed to grow up...and play in parks...not be found stiff and cold. They are supposed to outlive their parents. How come I was born on the sidewalk and survived...but this baby...

She rose from the sofa and glanced at the pile of cartons near the table. The only open one contained a stack of records, and Celia reached in without looking, wiped an old '78 very carefully, and then placed it on the turntable. Lady Day's voice, low and husky, crowded out the silence. Tessie did not really move but inclined her head slightly, to keep time to the rhythm. So Celia waited, in silence, listening for the one word or sound that might bring Tessie back to the way she used to be.

The sound of the record player with its mournful crying let Celia and the whole house know when Tessie was home. The stoop watchers charted her progress as she looked for a job.

"Late gittin' back today. Think she found somethin'?"

"Naw. Nobody hirin' now. She gotta wait 'til the weather break..."

"What the weather got to do with it? She ain't lookin' for nuthin' seasonal..."

"Still, she do better when the weather break. Found some a my best jobs when the weather broke..." said Mrs. Canty, who hadn't worked in ten years.

"...and what you think Celia gonna do now that Tessie's back? Think she quit school?"

"Dunno. They was regular runnin' buddies when they was little, but now, I dunno..."

"I know. They're different now as night and day. The makeup Tessie piles on in one hour would last Celia all year..."

"Celia'd be just throwin' good money after bad if she start buyin' makeup. Besides, Frieda'd pitch a bitch if Celia even looked like she wanted to hang with Tessie."

"Well, now, I dunno. What mama *say* and what a child *do* is two different things..."

And they continued the daily duel with the digits, only now the arrival of the runner held less interest than Tessie's comings and goings.

The weather changed. Light air crept in with warm rain to wash gray mounds of snow. The ice-cracked streets seemed less hostile, and almost overnight, it was as if winter had never happened.

The rising temperature meant more open windows and allowed the sound of Tessie's music to flow in, more insistently than ever. The beat filled the courtyard, finally overwhelming the other sounds.

Celia, unable to study, listened as Lloyd Price pleaded Stagger Lee's case for the tenth time. Finally, she closed her notebook, left her room, and climbed the flight of stairs to Tessie's place. The sound vibrated off the marble steps and seemed to scrape against the soles of her shoes.

...perhaps she's finally found a job...and decided to celebrate.

Her knocking went unanswered. She hesitated a minute, then touched the knob and the door opened slightly. She passed the small foyer and was in the living room before Tessie turned around.

"Girl! When you gonna stop sneakin' up on people like that?"

Celia did not hear the warning and said, "When are you going to learn to lock your door?"

"I'll lock it when I get a job and get some money to buy somethin' worth stealin', that's when..."

Celia knew then that it was time to change the subject but could think of nothing that would make sense.

Tessie paced the floor, pausing to tap her cigarette in the overflowing ashtray balanced on the arm of the sofa. She stopped, waved Celia to a chair, and then sat down on the edge of the sofa.

"Girl, be glad you in school 'cause there ain't nuthin' out here. Not a damn thing..."

She lit another cigarette, and Celia moved to empty the ashtray before Tessie added any more to it. She returned from the kitchen to find her pacing the floor again.

"You know, I keep tryin' and tryin', day in and day out... sometimes I'm so tired when I come in, I say to myself, just five minutes, I'll lie down for five and I'll feel better. But then, while I'm lyin' there, and five turns to ten and I'm still starin' at that damn dirty ceilin', and all this damn dirty broken-down furniture that I can't do nuthin' about, I close my eyes and start to wonder what it'd be like not to have to open 'em again, not to have to feel nuthin' no more..."

"Oh, Tessie, wait a minute, wait—"

Celia was about to get up from the sofa when Tessie snapped off the record player. The needle skidded across the surface with a high, whining sound.

In the sudden quiet, Tessie's voice was toneless.

"Wait? For what? What do you know about what I'm goin' through. You sittin' in some damn warm classroom with your 'siddity' friends. What do you know? I'm out there hittin' them bricks every a.m. and you tellin' me to wait? For what? What do you know?"

Tessie leaned over the sofa with her hands on her hips, her face inches away from Celia's.

"What do you know??" she repeated.

Celia stared in disbelief. Something in her shrank from the dimensionless gray eyes and the heavy makeup. And the thin laugh lines that did not come from laughing.

But more frightening was the faintly sour exhalation that hung in the air when Tessie spoke. It was a bitter odor from the pit of the stomach that spoke of cold coffee and stale cigarettes and an anger that threatened to enlarge and devour everything within her reach.

"Listen," Celia said quietly, "you've got it wrong...the wrong idea about me. I may be in school, true, but this is not what I wanted. Mother carried on so, I had to give up a scholarship just to keep the peace. She didn't want me to go away, she said. Something might happen. She never said what or to whom. So I didn't go. Shing a Ling took my scholarship, and she's changing the world while I shuffle home like a crippled puppy. Shing a Ling's doing something…not like those phonies at my school who talk black but won't look twice if you're not at least high yellow…"

She could have gone on about the big dark men on campus, posturing, strolling, invading, and dominating every scene that provided an audience. And unfailingly, they had dangling from their arms the high-gloss, high-yellow charms. Once, one of the charms actually smiled and said, "Thomas, this is Celia…we're in Bio together…"

Celia remembered Thomas glancing at a small space somewhere to the left of her forehead and grunting something that she could not interpret, while the charm continued to smile, laying up IOUs for the midterm.

She could have gone on, but she saw that Tessie had dropped her hands from her hips and was staring at her.

"Tessie, I'm sorry, I must sound like a fool. Going on about some stupid thing while your problem is food and money. You need a job, and I'm talking nonsense. Who cares about sit-ins and lay-ins and who sleeps with whom? None of that matters if your belly button is rubbing against your backbone. None of it matters." She leaned forward and pressed her hands to her head. "I'm sorry."

Tessie waved her hand. "It's all right. I guess I shouldn't have come at you so hard like that. It's the same old story…I was thinkin' how green the grass looked on your side, that's all."

Celia started to laugh, but the tight knot was still in her throat. "Grass. It feels more like gravel. Hard little stones beating against me, grinding me to pieces. If I had gone away, I wouldn't have to feel my mother's eyes on me watching, like she's waiting for something to happen. I wouldn't have to listen to her say, 'Don't do this, do that, don't go there, don't go too far, come straight home, what time will you be home, walk the straight and narrow, remember your leg is not too strong.'"

"Don't tell me your mama's still harpin' on your leg?"

"Yes, but it's not really that. I can't explain what it is she's afraid of. But her fear is killing me…"

"Look," Tessie interrupted, "whatever it is, you can't give in to it. Look at me. I lost my man and my kid, remember? I mean, I have some really bad days, but I snap back. You gotta do the same. You gotta git a handle on whatever it is you want, whatever you wanna do, then find a way to do it and to hell with everything else. Your mama ain't gonna change just like mine ain't gonna. Your mama's thinkin' she's protectin' you, standin' there like a big hidin' place, but that ain't what you need. You been hid too long as it is. She's like a big rock that you just gotta find your way around."

Celia looked at the cloudy eye shadow and auburn streaks. She watched Tessie exhale, the smoke wafting from her nostrils in a lazy stream. She wanted to laugh but she felt too tired.

"You remember when we were kids, I practically lived in the library..."

"Yeah, and I used to run to the Apollo every chance I got. Even back then, we tried to find our own way 'round things..."

"And nothing's changed, has it?"

Tessie put her cigarette out and looked at Celia. "Come on, girl, things are always changin'. Always. Trick is not to get stuck in one spot and let change pass you by."

The weather turned unusually warm and humid. The bright sunlight curbed the edges of the wind and softened its bite. The stoop watchers, encouraged, ventured out of their cocoons to observe the change with caution.

"This what they call pneumonia weather..."

"Anybody fool enough to take off their coats deserve what they get..."

Their remarks, as usual, were aimed obliquely at the young, who welcomed any change in the weather with changes of their own: three-quarter toppers and high-heeled slingbacks displaced maxis and suedes, which two months ago had been all the rage.

The stoop watchers shook their heads at the quick-change artists, condemning their frivolity.

"Double pneumonia'd teach 'em a lesson. Walkin' pneumonia be better 'cause that's long and slow. Give 'em time to think about what hit 'em."

Not one of them acknowledged the small current of envy that

flowed through the small talk; how it circled and turned back on its source, tightening its grip, making the sweat run until it seeped into the coarse wool of their patched winter snuggies, almost causing them to scream out from the itching confinement.

The snuggies were not due to come off for at least another three weeks. They were stuck with them—prisoners of fear, and habit, and old age. Meanwhile, they assuaged their pain by condemning the small freedom of others.

On campus, the sun poured unfiltered through the budding branches of the old maples and splashed against the long, narrow, uncurtained windows. Celia turned from the window and looked again at the blank paper before her. Beyond name, address, and date of exam, there was nothing.

...concentrate...concentrate on what's at hand...why am I thinking about summer...

The chalk scraped the blackboard as the instructor noted the time remaining. Celia blinked.

...I need one line...one good line and I can start and finish in twenty minutes...

She bent over the paper, blocking out the sun's glare with her shoulder, and began to write. Between paragraphs, she wondered about Tessie and what it was that kept her going.

11

Tessie was walking down the hill from the subway one evening when she met Willie. He fell in beside her and slowed to match her stride. He was tall and his long legs made him seem even taller.

"Good evening...anything yet?"

"No. Nuthin'..."

She glanced sideways at him and smiled, not knowing what else to say. She saw his thin, dark face and his concerned expression. He had recently moved into the next building, and every morning she saw him hurrying to the subway. But this was the first time he had spoken to her.

He always wore a suit and never carried his lunch, the way so many of the other men did.

She had a chance to look closely now and noticed that his fingernails were clean too.

The next evening, as they passed the Peacock, he invited her to stop for a drink.

"Little something to lift the spirits," he smiled, raising his glass.

She laughed with him. "Those stoop people don't bother me..."

They drank in near silence the first night. The evenings that followed, he spoke of his job as a draftsman and she listened attentively.

Then she spoke of her mother, her baby, and her first love and how they were all lost or dead or gone to a place quite beyond her reach but still within memory.

Once she began, the words came out, tripping, stumbling, like ragged prisoners newly released from a dark, damp dungeon. She spoke of death and deprivation and days spent wondering when her life would be put together again.

He listened, holding under his tongue the taste of whatever it was they were drinking, not interjecting a syllable, not daring to swallow lest he disturb his concentration, and all the while drinking in the wonder of her, trying to reconcile the fragility of her beauty with the hard, broken words she threw at him.

He listened for nights. Weeks. Longer than it ordinarily took for him to talk a woman into bed with his soft, sly, sexy accent. Every evening, he walked with her as far as the lobby, said good night, and left, leaving the stoop watchers in a fit of consternation.

And every evening, as soon as she rushed in, she signaled out of the window to Celia, who came up to listen to the latest details.

"He's beautiful, Celia, beautiful...and right here under my nose all the time. How come I didn't notice...? Oh Lord, how come I didn't see this big, handsome—"

"You were looking for a job, remember?" And they both laughed.

The old music did not stop, but Celia also heard Lady Day singing "What a Little Moonlight Can Do." She heard Nellie Lutcher sing "Fine Brown Frame," and she listened as Tessie talked about the Peacock Lounge, where Willie took her every chance he got.

The Peacock was another world, and last weekend was the liveliest it had been since Tessie had started going there.

Celia listened with her mouth open. "A robbery??"

"Yep...I was right there. And you know, everything woulda been all right if Phoebe hadda been cool," said Tessie, enjoying Celia's reaction. "She's the barmaid, and everybody call her feebleminded Phoebe. Always stickin' her titties up in the dudes' eyeballs... and she never pour a straight drink. It's broads like her give the barmaid profession a bad name."

Tessie paused to light a cigarette. "Anyway, me and Willie, we sittin' at the bar, not too near the door 'cause Willie don't like no draughts on his neck, you know, and Phoebe had just finished pourin' her usual sloppy two-for-one when these three dudes, out of nowhere, bust in the joint and say, "Don't not a motherfucker move!!"

"Well, you know, there's guns and there are guns, but these cats musta just knocked over the armory. Anyway, I bet you not a motherfucker moved. We all had our hands in the air. All 'cept Phoebe. She had hers on her saddlebag hips tryin' to look cute while everybody's pockets was bein' lightened.

"One of the dudes turned on her and starts pattin' her down, you know, lookin' for her stash, and the dumb broad goes berserk behind the bar—starts throwin' Scotch and shit. By now, they figure she got gold stuffed in them hills. They pin her down, rip her blouse and brassiere off, and girl, I'm tellin' you, Miss bigtime Phoebe was not only broke, she was bankrupt. I mean, not only did she not have no cash in her stash, she ain't had no tits neither! She flat as Willie's feet, and you know he got a bad case.

"The dudes, and everybody else, was shook. They threw the falsies on the bar, size forty I want you to know, and they got in the wind. All this time, Phoebe standin' there screamin' and hollerin' and everybody else so stunned, they even forgot to call the po-lice. They just stood and stared and wondered how the hell they could get all them tips back."

"But weren't you and Willie afraid," asked Celia as Tessie paused for breath.

"Naw. Maybe a little. Besides, nobody got hurt so it wasn't so bad, but all the next day, Phoebe wanted to know who the slick cat was that kept the jukebox jammed with "The Great Pretender." When she rang up that night, she told Tate that she hadda go out of town, but he knew she wasn't comin' back, so I asked for her job."

Celia's frustration grew. Tessie had been able to come and go to the Peacock as she pleased. Now she was going to work there, and Celia could not even walk on the same side of the street as the bar.

So she made it a point to do her homework near the living room window, where she could watch the activity across the street.

The door was in constant motion as bar traffic ebbed and flowed with players dueling with the digits. If someone hit, the party lasted until closing. If no one was lucky, the crowd thinned, drifting to other places where they could lose more money.

When the cash registers slowed, the Peacock became quiet and the silence caused Tate, the bar manager, to feel uneasy. He was a handsome, quiet 'Bajan who had adroitly juggled two full-time families for several years, and an uninterrupted cash flow was necessary for his lifestyle. He hired Tessie not because she was pretty but because he perceived in her a certain vitality that people responded to. This was what he needed to pull the action during the slow, early evening hours. When she worked, the bar was crowded and the tips were heavy even though the men knew she was interested in no one but Willie.

Women came because of the men. Even LeRoy the Runner made more frequent stops on his evening rounds. He drew the night players who bet heavy and hit big.

When this happened, the winnings seemed to burn a hole in the palm of the fortunate. Hustlers, boosters, and other parasites of the poor crowded in, and buying and selling took place on a grand scale.

"A mink ain't no big thing in the Peacock," Tessie said to Celia. "I see at least four or five of them a week, not to mention custom color tee-vees, sewing machines, industrial vacuum cleaners, you name it.

"But you should've been there though, a couple a nights ago, when that undercover sweetie, Mr. Peabody, hit his digit. He's a damn good piano teacher, I got to hand him that much, but ain't nobody supposed to know he sweet. Girl couldn't fool a blind man. One night he spent forty-five minutes winkin' and blinkin' at Willie 'til I asked him if somethin' was wrong with his eye that I couldn't fix.

"Anyway, right after he collected, he come trippin' in and announce how he been just dyin' for a baby grand. Now, why he had to say that out loud 'round all them bloodhounds?

"I spied when Joe and Turk eased on out. I had my eye on them. And don't you know, at four a.m., while I'm announcin' the last call for alcohol, here come them two guys slidin' through the door rollin', not a baby grand, but a damn concert grand. Where they cop, nobody know, but the crowd went crazy. They start movin' chairs and tables out the way like they gettin' set to party.

"Peabody nearly peed on himself, tryin' to hold the crowd back. He was jumpin' up and down and screechin' at the top of his lungs, 'Don't mar it, for heavens sake, don't mar it…'

"Then a fight nearly broke out 'cause some other fool wanted Joe to upright it so he could jam to Hamp's 'Boogie Woogie.' Naturally, Peabody wasn't havin' none a that but was too scared to say so. And you know how people are, they see Peabody is uptight so they eggin' this other dude on who kept hollerin' about how good he was 'cause he had been a killer on the keys 'till he got his thumb shot off in a stickup…"

Celia listened with her mouth open as Tessie went on.

"Everybody started screamin' as Peabody fell over the keyboard as if he had had a stroke.

"Someone in the crowd yelled, 'Cool jazz on a hot piano is just my thing, move out the way…'

"Now Peabody recovered quickly and, with hands on hips and stamping feet, declared: "I'll slap the black off the first bitch—man or woman—who comes near my piano!!"

"Your mama was the first," Dir-Dee-Valerie yells, "and I know you ain't slapped her."

"Dirty Valerie?" asked Celia.

"Yeah. You remember…we went to school with her. People

call her that 'cause when it comes to bathin', she is definitely and strictly a Saturday night gal. She a kinda steady in the Peacock. Talk about somebody gittin' serious with a jug, she's the Peacock's best customer. Puts away a fifth a day. Some mornin's you can even see her helpin' Tate roll back the gate. I kinda feel sorry for her 'cause she ain't much good for nuthin' else.

"She had to take her man to court last year for breakin' her leg, and the dude told the judge that there wasn't no fight. Said she slipped and he walked on her on the way out. When the judge fined him fifty dollars for the walk, who come up with the cash money but Peabody.

"Now the furtherest she walks is to the Peacock. She don't usually get loud with nobody, so it musta been that ninety-proof junk juice told her she could rank him and get away with it.

"Well, the joint got quieter than Woodlawn on New Year's day. All eyes is on Peabody now, knowin' he ain't about to take low from his ex-man's ex-woman.

"Well, he switches up to her, completely forgettin' about the piano, and looks her up and down and laughs. 'Sweetie,' he says, 'and I use that term loosely 'cause I heard you was once sued by the fresh air fund. How come you wastin' your talent in here? A powerful cleanup woman like you. I heard that back home you smelled so bad that when you walked by, skunks rolled over, buzzards fell dead, and rats left town. You were a regular pied piper. Too bad the board of health didn't understand. When they gonna lift that ban against you, girl?'

"But Dir-Dee-Valerie didn't back off. She give him the bad eye and said, 'You wouldn't be talkin' that talk if you-know-who was with me.'

"'Well, you-know-who ain't with you,' Peabody laughed, 'and it's a mystery to me how he stayed as long as he did. But then again, he always bragged about how you loved to have your mouthful.'

"I had to turn up the jukebox then 'cause things was gettin' thick. When Tate hears the music, he comes out the back and takes one look at the piano and another look at Peabody, who he cannot stand. 'Just get it the fuck on out,' he says politely, and Joe and Turk roll it out with the sissy marchin' in front like he leadin' a whole brass band. They charged him by the step all the way to his crib and cleaned him out of another five bills, but I hear he's happy. There's days when you can hear him down the block. It got so bad one night that Turk and Joe was thinkin' of stealin' the damn thing back, but they thought about the weight and decided ain't no point in bein' a fool twice."

Celia had heard Al and the twins talk about the Peacock but not like this. They had only spoken of Bird, Prez, and Dexter Gordon and how listening to their music while sipping a brew always managed to revive them after a back-breaking day. But Tessie spoke about the sounds of the people: the friendship and romance, the profanity, pretense, and small, harmless illusions that helped move them from one day to the next.

Celia passed the lounge—on the other side of the street—on her way to school every day. The brilliant neon blinked its welcome, but the window was so thick with plants, it was nearly impossible to see inside.

So she had settled for the sound of the music drifting from its core, loud in its mystery. Or jazzy and sweet, depending on the day of the week. Monday was truly Blue Monday, and the music stayed that way until Thursday, when the sound escalated in anticipation. Friday and Saturday, everyone within half a block listened to the Peacock's music, whether they were inclined to or not. On Sunday, the sound was lowered in deference to those nursing hangovers and other casualties, and Monday was Blue Monday all over again.

Monday was Celia's favorite day because someone, a Peacock regular, with just enough in him not to care, would usually sing along, voice rising, to let the world know that trouble was his middle name, that he had been done wrong from A to Z but one of these days his ship was comin' in and he was gonna kiss these Monday morning blues goodbye.

She never saw the singer, but the very sound was enough to make her feel what he felt without knowing why she felt it. The voice, weary and raspy, struck a chord though the bar was light-years away from the dust-dry geology and history classes she fought to stay awake in.

Celia was in the lobby when Tessie came rushing in from the hairdresser. She swept in, bringing with her the usual aura of excitement.

"Am I in a hurry, girl...got to get my shoes out the shop...big party tonight...did your mother finish my dress?"

"It's finished," Celia said without expression, "it's been ready since yesterday."

The dress had been finished and folded over the dining room chair when Celia came in from school. Frieda had gone downtown on a rare shopping trip with Al to buy sewing supplies. The note said she would return in one hour.

Celia looked at the dress and examined the workmanship. She held it to her and executed a timid pirouette. Without another thought, she had slipped the pale-green dress over her head. It didn't quite fit. Tessie had a fuller bust, smaller waist, and slightly larger hips. But the style, the color...

When Frieda came in, the dress had been returned to the chair, but when Celia went to sleep that night, she had dreamed about the dress.

She watched now as Tessie turned slowly in the lobby. "How does this look?"

The sheen in her hair was highlighted even in the dim light of the overhead bulb.

"How's it look?" she asked again.

"Very pretty," Celia murmured, wondering why Tessie wasted her money at the hairdresser's. Her hair always looked beautiful.

"Who's the party for?"

"Nobody in particular. You know how that joint is. They celebrate just 'cause it's Friday and it ain't rainin'..."

"Sounds like fun..."

"It ain't bad..." Tessie glanced at her. "You know, if you could get away...just for an hour..."

Celia stared at her, wondering for a second if Tessie were joking. Then she said, "You know I can't do that, I—"

"Well, one hour ain't gonna hurt nobody. You need to rest your eyes anyway. Take a break from them books." Celia looked at Tessie. She was serious.

...take a break...

Her stomach turned over with excitement....a break...Finally, she said, "...but how...how..."

"Think of somethin'..." Tessie said, trying to hide her impatience. She had to pick up her shoes before the store closed.

"Think of something like what?" Celia persisted.

"I don't know...don't they have evenin' classes or somethin'? You in school, think of somethin'...if you can make it, I'll see you around nine. I'll be lookin' out for you..."

Tessie swept out, heading for the shoemaker. Celia watched her retreating back until she disappeared around the corner. Then she climbed the steps, wondering how to begin to shape the lie that bit at the corner of her imagination.

Frieda looked up from her sewing.

"What time will you be back?"

She had long ago given up trying to follow Celia's irregular schedule of classes and settled for the knowledge that the last class ended sometime around three and she was usually home by four. Unless she stopped off at the library.

On those "late" days, as she preferred to call them even though Celia was usually home before dark, Frieda remained in the dining room, working at the table where she could see the clock. She would establish an "upper limit," the very latest time Celia might be expected to arrive home. If the hour came and went, Frieda would put her work aside and sit, immobilized by a nameless dread.

She felt it now as she said, "What time will you be back?"

"I'll be home around eleven-thirty."

"Eleven-thirty?? A lecture takes that long...?"

"Mother, they're serving refreshments afterward. And I think he may be showing a film. I'm not sure...but I just can't get up and run out. I have to show the instructor that I'm at least halfway interested..."

"Well, why does it have to be at night...why couldn't it be—"

"Mother, I will take a taxi back..."

Frieda heard the door close and wondered how soon after eleven-thirty the feeling would envelop her.

Celia left the house and strolled in the opposite direction, crossed the street, and circled back on the far side away from her mother's window. Halfway down the avenue, the loud, weekend sound seemed to leap out of the bar and wash over her in waves. She approached the side door, pulled, and felt panic when it didn't open.

"It's locked!" She felt the edge of fright crowding in. I've seen so many people coming and going through this door. Besides, Tessie said it would be open. Did someone, did Tate, decide to lock it tonight, of all nights.

She made an effort to remain calm. If she turned and walked away, she knew she would not come again. She would pass by, on her way to school, and it would remain a mystery forever.

She tried again, pulling harder. This time, the door gave a little, then opened rustily, as if it were out of practice.

Inside was dark, but through the thick cigarette smoke she could see people crowded three deep around a wide oval bar. A mirrored bank of bottles and glasses in the center seemed designed to reflect a benign image no matter what shape the viewer might be in. Large trailing plants hung from the low ceiling and swayed lightly when the door opened, giving the place a close, exotic feeling.

Tessie was behind the bar laughing and refilling a glass for a man seated near the end. She glanced at her watch, looked to the side door, and suddenly let out a whoop as Celia made her way to the bar.

"Girl, I was gonna send out a search party..."

Heads turned to focus on the object of Tessie's attention, registered little interest, and turned back to their drinks. The man at the end of the bar rose from his seat as Celia approached. When he spoke, his low voice was lost in the noise, but he smiled, showing bright, even teeth.

Tessie said, "Didn't you hear him? Sit down. This don't happen every day, I can tell you."

Celia eased into the seat, aware that he was standing behind her. She looked at Tessie's dress and thought of her own, also made by Frieda but double-buttoned at the neck. She looked at Tessie's hair and understood now why it needed the special treatment. In the dull, man-made fog, the highlights stood out like so many diamonds sprinkled in a crown of dark cotton. When Tessie moved away, Celia glanced at her own image in the mirror and saw that the lighting was no help. The buttoned neckline seemed to tighten at her throat, and she was wondering how to escape when Tessie returned and placed a small, fluted cocktail glass on the bar.

"Got just the thing for you, girl. Private recipe...called Brown Lady. You can down ten of these and still think straight in the morning. Sip all night long and never get loud and wrong..."

"Say Tessie," came the low voice again, "this Brown Lady's on me."

Celia barely heard him above the roar of the jukebox, but Tessie's ear, like radar, had been fine-tuned to detect the slightest ripple of an offer. Her smile was radiant.

"Hey, bet. Girl, thank the man..."

Celia turned halfway in her seat and looked directly at the man standing behind her. He was tall, thin, and stood slightly hunched over, hands jammed into close-fitting trousers. Even in the semi-darkness, she could gauge the smoothness of his dark skin and knew that the thick moustache covering his mouth was well cared for.

She stared at the coin-sized birthmark that stood out, lemon yellow, above his left eyelid. She wanted to speak but the words would not come. He returned her gaze with a detached curiosity until she looked away. Finally, she heard a whisper very near her ear.

"Enjoy...brown lady..."

The voice was soft, warm, and deep. She turned again, but he was moving through the crowd to the door. She had not thanked him. She didn't even know his name.

She looked for Tessie to ask who he was, but Tessie was already at the far end of the bar, smiling and refilling a glass. So she concentrated on her own glass, on the thick, creamy, sweet-tasting concoction that went down quick and easy, almost like a malted milk.

"So what you think of it, girl?" asked Tessie, making a rare pause.

"Nice. Very sweet. I can hardly taste the alcohol—"

"Not the drink, girl, the place...what you think of the place?"

By the time Celia could think of an answer, Tessie was gone again.

She made an effort to relax and not swallow the second drink quite so fast. More people were coming in, joining the already crowded and close-knit groups. She watched the men, posed in fraternal knots, maneuver to rest an elbow or at least a hand on the bar. The gleam of gold watches and diamond rings cut through the smokey air. The women, proud possessors of high cheekbones, high behinds, and high heels, caught the flash in the amber mirror as the men watched from the side of their eyes and, between sips of cognac, spoke of current events in important tones.

A woman, oblivious of the crowd, leaned over the jukebox, studied the selections, and pressed a button. She turned from the machine and stood rocking slightly with eyes closed and palms pressed to her face. She followed the song silently at first, moving her mouth. Then she began to hum and finally, the sound came: "Tomorrow night? Toomaaarrroooh naaght? Will you remember what you said tonight...?"

It was warm with memory and rose in waves through the heavy air. She opened her eyes and began to snap her fingers. Celia could hear the sharp clicks above the music.

"Toomaarooohh...?"

The woman was alive now, smiling and bending slightly at the waist as she danced. She had found her own interpretation of the song: Either her man was coming back or he wasn't. If he did, it would be fine, her dance said. If he didn't...well...the feeling, bad as it was, wouldn't last forever.

Her age, to Celia, was indeterminate, and her movements seemed to express an attitude, a belief that a man was like a bus—if you didn't catch the first one, no big thing. Another would be along in due time. In due time.

But Celia looked closer at the woman's face as she swayed to the beat, and she knew that the attitude was a lie. The face spoke of a loss of love so strong that it sank to the marrow of her being and remained to plague and haunt and change.

The woman moved and sang, smiling and gliding expertly in the half-dark, but Celia knew that she was in mourning.

When would it end? How did it begin? Would it last as long as her own mother's sorrow? Celia thought of her father and wondered about the man for whom this woman danced. Had he, too, been snatched from her against his will? What were women like these left with? What did they have except the dance of despair and small memories wrapped in old, yellowed news clippings hidden in the bottom of closets.

The record clicked off. The woman executed a slow, final turn and wriggled through the crowd to the bar, her face a bland, drained mask. All around floated bits and pieces of the most current event.

"What you think a them Feds in Alabama...?"

"Four hundred marshals...wonder what it costin' to keep 'em there?"

"Four hundred...man, you talkin' big money...serious tax shit... probably coulda sent up a satellite with that bread..."

"Now take them Russians...got that thing into the air last week and surprised the hell outta us..."

"Us who? You and me is us, and us ain't never been a part of them. Since when is you and me a part of them...?"

"Well...them...surprised the hell outta them. They so busy lightin' bombs under buses, they ain't got time to deal with no facts. And the fact is the Bear is growlin...he gonna start takin' names and kickin' ass if we don't watch out..."

"You mean if *they* don't watch out..."

A man held up his hand. Tessie spotted him at the end of the bar.

"...same?"

"Same, baby, and hit yourself a taste."

He raised his glass. "Now, what I wanna know is where you all get this 'them' and 'us' bullshit from. I'm an American. Born and raised here. I didn't come over yesterday. I fought in the war. I wish one a them would try tellin' me where I can and can't go..."

Celia caught the flash of diamond as he raised the glass to his soft, unlined face. No one acknowledged him, the local loudmouth who talked bad but had his shuffle down to a precise science. They knew that dogs were eating children in Selma and women were being raped by men sworn to uphold the law of the land.

They knew and were angry with themselves and with this man who had unwittingly held up a mirror which cost them a piece of their humanity each time they dared look into it.

For the mirror said they were insignificant minutiae moving underfoot, having no hand in the day-to-day management of their lives—even on the reservation—and no voice in the decisions of cartels and conglomerates, trusts, treaties, and other treacherous activity. They were impotent and so spent this time in liquid solace, blurring the line between reason and rage.

And Tessie was kept busy with refills.

The dance lady with the bland mask also raised her glass. "It's a damn shame," she said aloud. She had reached the level of slight intoxication where it was perfectly all right to speak aloud to no one in particular. "A damn shame," she repeated, "don't stand a chance."

At the other end of the bar, Celia watched the high cheekbones bend low. Surely the mask, they seemed to say, did not mean them.

They had successfully infiltrated the fraternal knot and had engaged in an animated discussion of civil rights: the discussion being of course a prelude to their own personal right—a right to a good night, and a good man. If not a good man, then any man, and they'd make him good.

The high cheekbones had come with wet lipstick and powdered faces. They were dressed to kill and aimed to score. Surely, the mask did not mean them.

Doubting faces took refuge behind double Scotches, and the delicate goblets were not lowered until James Brown pleaded from the piccolo: "...please...please...please..." And they remembered other nights and were reassured.

Celia stared in wonder. The women, to her, were all beautiful and all dressed to the minute. Yet they strove desperately to conceal an unnamed fear that seemed to flow from their pores like perspiration, ruining perfume and powder.

This was not what she came to see. She eased off the stool and caught Tessie on the run to say good night.

"By the way, who was that guy...?"

"What guy...?" Tessie, busy, had forgotten already.

"—who bought my drink..."

"Oh, him." Tessie looked at her quickly. "Why you wanna know?"

"I'm curious," Celia replied, feeling vaguely annoyed. Tessie was asking too many questions before favoring her with a simple answer.

"I'm curious," she repeated.

"You more than that. Look girl, you can't go gettin' glassy-eyed over every cat that picks up a tab. In here, that's light stuff..."

"Perhaps. But if I see him in the street, I want to be able to thank him..."

Tessie shook her head and laughed, and Celia watched the highlights shimmer in the amber mirror. "Forget it, Celia. You ain't hardly gonna see him walkin' down no street...anyway, his name's Jonrobert and I'm tellin' you, he won't remember you from a hole in the wall..."

The remark was not quite what Tessie meant, so she said, "I'm surprised he stayed as long as he did. He's usually in here twenty minutes tops..."

Celia raised her shoulders slightly in an attempt to appear unconcerned. "I didn't expect him to remember me. Anyway, I'd better be going..."

Tessie looked at her watch. "What you gonna tell—"

"I told her I went to a lecture...that I'd be coming in a little late..."

Tessie shrugged. "That beats a blank...did you learn anything?"

Celia glanced around and did not answer immediately. She wondered how to make Tessie understand that, despite its bright, glittering exterior, the Peacock was a profoundly sad little place, haunted by frightened people who clung to their mutual sadness for survival. They were all actors: dressing, drinking, dancing, and dealing. She wondered how she could get Tessie to understand how disappointed she felt, now that she had seen the interior.

"Celia, you all right?"

"I'm fine..."

"Them drinks didn't get to you, did they? Sometimes you go off into yourself so quiet, you scare me..."

"Sometimes I scare myself..."

Tessie stared at her and then folded her arms and leaned across the bar. "Listen to me. You been in that house and in them damn books too long for your own good." Her voice was low and had the ring of one diagnosing a terminal condition. Celia tried to ease away but Tessie reached for her arm.

"Wait...listen...I'm goin' to a party next Friday. At Joe's...

remember the one who took the piano? He's a lot of fun. I want you to come. Try to think of something. Another lecture...okay?"

Celia looked at her watch as the door closed heavily behind her. She moved away from the bar, retraced her steps, and walked slowly past stoops crowded with loungers trying to beat the heat of the summer night, past a knot of hard-kneed poker players sitting and balancing a makeshift card table between them.

She listened as their voices rose and fell.

"Wham! Two aces showin' and nobody goin'. Must be got somethin' up y'all sleeves. Wham. Read 'em and weep..."

The cards hit the deck and the table trembled.

The dealer was a dark rangey man whose face was partially hidden by a ragged wide-brimmed straw hat. His voice, deep and low, carried through the small group.

"I say, putcha money where yo' mouth is..."

They passed paper cups and side bets and tapped their feet to the beat of the Peacock's music. Under the streetlight, they functioned in a closed and private world, held together by cups and cards.

For a fleeting second, Celia wished she could know all there was to know about poker and liquor and the language of gambling. It didn't matter that she would be the lone woman in a group of rough, rowdy men. Nor did it matter that these games often disintegrated into razor contests where a face was reshaped faster than an ace dropped in error. In the shadow of the Peacock, these men were held together, whereas the women inside seemed torn apart by a common desperation.

She retraced her steps and fumbled in her purse for something to clear the taste of Brown Lady from her tongue.

12

Al lit another cigarette, waiting for the right moment. Frieda's agitation was tapering off, but he had to say what was on his mind before she became too exhausted to listen. Meanwhile, he busied himself setting out the glasses and ice. He cleared a space on the dining room table overflowing with fabric, patterns, and pins.

It's only a party, he thought, a birthday party for Tessie's friend. Why the big blowup? So she don't like Tessie hangin' 'round the kid. Bad influence. Tessie ain't that bad. Ain't that good, but damn sure ain't that bad either. Seen a whole lot worse. Kid just had some bad breaks, that's all. And Frieda raisin' all that commotion over nuthin'. 'Bout time for the kid to get out, to let her hair down, shit...

He gazed at Frieda, thinking of the irregular, late-night meetings, her guilt and her rage, her pleading with him not to tell anyone.

And he had acquiesced because of his need for her, his love, his perpetual hunger for the taste of the caramel-colored belly button hidden in the soft fold of her stomach.

But sometimes his nerves felt as if they had been held too near a grindstone. And his arms ached even while he held her, because he never knew when he would hear again the faint sound of her hand on his door.

He placed the glasses on the table and thought, still...I shoulda spoke to Celia that night I pinned her slippin' outta the Peacock... but she looked so upset, and got in the wind so fast...shoulda said somethin' when she come to me 'bout this damn party, but she was upset again. Now Frieda's upset...between the two of 'em, I ain't never seen so many upset women in my life. Damn!

He knew that was not true. He thought of Evie, who once looked like Frieda, and knew it wasn't true.

He slammed the ice into the glasses and watched as Frieda sank, exhausted, into a chair. Then he asked, "Chaser? On the rocks?"

"Chaser, I guess..."

"You guess. Don't you know?" He could see that he was in for a rough time.

"Right now, I don't know anything," Frieda sighed. "Imagine that floozy asking my child—"

Al looked at the ceiling. Where did she hear that word? On one of them soap operas? Another twenty years and she just might get around to sayin' damn, but I doubt it.

"Listen, Frieda, I know how you feel, but listen..."

He glanced at the clock as he poured the drinks. Celia would be home in another hour—he had to talk fast.

13

The confusion of music and laughter could be heard in the lobby. Tessie simply held up three fingers and Celia followed as she started up the stairs.

At the end of the corridor, the door opened and two men approached. "Tessie, baby, what it is!" They had to shout to be under stood. "Music louder 'n a mother out here. Back in five, baby..."

They disappeared, and Celia and Tessie entered the apartment. Disembodied elbows poked at Celia in the dark. Heavy, moving feet stepped on her toes. The odors of cigarettes, perfume, and perspiration crowded in, and she felt excited and dizzy. Tessie, who seemed to know everyone, immediately abandoned her.

"Back in five, honey," she managed to shout, "gotta find the little boys' room..."

She disappeared, leaving Celia to edge through the crowded darkness alone. There was an open window at the far end of the room, and Celia made her way to it. She leaned against the sill, feeling a peculiar mix of intimacy and anonymity as she waited for Tessie.

A voice behind her, so low that she might have imagined it, whispered, "Soloin' tonight, baby?"

She looked out of the window. Jonrobert was sprawled on the fire escape, his back to the window ledge. Celia stared in surprise, unable to speak.

"...asked if you was soloin' tonight," he repeated.

Celia still did not answer immediately. It was obvious that he did not remember her, but she felt a sudden constriction in her chest and her mouth went dry. Finally she said, "I'm not alone, if that's what you mean..."

His eyes were on her, and she felt the need to explain her presence in this loud, raucous atmosphere where clearly she did not belong.

"...I came with Tessie..."

"Willie's woman?"

"Willie's girlfriend," she replied firmly. There was something, an air about him, that, despite his handsome looks, seemed to repel her.

Jonrobert smiled. "You mean Tessie, who works in the Peacock?"

She shook her head, watching him.

"Well, that's Willie's woman..."

She did not answer.

"Name's Jonrobert," he said after a long pause.

"John Robert?"

"No. Jonrobert's my first name. Last name's Stevens..."

He remained in the same sprawled position, one leg curled under him, his eyes still on her.

"I'm Celia," she said quickly. Then she realized that he had not asked.

"...and you know Tessie. You don't look like a friend of hers. What do you do?"

Celia wondered what a person had to look like in order to be a friend of Tessie's and what it was that person had to do. She couldn't think of a lie fast enough, so she settled for the truth.

She looked around and then said, "I'm in school." She hoped no one else heard her.

"You in what?"

"...and Tessie and I live in the same building and she—"

"Never mind. You just checkin' out the other half tonight, is that it?"

"Not...exactly..."

"Well, how do you like it?"

"I...it's too early to tell..." Why was he asking her all these questions, she wondered, and where was Tessie.

Jonrobert shook his head and started to smile. "Too early. I see what's happenin'. You ain't had a taste yet. We gotta fix that up right fast."

He climbed in through the window. She saw that he was taller than she had thought. He was also very quick. He pressed against her in the crowded room, cupping his hand over her breast as he passed. She tried to back away, but his arm slipped around her and he held her.

"Don't panic," he whispered, "just wanna see if you was all you. I don't waste no time with no might-have-beens..."

He released her and disappeared into the crowd, leaving her standing in the middle of the dark, hot, sweaty room. She was trembling like a leaf. "Where on earth is Tessie? I've got to get out of here..."

She did not move. Instead, she watched for him and saw him approach, taking long easy strides as if he were alone in the room. He wore an easy smile. "Baby, you look like you ready for a quick flight. Here. Take a sip of this before you take off."

She hesitated, confused. He had seemed so nice in the Peacock. He put his hand to his heart. "Trust me, baby, poured it myself. Guaranteed free of LSD."

He smiled again, and she took the glass and put it to her mouth, her eyes still on him. The stuff was straight and strong and felt like fire, but she did not stop drinking until the glass was empty.

He stared at her, no longer smiling. "So what you prove? That you got somebody willin' to drag you home tonight if you flake out? You damn dumb broads, first time around, you all alike!"

Celia stopped shaking. Now she felt suffocated. "It's not the first time," she said, trying to control her voice. "Perhaps it's not important for you to remember, but you bought me a drink in the Peacock last Friday. I've been meaning to thank you."

She tried to keep her voice steady, tried to remain calm, but she felt her throat closing and was glad it was dark and he couldn't see her face.

He stared at her but did not answer. Then he pressed her arm and guided her back to the window. "Come on. Let's sit on the fire escape."

"Why outside..."

"'Cause this joint ain't exactly air-conditioned. A little breeze might help keep your head together..."

He helped her through the window, holding her by her waist.

"Do you usually sit on fire escapes?"

"Not usually. Matter of fact, I was just plannin' to leave before you came in..."

Some part of her wanted to tell him not to stay on her account, but as soon as he sat beside her, the thought vanished. She lay her head on his shoulder, heard his voice, and when she felt his breath near her ear, she felt dizzy.

"So...you in school..."

"Yes..." she answered, wishing he would talk about something else. Then she thought...if I had gone away, I never would have met him...

She felt his hand in her hair and she closed her eyes. His voice came soft against her ear. "Baby, let me tell you, whatever you studyin' you do better to take a quick lesson in slow drinkin'. I remember you now...had that pretty malted milk last week...I remember now..."

He slipped his arm around her and she started to laugh, quietly at first, then she could not stop. He began to shake her.

"Relax, will you? It ain't that funny. What woulda happened if I had filled that glass to the top?"

She raised her head to apologize, to tell him how nice he was, to let him know how handsome she thought he was. But he was looking beyond her, down the street, where several men had quietly emerged from three parked cars.

Celia could feel his muscles tense, turning hard as stone. He jumped up suddenly, pulling her with him. "This is it, baby. Let's go roof hoppin'. We sittin' on hot stuff!"

"What are you—"

"You heard me!! Let's move. Next stop is tar beach. The man is here!!"

He watched the men as they casually crossed the street, trying to conceal their urgency, their excitement. They disappeared into the lobby below. In a few minutes, he knew, the regular squad cars would arrive.

Celia searched his face. He was teasing, surely. But he was like marble. Only his eyes were moving.

"You mean," she whispered, "those men are policemen. They're coming here?? To *this* party??"

She did not, could not, believe it.

"What you expect? Ain't the first time. Won't be the last. These people should know by now that coke, smoke, and noise don't mix. Damn sound loud enough to take the fuckin' roof off!"

"Coke??"

"In the bathroom. And I ain't takin' no weight for nobody. Now you comin' or you stayin??"

His moves were deliberate and furtive and reminded her of a sly black cat. She tried to keep up with him but stumbled several times as they made their way up the fire escape, and Jonrobert had to push and pull until they reached the ladder that led to the roof.

The wail of sirens cut through the night and the sound seemed to cut through her head. Windows were thrown open and shouts and screams filled the air.

She stared, eyes wide, in mute surprise, as if she had never in her life seen a ladder. She felt her head was about to burst, and the whole fire escape appeared to dip and sway. "I can't climb that! I can't do it...my legs...I can't...my legs...I'll fall!"

She began to cry and Jonrobert was dumbfounded. "What's wrong with you?? You was walkin' all right before. What're you talkin' about...come on!!"

"I can't!! I can't!!"

Her crying grew louder, and Jonrobert's surprise turned to fury. "You damn, dumb—I oughtta leave you right here!"

She did not hear him. She was thinking of her mother, of jail, of the disgrace. She became hysterical and clung to him, screaming. She did not feel it when he pushed her against the wall, held her at arm's length, and struck her sharply across the mouth. Her head hit the wall and she fell against him, her breath exploding.

"Now, come on, dammit!"

One foot, one rung, one foot, another rung. The ladder stretched to heaven. Her arms were being pulled from their sockets. Her left sleeve was ripped off at the shoulder. The concrete tore her stomach and took the skin off her knees as he hauled her over the edge of the roof. She opened her eyes and found that she was still clinging to him.

Oh God, she thought, I hurt...

She began to whimper. She tried to bury herself in him even as she felt his hands on her stomach trying to push her away.

"Baby, come on, lighten up, hear? Everything's gon' be all right."

The sweat poured down his dark, angry face. She smelled it,

felt it, tasted it, and held onto him tighter as they made their way across the adjoining roof.

They stumbled, out of breath, into the shadow of the stairwell. "Now look, baby, ease up, come on, mama..." His voice was soft again and he had his hands in her hair. She barely heard him. She could barely breathe. She was only aware of the heat of his body and the taste of his mouth as his arms closed around her.

14

Before the police joined the party, Tessie had made her way through the crowded darkness only to find the bathroom locked. She turned away to look for Celia when the door opened behind her.

"Say, hey, if it ain't pretty Tessie...come on in..."

Tessie smiled as Big T made a deep bow at the bathroom door. He had some trouble straightening up, and she knew at once that he was high.

The gold spoon glittered at his neck as he stepped out of her way. He was a regular at the Peacock, loud, bold, and easy on the money, which seemed to attract a lot of women. But Tate had had to warn him more than once about using the men's room to "get straight," as he had put it.

He stared at her now as he rubbed his nose and made a loud snuffling sound. The veins in his forehead stood out, and his eyes were red and glassy. Tessie tried to smile even though he looked hideous.

"Just gittin' straight, mama...just gittin' straight..."

"Yeah, well, to each his own..."

"Say, mama, you down?" Big T asked. He knew better, knew that Willie would probably come looking for him if he found out that he was fooling with Tessie, but right now, he felt good, he felt bad, bold, and dangerous—he could wipe out a thousand dudes with one flick of his x-ray eyes.

"Come on, man" said Red, "be cool."

"I *am* cool," said Big T, assuming his George Raft shoot-out stance. He was raised on George Raft movies and worshiped everything about him, even his mile-wide lapels.

"...as a matter a fact, they don't come no cooler, they don't come no badder, and—"

"—they damn sure don't come no dumber," said the plainclothesman who was standing in the doorway. "Well, bust my ass if it ain't Big T. What's happenin'? Into a little sociable one and one?"

The tiny ashtray had been strategically placed in the tub to be washed away in an emergency, but the emergency was here and they had been caught cold.

Big T, already out on bail, had the most to lose. He motioned to the detective to come in, whispering, "Man, what you see? You don't see nuthin' but this three yards I'm puttin' in your palm, nuthin' at all..."

The detective looked at the ashtray and laughed good naturedly. "Come on, Big T. You walkin' with a felony load there. Take you down on this and you max out. Y'all gotta do better than three hundred—"

Big T was amazed. "What you mean y'all? Them three bills was *me* talkin' to git *me* walkin'. What you mean y'all?"

The detective leaned against the door. "Stop talkin slick. You know if one walks, you all walk. If one rides, you all got to ride. Now let's get it together!"

Big T turned to the other two men. His high had crashed down and he was sweating profusely. "Okay, you tight motherfuckers, you know you sittin' on money's mammy. Loosen it up! My ass ain't seein' no slammer tonight!"

The detective put a thousand dollars in his pocket and turned the tap on. The five of them watched in varying attitudes as the powder dissolved and drained away.

Then the detective looked at Tessie, at her face turned ashen, her eyes wide and her mouth pressed in fear. He smiled, and something in him labored to come alive.

At last, he thought, something different, someone who's really afraid...not like those worn-out whores down at the truck stop who laughed in your face while you kicked their ass...no respect for the law...here was something different...

He moved close to her and his breathing was audible. Finally he said, "I know you don't walk with that kind of change. You work in the Peacock, where lies 're long and tips are as short as a pup's prick..."

The three men laughed obediently. Tessie did not blink. Her fear was real, and for the first time in a long time, the detective felt the faint undercurrent of arousal.

"I'm letting you walk tonight, but you be ready for me tomorrow, understand? And every weekend after that 'til I get tired of fuckin' you..."

Tessie opened her mouth in shock, but before she could reply, the three men assured the detective that she did indeed understand, yes sir, and would be ready if they had to get her ready themselves.

"She's real grateful for the opportunity," Big T assured him.

"She ain't hardly gonna forget the favor you done her," Red said.

The detective backed out of the doorway and motioned for the four to follow him. He led them through the confusion and down the steps. They entered a patrol car and were driven three blocks. Big T, Red, and Lefty stepped out. The detective pulled at Tessie's blouse as she tried to follow.

"Get your hands...off me, you greasy—" Her swing was wide, but she caught him on the side of his face just above his mouth. He pinned her arm and pulled her back into the car.

"Help me! Don't let 'im do this! Help me..."

The detective had his gun out. "The woman's hysterical. I'm takin her down for resistin' arrest. Anybody got anything to say?"

Through the window, he called out, "ain't nuthin' but a game, Big T, you know that. Ain't nuthin' but a game..."

He made a U-turn, and the three men watched as the car disappeared into the dark entrance of the park.

Big T pulled out a silk handkerchief and mopped his forehead. "Damn, that was close! Come on, let's find us a bar. I need me a taste in the worst way..."

"What you think gonna happen to Tessie?" asked Red nervously. He was concerned, not just for Tessie, but for himself when Willie found out.

"Listen," said Big T, "if we stick to a story, sayin' we don't know nuthin', then what could the cat do? It's his old lady...shoulda kept his eye on her himself."

"I don't know," said Lefty. "That Willie is one evil West Indian. I don't trust no nigger that smile with even teeth, and that one got the most evenest teeth I ever seen."

"Man, we just gonna have to worry about that when the deal go down, that's all. Besides, that ain't nuthin' compared to what woulda happened to me," Big T said. "I'm already feelin' the heat 'cause of a jive junkie. I don't need no more weight on me right now."

The three entered a bar and ordered a round of drinks. "A whole grand," sighed Lefty. "Tough break, but we got off. Too bad you can't beat your other case this easy..."

Big T stared into his glass. "You know, I was thinkin' maybe I oughtta fire that jive ass know nuthin', do nuthin' lawyer and defend my own damn self. God knows I got a good case..."

He maneuvered into a more comfortable position on the bar stool, took note of the number of people within earshot, and began to tell the story for the hundredth time since he had posted bail. He also wanted to take their minds off what might be happening to Tessie. Their fear was making him afraid. He sipped his drink and said, "...there I was, settin' in my own livin' room. Mindin' my own business, figurin' to enjoy a little tee-vee before I stepped out to tackle the night track. Well, you know how it is when them jive commercials come on, everybody and they mammy git up and run to the kitchen for a beer. You do that yourself.

"Well, I run to git me some more ice 'cause I was sippin' Chivas at the time. I comes back to the livin' room—my crib's on the ground floor, you know—and what I see but my tee-vee movin' 'cross the floor. And headin' for the window...

"I look a little closer, and I see these hands through the blinds pullin' my set by the cord. By this time, it done picked up speed and I knew I had to git on the case.

"So I grabs me the first thing handy which was a baseball bat. When I smashed it through the window, how was I to know the motherfucker's head was in the way? I mean, all I saw was his hands. So here I knock off a junkie—tryin' to defend my property rights—and I git hit with a bullshit manslaughter rap."

The bartender poured a round in sympathy. "Don't sweat it, T. Ain't no way you gonna see the joint. That's about the coldest shit in town...wastin' taxpayers' good bread every time you show up downtown..."

"Shouldn't happen to a dog," agreed Red, as he quickly swallowed his drink.

The bartender was about to pour a refill, but he stopped as the door swung open. "Speakin' a dogs! What the hell...??"

They all turned to follow his gaze and stared in shocked silence as Tessie stumbled toward them. She moved like a drunk woman. Blood streamed down her legs and flowed from a gash on her face.

"...please..." she cried, "take me to the hospital...help me..."

15

Frieda stalked the room in a rage. She circled the bed, unable to believe her eyes.

"What do you mean, 'nothing happened.' You come crawlin' in here, barely breathin', and you tellin' me nothin's the matter??"

Celia lay across the bed, not moving. "I don't want to talk about it, mother..." Her voice was just above a whisper and held a slight tremor. Frieda stopped in her tracks. "If I looked as bad as you, I wouldn't want to either, but you're goin' to whether you want to or not...what happened to you?? Look at your dress. And your hair. And not only that, your face is swollen. Please, Celia, what happened?"

Celia tried to blot out the hysteria rising in her mother's voice. Why couldn't her mother just go away, dissolve, disappear, so that she could be alone with her thoughts. She pretended to sleep, but Frieda's voice cut through the red rimmed fog.

"I knew I should have followed my own mind, but oh no, I had to listen to Al. You're old enough, he says. Old enough for what? You look as if you were in world war three. Well, listen to me! Never again will you go roamin' with that floozy, you hear me? Not ever again. Not even to the corner..."

Frieda's voice reached the breaking point, and she ran from the room and slammed the door.

Celia heard the noise and thought her head would fall off from the vibration. Every bone in her ached, and she had to turn over by inches.

She sat on the edge of the bed for some minutes before easing onto the bench near the dressing table. Her reflection shocked her. "My God...what happened...to me. He'll never look at me again..."

Her jaw was indeed swollen, and the left side of her face was beginning to puff out. "What if this never goes away...he will never look at me again..."

Then she saw the bruises. Her neck, shoulders, and breasts were crisscrossed with mouth marks, purple, welted, and beginning to rise. She closed her eyes to the mirror.

"What if he doesn't want to see me again..."

Through her terror, she heard his voice in her ear, every sound and syllable. And his exasperation, "What the hell you doin' with so much hardware on, baby?"

And she remembered feeling ashamed and confused. The girdle—as thin as she was—that Frieda insisted she wear because "all nice girls wear them to hold themselves in," and the cotton bloomers and undershirt set, and heaven knows what else that he felt had slowed him up and that she definitely did not need.

And the other sounds that she had never heard before, coming from somewhere deep within him, that said he had run a hundred miles but could not stop now.

And the soft wonder in his voice when he said: "You never been...before? Ah...you never...ever...had this...ever...aah, baby, it's yours...take it...come on, mama...take it..."

At first, she was slow and stiff and awkward. Then wild and greedy. She lay on her back and her hands pulled at his hair as the soft, warm pressure of his mouth drew on her breasts and stomach and explored places she had only dreamed of.

When he entered her, she came apart, luxuriating in the pain, dying in a thousand small explosions. Finally, she remembered the sheer, absolute, all-encompassing, magnificent weight of him.

* * *

She moved away from the mirror and lay down, fully clothed, under the bed covers. Her dress was torn and held a close, unfamiliar odor, but her skin felt alive, every pore open and alert to the slightest sensation.

"...what if he doesn't call..."

She closed her eyes to hold the tears in place, to keep the ache from spreading. Her mind raced...there was something else, what... what was it...

"Next time," he had said, "Next time, baby, leave some a that armor home..."

...next time. He did say next time. She wanted to smile but her mouth hurt. She tried to relax and think of other things. Tessie.

...nothing bad could have happened to her because I feel so good...I never knew I could hurt so much and feel so good at the same time....

She thought about this, the contradiction of her condition, and was suddenly terrified, convinced that something was wrong with her. She began to cry finally, to relieve the pressure of the confusion. She pulled the covers over her head, intending to lie there until "next time."

16

Al found Willie's name on the mailbox and pressed the button above it. The buzzer sounded, and he made his way up the narrow staircase to the third floor. He paused a moment, listening in the quiet to the somber notes of Charlie Parker filtering through the door, and wished that he were coming to visit under different circumstances.

Willie opened the door before he knocked.

"Say how you doin'," Al said quietly. "I'm sorry to bother you but I'm Celia's...uh...I'm her uncle and...she went to a party with Tessie last Friday and come home lookin' like she had an accident..."

"An accident?"

"Yeh, you know, like maybe she had got jumped or somethin'. She ain't talkin' and I can't find Tessie..."

At the mention of Tessie's name, Willie cut him off. "Look man, come on in. Didn't mean to keep you standin' in the hall. Come on in."

He turned and Al followed him into a fairly large, well-kept apartment. One wall of an alcove was filled with books and nearby was a draftsman's table. A large wicker basket held several rolled blueprints. The sound of "Yardbird Suite" faded away in the silence, and Al hummed a few bars as he watched Willie head for the large liquor cabinet.

"Grab a seat. How 'bout a taste..."

"Don't mind if I do..."

Al saw Willie's hand shake slightly as he filled the glasses and wondered what he had to be nervous about. He pretended to look for a cigarette and casually checked his back pocket to make certain that he had not come unprepared. Just in case.

He sat patiently while Willie took another drink, straight, no chaser.

"An accident?" Willie repeated.

"Yeah," Al said slowly. He was beginning to wonder if Willie might not be the one responsible. Maybe he was the reason why Celia was walking around the house like a zombie.

He saw Willie's hands on the glass—neat, clean nails drumming a nervous staccato against the rim—and suddenly he was filled with a deep, murderous rage. He was halfway out of the seat, his hand in his pocket, when Willie looked at him.

"It wasn't no accident, man. Tessie's in the hospital. Doctors say whoever did it messed her up. Really messed her up. Can't have no more kids. She's cut up inside and out, man. And ain't talkin'... can't talk, really. She just layin' there. They keep her doped up most of the time, to stop her from screamin'. She...she..."

Willie put his hands to his face as Al sat down slowly.

"What you sayin', man? How...how this happen?"

"How? I don't know exactly. But I heard she had been with Big T and his boys, so I waited in the Peacock and followed him into the bathroom two nights ago. Had my knife ready to take his fuckin' tonsils out, but he swore it wasn't him. Checked Red and Lefty and they all said it was Purcell."

"Purcell?? You mean that greasy pig always runnin' around disguised as a bum?"

"Yeah, that's him. That's the one..."

Willie raised his glass and Al watched him, wondering what held him together. The pain was visible in small knots near his jaw. They moved back and forth as he swallowed.

"Listen," Al said, "lemme run to the store, pick up somethin' else for you..." On the way there, if he ran into Purcell, he would kill him.

Willie waved him back. "Nah, nah, plenty more where that came from. Don't worry about it..."

He looked again at Al and after a minute answered the unasked question. "Don't worry about it, man. Everything's gonna be taken care of...Everything..."

"I know, but—"

"—so, if anybody ask, just say Tessie got mugged. I'll take care of the rest..."

"Yeah...okay. I understand. Anything you want me to do, just—"

"No. Thanks. You know...some things gotta be done solo..."

Willie offered him another drink, but Al knew the visit was over. He walked to the door and turned. "I understand, man, I understand..."

Al stood on Willie's stoop for a few minutes trying to collect his thoughts, trying to decide where to go. Finally, he lit a cigarette and headed toward the avenue.

The early evening crowd was out, and the street, fresh washed from a heavy afternoon shower, glistened as the strollers hurried to get in on the last few minutes of happy hour. Several persons spoke as he passed, but he neither saw nor heard them.

He moved slowly, wrapped in the horror of his own remembrance: ...nuthin' changes. Nuthin' ever changes. Man can run a million miles and end up in the same shit...

He flicked the cigarette into the gutter and headed for the liquor store. He knew he could not get through this night without getting cold dead drunk.

...maybe, if Tessie hadna been so pretty...maybe if she didn't have them funny lookin' eyes that kept half the dudes hopin' and the other half hoppin'...maybe if...

...hell with that...you mean, a woman, a black woman, ain't allowed to be pretty without gettin' popped...it don't make sense... it don't make...

He thought of Evie: In another time and place, and everyone had called her Evangeline, except him. She had asked him to call her Evie. Her mother had picked the name from a book no one had ever heard of. She was as fragile and beautiful as a butterfly, with black hair braided against burnt brown skin. A face alive with laughter.

One morning, walking along a road overgrown with hyacinth and surrounded by the warmth and softness of spring, he told her he would find the book and they would read it together someday.

"...but you see what happened..."

He was talking aloud now as he walked. People who knew him and those who didn't gave him a wide berth.

...I remember...that place way in the middle of nowhere where your folks took you after it happened. Place for the colored, they called it. Crowded with people more animal than human. They stuck you there and left. Like what happened was your fault.

And you walked them long halls day and night and day in that dirty robe and nobody to comb your hair...nobody to care whether you ate or not...way in the middle of nowhere...

...if only I coulda gotten there...one more time...things mighta been different...

...but one night, you just curled up in a corner and that was that. Just left us...left me...

He stopped in the middle of the street, tore the wrapping off the bottle, and tilted it toward his face. When it was half empty, he started walking again, directionless.

...thought I was gonna lose my mind...you dead...dead... nuthin' left...

...then the talk...not even whispers...loud talk...with that cracker braggin' on you...

He was surprised at the vividness of memory. The hot, humid closeness of an old Georgia night pressing in as he walked and waited, waited and walked.

He remembered the narrow flow of sweat trickling down the small of his back that made him shiver in the heat. He even heard again the myriad sounds of the night creatures, invisible in the darkness.

And finally, he saw again the look of absolute astonishment on the face of the man who had destroyed her.

...caught 'im good. Hair in one hand...blade in the other. His head nearly come clean off. Left 'im there hangin' by his heels, just like a pig...'til everything drained right on out of 'im...

...I did right by you Evie...more than your papa or your brothers coulda done. They may as well had done it 'cause they hadda leave anyway after that. And I was right behind 'em...different direction...

...ah, Evie, girl...

He found himself at the entrance of the park. He stared at the old fashioned streetlamps hooked like shepherd's staffs, standing helplessly on either side, their elegant globes long smashed and the wires ruined by time and weather.

He stared beyond into the dark forbidden expanse which seemed to open and close in all at once like a dark, formless maw. He put his hands to his mouth to keep from screaming and turned abruptly and headed home.

17

June 1961

Willie stood inside the door of the Peacock Lounge long enough to adjust to the smoke-filled darkness. He had been in the bar only once since Tessie had gone to the hospital and that was to flush out Big T. Now he scanned the faces carefully and spotted a heavyset, balding man near the end of the bar.

Willie moved quietly and slid onto the stool beside him. Reggie looked up. "How's it goin', Willie? Sure am sorry to hear about

Tessie. Place ain't been the same since she gone, and nobody got the scoop. What happened, anyway?"

Reggie was one of those who did not believe in beating around the bush. Willie knew this, so he ordered a double gin and took a long sip before he answered.

"Don't really know, Reggie. Seem like she got caught comin' home from a party...she was pretty bad there for a while..."

"Damn!" Reggie slammed the bar with his fist. "If these ain't hard times, man, I don't wanna see 'em. Cat strung out, he take off King Kong's mammy for a quarter when his habit come down... hard times, man..."

Willie raised his glass again. The drink was strong and slightly bitter, but he went through the motions as Reggie spoke.

"...and they talkin' that talk 'bout not packin' a piece. Shit, every law abidin' citizen oughtta have one. I mean, if everybody walked with some weight, you know, crime would disappear overnight. No more muggin's, robberies...them junkies forced to stay cool 'cause they know everybody equal and everybody bad. Now if Tessie hadda had some weight on her that night..."

"Matta fact," said Willie, his voice dropping to a whisper, "that's what I wanna talk to you about. I gotta get her a special. She home now, and you know I can't be with her twenty-four hours..."

Reggie inclined his head. "When you need it?"

"Shoulda had it years ago, but I'll settle for tomorrow..."

"Cool. Be here after the last figure. Got somethin' comin' in from Chicago..."

"What kind? She don't need nuthin' she can't handle. And nuthin' too light neither..."

"They thirty-eights. Just right. Guaranteed brand new. Ain't been out the box. Seein' it's for Tessie, I'll put you in for a half a yard..."

Fifty dollars was excellent for a brand new handgun, but Willie knew that it was always good politics to bargain a little. "Man, gimme some slack. Half a yard is a lotta bread..."

Reggie shrugged. "What can I say, Willie. There's a war on. Cats is buyin'. I'm supplyin'. If it was anybody else, I'd be askin' anywhere from a yard to a deuce and a quarter and gettin' it. People glad to pay it too. Besides, you pullin' that long bread down the great white way. Big-time draftsman's gig and all. You kickin' 'em in the ass and can give up fifty without even blinkin'."

Reggie rose from his seat and signaled for the check. "I'll be glad when Tessie git back. I don't know where Tate got this excuse from..."

He wrinkled his face and maintained a stony silence as the not-so-new barmaid rung up the tab.

She was thin, sallow, and frumpy, with a pitted face and a voice that could beat out sandpaper.

Reggie groaned as she flitted away.

"I mean it's cool for Tate to hire the handicapped, but there gotta be a limit, dammit. This broad so ugly, you forced to take a drink just so you can look her in the eye."

Reggie expressed his opinion loudly, causing Willie to look around.

"Be cool, man, maybe that's Tate's woman..."

"Shee-it! If it is, all his taste is in his mouth. I mean, if he got one for blow and one for show, this one definitely ain't the star. Her mug could stop a clock. Matta fact, me and the dudes been wonderin' if we should chip in for one a them gift certificates for plastic surgery or just forget it and give her a banana..."

Willie wanted to laugh as Reggie walked away, but then he remembered Tessie's face—the scar and all the other things he had pushed to the back of his mind and had refused to think about until now: Her sharp and sudden changes from rock-hard silence to screaming hysteria. The denial. The loss of loving and the loss of love. He thought of these things and a dull heavy fear crept in. He sat there, mesmerized by the unfamiliar sensation.

Of course, she wasn't ready. He knew it. She knew it. The doctors knew it. But one night she had tossed and turned so badly that he had reached out to hold her, to let her know that he was there, and she had woke screaming, tearing at him in the dark. He thought of the loss of love and the pulse near his temple began to bother him again. He closed his eyes to relieve the pain and was assailed by the vision of Tessie.

At first, when he saw her, he had been careful always to keep just slightly behind her so he could watch her walk. Head up in the morning, fresh and pretty, going to look for a job. Head down at night. No prospects, but still pretty. She walked with her shoulders held back and never lost her stride. She seemed proud and defiant, and he loved it.

He dreamed about her. Day and night. Did she sit with her legs crossed at the knees or at the ankles? Probably at the knees. Only fat women sat with legs crossed at the ankles, and Tessie was not fat, at least not in his book, because high behinds and big legs did not count as fat.

Finally, one evening, he counted to ten, held his breath, and fell in step beside her.

Truthfully, he knew now that he hadn't been prepared for her. He was accustomed to women acting cute, smart, strong, dumb, or desperate, or if they were really creative, perhaps they combined two or three out of the five. But Tessie played none of these roles. She had a basic, hard-edged innocence that at once intrigued him and made him suspicious. He tried to cut through with his arsenal of wit and sharp words, but there was nothing to cut through.

He opened his eyes and lifted his glass, hiding behind it.

...it ain't over, baby, just hang in, hang in. We gonna do all the things we used to...

He thought of their first month together. It had been nothing but talk. Talk that threatened to wear him out. He had even begun to doubt himself. Was this what she wanted?

Then one night, as they sat cross-legged on the floor in the semidarkness of his living room, listening to the smooth pain of Lady Day and trying to understand what she really meant, Tessie sighed and threw up her hands.

"What's the matter?"

"I don't know...tired, I guess...and scared, mostly..."

"I can understand that. Looking for a job ain't never been easy..."

"...oh, it isn't that. I mean, it's not only that..."

"What is it?"

His voice was a whisper, and he leaned over to touch her leg. His fingers found the place behind her knee, and this time she did not try to move away.

"What is it, baby. What are you afraid of..."

"This. This. I can't go through no more hurt. No more..."

He held his breath. He could barely see her face in the dim light and wondered if she were about to cry. Or worse, push him away again. Finally, he whispered, "Tessie, listen to me. There ain't no guarantees. I'm comin' into this thing just like you are, baby..."

"You are...?"

"Yes..."

"Willie..."

"Yes?"

"How do you feel...I mean...about me?"

"How do I feel? Nervous. I feel damn nervous. Sometimes I can't think straight. I mean, I haven't even made love to you yet, but if a day goes by when I can't see you, it's like a day that didn't happen..."

He stopped talking when she touched him. She uncrossed her legs for an instant and then closed them around his hips, drawing him to the center of her.

When he finally felt those legs wrapped around him, he wanted to cry. It was heaven and Christmas and his birthday and she was all good things come to him at once.

Gift wrap, he thought then. She was like gift wrap. Tight and fancy.

He wanted to cry.

Later, he remembered her hands on the small of his back, nails pressing, and heard her crying.

Still later, he tried to remember the exact instant he had come to love her, tried to reconstruct it, but it was like peering at a point in time through silken gauze. Memory was a maze of elusive, indefinable images. He gave up, concluding that he had loved her, or the idea of her, all along and meeting her had only been a matter of time.

Now, he stared beyond his drink into the mirror as if concentrating on the music. He appeared utterly absorbed but was really locked in a tremendous battle to control the rage and the tears that surfaced each time he thought of her. He wished Reggie were still there to distract him. He remained perfectly still until the pressure subsided; then he drained his glass and rose from the bar stool.

He was tall, with soft, dark features, and moved with a quiet, fluid grace that a lot of women liked. They thought the way he moved was sexy, but Willie knew he walked that way, easy on his toes with slightly swaying hips, because his feet hurt.

The women lounging near the door watched him through narrow eyes. They shook their heads as he approached and clucked their condolences.

"She home," he answered quietly. "She comin' along. Comin' along." And he padded out.

The temperature hit ninety the next afternoon, and the air conditioner in the Peacock chose that time to quit. The regulars—true to their mission—lined the bar as usual, and several looked up expectantly as Willie entered.

They sighed and returned to their drinks as he edged by and took a seat at the end of the bar. Reggie had not yet arrived. The last figure was not out and Willie could almost touch the tension in the air.

Everyone drank quietly, afraid to make a sound lest the number runner pass and they miss the signal. The door burst open again and all heads turned. Disappointment was audible as Tacky Jackie waddled in.

"Sorry I ain't who y'all think I oughtta be," she yelled in a voice two registers above the jukebox. "But ah'm waitin' just like y'all is. Ain't no picnic when you got ten dollars swingin' on six-oh-oh and six-oh is leadin'. Dammit, lemme calm my last nerve. Gimme a double gin!"

Numerous patrons rushed to pay for her drink, and Willie smiled and shook his head at Jackie's talent for creating confusion. She was an extremely obese woman of nearly three hundred pounds, and there was a man and a story for every pound over the first hundred. Willie and everyone else still remembered the uproar when a man had died in her bed.

The stoop watchers had swung into high gear, stretching scandal for months by pinching off pieces of small talk to send out in breathless dispatches.

"...makin' love, they say..."

"...musta been a hard nut to crack..."

"...heard she so good, poor man had a seizure..."

"Hush your mouth..."

"That too. Undertaker caught hell tryin' to git them lips back together..."

"Ummm, mmm. What she got?"

Services for the deceased had been brief. The man's outraged widow had ordered a sealed casket and immediate cremation.

And still the talk rolled on.

And the myth grew like magic and Jackie became a star. The truth was, as Willie knew, that the unfortunate lover had died of asphyxiation, having swallowed one of Jackie's dime-store earrings, which she had not taken time to remove.

The door of the Peacock swung open and LeRoy the Runner strolled in. With a no-nonsense air, he motioned to Jackie and she followed him to the rear of the bar. In passing, he held up his right hand, fist clenched, no fingers showing.

Zip! Zero! Nuthin'! There was a split second of silence and pandemonium broke. Jackie had hit. She had six thousand dollars. Several others in the bar had money coming because they had "rode her luck," betting heavily on the last figure of Jackie's number.

"Thank you, *Jesus*!!" Jackie screamed. "Set up the bar and run it 'til I say stop! I ain't goin' to no damn face-to-face tomorrow. That welfare bitch can kiss my ass!"

She was delirious with excitement. She felt rich and in control. "Thank you, Jesus," she shouted again.

Tate turned up the jukebox, and Little Richard split the air with "Tootie Fruity." Everyone fell in for the madison, and all drinking habits changed.

"I'm havin' me a double Chivas Regal, and Jesus ain't had nuthin' to do with it," shouted Red as he elbowed his way to the bar.

Outside, the word spread faster than fire, and the door of the Peacock strained on its hinges as the local population, poised for such events, poured into the already packed bar.

They roared approval as Jackie climbed up on a table and set the madison in motion. Hands clapped and fingers snapped.

"Go on, girl. You got the juice."

"And I'm gon' turn it every way but loose."

Jackie threw her head back and slid into a heavy gyrating motion. The fat moved in old folds and the table groaned under the weight. Tate made a note to charge her double when she broke it and meanwhile kept a sharp eye out for any glass that needed refilling.

Willie watched, fascinated, and did not hear Reggie approach.

"What's happenin?"

"Nuthin' too tough. Jackie's in the money...six grand..."

"Yeah, it's all down the block. Ain't gonna last, though. Heard she even bought the cook a pork chop sandwich..."

He looked around him. "Been waitin' long?"

"Not too long," Willie replied, noticing the casual way in which Reggie held the brown bag.

Reggie caught his gaze. "Man, don't git uptight. You know this the best way. Nobody care what you carry in a paper bag. Could be a container of milk for all you know..."

"Well, is it?"

Reggie laughed. "Ain't exactly, but it'll sure homogenize a dude. Mix him with the four winds in a hurry."

He placed the package on the bar near Willie's glass. Willie laid down five ten-dollar bills.

"Tessie be glad to see this," Willie said. He drained his glass and tucked the package under his arm. Suddenly, he began to sweat profusely.

...suppose I drop it and the bag tears...suppose the piece falls out...suppose...

Fuck it. I'm in it now and ain't no turnin' back...

He left the bar and, like a fish swimming against the current, made his way through the mob to the door.

18

A week after Big Joe's party, Jonrobert parked his car a block from the school and waited. An hour later, Celia emerged from a side door of the library and made her way down the crowded walk.

He watched her for half a block before he put the car in gear and cruised slowly behind her. Finally, she caught the hard stares of the other students and looked back. The window slid down, and she heard his voice.

"...where you been? Playin' hooky?"

Without hesitation, without a word, she pulled at the door and almost tumbled into the car.

He drove north, up the tree-lined street alive with chattering students. At the hill, he turned and headed for the drive.

"So," he said, breaking the quiet, "how you been...?"

"Fine," she whispered. She did not look at him.

"This is fine?"

She did not answer, but stared straight ahead.

"...hate to see you when you ain't..."

Still, she could not answer. Her mind had closed, and the myriad questions that had assailed her since last seeing him dissipated as soon as they rose to the surface of her consciousness. But she felt a fever of confusion.

...never thought I'd see him again. I had given up...then started hoping and gave up again. I prayed so hard, my knees and my knuckles ached...prayed night and day...and in between, prayed for the strength to pray some more. And running to the hospital...Tessie... poor Tessie...

She was suddenly angry.

...all of it is his fault...maybe I could have gone back for her... could have warned her...now he's here acting as if nothing had ever happened...

Jonrobert eased the car into a diagonal parking slot on a bluff overlooking the river. The sun's rays reflected a fiery orange off the intricate steel cablework of the bridge. Below them, a tug slid smoothly against the tide.

He lit a cigarette and leaned over the wheel, staring at the water. "I called you," he said quietly. "Last time, I thought your mama was gonna come through the wire. With a pistol."

Celia turned in surprise. "You...called me...?"

"Yeah. And when I couldn't get to you, I popped into the Peacock, lookin' for Tessie, figurin' maybe she could front for me. But man, when they pulled my coat. That was a trip. They took that chick on a cold trip..."

He cursed under his breath. "Well, word is whoever did it

gonna git it. I'm damn glad you were on that fire escape with me. I kept thinkin' it coulda happened to you...it coulda been you..."

Celia looked at him. In all the confusion of running back and forth to the hospital and school, that idea had never once occurred to her. Tessie, she knew, was bound to attract a lot of things, including trouble, but not her.

She glanced again at him, trying to fathom what it was about her that interested him, what unknown chemical configuration had come into play that had drawn them to each other. She listened to him, the soft sound of his voice and the smooth flow of his words.

"...and knowin' what I know about you, which ain't much but enough, I'd have to track that dude and take 'im off." He crushed the cigarette and turned to her.

The sun cast his dark profile in bold relief and colored his eyes a strange shade of red-flecked gold. He had even features and perfect teeth. He was so handsome that it frightened her to look at him, yet she absorbed every detail.

"You know..." he whispered, "you pretty hard to track yourself, but I figured if I worked it right, I'd run into you sooner or later..."

When Celia spoke, her words came in a rush, as if she had been holding them in some small place and now the place had become even smaller.

"...I never thought I'd see you again," she whispered. "Mama never said a word. I thought you had forgotten about me..."

"You believed that?"

"I didn't want to, but I...I didn't know what to think..."

She lowered her eyes as he moved near and she began to absorb his closeness, breathe in his familiar essence, the essence which she remembered and which had kept her awake all those nights. She felt the fine softness of his moustache as his mouth brushed her neck and closed over her ear.

His voice was a whisper. "Listen...baby...listen...open your eyes. I'm here. I'm back...look at me..."

The sound of him washed over her and the tightness in her chest suddenly eased. She felt light-headed and filled with an overwhelming exhilaration. Her arms went around him and her fingers twisted and pulled at his hair.

"Jonrobert...oh...Jonrobert..."

He held her face in his hands, forcing her to look at him.

"Baby, wait...listen to me. I wanna apologize for what happened on the fire escape. I shoulda known you never been anywhere. And when you started screamin' about your leg, I didn't understand, I—"

Celia opened her eyes and slowly eased away from him. She curled her leg under her and looked away.

What had she said about her leg? She could not remember. The euphoria washed away, and she felt an intense weariness. Finally, she said, "It's been like this since I was born. I don't know what—"

"—baby...it ain't no big thing..."

"What?"

"I said it don't matter. Nuthin' matters...'cept that I met you and I wanna keep on seein' you..."

His arm came around her shoulder, and she buried her face in his chest.

"Jonrobert...I'm glad. I'm so glad...I—"

She couldn't finish. All the words and thoughts and prayers from daydreaming and night dreaming ran together, and she could not finish. All she knew was that he was here, beside her, and she had heard him say that she was all right. She was all right.

19

Celia did not see the inside of a classroom for the remainder of the term. Now, as they cruised along the expressway, she worried. The semester would soon be over. What excuse would she have to leave the house every day?

...summer school...perhaps repeat the courses I failed, she thought. Heck with it...I love him and I don't care about anything else...I can't even think straight...let alone think about class... I love him...I'm not letting go. Not again...

"You dreamin', baby, wake up..."

She opened her eyes and sat up. They were still on the expressway.

"You ain't lettin' go...of what?"

She did not answer but saw that he was smiling as they approached the exit.

"Where are we going?"

"If you promise to keep quiet, I promise to show you..."

They parked adjacent to a wholesale auto accessory supply store. The area was deserted but for this building, which covered the entire block. Jonrobert turned the ignition, and Celia followed his gaze. They sat for some minutes in silence until she finally asked.

"What's that?"

"That," he said, "is the beginning of my life..."

"What do you mean? What kind did you have before?"

Jonrobert was silent; then he turned to face her directly.

"Well...no point in dancin' 'round it. I'm gonna say somethin... a lot of things...and I don't want you to interrupt 'til I'm finished, you understand?"

A fine apprehension rose in her as she shook her head. "I don't know if I can do that...I don't understand..."

"You don't understand 'cause you don't know. You don't know anything about me. Or the life."

"Your life...?"

"My life. The life. For a while, it was one and the same..."

He took a deep breath and said suddenly, "You know what a player is?"

She shook her head slowly, afraid that he might laugh at her. A player, to her, was someone who worked in the theater or perhaps someone who won or lost at cards.

...maybe he should laugh, she thought. I've been seeing him all this time, going to bed with him, using the same toothbrush... and now he's telling me that I don't know him...he's right...but it isn't because I don't want to...each time I started to ask, there was always something that...stopped me...

"Well," he said, "I'm gonna start at the beginnin'...

"When I stepped off the Hound in my light-green pin-striped suit and inch-thick brogans, I had one thing in mind. I came here to make it. You know...just make it....Well, who was there waitin' for me at the station but Thomas. Mama had written to tell him I was comin'...and for him to look out for his little cousin.

"Only thing, his name wasn't Thomas no more. He had changed it to Pierre. He also changed his suits every hour on the hour. Imagine a dude practically born behind the plow, could hardly speak English, but had everybody, includin' the V squad, callin' him Pierre.

"He was a smooth lookin' cat though, and that was his ticket. Showed me around...flashin' more cash than a government printin' press...

"Then he showed me his enterprise. Stable of eight broads... they worked hard and he lived royally. Boss pad complete with a maid servin' him Remy on the terrace. Which was nice, but I wasn't into that. I mean, I wanted somethin', but not that...

"So I went into a lotta things, dispatched cabs, pumped gas figurin' to get my own station, had my own gypsy cab for a while and was doin' okay 'til I had to face down two dudes early one Sunday mornin'...

"Thought they was drunk when they climbed in, you know, 'cause one was actin' so stiff, and the other, he could hardly get the door closed, he was shakin' so bad...anyway, I didn't drive three blocks before they pulled the pistol.

"Shit, I saw that and I put that pedal through the floor. Cab jumped the sidewalk, ran over a mailbox, spun around, hit a phone booth, and finally stopped against a newsstand.

"One dude was out cold, and the other had his arm pinned somewhere. He was cryin' like a baby, and the piece was nowhere in sight. So I pried him out and broke his other fuckin' arm. It ain't easy tryin' to make a honest hustle out here, lemme tell you..."

Celia's mind was racing...an honest living...that's how he was able to spot those plainclothesmen from the window that night... an honest living...

Her head felt ready to burst, but she made an effort to listen.

"Anyway, Thomas had been talkin' to me all along, off and on, and I listened but just wasn't interested. Well, after that Sunday mornin', I knocked on his door with a mile-wide smile on my face.

"So, he set me up. I went for it. Why not? Long bread, short hours, and hard workin' broads. Stashed more cash money than I ever seen in my life. But I don't know what happened, or when... seems like the more that went down, the more stuff got on my nerves.

"Saw Pierre go after a babe once...wore her down, wore her out, then threw her out. Like an old paper bag. All in six months. Threw her out and then he complained.

"'Hadda git rid a her,' he said, 'bad for morale. From now on, we deal only in cream, no more fuckin' cocoa—then white broads come your way, they easy to work 'cause they fucked up already and come to a black cat for the finale. Everybody know that. Thing to do is milk 'em for all they worth. Git everything. Git it all while the gittin's good. Then cut 'em loose.

"'But them black broads. They another story...black bitch git slick quick and slow down fast. Had one, long time ago, so lazy, couldn't hardly keep both my feet on the ground. Had a keep one steady up her ass. Shoulda known then not deal no more cocoa.'

"That's how he complained," Jonrobert said, "but I knew he was jivin' 'cause when money talks, bullshit walks. If the price was right, Pierre'd deal cocoa and cream and anything in between, even sludge if he had to...

"It was lousy. The more I saw, the more I wondered what the hell I was into..."

...and what am I into, Celia wanted to ask. What on earth am I into? She felt dizzy as the sound of his voice wove in and out, at once hard and soft.

"...and mama wasn't helpin' matters none by writin' every other week askin' between the lines what kinda work I was into to be sendin' her that kinda bread..."

He paused to light a cigarette. He did not look at her.

"Somethin' like that really mess with your mind if you ain't cut out to play, and I just wasn't cut out...

"I was lookin' for somethin' different all along when I ran into you..."

Celia said nothing, but Jonrobert had expected no reply and he went on without a pause.

"...and there was somethin' else...somethin' I tried to talk about with Thomas, but he didn't know what the hell I was sayin'... I was bothered by the smell.... I mean, most of the broads strolled clean, but...you know...like when a man's been foolin' around and his number one finds out. Well, nobody has to pull her coat... she can smell another woman on him. Don't matter how much water a cat throw on after he gets outta bed, soon's he's dry, it comes out of his skin somehow...

"And just like a woman can smell another woman on her man, I smelled other men on those girls, it was—"

"What about the money?" Celia asked.

"What—??"

"You know—the money...did you smell it on the money they brought in?"

The question surprised both of them. He stared, and then reached for her as she drew away.

"Look Celia, I was hopin' you'd—"

"—I want to go home..."

"Home!"

"Yes...I'm tired..."

"Lemme ask you one thing before we go. How come, when the money was bein' spent and we was goin' all them different places, you didn't think to ask me where it came from then?"

She could not answer and did not look at him. She had avoided looking at him the whole time he spoke, had closed her eyes and hoped, when she opened them, that it would be someone else telling her this tale.

From the very beginning, the relationship had had for her a surreal quality. He had touched her and she had come alive; he had loved her and she came to love him, to worship him. But she had drifted, mesmerized by the experience, asking no questions because she did not want the dream disturbed.

She thought about it now: how she had, in her daydreams, constructed this fragile bubble, this translucent, glimmering globe, around him and allowed only her dreams to grow inside.

Now, as he spoke, each word hit against the thin membrane and seams appeared where there were none before. Now, in her mind's eye, the bubble began to float, at first grazed gently by reality but then, finally, blown off course forever, whipped by the hard and bitter words.

She saw it break and watched the dream die. The fragments scattered to the wind, and she knew she could not gather them together again. She felt betrayed, as if she had been robbed and left at the scene of the crime to figure out why.

She closed her eyes—the easiest thing to do under the circumstances—and worked hard at allowing the spinning pieces in her mind to go blank—at least until she got home.

20

There was a note on the dining table when Celia came in. Frieda had gone shopping for supplies.

"Thank God," she murmured, "I can go straight to bed without having to pretend I'm doing homework for an hour..."

In the bathroom she wrung out a steaming hot towel and pressed it to the side of her neck, holding it in place until she felt the pulse slow.

In her room, she lay across the bed, trying to catch her breath and, at the same time, ignore the small voice within, which had now assumed choral dimensions in the silence. She looked in the mirror and experimented with the sound of her disappointment. Damn. Damn it. Damn him. Damn.

Before she met Jonrobert, she had been repelled by the sound of profanity, believing that only the dull and ignorant needed it to fill gaps in dull and empty circumstances. It was the song of the street corner and sounded sad and powerless when a man called someone's mother "out of her name" and followed with suggestions as to what one could do with her.

When such exchanges occurred, Celia usually walked quickly because bullets were known to turn corners when a mother's son got mad enough.

But Jonrobert was different. The casual flow of the language as it rolled off his tongue was unlike anything she had ever heard. His "damn" was soft and his "shit" sounded sweet.

She closed her eyes, feeling the heat rise as the other words, especially when they were in bed, came to mind. The beat near her throat grew strong again, threatening to enlarge and choke her.

...the clothing...the language...why couldn't I connect it?

I've seen men who dressed like him, but they were always on corners, doing nothing...Jonrobert never hung around, but I never knew what he did...

Then Tessie's laughter, the night in the bar, came to her. "You ain't hardly gonna see Jonrobert walkin' down no street—"

She put her hands to her head.

...Tessie knew...and she didn't tell me...

She concentrated on the image in the mirror, staring hard, trying not to blink or otherwise disturb it. When she could no longer do this, she was forced once again to focus on him.

"Jonrobert is a...was...a...I still can't believe it..."

The earlier feeling of numbness began to dissipate, and she wondered now why she felt only a cold curiosity. The man she loved had used women and, so far as she could tell, had made a lot of money from them. Why had she felt no anger? She examined her image carefully, trying to detect the smallest flicker of moral outrage for what he had done.

She felt none. She thought instead of the girl her mother had been: young, working in a strange kitchen, eating leftovers, dizzy from the heat and the smell of lye soap, walking miles and miles and miles before sunup and after sundown.

And the woman for whom she worked had looked at Frieda's blistered fingers and swollen feet, had looked through them, and had seen nothing.

Her mother, and people like her, were fixtures designed to ease the imagined burdens of useless lives.

The numbness gave way to an old anger. It should have been easy to excuse Jonrobert, to rationalize that turnabout is fair play, that Jonrobert and Pierre were only the newest players in a game as old as time where possession translated into a small show of power and nothing more.

But forgiveness and fair play were not her immediate concern.

"...if he's a pimp...what am I...what do I mean to him? He said he loved me. What does it mean?"

I love him.

She thought of motherly love, brotherly love, blind love. But *love* love, which had caused lives, battles, and fortunes to be lost, was an unquantifiable abstraction.

...maybe it has no meaning and people are searching so hard for nothing...maybe I'm only supposed to feel it, not understand it...

...I see now why all those times when I asked him, begged him, to tell me why he loved me, he couldn't say...he would only smile and say, "When I find out, I'll let you know..."

Which, after a time, had satisfied her. Because by then, her appetite had grown large and she had neither capacity nor inclination to consider the question in depth. She did not understand what she felt, only that she was overwhelmed, swallowed up in a twenty-four-hour, seven-day-a-week, day-in, day-out feeling that reached into deep and vital parts of her. It interfered with respiration and digestion; caused her heart to race and her pulse to slow; made it impossible for her to eat; made her temperature rise and sweat run down her arms and collect embarrassingly at the tip of her elbows; caused her at night to rock herself into an uneasy sleep where nightmare phantoms of fast, beautiful women lured her man away. She awoke, dizzy from dreaming, freezing in her own sweat, and his name was hot on her tongue: Jonrobert... Jonrobert...oh Jonrobert...I love you...I love you...I love you...

For several days, her mother had looked at her warily: then she finally asked, "You sick?"

And Celia had answered too quickly that she felt fine.

Now, she felt like screaming and smashing the image in the mirror.

21

Celia let herself into Willie's apartment with the key he had given her. At the sound of her footsteps, Tessie turned off the television. She sat propped up on the sofa and an assortment of medication filled the small table nearby.

"My God," she said as Celia walked into the room, "you look like hell just opened up. What happened...?"

Celia set about preparing the gauze, tape, and oil needed to change the dressing on Tessie's face.

"I'll tell you later…"

"I got time…"

Celia gingerly peeled off the dressing, and Tessie tried to read her progress in Celia's eyes.

"…look any better?" Tessie finally asked, unable to remain silent.

"A lot." Celia murmured as she prepared a new dressing. "I think this stuff mother got for you is finally beginning to work…"

"Well," Tessie sighed, "at least it doesn't itch any more…"

When Frieda learned about Tessie from Al, she had been so relieved that the worst had not happened to her own child that her attitude softened and she even went to the hospital to visit her. She looked at the wound and knew that once it had healed, Tessie's face would be drawn into a perpetual, lopsided frown.

She sent Willie down to La Marquetta under the bridge to visit the Candle Man, a dim narrow shop next to the notions store where she bought sewing supplies.

The candle store, with no electricity, was lit by a vivid display of votive lights, and the air was heavy with the smell of oils, herbs, incense, and dried flowers. The Candle Man also stocked minute samples of soil and dust from places as far apart, he said, as Africa and Antarctica: These were packed in inch-square brown containers labeled in a code only he understood.

He was eighty-four years old and knew things that had long been forgotten or were never learned by others.

Willie returned with the small jars of almond oil, aloe, and white willow bark, and Frieda showed Celia how to apply the mixture to Tessie's face.

Now the stinging sensation was gone and it didn't hurt as much to talk.

"It's getting better," Celia said. "Pretty soon, you'll be looking in the mirror again…"

"I don't know about that…" Tessie said. Then her voice dropped to a whisper. "You don't know…what that man did to me…even Willie doesn't know all of it…I can't tell him…

"Since I been home, I keep thinkin' and thinkin' that if I had just kept quiet…you know…maybe closed my eyes and gritted my teeth, it would've all been over quick like, 'cause he wasn't raisin' no hell...but all I could feel was this fat, greasy pig huffin' and puffin' and beggin' me to tell him how good it was. I don't know what happened to me...all of a sudden I found myself...laughin'... a screamin', cryin' kind of laughin'...then it was like I had stepped outside of me and everything that was happenin' was happenin' to another person...and I heard that person laughin'...tellin' him how small he was...kept sayin' it 'til he pulled his gun and said he'd blow my head off...next thing I knew, he had a bottle or somethin' in his hand. When I passed out, he musta thrown me out of the car..."

Tessie's voice rose and a sudden pain cut through Celia which she didn't dare acknowledge. She looked at the line running from Tessie's left ear to just below her cheek. The heavy scar tissue did not form, and the line was thin, barely visible. If Tessie cared to, she could have looked, and the mirror would have told her that, despite the mark, she was still pretty. But she was terrified and spoke only of the crushing, psychic damage which had reduced the face in the mirror to a smudgy cypher.

Celia tried to apply another layer of the mixture and somehow dull the horror of what she was hearing, but Tessie pushed her hand away.

"...you know...I wish he had killed me..."

Celia stared at her. "What??"

"Look at me...all cut up like a wino...like my mother....A long time ago, she was a woman you could love, but somebody got to her too....Now look at her...look at me..."

She rose from the sofa and began to move about the room. Celia watched her awkward steps and knew that the effort was too much for her. Tessie stopped suddenly and cried again, "Look at me! You think this stuff is gonna help??"

"Tessie, maybe you—"

Before Celia could move, Tessie, in one swift motion, swept the accumulation of jars and bottles off the table.

"Tessie!! What are you doing??"

Tessie stood in the middle of the room and pressed her hands to her face. "Look at me!!" she screamed past Celia. "He should've killed me!! I should've killed myself!!"

"Tessie, please! Don't talk that way!!"

"What way? You don't know...you don't know what happened..."

She moved back to the sofa and sat down. "I feel like...like... everything's over...gone..."

She leaned back and closed her eyes.

"Everything's gone..."

"No. No, it's not, Tessie...these things take time. In a few weeks, you'll be feeling better. Give yourself a chance..."

"Ain't that much time in the world, girl. And I'm...tired... I'm so...tired..."

Her eyes remained closed, and Celia watched her agitated breathing and then her tears again as she struggled with her turmoil.

Celia rose from the floor where she had been kneeling and reached for the phone. Her hand was shaking as she dialed. She prayed that her mother had returned home. Willie was too far away.

There was a half ring and she heard Frieda's voice. "I just walked in. Where are you?"

"Mother, I'm at Willie's. Tessie's not...she's not...oh mother, I don't know what to do..."

"Unlock the door. I'll be there..."

Celia returned to sit on the floor near the sofa. She let some minutes pass before she spoke.

"Tessie, listen. I know that nothing I say can ever change what happened, but you can't give up. Everything's not over. You have a wonderful man who loves you...you can't give up..."

Tessie looked at her. "Celia," she said slowly, "I just can't explain what I'm feeling—"

They started in fright when the door opened, and although Celia was expecting Frieda, she too stared wide-eyed, listening to the movement through the alcove, and sighed when her mother appeared in the door of the living room.

"What's happened..."

Without waiting for a reply, Frieda set about collecting the scattered bottles and jars from the floor. She placed them on the small table and then sat down next to Tessie and gathered her in her arms. "You not feelin' so hot, are you?"

"No, I..."

"It's all right...sometimes, things happen to us and there's never no warnin' and when it happens, it feels like we're gonna die. But somehow we live through it and go on livin'. I mean, we survive, Tessie...you hear me. We survive....You gotta make up your mind...to survive. If you don't do that, none a this medicine is gonna help...you gotta make up your mind...Willie's stickin' by you. And Celia and the rest of us...we're all here."

Celia watched her mother as she held Tessie, rocking her gently, and knew that when she and her mother left, Tessie would cry again. She would bury her sorrow in her pillow at night and in her smile when morning came. She would cry often and alone and out of earshot, where Willie would not hear the sound of her anguish and be reminded of her humiliation.

Celia became aware of the sound of her own tears and wanted to close her eyes to the two women on the sofa, but then she would have to confront her own pain, open her mouth, and scream, in order to relieve the vibration caused by the grinding of her teeth.

22

When Celia heard the phone, she picked it up on the second ring.

"Hello...?"

"Hello back...it's been three weeks. I been thinkin' about you..."

The sound of Jonrobert's voice, soft and low, took her by surprise. She eased into a chair, holding the phone close.

"Jonrobert...how did you—"

"Your mama just left the house. With killer."

"His name is Al..."

"I don't care what his name is. He looks like a killer to me..."

She wanted to laugh with relief. She was hearing his voice. He could have been translating Sanskrit and she would have been happy to listen.

"Look, baby, I'm sittin' at the bar. I can see everything from here. What time's your mama comin' back?"

"I don't know...she never goes very far..."

He heard the fine tremor in her voice, so he said, "I didn't mean that. I gotta see you but I ain't comin' there. Why don't you come to the house. I wanna talk to you..."

The soft rhythm of his voice flowed into her, and she wondered how she had managed to let so much time go by without seeing him. She was going to call him, had to call eventually, she knew, if only to hear his voice. She had no idea what she would have said.

"I...want to see you too."

"Baby?"

"Yes?"

"Come on. I'll meet you there."

Jonrobert opened the door before she knocked. He gazed at her and then stepped aside to let her pass. She walked slowly into the apartment, uncertain where she should go. In the middle of the room, she turned and held up her arms, as if to fend him off, although he had not moved.

"You sorry you came?"

"No..."

"Then what's the matter..."

"I don't know..."

"Come on...don't lie..."

"Don't lie? Me? If anyone was lying, it was you!"

She was confused. Why were they fighting? Was he as frightened as she was? She did not have time to consider this because all at once she was indeed angry. She was sorry she had come. She was sorry she had ever met him.

He turned from the door and took several steps toward her. Still he did not touch her. When he spoke, his voice was almost a sigh.

"Look. I know what you thinkin' and it's my fault. I was wrong to put all that on you at one time, but I was tired. I didn't know no other way to give it to you, so I laid it on you straight...these three weeks we didn't see each other, you know, it didn't have to be that way. If you had understood, it didn't have to be that way..."

She looked at him, amazed. "If I had understood," she repeated. She wanted to scream. "What was I supposed to understand? That you never meant to live off those women?"

She stopped.

...at the sound of his voice, I came running. I couldn't get here fast enough...for what...what guarantee do I have that he's going to change. He's too smart and too fast for me...I could never keep up...never. He lived off women...what do I have to give him...I know those women must have been pretty. Why does he want me...I'm a fool...I quit school because of him, I cut my hair because of him, and now, the minute he says the word, I come running, I come running...

She heard his voice again and panicked, wondering if she had missed anything he was saying.

"—you worried that somebody else paid for that car. You forget you rode in it..."

"If I had known, I would have walked..."

He looked at her as she stood in the middle of the room, her hands on her hips. The situation was slipping beyond his control, and if he did not turn it around, he knew he would not see her again.

"Look, Celia, what happened, happened. It's past. I wanna go on from here. And I want you with me..."

She was silent, and he wondered what she was thinking. Several minutes later, when she still did not respond, he grew angry: ...well. Hell with her. Thought she was different, thought she would understand, but seem like all she wanna do is rub my face in my shit. Well I ain't lettin' her or nobody do that. Nobody...

He watched her watch him. He knew how he felt; but beyond his feeling for her, he knew nothing, he had nothing. It was like stepping off the edge of the world into a deep, vast sea of darkness. He had allowed her, against his will, to become his anchor, his beacon in this darkness. Now he was drowning, and she was standing there undecided about throwing him a line.

...well, fuck her. He closed his eyes. Despite his anger, he nearly laughed, because that was what he wanted, really wanted, to do.

...she knows it's nice and she knows it's been three weeks, and now she's standin' here givin' me a hard time.

He wanted to hold her. He wanted to feel her moving and crying under him, feel her clinging to him with all her being and hear her talking out of her head. He knew that when he made love to her, he could drive her out of her head. When it happened, he felt a soaring power, a unique control, and he loved her because she made him feel that he was the only man in the world, the only man...

Suddenly, she sat down and bowed her head. He moved toward her and was amazed to see the tears. What had he done?

She looked up, shaking her head in a slow, nervous motion.

"I'm sorry I ever met you," she said quietly. "I'm sorry. I didn't know who you were, or how you were. These last weeks, I tried to figure it out, I tried...even on the way over here, I tried, but this is beyond me...I don't know the answer...and, three weeks is a long, long time. I love you and I can't think beyond that..."

She leaned over and her face was very near his.

"Jonrobert," she whispered, "if you hurt me, if you treat me the way you did all those—"

She drew away and started to cry again.

The sound of her voice, small and sad, beat him further into his confusion. He wanted to scream...stop it, I can't stand it, I love you, you bitch, and look what you're doin' to me...

Instead, he said, "It's been three weeks, baby...three weeks... did you mean to stay away forever?"

His mouth was near her ear and she turned to face him, to bury herself in the source of his breath sounds.

"I love you, I love you," she murmured, knowing that the simple phrase did not say nearly enough. Tears would not say enough. If she gave her life, that would not say enough. "I love you," she repeated softly.

They held onto each other, standing in the middle of the room, hands gliding light and smooth, like two sightless persons sensing and enjoying the extraordinary qualities of each other for the first time.

She felt the pressure of the small copper buttons on his shirt. The flat belt buckle, the crease in the cotton sleeve. And she wanted all of these to melt away, so that there would be no barrier between her urgency and that very essential part of him which, she knew now, she could not live without.

She felt the speed and nimbleness of his fingers as her blouse and brassiere came off. She strained to hear him as he gazed at her bared breasts:

"Cupcakes...babies...how my babies been..."

The palm of his hand closed over one and the drawing warmth of his mouth enveloped the other. Then, very quietly, he drew her to the floor. She lay under him and he pressed in hard and heavy, as if to meld her to him by sheer weight alone.

"...Jonrobert, wait...Jonrobert..."

He did not answer directly, but whispered, "sweet thing, sweet thing, sweet thing..." and kissed her arms, hands, shoulders, and ears until she rose above and beyond the pain, raised her hips, and locked into his furious rhythm. Every move was like a death stroke, each breath, each bite, each scratch, a final paroxysm. She drank the salt of his sweat and wanted more. He ingested and consumed the very essence of her and wanted more. Her head whipped from side to side, and he knew, before she knew, that she was going to scream. He cupped the palms of his hands over her mouth and pressed both elbows into the rug.

"Come on, baby, come on...I'm with you...I'm with you... I'm with...aaaaahhhhh, goddamn, fuck it, fuck me...baby..."

His hands slid away from her mouth. She did not scream, but gasped for breath, taking in lungfuls of air. He heard her voice, heavy, yet whispering, like rain against a window: "...push...push... open me up, Jonrobert, open me up, honey, push it...push..."

Much later, in the shower, their bodies slippery with soap, they glided against each other, colliding softly and easily under the warm spray. The scratches and bite marks stung both of them, and they laughed.

"What do I tell mother this time?" Celia asked. "I can't hide these..."

Jonrobert gazed steadily at her, the spray hitting his back and splashing in her face, causing her to squint.

"You ain't tellin' her nuthin'," he said. "We gonna tell her together. We may as well. We ain't gonna make it apart from each other, so we may as well make it together..."

23

The tap on the door was so soft that Al knew before he opened it that it would be Celia. He pulled on an old shirt and made his way through the small, cluttered kitchen. He was glad she was coming to see him. Now maybe he could really sit down and talk to her about that party. Between her going to school and running to see Tessie, he hadn't had a chance.

He opened the door, looked at her face, and changed his mind again.

"What's wrong?"

She looked over her shoulder before answering. "Could you... could you come downstairs a minute, please...?"

"What happened?"

She hesitated, then said, "I brought...someone home...to meet mother..."

She could not finish, and Al watched as she stood in the doorway, wringing her hands.

"Okay, just gimme a minute. And lighten up. It ain't that bad..."

In the bedroom, he snatched a clean shirt from the drawer and fumbled on the dresser for the hair brush. Then he took a quick, two-fingered dab at the can of Nu-Nile and worked it into his unruly hair. He wanted to be presentable when he met the boy.

He had often wondered when this day would come, and what Frieda would do.

...wonder what he's like? Did she meet 'im at that party?

...probably met 'im in school...or the library. Yeah...the library. He's one a them brainy ones with glasses and a pipe. Hell, it don't matter. He could come straight from heaven and Frieda'd still pitch a bitch. Probably carryin' on right now...

He buttoned his shirt and glanced in the mirror. He was not satisfied, but what he saw would have to do.

Celia was standing in the hall exactly where he had left her, afraid to come in and afraid to go back downstairs.

"Come on, it ain't that bad..."

"Yes, it is..."

"Well, let's see...let's see..."

He led the way down the short flight and paused for her to catch up. Together they walked into the apartment.

Frieda was standing near the window in the living room. Her face was tight, and she made no effort whatsoever at pretense. Al saw that the window was open and moved quickly to be near her. As Al crossed the room, Jonrobert rose from the chair and offered his outstretched hand.

They shook hands stiffly as Al eyed him casually.

...forgit the library. This cat ain't read a book in his life...she met 'im at that party...look at that loud, silk shirt and those damn tight pants...and where the hell he git them pointy-toed crocodile kicks from? This motherfucker look like a pimp...if he was at that party, probably *is* a pimp...

Al glanced at Frieda again, and the pity and anger welled up inside him.

...this what she kept this kid here for? Afraid to let her go away 'cause she wanted to keep her safe? From what?...this cat's a pure pee-eye pimp...

"So," he said, forcing the sound from somewhere within him, "how you doin', Jonrobert?"

"Not bad. I was just sayin' to Celia the other day that I—"

"He's opening his own business," Celia put in quickly. "Right down the block."

"Is that so," said Al, envisioning a numbers spot or an after-hours joint where God knows what would go on. "What kinda business you thinkin' about...?"

"Auto repair," Jonrobert said quietly, staring back as Al continued to scrutinize him.

Al nodded. "...auto repair...that's good...need somethin' like that around here..."

"Well, yeah, I was thinkin'—"

Al cut in again,"—you sound like a home boy...where you from?"

Jonrobert relaxed and started to smile. "Man, my hometown so small, it ain't even on the map, but it's—"

Jonrobert usually glanced down when he smiled, and in that quick second, Al caught a flickering impression, a vague shadow of something that he had worked hard for many years to forget. He glanced at him, looked again, and his heart nearly stopped.

...it can't be!...it can't be!

Words froze in his throat, died on his tongue, yet the thought beat against his brain in a babble of confusion.

...it can't be. Dammit. It can't. I put him on the train myself. That letter come, and I took him to the station myself.

Al stared wide-eyed at the mark on Jonrobert's face. He remembered the crowded station, people pressing everywhere and him rushing with the little boy clinging to him in a terrified silence, unbroken since the night of the fire.

He remembered trying to explain it all to the old pullman porter as he pinned the tag on Jim-Boy's shirt, but there hadn't been enough time. All he knew was that the boy would never get well if he stayed.

The porter had lifted the child out of his arms and said, "Sometimes things got a way of knockin' us out soon as we git here, soon as we open our eyes. But don't worry. I'll see he gits to his folks in one piece. Even if he gits lost, can't stay lost—not with a patch like that on his face."

Al stared at the lemon-yellow mark on Jonrobert's eyelid, and the memories bobbed to the surface of consciousness, like bloated bodies frightful in death.

The little boy, the ball, the man in flames. And a sound came back, mournful and low and formless, with no beginning and no end. There was no real end, because Frieda had never really stopped crying. The sound and her sorrow had simply been submerged, thinly veneered by time and his own feeble attempts to make her forget.

He glanced quickly at her. She seemed unaware of his presence and was concentrating on Jonrobert, locking him into a gaze at once murderous and frightened.

Jesus, Al thought, suppose Frieda finds out and the screamin' and hollerin' start all over again...if she don't start hollerin', she might maybe do somethin' else...

...how did this happen? How in the hell this boy find his way back anyway? Fifty million places to go, and he come back here. To this very spot. Just like a fuckin' homin' pigeon...

He don't know the hell he caused...or the hell he gonna cause, if he decide to hang around...and from the look on Celia's face, the motherfucker done did more than hang. Shit! Gotta git to Sam and Dan and pull their coat. Shit!

Al lowered his eyes and, without a word, turned and walked out.

* * *

Frieda stared in amazement as Al turned. She listened to his retreating footsteps and heard the too loud sound of the door as he slammed it behind him.

Seconds before, it seemed to her that he had nearly stumbled as he left the room.

...why would he leave...he knows I can't do this alone...how could he leave me...with this...this...

She drew a deep breath. ...it's almost like somethin' scared him. No...no...this boy is nothing compared to him...yet he jumped back as if he'd just seen a whip snake...

She remained where she was standing although Jonrobert had returned to sit beside Celia. It was like watching a picture in slow motion through a lens frozen open. He shifted and raised his arm, bringing it up to an arc-shaped position, and the light caught the bright peacock-blue splash of silk as he lowered his hand.

Frieda's chest ached. ...did he intend to place that arm around Celia...my child...my baby...while I'm watching...is this rough, slippery...man going to...lay a hand on...my baby...

The light scattered as he gestured. "...you got a real nice place here, ma'am..." His voice was strong in the silence, and Frieda wondered if he expected a reply. She was nearly mesmerized by the way he was dressed.

...I've been sewing for years and never saw colors like that... where did she meet him...at that party...that terrible party... this is the boy who kept my child out all night...didn't allow her to come home...

She cleared her throat and said, "Young man, you have to excuse us. I want to speak to my daughter. Alone."

There is something about language that kills. It was not "Celia" whom Frieda wished to speak to, but "my daughter." To call her by name would have indicated a commonality, a mutuality. Frieda and Jonrobert both shared someone named Celia, but only Frieda could claim her, absolutely and exclusively, as "my daughter," thereby shutting out everyone and everything else. There it was. The stiff, formal, declaration of war and the opening salvo, meant to be a warning shot, caught him between the eyes. She watched as he blinked, stole a glance at Celia, and rose quickly from the sofa.

"Ma'am, I wanna explain somethin'...me and Celia..."

Frieda held up her hand. "Another time...not now."

She watched him touch Celia's face lightly and whisper, "Baby, I'll call you later."

Then, in a clearer voice: "So long, ma'am...it's a pleasure meetin' you..."

The door closed a second time, and now Celia felt the room grow large.

...well...perhaps, it's better this way. Not easier, but better... I'll be able to explain how we—

She watched her mother move from the window and, ever so slowly, cross the carpeted floor. Frieda moved so silently she might have been floating. After what seemed like forever, she was standing near the sofa, bending low so that her face was level with Celia's, so close that if she blinked, Celia might have felt the disturbance in the air around her mother's eyelashes.

"...I see," Frieda said quietly "...that your face is bruised... again..."

24

As usual, Al had trouble catching up with the twins. It was Saturday night and they could be anywhere.

He thought about it before making a move. "Ain't no point runnin' 'round like a chicken with its head cut off...could wait 'til Monday when they back at the store. Hell no, too long. Somethin' gotta shake right now...better peep Bubba. Maybe one of 'em over there..."

He walked into the shop and Bubba was hard at work cutting the hair of a restless seven-year-old. The boy's mother sat patiently thumbing through a year-old magazine while Bubba labored to complete a task in one hour that ordinarily took twenty minutes.

Three old men were seated near the window, passing the time of day hunched over a battered chessboard.

Bubba looked at Al brightly and snapped the air vigorously with the narrow scissors.

"What's happenin'...?"

"Nuthin' to it. Seen Sam or Dan...?"

Bubba's expression changed. "Ain't seen neither one..." Al shrugged, "Well, if you do, tell 'em I'm lookin' for 'em. Either one of 'em. Tell 'em it's important. I'll be hangin' in the Peacock a while..."

He left, not at all sure that Bubba would deliver the message. Bubba's attitude had changed radically, along with the hairstyles. Those raggedy Afros, as Bubba called them, had made a big dent in his business. For a while, he had had three empty chairs where once there had been a waiting line that extended out the door.

"Damn raggedy bunch a picky heads," he would fume on the really slow days when he stood idly in his doorway watching the passing parade.

The brothers' heads were styled with a vengeance, but the ones which caused him the most heartburn were the full, furious fros—blown out, sprayed, teased, and greased, so that they stretched shoulder to shoulder and required two umbrellas to keep off the rain.

At those times, Bubba would yearn for the forties, the old days when he had cut hair in Chicago.

Those had been fairly good times until a particular customer had come in one day demanding a "conkadour." None of the other barbers would touch him because he was a known hit man, notorious for his accuracy.

But Bubba thought of the potential tip and dusted off his chair. "Right this way, sir, for the finest, deepest, waviest waves this side of the Atlantic Ocean. Last cat looked in my mirror damn near got seasick, yes sir, right this way."

In those days, they were using the hard stuff. Depending on how one mixed it, it could straighten out a hunchback or put a crimp in a rock. And Bubba never read labels.

After an elaborate preliminary involving several snaps and flourishes of the towel, Bubba laid it on heavy and began to pull it through, using a steel comb. Two minutes of this and the hit man's hair was in the comb and the comb had curled. There was hair in the towel and the rest was on the floor.

Bubba turned the mirror to the wall and stepped back to survey the damage. A minute passed before he managed to murmur something irrelevant about the weather being hotter than a Mississippi mudbath. Then he excused himself and strolled casually to the bathroom.

In the stall, his fright translated into the strength of King Kong as he bent the rusty bar over the window. He started running and, some say, arrived in New York two days ahead of the Broadway Limited.

Still, those were some good years, he thought now, as the little boy squirmed in the chair. Bubba was tempted to cut a large Z-shaped design in the top of the boy's head, but quickly squashed the idea. There was no point in losing another customer.

Thank God, he thought, for them Muslim guys. Or maybe I should thank Allah. They like their heads neat, the way a man oughtta look. Yep, them fellows are all right with their bow ties and nice suits...

...I don't go along with some a their yakity yak but least they got a program to yak about...know where they goin'...some a these other dudes drop in to shoot the breeze don't know they ass from they elbow...still talkin' that old-time if-a-woulda-coulda bullshit... if I hadda good woman...If I woulda had some extra change on me a few years ago...don't mean nuthin'....Now, these Muslim guys is different. Hear they kin have more'n one wife and all the women work. Yup, they ace with me.

He glanced in the mirror as the tiny bell near the entrance jingled almost imperceptibly above the drone of conversation. He watched Jonrobert close the door and move toward the other, vacant, chair.

"What's happenin'...just had you in mind..." Bubba smiled.

"Yeah? Nuthin' to it..."

"Grab a seat. Be right with you."

Bubba was always glad to see Jonrobert. He dressed well, drove well, and tipped even better.

...even brought that skinny college girl in for a haircut...he sighed as he unfastened the cloth....I didn't wanna do it, but the price was right and it was her head. He wanted me to give her a mini-fro. Now what in the world was a mini-fro. I damn near scalped her before I got the hang of it. And she smilin' and gigglin' like teeth goin' outta style. Love is a bitch. But she did look good when I finished. Short hair and all...looked damn good...

He took another deep breath. Events were moving far too fast for him, and he felt age creeping up his spine. What with college girls going with players, Negro men having as many wives as they wanted, and that Elijah Muhammed calling for a separate state. What next?

He glanced at Jonrobert as he leaned back in the chair and noticed the fine lines of fatigue that played at the corners of his mouth. He decided to dispense with the usual snap and flourish of the towel and instead reached into the steamer for a warm cloth. He carefully folded it over Jonrobert's face and said, "Be right with you...relax a while..."

Jonrobert closed his eyes and tried to concentrate but the small talk cut in: "Listen," one of the older men said, pointing to Jonrobert, "I bet you young dudes think you facin' bad times now, with all these march-ins, sit-ins, pray-ins, and lay-ins, but man, you ain't seen nuthin'. Lemme tell y'all 'bout the time me and my boys kicked Jim Crow's ass...A. Philip Randolph was behind us then, and man—"

Jonrobert nodded from behind the towel. He preferred to remain on the periphery of conversation but knew that he had to at least appear interested. His shop was going to be right down the block. Some of these men would be his customers.

"Randolph. I don't know that much about him, but I heard he was a heavy cat..." He made a mental note to have Celia fill him in. His eyes remained closed after Bubba removed the towel, and now he listened to the tiny, metallic clicking of the scissors near his ear. The talk flowed around him.

"...black man's solution lies within the family structure..."

"But a cat gotta hook up with the right woman. Somebody in his corner, he—"

"Awh, these women lookin' for one thing in a man—a big paycheck and a big—"

"Well, they can't have both now, it's either one or the other—" Jonrobert listened quietly and wanted to smile. There were, he knew, as many opinions about women as there were women. Despite his best efforts, he tuned them out and concentrated on his own feelings. How easily he had come to depend on Celia to fill in the gaps in his experience. It had happened so smoothly, as if she had been a part of him forever, and he could not remember not knowing her. She had eased in, somehow, quiet and careful and full of wonder, as if she were stepping ashore on some new and strange land.

He sighed. He wished it had been like that but he knew better. He wished that fate—or whatever it was that made things happen—functioned less erratically, that the good things could have happened in one long, unbroken progression.

But there had been the detour with Pierre. And the women… playgirls, they liked to call themselves…and everybody else was daddy…

He brought his shoulders up in a shrug. …fast jive times. Scene was tough as a Turk's toenails…wring you out in a minute. Ain't even twenty-five yet and it was killin' me. And that damn dumb Pierre, spending as fast as he rake it in…how long he think that's gonna last…one a these days, one a them broads…

He was tightening up again and made an effort to relax. He concentrated on Celia and a minute later felt the smile near the edge of his mouth. He opened his eyes halfway to see if Bubba had noticed, but Bubba was working intently with the scissors, listening to the other voices.

He closed his eyes again.

…like a quiet kind of music…ain't that funny…

He thought of Billy Eckstine and wanted to whistle a few bars of "Cottage for Sale"…

…Celia couldn't dig it…comparin' her to the music…thought I was jivin' her…

He remembered how he wound up having to go through his entire record collection before she understood that her laughter was the waterfall notes of Erroll Garner and that her tears went through him like some deep Don Byas riff.

…especially after love…she held me and cried after love…

Then his mind clicked over to the sounds he had grown up with. In North Carolina, the folks worked hard, and what little sweat was left over spilled out in the juke joints on the weekends, staining the checkered tablecloths on Saturday night and dampening the tattered Bibles on Sunday morning. He went to both but could not stay. Something about the fearsome sound and the people's response to it caused him to want to back away, to move away just enough to put space between himself and the source of the heavy, bloody, gutbucket sounds.

Saturday nights were one thing: He always left after an hour. Those times were all right. He could widen the space and diminish the volume simply by walking out.

Sunday mornings were something else. His mother controlled that.

"Nobody sleep under my roof on Monday who don't go to church on Sunday," she said in her quiet voice. Quiet but firm.

His father was dead, killed in a mill accident before he had had a chance to become a memory. So he had been alone with his mother with no one else to absorb her attention and her confusing lamentations.

"Gonna make me proud someday, I just know it!"

He had looked at her, and listened to the agitation lurking just below the skin of her tongue. What did she mean? Did she have a blueprint? A detailed plan for his life.

And her agitation seemed to grow as he grew. "...gonna make up for everything that happened..."

"Everything like what...?" he finally asked when he had gotten old enough to do more than just nod his head politely. "Make up for what...?"

"Don't you know!" she whispered, staring at him so intently that he had wanted to close his eyes to shut out the fear and madness lurking in hers.

In church, the time she controlled, some of the agitation spent itself in the powerful recitation of someone else's sorrows.

By midweek, it would begin to build, and on Sunday, her time, he would have to listen all over again.

He thought at first that he could balance it out. Saturday night against Sunday morning. Until he realized that the jukebox sounds and the wailing sounds he shrank from were inextricably bound by the same secret pain, the same longing for an answer that kept slipping just beyond the edge of memory. It reminded him of a giant puzzle whose pieces were piled high in a jumble. If he grabbed the right one, everything else would be easy. He needed to find it. Somehow. To push the pain away.

So he had used the expectation of a job as an excuse, kissed her goodbye, and headed for the promised land, looking for the missing piece through the tinted windows of a Greyhound.

Her agitation followed him in her letters; though without the sound, the soft curve of sadness to wrap around the words, he thought he was less affected. But he had absorbed the melody from her song of sorrow and made it his own, and mornings, while shaving and showering, he found himself wondering.

...make up...for what...what is it...?

At times, when something in Celia's laughter cut through the sound, he was able to breathe easier. Some of her notes managed to slip through, and he found himself whispering to the mirror in the morning... "ain't nuthin' to make up for but lost time. This the Big A. Everything here for the askin'. Don't settle for nuthin' less than what you want..."

And he had wanted more than the thin smile he had seen on the salesmen's faces when he and Pierre had outfitted themselves in the gaudy suits and preened before baroque-style mirrors in decaying stores.

125th Street. Blumstein's. Frank's. The Palm Cafe. Herbert's Home of Blue White Diamonds. Harlem had been the absolute limit of Pierre's orbit, and Jonrobert watched him pay twice the price for the privilege of riding high.

...but I knew it hadda be more to it...those nights workin' the pump...used to watch those long shorts pull up...fill 'em up... check the oil...checked the dudes behind the wheel too...cool. Looked right through you...the way real money supposed to do...

Now Pierre...he'd be lookin' everywhere to see who was diggin' him. Pull up to a red light, lay on the horn, and check out the winos to see if they eyein' him...

...but those others...cool...real money...

He wondered how the cool ones had gotten to be that way. Of course money helped, but it went beyond that. It was something else. At odd moments he would watch Celia when she wasn't looking and he saw it in her. An air, an attitude so untouchable at times that it annoyed him and made him more than a little envious. But then she would laugh, and he would hear the music...

He opened his eyes and straightened up in the chair. Bubba had unfastened the towel and was brushing his neck and shoulders delicately with the soft whisk broom, a ritual he performed only on the best customers.

Jonrobert handed him five dollars, ignoring his profuse thanks.

He lingered in the doorway outside the shop for a few minutes and wondered how he was going to contact Celia. The battle lines had been drawn, no doubt about it, but he'd just have to find a way around them.

...her mama...acts crazier than mine...and that mean lookin' dude...King Kong killer from jump street...eyein' me like he seen a ghost...

25

September 1961

Shortly after the four-to-midnight shift came on, and the uniformed policemen and unmarked cars fanned out in widening circles from the precinct, Willie peered through his binoculars, as he had been doing for weeks, at the comings and goings in the Peacock.

His third-floor window was situated diagonally across the avenue, and he watched as a battered gray sedan pulled to the curb.

None of the occupants emerged.

"Damn dumb narcs. Even a blind man could pin 'em." He relaxed his vigil and went to get a beer. Nothing was going to happen as long as the car remained there. No pushers, no boosters, no runners, no buyers, no sellers, no players, no nothing. The bar was in for a slow night.

Willie returned to the window.

"Dammit, the car's gone!"

Willie snatched up the glasses and focused with trembling fingers. His hand froze. In the shadow of the Peacock, there was his man.

Detective Purcell stood in the door of the bar, jacket open, no tie, and buttons on the paisley-print shirt straining against the fat belly. His porcine features had a look of indecision. Willie wondered if the man had already gone into the bar and inquired about Tessie. If he had, Willie would have to move fast. If he hadn't, he'd still have to move fast.

The detective lit a cigarette. Willie watched as the match flared and illuminated the beefy nose and thin, loose lips. Then the man turned and entered the bar.

Willie lowered his glasses, went to the closet, and took down the brown paper bag. He went to another closet and took out a silencer.

In the living room, Tessie was dozing in front of the television. She was still propped up on several pillows. Willie looked at her and wondered if he should turn the set off.

He touched her face lightly and whispered, "Back in five, sweetheart. Gotta take care of a little bee-eye..."

She opened her eyes, alarmed. "Where you goin...?"

"Ask me no questions, I tell you no lies.... I said I'd be back in five, but this won't take but a hot minute..."

He kissed her and padded quietly out the door.

The detective's body was discovered one week later by a wino wandering through an abandoned building.

At first glance, the corpse resembled a pile of plaster-coated rubble, but then the wino saw the shoes that had burst off feet purple and swollen beyond the size of melons. He saw that the lower half of the face and all of the fingers had been devoured by rats and that the area where the chest should have been appeared to heave and throb under the natural activity of a million maggots.

The decomposition was so advanced that the wino was not horrified by his discovery (it resembled nothing *he* knew), but he was furious at the indescribable stench that had knocked down his high. He retreated in a sulk and, for spite, said nothing to anyone for an additional week.

Then, under the fresh weight of a half gallon of Gypsy Rose, the wino started to blab to the plainclothesmen who had saturated the area for the last two weeks.

"...man, you ain't safe no place. Guess what I seen a few days ago..."

The forensic examination determined that the detective had been shot twice at close range with a .38-caliber revolver while he was in a standing position and that four additional bullets had hit him after he had gone down.

The poor condition of the tissue made it difficult to pinpoint the exact time of death. More difficult to explain were the four-ounce foil of cocaine under the belt buckle and the bloodstained three thousand dollars in his back pocket.

So the investigation was quiet. Purcell was last seen two weeks ago Friday in front of the Peacock. He was on his own time, no partner, no backup. It was assumed that he had been killed within the following twenty-four hours.

The detective had had a reputation for beating up whores and shaking down pimps which could have, by a long stretch, accounted for the money, but the four ounces was too much for personal use or ordinary street sale.

Again the word went out and the network came up empty. In the Peacock, when a strange question was asked, no heads turned but tongues curled, jaws went tight, vision blurred, and ears waxed over.

"Serve the sommabitch right," the very night air seemed to say, and the street closed in on itself.

Through it all, Willie frequented the Peacock; he dropped in every night after work and didn't miss a beat. He saw the faces, fresh and foreign and always in pairs, smiling tightly in the heavy silence.

...damn, he thought, three thousand, cold cash, motherfuckin' dollars and four oh-zees...that's what the bastard was talkin' when he tried to cop that plea...shoulda stripped 'im...fuck it...what's done is done...

Willie knew he didn't have to leave, but a short vacation seemed in order anyway.

PART THREE

26

As soon as Willie stepped off the plane, the heat closed in through the palms and he felt the fatigue that had lain in his chest like a fist. For a few minutes he stood trying to absorb the surroundings but soon gave up and moved with the crowd into the terminal. Inside was cool and pleasant, but he had no wish to linger. He took off his jacket and walked across the damp, marbled floor to the line of waiting taxis.

As he climbed into the car, the driver narrowly eyed the American-made suit, tie, and expensive shoes and wondered aloud why there was no luggage.

Willie gave him a hard stare along with the address of his mother's house; then he settled into himself as the car took off with a noisy display of gear shifting designed to impress the foreigner and produce a bigger tip.

Fifteen minutes into the ride, Willie opened his eyes as the tiny taxi jerked sharply to one side. A creaky, overburdened bus had met them on a narrow, winding curve.

Both drivers let out a stream of invectives, mostly for effect: "Wha' wrong wid you, boy, you mama birth a blind monkey or what?" shouted the bus driver.

The passengers cheered and jockeyed for a better view. The taxi driver flicked his thumb nail under his front tooth and yelled back. "Man, go kiss you own ass! Is a good thing me in a hurry, else me tell you to kiss mine!"

He did not wait for a reply, but engaged the clutch and crept forward so close to the bus that Willie, with one eye closed, swore that he felt the paint peeling. On the other side of the taxi was the sheer drop of the cliff.

He made a note to double the tip if he arrived in one piece.

The car passed the bus and continued its struggle up the narrow road. Willie glanced out of the window to his right and saw only the tops of the trees. The cliff seemed damn near next to heaven. It hadn't seemed that high when he had left. He stared straight ahead and tried to think of something else.

The road leveled gradually as the car passed through what appeared to be a tunnel carved out of giant ferns. Overhead, the thick, blue-green fronds overlapped and intertwined, admitting only the thinnest threads of sunlight. Through the tangled mass, the air took on a cool, sea-moist quality.

Willie stared at the lacy pattern on the road and windshield. The driver glanced at him in the mirror and wondered why the stranger was so tense, as if all the pressure of the world had settled in the core of him and was now ready to spill out.

He nodded his head. "You comin' a relax now..."

It could have been a question or a statement, but Willie, lost in himself, did not reply.

The house appeared much smaller than he remembered. The yard still needed sweeping; the chickens squawked loudly and scattered at his approach, heading for the kitchen garden. The mango, lemon, and eucalyptus trees still bloomed in profusion, spreading a panoply of color and fragrance over the landscape.

Inside, the rooms seemed cramped. The doll-like furniture was still precisely arranged on the clean-swept, uncarpeted wood floors.

He was shocked by the change in his mother and could not hide it. In ten years, her hair had turned completely white, but in all her letters to him, she had not mentioned it. She looked in his face, saw the confusion, and said simply, "You been away long, too long, son," and held him as he struggled with his tears.

* * *

He had planned to stay only long enough for the excitement over the killing to subside. But one week slipped into another and another. Finally, he wrote a long letter full of love to Tessie, describing how sick his mother was; he felt ashamed because the old lady was healthier than he was.

For several weeks, he sat on the porch, hours at a time, distilling the flavors of mango and lime and sugar cane and remembering how large the leaves of a grape tree could grow.

At night, he was unnerved by a nameless silence, but the loud racket of the crickets soon crept in and he eventually forgot that there was no television and was finally able to fall asleep.

One morning, just before daybreak, he strolled up and down the beach, feeling the sand, cold, wet, and clumpy, slip between his toes. He watched the night fishermen as they came in, dragging the long, narrow boats through the rough, noisy surf. The last man spread his nets to dry and headed home, leaving Willie alone once more.

A large gull wheeled out of the empty sky, skimmed the mirrored surface of the water, and rose again on wings that barely seemed to move. Willie shaded his eyes and squinted at the bird until it turned into a speck and then disappeared.

"Now that's cool. Really cool. What a life."

He thought of his own, and his mood changed. "This sure ain't nothin'…said it when I left and I wind up sayin' the same thing when I come back. Ten long years later…"

A pink crab scuttled sideways away from Willie, urgently heading for some secret destination. Willie's first impulse was to smash it with a rock, change its plans, interrupt its destiny—the way his own had been interrupted.

"Ah, let it be. It ain't his fault. Ain't anybody's…"

He thought of the boys with whom he studied. All had left as soon as possible, fueled by ambition. England, America, Canada. If they returned, it was expected that they would have half the world in their pocket. He remembered the letter his mother had written to him when Leo, the quiet one in the group, returned from England a doctor. The letter was practically a novel. She had also written to him when Marcus returned, but the letter had been vague and brief. Willie heard the story from someone else.

...Marcus did the right thing. I woulda stayed and fought for my share too. Day after the funeral wasn't soon enough. Especially since the battle was on long before his mama died...Well, Willie boy, there's them that has and them that has to get. I wasn't doin' too bad 'til I had to blow that fuckin' cop away. Wasn't no big thing though, I'd do it again if I had to...

Question is, what next...where do I go...to start over...

He opened Tessie's letter and read for the third time how she missed not being able to sleep next to him, especially since the weather had turned so cold now and the extra blanket was no help, and what the hell, if he wasn't coming home to burn his log in her fire, then he damn sure better be looking for her to come down there.

He was elated. She was speaking of love again. Making love. Talking love.

The rest of the news was the same. Celia was fine. Tacky Jackie had taken on yet another man, swearing that this time was it. LeRoy the Runner was still running...the Peacock had gotten back in stride and was jumping...

Willie slipped the letter into his pocket and turned onto the road leading away from the beach. One hour of slow walking brought him to the edge of town. He walked even slower, trying to decide what to do, and did not see the tall man approach.

"T'rass, mahn! My eye see wha' eye see? If e ain' Willie-too run-run! Bad foot an' all. Mahn, how you keepin'?"

The big man clapped him on the shoulder, nearly bowling him over. It was a few seconds before Willie recognized his old friend.

"Marcus! Well, damn if it ain't my man. My main man! Been hopin' to run into you! What the hell you up to? Must be somethin' slick, you still down here!"

Marcus laughed. "Slick as goose grease and gettin' slipprier. Wha' tis is wah tis. Stateside? Me ain' never goin' back, mahn. Is gold right here bein' discovered..."

Willie shook his head in wonder. As tall as he was, Marcus seemed to tower over him. When he laughed, ropelike cords stood out in his neck and glistened dark brown in the sun. Willie looked at the wide shoulders and heavy arms and was glad to be on the right side of Marcus's friendship.

"So, Willie-boy, this call for fete. Come on, let we wet ya whistle and we talk more..."

Marcus led the way into a rum shop, and they stood at the end of a long bar. It was not quite noon, but the dark interior was already half-filled with men, some arguing the political situation so passionately that Willie expected a fight to break out at any moment.

Others concentrated on a game of dominoes. All were drinking and listening to the sound of calypso. The only woman in the bar was the owner, a short, round woman called May-Mae.

"The best you got," shouted Marcus, "for two lost home boys..."

"Soon come," she called above the noise of the politics and the din of the ancient piccolo.

Willie meanwhile watched the overhead fan with its huge wood blades barely moving through the thick air. His shirt clung to him and water streamed from his arms. He was glad when three men vacated one of the tables outside. He and Marcus edged through the crowd toward it.

"Marcus, you lookin' like a cool million. What you up to?"

Marcus offered another round. "Willie, ya ever know when I was up to anything but no good. Yes, mahn, no good plenty good. But, tell me—no, I tell you—ya here quick, quick. Nobody know ya comin—so who ya kill?"

Willie steadied his hand as Marcus laughed. Then: "Mahn, don't look so. But truth be, you ain' home for nuthin'. Who weddin' you come? Who funeral? Ah, you come so silent in the darkness, ah nearly miss ya if ya didn't smile."

Sweat covered Willie's forehead. He swallowed the best May-Mae had to offer and half a second later felt as if someone had stocked a blast furnace in the middle of his chest.

...I ain't hardly smilin' now, dammit...and I ain't hardly gonna let this gold-tooth sucker peep my hole card...

He took a deep breath and poured another drink, all the while telling himself to take it slow and steady and don't break loose.

"Things got tight in the Big A, Marcus. I was just gettin' my thing together when up pops two broads, both with a little somethin' in the oven. Now I coulda laid in the cut with one, you know, maybe slid and jived, but two? Too heavy. Couldn't take the weight, so I took a walk. Grabbed the first thing smokin'."

A faint breeze stirred from the ocean. Willie felt more at ease as his shirt began to dry and cling to him less. He looked Marcus in the eye.

"It really was rough skippin' out like that 'cause one of 'em I really dug, you know?"

Marcus did not answer but poured another drink for both of them. A minute later he looked at the sky and pursed his lips.

"Rain comin' heavy, heavy..."

Willie looked at the bright-blue sky but knew better than to question the forecast. He had heard his mother make the same pronouncements too many times. He only asked, "How soon?"

"Hour. Hour and a half." replied Marcus as he rose from the seat. "Come, let we lift ya, no?"

Marcus straddled a bright-yellow Honda, and Willie climbed on behind him. The crowd of men and boys made way as Marcus revved the motor and glided away from the shop.

They hit the open road and Marcus shifted into high gear. Willie caught fleeting glimpses of trees, houses, bicycle riders, herds of goats, and scattered bands of schoolchildren, fast receding into the background.

"Hey, Marcus, my man, are we in a big hurry? You said that rain ain't due for another hour..."

Willie's voice trailed in the wind, lost in the roar of the motor. He tapped Marcus on the shoulder, hoping to slow him down. Marcus's hand edged back slowly, holding what appeared to be a huge, lighted cigar. A whiff of the pungent aroma, and Willie scooped the offering from Marcus's hand.

"This is the biggest damn joint I ever seen," said Willie. "How the hell do I smoke it?"

He contemplated the logistics for less than a second and jammed the joint in his mouth the way a child would suck on a banana. He inhaled deeply and heard Marcus's voice from far away. "Ganja heavy, heavy shit, mahn. Dat bomber blow your head off, sure. Mind yourself!"

"Mind myself? Shee-it, baby, dig it, mind yourself 'cause things is cool with me. Matta fact, why you slowin' down? We got to keep on gittin' up...got to stay...in the ...wind..."

Marcus had, in fact, speeded up, and Willie, ingesting huge puffs, sailed along as if in a dream. The roar of the motor seemed like the purr of a kitten. A pink cloud wafted him along above the jarring vibrations as the motorbike cut along the rutted path.

Willie gazed with intense interest over Marcus's shoulder, staring in wonder as the trees appeared to bend and part just as they approached. "Now...that's what I would call co-op-o-ration," he emphasized loudly, as if addressing a mass rally. "But the only thing I don't like is you keep changin' colors on me..." he went on, still addressing the trees.

He was about to leap from the speeding cycle to reprimand the blue ones when Marcus suddenly turned off the road onto a narrow path overgrown with thick foliage. It did not occur to Marcus to slow down; he ducked his head low from habit, but several branches caught Willie, whipping him in the face. The cycle roared to a halt in front of Marcus's house.

Two servants who came out to greet Marcus watched in amazement as Willie dismounted, advanced furiously on the nearest tree, and delivered a kick to its trunk. Marcus, remembering Willie's bad feet, rushed to restrain him.

"Mahn, you was flyin' before, but you come down now, yes? I tell you dat bomber bad..."

Willie stared at him blankly and broke from his grasp. He spied a broken tree limb on the ground and, with a screech, rushed to seize it. The servants melted back into the house. Marcus did not move. He watched silently as Willie crouched low and darted behind the tree.

Marcus saw the shadow of the tree. Willie, his eyes blazing, saw only the shadow of a crumbling stairwell and heard his soft, catlike footfalls as he raced through the burned-out, abandoned building in an effort to head off the detective.

Willie leaped out from behind the tree and jabbed the air with the limb.

Facing the blackened doorway, the detective, hypnotized, drew nearer. The gun in Willie's hand recoiled, and he nearly lost his footing on the carpet of broken glass and plaster. He twisted and turned, flailing the tree. "You...bastard...messed up my woman, she ain't a woman no more! Fucked over her so I can't even touch her! No more, you lousy bastard, no more. I got somethin' with your name on it, and the last one gonna blow your balls off!!"

The last shot made a sharp, pinging sound in the hallway.

Willie waited in the silence, listening as snatches of music from the Peacock drifted across the street and echoed softly off the blackened walls.

He squeezed the trigger three more times and removed the silencer. Without looking at it, he stepped over the body, retraced his steps, and slowly made his way out of the building. It had begun to rain, but he walked casually until he approached the Peacock from the opposite direction.

Marcus watched Willie fall to his knees, a spray of saliva on his chin. He began to tremble. "No more!" he shouted, "No more, you bastard..."

He was seized with a violent spasm that threw him to the ground. He grasped a clump of leaves, pulling them up by their roots. Then he rolled over and lay still.

Marcus felt the first heavy drops of rain as he knelt beside his friend and cradled his head in his lap.

"Well, Willie-boy, you home for good. Just...like...me..."

Willie came to himself two days later. When he awoke, he was alone in Marcus's house. Except for the servants murmuring out in the garden, everything was quiet. He lay still for a time, gazing around the unfamiliar room. His clothing, washed and pressed, was hung in the half-open closet. His underwear lay on a chair next to a marble washstand. His wandering gaze came to rest on a silver jug on the nightstand. He watched the frosty sweat run down the side of the jug, and suddenly he was overwhelmed with an aching thirst.

He reached for the jug, but fell back on the bed, exhausted from the effort.

"What the hell is happening to me?" he wondered aloud, frightened. The murmuring stopped and a young girl peered through the window. She was smiling, embarrassed to be in charge. "Good day, Mister Willie, how you keepin?"

Before he could answer, the girl disappeared from the window and came into the house. She entered the room with a covered tray and a stream of conversation. Willie interrupted her.

"Where is Marcus?"

The girl fell silent and stared at the floor. Willie knew better than to ask again. Instead, he wondered aloud if he shouldn't be getting on home, his mother was probably worried...

The girl brightened at this and began to chatter again, happy to be able to impart some important, harmless information.

"Oh no, sir, your mama, she not worryin'...Mister Marcus, he say, visit your mama. She not worryin', no sir!"

She smiled again and Willie wondered about her teeth—so white they didn't look real. Suddenly, the girl threw back her head and stared at the ceiling, pressing a finger to her lips.

"Aaaah, Mister Marcus, he now come..."

Willie followed her gaze and stared hard at the ceiling, but he could see or hear nothing.

One minute later, the very faint sound of a car's motor drew his attention. It grew louder, and the girl left the room as the car pulled into the drive. Willie heard the door slam, and a second later, Marcus strode into the room.

"Ay, Ay! Me see you now! Eye open wide, wide. Is good."

Willie shook his head as he threw back the covers and began to put on his underwear. "My eyes are open now, but damn, man, what the hell happened?"

Marcus sprawled in the chair by the bed. "Aah, you treat splif too, too light, mahn. Is a serious business, I tell you."

"No stuff! Man, I had some in my time, but nuthin' ever got to my knot like that..."

Marcus laughed. "You just get a taste firsthand, mahn, fresh. By time this stuff reach the States, it done mix down wid all kinda bush 'n shit. New York eatin' the appetizer. Down here you get main dish."

He rose from the chair. "Well, how you feelin'...kin walk now?"

"I'm all right, man." Willie was embarrassed by Marcus's attention as he rose from the bed and struggled into his clothing. Marcus strolled to the door and called out. "Phenie, please bring some drinks out to the patio..."

Marcus left the room and Willie followed. His legs were still shaky, but he managed to keep up without falling. They walked through the house, a low, sprawling, one-story, four-bedroom affair. In the sunken living room, Marcus slid glass doors open, and they stepped onto the tiled patio.

Willie blinked at the blue water in the oval pool. "Marcus, I got no words, man, no words at all. You truly got it together. Why, man, just two years ago you was nickel 'n dimein' it in the Big A, gettin' on everybody's nerves about how you were gonna make it if you only got a break..."

Marcus tasted his drink and put it down. He did not smile.

"Break come, Willie, but not the way I look for it. Not the way I want. Remember the time my mama so sick here I hadda bum fare from you to get down to her? Was no help, Willie. Old lady gone within the week. Before I come, was only neighbor to nurse her, clean her, and thing...

"But I tell you, when she pass, a billion relative does show up. Well, I look at this army come to lower one body into the groun' and I say to meself, Marcus boy, somethin' fishy and it ain' fish, no mahn...

"'Cause body ain' cold yet when come to find the old lady had so much piece a paper sayin' she own so much piece a land an' thing. Well. Is a wonder, Willie, you ain' hear the shout in New York! I mean, brother, sister, uncle, cousin, all in a big melee for their handful a dirt. And me, the son, they ain' even see, they so wild!

"Well, I tell you, I so disgusted, I ready to run back to the Big A and leave the dogs fight over the bone, but you know what stop me? Boy, me ain' had coin one! Run where? On what? I sure can't walk water. With no money, is to stand and fight, is all.

"So. The smoke clear. Here me and two dozen cousin standin' fron' the magistrate. Rumor flyin' high and wide. Me hear a cousin burn black candle on me mother grave. Some other one caution me watch and don' eat soup from none a them. Some say magistrate is a cousin of a cousin but is no cousin to me.

"Willie boy, I tell you I sweat tears while that man shuffle and ruffle them papers that day.

"But cousin of a cousin or not, he fair! He just back from big education in England and see I just back from the Big A and he *know* I an honest man. Just like he."

Willie stared at Marcus; then he shook his head and smiled. "Man, you sure got a way of making your stuff smell sweet."

Marcus shrugged. "Mahn, is too sweet. Me thinkin' a bottlin' it." Then he became serious again. "Was a happy day when the magistrate declare for me, Willie, and I tell you, I been happy up to now. Every inch a that land I got under cultivation..."

"Cultivation? What—"

Marcus looked at him and then said, "What just blow your head off?"

"How much land is it?"

"Near three hundred acres, give or take, scattered here and there..."

"Jesus," Willie breathed, remembering what just one joint had done to him. "Jesus!"

Marcus put his drink down. "Come. Let we take a swim, then we go for a ride..."

He saw Willie hesitate at the mention of a ride, so he said, "Look, mahn, no speedin', no smokin', no nuthin' but talkin'. Is a serious business comin' here soon. Very serious. And I wan' talk to you...with your head on straight."

27

October 1961

The Peacock was jammed. Weeks had passed since the killing, and it was no longer news to the bar crowd. Tessie still had not returned, and Tate replaced the frump with two male bartenders, one a handsome baritone and the other, just handsome.

Female attendance doubled, and Tate's predilection for the intense, short-term affairs on which he thrived, in addition to his two families, increased in geometric proportion.

To accommodate the surge, he had the oversized, semicircular booths torn out and replaced with small, square tables and chairs which held more people in less space.

Al, Sam, and Dan sat at a table squeezed in near the rear door. They drank quietly, watching both entrances as the crowd and the music moved around them.

Suddenly, Al nudged Dan imperceptibly and whispered, "He's here."

They watched Jonrobert make his way through the crowd directly to the table.

"You lookin' for me?" he asked, glancing from one to the other.

"Have a seat," said Sam, drawing up a fourth chair.

Jonrobert sat down. In the small space, it was difficult to place hands or elbows on the table and not touch.

"What you drinkin?" asked Dan.

"I'll pass for now," Jonrobert replied. "Got the word that you all wanted to see me..." He gazed at the three men around him.

"We wanna talk to you," Sam said.

"What about...?"

"Celia," said Dan.

"Celia??" Jonrobert repeated, surprised. He could not see their faces clearly in the dim light, so he waited, silently. Behind him, a thread of sound rose from the baritone at the bar, catching the tune from the piccolo, then overwhelming it. "...don't do this to me, baby, you all I got...don't do—" The melody wafted through the crowd, winding its way around the tight bodies jammed together impersonally in the dark.

Jonrobert felt an acute sense of apprehension dissolve into an undercurrent of anger and he had difficulty concentrating on what was being said.

"...we gonna put it to you straight," Sam said, with no preliminaries. "We don't want our niece hooked up with no hustler..."

"Hustler! I'm outta that, man. Been outta it. I'm—"

"Maybe. But you still bad news..."

Jonrobert started to rise from the table, but Dan held out his hand. "There's more."

"Well, I don't wanna hear it. You got the wrong man!"

"—and we tellin' you that you got the wrong girl!"

Sam interrupted, "Whoa...hold it...let's begin at the beginnin' so he'll know what this is all about..."

"What's what all about? What's goin' on?" Jonrobert looked from one to the other.

After a pause, Al said, "Okay, it's like this. We know you from North Carolina, from Milfield. And we know your mother's name is Sara—"

"So what? You the FBI or you takin' the census?"

"Neither one, so let me finish. You had a grandmother up here years ago..."

"So? Everybody had a grandmother—"

"But yours got killed in a fire. Remember?"

Jonrobert closed his eyes an instant. "Yeah, I—"

"Do you remember the man who tried to save her?"

"Yeah," he said slowly, "last I remembered, he was on that fire escape. I couldn't see nuthin' else 'cause of the crowd. I don't remember much else..."

There was a silence in which it seemed that each man was struggling to recapture or let go of the same memory. Finally, Al said, very quietly, "The man who died tryin' to save your grandmother was Celia's father..."

Jonrobert leaned over the small table, straining against the deep rhythm of the baritone. "What did you say?"

"I said—"

"Wait a minute...I...this ain't for real...it can't be..."

He leaned back again, listening, waiting for confirmation of his disbelief; he expected all three of them to laugh, the light hand on the shoulder would be felt, then the whisper that it was all a joke, anybody can take a joke, man, now let's have us a taste to the joke, come on, I'm buyin'...

Nothing came. He was all alone with the sound of the baritone crying: "Don't put me on the spot, you all I got—"

His own impulse was to laugh, to show them that whatever their game was, he wasn't going for it. But this laughter did not come either, and he was surprised at himself. He strained to pay attention as Al's voice filtered through the noise and music.

"—and Celia don't know nuthin' about this...this connection yet. But her mama, her mama went crazy 'cause a what happened, and it took her a long time to pull out of it. She was there when it happened..."

"How do you know?" Jonrobert asked, pulling at the last thin straw of doubt.

"Because all three of us was there..." said Al. "I got your mama's address from a neighbor and I personally put you on the train..."

"I know you thinkin' this is somethin' that happened so long ago, her mama won't remember you," Sam said, "but you still got the same mark on your eye. That didn't change none."

Al and Dan looked uneasily at Sam, hoping he wouldn't spin his tale out too far. They knew Frieda never saw the little boy in that sea of people that night. But still, there might have been someone else, some of the old-timers that hung around Bubba's who had a talent for minding everyone's business but their own. They might have seen him, and like Sam said, moles and marks don't change.

Jonrobert shook his head, trying to understand. "But what did I have to do with his dying?"

"Everything. It was your grandma, and Celia's father was your friend. He never woulda known nobody was even in the house if you hadna told 'im..."

"And let's look at it this way," said Sam. "The woman lost her husband and ain't been right since. If she finds out about you, all hell gonna break loose..."

"How she gonna find out?"

"We gonna see that she don't," said Al quietly.

"So what you tellin' me is I gotta stop seein' Celia. I ain't goin' for it..."

"You gonna have to. When the deal go down, and she find out you caused her pop to kick, what kinda relationship you gonna have left?" asked Dan.

The baritone started in again. The tune was softer and sadder, and Jonrobert wanted to jump up, wade through the crowd, and smash his face, pushing the words back down his throat. He wanted to do that to the three men seated around the table watching him. Make them eat their words and restore his sense of balance.

"Leave Celia?" he repeated. "You dudes must be crazy."

"Well," said Sam, "that should tell you we ain't shuckin'. If we crazy, then you really in trouble..."

"Look, man," Al said, "we laid it out on the line so you could see. It's no win any way you try to deal. Even if you ain't in the life no more, if her mama finds out about this other thing, and go off again, you think Celia can work with that? Everytime she look at you, she gonna remember her pop and think about her mama.

It ain't gonna work, man, no matter what you say. Do yourself a favor all around and quit the scene..."

They left him sitting there. The bar was so crowded that as soon as they rose, three women who had been wedged in near the rear door slid into the seats, looked at Jonrobert, and immediately entered into keen and subtle competition for his attention.

He glanced at them. They were overdressed and animated, excited at having struck gold so early in the evening. He could have, had he been merely angry, played them off against each other, making the pretty one think she was smart and the smart one think she was the really attractive one, and then go off with the third, who was neither, and teach her a quick lesson in the futility of picking up strange men in strange places.

But his feelings had been pulled beyond anger. He felt now only a dull amazement. He rose slowly from his seat and made his way past the baritone, who by now was sounding like a sick soprano crying for his own lost love.

Outside, he leaned against the car for a minute, idly watching the neon tail feathers of the peacock change from yellow to blue to red, then blink out, and come on again in a shower of color. Finally, he turned the key in the lock and slid behind the wheel. The interior held the faintest trace of Celia's perfume. And the leather headrest was still depressed, although it had been hours since she had been in the car. He touched the indentation lightly, not wanting to disturb it.

"...ain't this a bitch?...ain't this a bee-eye bitch??"

His voice sounded loud in the small space, and he glanced around to see if anyone outside had heard.

He stared at the headrest for several minutes, as if expecting a reply, a disembodied murmur reassuring him that it was all a dream.

He knew better.

Elliptical fragments scurried across his awakened memory, and isolated events suddenly became clear and whole to him: the years and years of backing away, running; the fright of noisy places; the dream of doors closing and walls falling; the fear of being trapped, unable to get out; his mother's strange pronouncements. Noise, noise, and more noise. The press and smell of people closing in. And worst of all, the sound of the siren as the ambulance pulled away, and him screaming and running, running, running, until he felt his heart grow large and he thought his chest would burst, and more screaming: "Granma! Granma! the ammalambs got my Granma!!"

The shower of light from the neon bird exploded against his closed lids, and he opened his eyes. His vision seemed blurred and he blinked rapidly to bring things back into focus. Then he sat, immobile, for some minutes, watching the colors bathe the seat beside him and highlight the empty headrest.

"God," he murmured, "how'd this happen? How did this..."

He stopped and held his breath long enough to force down the bitter taste that rose to the back of his throat. He swallowed hard, and kept swallowing until the nausea was under control, but now his chest ached. He wanted to lean forward and rest his head on the wheel, but he knew his vision would blur again and this time he would not be able to control anything.

For another minute, he remained perfectly still; then, finally, he put the car in gear and moved away from the curb.

28

October 1961

The weather turned unusually cool although summer had officially ended only two weeks before. The oppressive heat that rose in shimmering waves from the pavement subsided before a brisk wind, and the stoop watchers were grateful. Now they were able to come out earlier, stay later, and gather twice as much news.

Their hero, Adam Clayton Powell, Jr., had become chairman of the House Committee on Education and Labor. They had cheered and clapped, but beyond that, they did not know what to make of it. Did it mean better schools? More jobs? And what about Kennedy's new Peace Corps? Was that a job, a vacation, or like going away to the Army? They shook their heads vaguely. Meanwhile, the rest of the nation geared up for the latest offensive in the civil war as the Freedom Riders targeted Alabama.

These were large issues, far beyond the stoop watchers' ken. They knew little and spoke less. What mental energy they did possess they expended on something they knew and felt comfortable with—like attempting to unravel the circumstances surrounding Celia's strange behavior.

For a week, the courtyard had been filled with the sound of her anguish. They strained to listen, especially at night, when all the windows were open and the slightest whisper was lifted and carried on the wind. They listened, breath suspended, and when they heard nothing beyond the crying, they immediately set about filling the gaps:

"Maybe she pregnant..."

"Naw. Gotta have a man for that..."

"She got one. Ever see that fancy El-dee drop her off some nights?"

"Ain't seen it lately though..."

"That's it. The nigger done hit and split..."

"Shit!"

"Well, serve her right. Always thinkin' she too good to talk to us. Flyin' in and outta here with her nappy head, and ain't got time to tell us how poor Tessie doin'..."

"Yeah. Poor Tessie. She was real regular, but that Celia..."

"...serve her right, whatever it is..."

Celia, meanwhile, in the sanctuary of her room, read and reread Jonrobert's letter for the hundredth time. It was less than two dozen lines, but she studied each word and each character. She turned the paper upside down, and backwards, searching for the secret message that surely must be there, if she could only find it.

She pressed it against the mirror, held it under the light, folded it, and smoothed it out; when the words began to blur from the salt of her tears, she pushed it under the glass covering on the dressing table in order to preserve it:

Dear Celia

I thought about calling you but if I heard your voice I knew I'd never say what I have to say

first of all remember I love you

remember how I loved you and that will help both of us to get thru
the days to come
I heard some news the other night that was so bad I had to back
away to think about it and figure out what kind of person I am
I can't go into it with you but god knows I wish I could just so you'd
understand
I already caused enough damage to last two lifetimes and I have to
find the best way to deal with it
go back to school and whatever it was you were doing before you
met me but don't forget me because I will never forget you
no matter what happens remember I will always love you

forever
Jonrobert

The letter was undated and postmarked New York. The stationery was plain, white, and unlined and it did not match the envelope. She saw that his handwriting was large, bold, and slanted to the left and it was uninterrupted by periods, commas, capitals, or other devices designed to create time for reflection. His signature sprawled across the entire bottom half of the page in bold, angry strokes.

She studied the paper until her senses dulled. Twenty-four hours later, she was able to repeat the contents with eyes closed, turning each sentence, inverting, juxtaposing, shifting emphasis, until, finally, all the words ran together and she was left with nothing except the knowledge that she would not see him again.

In the days that followed, the numbness gave way to a crushing ache that pushed into her bowels. She spent hours in the bathroom and the rest of the time in bed, piled high with blankets.

She lay under the blankets as the crisp autumn air was temporarily displaced by the false heat of a late Indian summer. She lay there, cold and still as ice, while outside, the short and sudden burst of warmth breathed new life into waning summer affairs, making other fools believe that they had been spared, that their love and theirs alone would last forever.

Frieda faced the three men across the tiny table in Al's kitchen, waiting for an answer.

"What do I do now," she demanded.

"Well, you said you didn't like him," Al reminded her. He shifted in his seat, trying to avoid her drawn face.

"Yeah," added Sam, "...and we were supposed to take care of him..."

"Well, what in the world did you do? Kill him? Celia's been in that room now for nearly a week, and I can't get in there to change the linen let alone change her mind. What did you do??"

"Take it easy," Dan said, "take it easy. We had a talk with him, that's all. A little light converse and the cat come up slack..."

"Yeah, you know, we asked him about...you know...his intentions and all...like marriage and stuff like that...let 'im know we wasn't gonna stand still for no stuff..."

"Well, apparently, he didn't stand still either," Frieda replied. "He sent her a letter and disappeared."

"A letter??" the three asked in one voice.

"What did it say?"

"Did you see it?"

"You sure it's from him?"

They had not anticipated this development. A letter. A double cross. He was supposed to leave and not see her again. No one said anything about writing.

The men looked at each other as Frieda pushed her chair back and began to pace the floor.

Al could barely contain his anger. "Slick motherfucker," he breathed, "I just knew his middle name was trouble..."

Frieda turned around. "What...?"

"Nuthin'...just wonderin' about all this trouble. What we need is a little taste, and we can discuss this like civilized people..."

He rose from his chair, but Dan was already at the refrigerator wrestling with the stubborn ice tray. Sam was busy at the cupboard trying to decide which four glasses they should use. There was nothing for Al to do but turn to Frieda.

She had stopped pacing and stood near the window, her back to them. Al studied her, as he always did. There was nothing to see out the window except the blank wall of the adjacent building. If a whole vista were spread before her, he knew she would still see nothing except Celia curled in the corner of her bed.

He studied the line of her back, the small waist, and the wide, still solid, hips. He knew from the high slant of her shoulders that an old tension held them in place and he felt the pain move across the room to envelop him.

Why, he wondered, had this boy come back. Why had Noel ever befriended him in the first place? He knew there were no answers, but it was easier to dwell on this than face his own dilemma.

Three weeks earlier, when Celia knocked on his door and brought him down to meet Jonrobert, Al's rage was so intense and immediate that he actually frightened himself. He couldn't determine if he had been angry because he'd been afraid or afraid because he'd been so angry.

After the encounter, he planned the next move with Sam and Dan; then he went home.

Frieda knocked on his door as soon as he had closed it. It was a crisis and he had expected her, but he hoped somehow that it wouldn't be her.

Maybe, he thought as he opened the door and she came in, maybe she'll have a drink, cry, and fall asleep, like she sometimes did.

...but nuthin' else...I can't take nuthin' else...not tonight.

They had one drink, and he was the one to cry.

On the edge of the small bed, he hid his face in her lap, and the folds of her skirt felt the weight and heat of his love and frustration. He felt her fingers in his hair and heard the sound of her from somewhere.

"You been my strength, Al...a part of me. I don't know why you walked out on that boy, but don't let go now. Not now..."

Don't let go. He absorbed the sound of her as a man drowning would take in air.

How could he put into words what he had felt when he first saw her? Frieda and Evie could have been twins—small, brown, round, and delicate, each with the same half-hesitant smile in a beautiful face. He was convinced that Evie had come back to him in Frieda, and he transferred a memory of a lost love to love for this woman.

After the first shock, he came to love her so much that whenever she was near, his chest ached because no breath came. But she was married to Noel and Noel was his friend, so that was that.

But Noel met Jonrobert and the fire changed everything.

...God knows I didn't mean to feel like I did when he died. He was my friend...

For days after, he had functioned in a fog, going through the mechanics of whatever had to be done, although a vital part had been cut out of him. He remembered very little of that period except the joy he had felt when he went to the hospital and lied his way through a maze of red tape to snatch Frieda from the evil that threatened.

"...so this is your sister. What proof do you have?"

"All the papers got burnt up in the fire, ma'am...but she's my sister all right. I can bring in the whole block to swear to that..."

"That won't be necessary," the administrator had said, struggling to contain a vision of a black horde, ragged and unwashed, descending on the hospital. "How soon are you prepared to take her home?"

"Today, ma'am, if it's not too much trouble. The baby too."

"The baby too, of course. No trouble at all. You understand, of course, that your sister forfeits the benefit of long-term institutional care once you assume responsibility..."

"...long-term institutional care." He was silent for a moment as he thought of Evie. "...of course...yes ma'am...I sure do understand that..."

He twisted his cap in his hand and grinned at the woman whose face he had wanted to split open. He wanted to laugh and do more than that to show the world that he had not failed a second time.

"...got there in time, this time, dammit!"

And a month later, he could not describe his elation when Frieda had finally been able to say: "...I'm gonna name her Celia. After Noel's mama. He would've liked that..."

Which was fine with him. It sounded almost like Evie. Close enough.

He worked to take care of them. All day and half the night. Without letup. Like a dog. A mule. A horse. Surely Noel would forgive and Evie would understand.

Now, as he watched Frieda, he felt the small prickle of guilt nibble at the thin layer of his subconsciousness where it had lain embedded all these years. It was like an insect that had burrowed beneath the skin and now was surfacing to bedevil the host.

* * *

Frieda turned from the window. "What am I going to do?"

"Sit down and have a drink," Dan said.

"No. Not now. Do you know she's not eating. She refuses... look, I don't want her to end up like I did..."

"This is different," Al said quickly.

"Is it? I don't care what caused it. The result is the same."

Sam put down his glass. "Okay. Okay. We just gotta talk to her, that's all. Make her see there's other fish in the sea..."

"...plenty more where he came from...but no matter what, this one ain't comin' back..."

Frieda looked from one to the other as they drank, and she wondered about their nervousness. She watched as Al opened a second bottle and filled each glass to the brim. He caught her gaze, looked away, and then said, "...you ain't joinin' us? Come on... come on, now..."

29

December 1961

Jonrobert gritted his teeth as he waited for Pierre to open the door. He knew it would take at least five minutes before anyone responded to the bell. If he listened hard enough, he could probably hear the muted scrape of the cabinet doors closing as someone rushed to hide the money or drugs or whatever. Then the music, soft and deceptive, would flood the silence, and finally, the small, round peephole would slide open and the familiar voice would filter through.

He glanced at his watch and grew angry as the second hand completed several revolutions.

...hell with 'im, he whispered and turned away.

He was halfway to the elevator when the door opened and Pierre called out.

"You got no kinda patience, man. Where you in such a big rush to? Come on in."

Jonrobert turned to face his cousin, a medium-built man of

thirty-five with smooth, brown skin, regular features, and extraordinary light-brown eyes. Whereas Jonrobert was handsome in a rugged fashion, with thick mustache and lean muscularity, Pierre's looks tended toward softness. His face and features were baby-smooth and his smile was endearing; his eyes he used the way a spider would, to ensnare his target of the moment.

"Come on in, man..."

"Ain't stayin' long..."

"Well, take five at least..."

Jonrobert entered the small foyer, which opened onto a large living room. It contained two huge sofas, three chairs that someone swore were French provincial, and a Baldwin grand, highly polished, which no one, with the exception of the deliveryman, had ever touched. Beyond the living room, near the terrace, was a small dining room crammed with a blue flocked-velvet dining set designed to accommodate the likes of King Arthur and sundry knights in a squeeze. Dominating this entire ensemble was the floor-to-ceiling stereo system, which, mercifully, was turned low.

Jonrobert sat on the edge of one of the sofas. Pierre sat facing him.

"Want a hit?"

Jonrobert waved him away. "Naw, man," and he was quiet for several minutes. He had intended to ask Pierre to let him keep some of his things here, his record collection and perhaps some of his clothing. But he looked around and saw that that was impossible. Pierre could not fit an extra safety pin into the mélange that surrounded him.

...hell with it...ship it on home and explain to mama the best I can...

"You mighty quiet," said Pierre, eyeing him casually. "That broad... you ain't still thinkin' 'bout her...it's been a while, man. Don't you know better?"

Jonrobert remained silent, listening to the deep, spiritual, melancholy of Otis Redding. "Dreams to Remember." The song was a perfect mirror of his condition. Suddenly, he rose from the sofa. "Man, this shit is for the birds!"

"What shit?" asked Pierre. His smooth voice hid the defensive attitude. All of his stuff was first-class. What was his crazy cousin talking about?

"What shit you mean?" he asked again.

Jonrobert took a few steps, found that he had no room to pace, and sat down again. He did not respond immediately because he had no answer. Instead, he sighed, "I'm up against it, man. Up against it."

"Yeah...I can see that, but what's eatin' you...it ain't just that broad..."

"Naw...but she's a big part of it. The other thing is I got this letter yesterday. Got turned down for the rest of the seed money I needed..."

Pierre leaned back and folded his arms. "I told you I'd stake you. But no! You had to go bustin' your ass downtown to borrow your cash. SBA. You know what that stands for? When chumps like you show up with your hat in your hand, they change the sign. SBA mean 'stick it to your black ass,' that's what it means...

"Plenty stash right here in Harlem. Probably a million dollars right on this block. Told you you didn't need to be shufflin' downtown. Now look what the man is tellin' you...after you done filled out a thousand forms, with umpteen copies, been checked out up to your eyeballs, after you done smiled and grinned, they finally send you this letter. Stamped 'ain't qualified.' Just like that broad told you..."

Jonrobert felt the fine hair rise at the nape of his neck. "Leave her outta this," he said quietly.

"Well, it's true, ain't it," Pierre went on. He could not hide the huge satisfaction he felt.

"You know...I knew a dude like you once...tried to make the same moves you makin' today...worked hard...stayed straight up... stashed a little cash...even had one a them broads that was goin' somewhere. Real class, he called it. Only thing was, she had too much class for him...I mean, he wanted to do right but just didn't know how..."

Jonrobert felt his anger rising as Pierre went on expansively.

"...now...you know 'bout love, 'cause you was in it, right? Well, these two was in love, as you say, deep. Took care a business and couldn't do enough for each other. But hard as she tried, and he tried even harder, it just didn't work.

"She couldn't dig his runnin' buddies and put the clamps on 'im to cut 'em loose, but then when they'd git 'round her siddity friends, she be embarrassed when he make a wrong move. I mean, what he know 'bout tellin' a salad fork from a barbeque fork. The dude worked as a night porter in the hospital. And she a school teacher, shoulda known how to be cool, but she laughed loudest in the cover-up. Now...the cat wasn't slow...he peeped what was goin' down and finally hadda take a walk...called it a day."

Jonrobert gazed thoughtfully at his cousin for several seconds, then he looked away. "Well, that ain't *my* story and I ain't here to tell it!"

"Yeah...I know...I know...you feelin' low 'cause of your financial and business reversals...." said Pierre.

The laughter was there though neither of them actually heard it. It took shape easily within the slight pause of Pierre's words. The hollow sound floated and danced; then it slapped hard against Jonrobert's face. He rose from the sofa and reached for his coat.

"Where you goin', man? Back to knock some sense in her? Let her know what a good thing she gave up?"

Jonrobert turned suddenly and started toward Pierre. He took a quick step, but then stopped. Pierre had sprawled back on the sofa, both feet resting heavily on the glass inlaid coffee table. His bloodshot eyes were half-closed, and his hands were busy keeping the folded bill to his face. He heard and saw nothing as his fingers pushed the powder down the crease of the dollar bill. His expression was preoccupied and the snake-colored eyes were empty.

Jonrobert's anger drained away and he shook his head. "I see you takin' a lickin' yourself. When *you* gonna call it a day?"

"...anytime I want to, man...anytime..."

"Yeah...and I got cash money ridin' on the time and the date..."

He started for the door again. It was useless trying to reason with a dead man.

The rug in the corridor felt thick under his feet. The hall was quiet, and he wondered what went on behind the doors of the other apartments. Everything seemed so closed, so secure and private. How were those other, mysterious, lives managed? What dreams did they remember? Did the men work hard? Did their women love them? What about the children and homework and television and Coney Island and church on Sundays?

He tapped the elevator button and waited in the silence. That's why he had come to see Pierre. Not to store records and clothing but to speak to someone who might perhaps tell him the reason for his pain. Connect. Close the yawning gap that daily seemed to grow larger in his aloneness.

But his cousin was in another realm and had stepped out just long enough to mirror his predicament. His chest ached, and he leaned against the elevator door. The steel felt cold against his forehead.

It had been over a month, but he still had trouble absorbing the impact.…it was her pop and my grandmama…

And I got down over the roof. Why didn't I stay with her. Did she call me? Scream after me, or what…

He felt the vibration in his forehead as the elevator approached and slowed. He stepped back, composed himself, and moved into the empty car. In the lobby, he nodded to the doorman and walked out into the cold night air. It had begun to snow and the flakes hit soft and wet against his face.

He should have known that Pierre would be of little help. He strolled the few blocks to his car.

…he's my cousin and I can't talk to him…Celia was…she was my life, and I couldn't talk to her when the deal went down…

He glanced at his reflection in the glass of a candy store.…no talkin'…just keep walkin'…why couldn't I have told her…but her pop died…her mama went crazy…'cause a me…damn…'cause a me…

He reached the car and was suddenly overcome by a feeling of terror. It brushed him swiftly and quietly in the wet air. The ground seemed to rise up, and the space between the houses grew smaller. He imagined himself standing in the entrance of his auto shop, the door closing, squeezing, pinning him against the wall. Flames were advancing, forming a semicircle and licking at his face.

When he opened his eyes, he was in the car, his hands sweaty on the steering wheel.

…what if we hadda got married…and she found out after…

He folded his arms over the wheel and watched the snow hit softly against the windshield, one flake building on another until the entire window was covered. He should have felt a measure of comfort, wrapped cocoonlike in the silence, but instead the sides seemed to be closing in again and he wondered what was beyond the snow that might be pushing in.

He suppressed a powerful urge to smash his fist through the window to stop the pressure.

If he could only see her and explain, but he did not know what it was he should be explaining.

The whole thing seemed like a battle much too large for him. It was a major assault carried over three generations and several fronts, and he did not know whom he should fight and whom he should defend himself against.

He fumbled for the switch and the wipers made a low whirring noise as they cleared a semicircle of glass. The avenue stretched before him, white and deserted, and he felt alone on the earth, a wandering, solitary figure with no connection to anything except his own pain.

30

January 1963

When physical pain eases, the memory of it diminishes accordingly. A pain of the heart is a different matter. Long after the cause disappears, pain is kept alive, nurtured and fed by the sufferer because the pain is the only remaining link to the one who caused it.

Celia went back to school (because Jonrobert's letter said that she should). She had regained some of the weight that she had lost but still had trouble eating. It was weeks before she adjusted to the capping of her teeth, which she had ground away in her sleep.

Her pain congealed into a dull knot, settled in a private part of her, and, like indigestion, surfaced periodically to remind her of her past indulgence.

"Where you been, girl?" asked James as he eased into a chair next to her in the library. "Ain't seen you around."

"I haven't *been* around," said Celia. She did not smile. All the neighbors who had ears, including James, had heard her crying and had reached the correct conclusion, and now here he was, handsome, arrogant, and stupid as ever, preparing to reopen and examine her old wound.

"You sure you all right? Look like you lost a little weight..."

James had lost interest in revolution and had become instead expert on the size, shape, and weight of the female population on campus. He divided his time between cafeteria, lounge, and library and carried the minimum number of credits that enabled him to remain in school. Despite James's lack of progress, his father was proud of his college-boy son and had even allowed himself to be talked into buying James a car, which only pulled him further away from the task at hand.

James's goal, now, was to remain a career freshman.

Celia did not look at him. "I'm all right," she said as she opened her notebook and spread the papers on either side of the table in front of her. James's aversion to schoolwork forced him to move back.

"Well, okay, long as you all right," he said hesitantly. He had never seen so many notes, and it made him nervous. Then he brightened: "Say, any time you want a lift home, lemme know, okay, just lemme know...I'm pushin' a bad set a wheels now..."

"I will, James, and thank you."

The finality in her voice seeped through to him and he stood up. "Look, I just remembered something...gotta run. Be cool..."

On the rare days that she spotted James riding alone, she pretended not to see him, preferring to walk. She plodded through gray February snow and indifferent March winds, holding tightly to the hope that Jonrobert would return. On days when her fingers lost sensation from the cold, she walked, just in case the long-lost, familiar, dark-green Eldorado should cruise by.

Once she thought she saw the car as it eased to a stop at a traffic light. She ran out into the street, her heart pounding louder than her footsteps. The light was changing as she ran up to the window on the passenger side.

Even before she looked in the window at the amazed face of the old woman behind the wheel, she knew it was not Jonrobert. He never cruised to a light. He always pulled up fast, squealing to a sudden stop as if traffic lights were not a part of his world. And once the light changed, he usually accelerated, screeching away in a noisy cloud.

The old woman behind the wheel stared as Celia moved silently away.

So she held on, by turns, to anger, frustration, and despair, and more practically, she held on to her short hairstyle and kept Frieda busy sewing the latest fashions for her. She wanted to be perfect when Jonrobert's car stopped again.

April is a bad month for love and devastating for those who pretend they can do without it. The thin veneer of whatever it was that held one together through the drama of Christmas, the trauma of New Year's, and the depression of winter dissipates under the pressure of changing temperatures and rising expectations.

It is difficult to ignore the excitement of renewal, of coats coming off and windows opening to expel the stale ghosts of winter. The heavy accumulation of fat and lethargy, nature's protective devices, is sloughed off, and the blood, thin and free, quickens in the veins.

But sometimes, secretly, silently, suddenly, the heart stops a beat away from fulfillment. April is a bad month.

Celia's anguish leveled off to a point where she was able to concentrate on her studies. She accelerated, doubling her courses—not to make up for time lost, but to dull the raw edge of time's passage. She retreated once again to the library, built a mountain of books, and buried herself within. She involved herself with nothing and no one, and she avoided the dim-lit coffee shops that had sprung up overnight like mushrooms in the shadow of the university, where talk of revolution and romance were laid out like snares for confused or bored young coeds.

She moved in solitude under her mountain and was not surprised to learn that she had completed all the course work on schedule. It was as if the interlude with Jonrobert, a minor aberration in the sequence of time, had never occurred.

She lay on her bed on graduation day staring at the ceiling. Her dress hung in the closet.

"You worked so hard," Frieda said, choosing her words carefully, searching for the smallest hole in the wall of indifference. "How will you get your diploma?"

"I'm not feeling well, mother, I'm sorry. They can mail it..." She closed her eyes and pictured the vastness of the reviewing stand, the rows upon rows of spectators, cameras, programs, handkerchiefs, and hats. Pomp and circumstance that held no meaning whatever for her without Jonrobert to smile and wave and single her out from a hundred other purple robes.

Even Tessie had gone. Joining Willie wherever he was because he wasn't coming back. He skipped out on a big bill, Tessie had said, and no need to spread that kind of news around, so she was going to join him.

Celia had helped Tessie pack, and Al had driven them to the airport. Unknown to Celia, the rest of Willie's belongings had been shipped by Groovy Movers long ago to Marcus's address.

Celia and Tessie and Al sat in the airport lounge for forty-five rainy minutes drinking and trying for meaningless small talk. Five minutes after takeoff, Celia remembered nothing except Tessie's promise to write.

What did a promise mean? She herself had promised to keep in touch with Shing a Ling, but meeting Jonrobert pushed out of reach every promise she had ever made.

She thought of Shing a Ling now and wondered if she had survived the long march through the barking dogs and cattle prods. Had she earned a diploma along with her combat medal?

Celia turned in the bed away from the window.

...if I had gone away to school...I never would have met him... never. I would have fought in the war...

If I went to Toogaloo...
I'd show those folks
a thing or two
I'd show those folks...

The pain returned and she drew it around her gratefully, like an old shawl.

31

September 13, 1963

Dear Tessie,

I know it's been two months since I received your letter and I feel terrible not writing to you before now, but the truth is I had been having a pretty hard time trying to find a job and I didn't want to bother you with depressing news. I know it must be hard for you to relate to this now. If I were surrounded by sea and sun and sand every day, I would have trouble relating too.

I gave your mother the money you sent, and she seems to be doing okay. Everything and everyone is still the same, the stoop watchers are still watching, though heaven only knows what.

Anyway, on the job front, things were looking pretty grim for a while, probably because there are so few options for English majors who don't want to teach or go on to graduate school, and even fewer for blacks. I must have left at least a hundred resumes all over the city, half of which probably ended up in the wastebaskets before I even got out of the door.

My haircut was not helping either, and mother was very upset. But I'm determined to keep this style because you know Jonrobert persuaded me to cut it and this is all I have left of him. I just wish mother would try to understand.

Anyway, the good news is that I have a job. A real job. It's with a small magazine publisher and I'm to start Monday. Keep your fingers crossed and tell Willie hello and thanks for the invitation. If I last long enough to earn a vacation, I'll be seeing both of you then.

Love,
Celia

The first week on the job—after three interviews and high expectations—the first person Celia learned to dislike was Sophie, the head of the copywriting department. Sophie was a short, angular woman who thought that Hobson Publishing was the sun that supplied all of mankind's needs and that she, in some large manner, was one of the rays.

"We had some girls in the stockroom, but it didn't work out,"

Sophie said, intimating that Hobson Publishing was setting a precedent by hiring Celia as a copywriter trainee. Celia gazed at her steadily, and Sophie knew that Celia knew she had not been hired because of any particular generosity on the part of Hobson and company. They probably hadn't even read her application—beyond her name and whatever arcane symbol they had appended to facilitate separation of the haves and the have-nots.

They both knew that it was the cry of alarm being heard in the streets, and on television at dinnertime, that had got Celia hired. It was the clenched fist raised high that no one wanted to see. It was the threat of violence, real and imagined, that propelled company recruiters to black campuses with orders to bring back ten tokens, dead or alive, one for every other department. No one wanted to step off the 8:20 from Larchmont to find Grand Central in flames...

When the agency called and said that they had "wonderful news," Celia should have been elated. Instead, she had braced herself.

"...and the policy of this company," Sophie was saying when Celia tuned back in, "is to acquaint our new employees with every phase of our operations so that eventually they will be able to write an intelligent magazine article."

Eventually. The word was not lost on Celia. "Eventually" translated into hard labor in the mail room, distribution, shipping, typing, filing. So she was surprised when Sophie said that she was being assigned to work for the sales manager.

"As his assistant?"

"As his secretary," Sophie enunciated clearly so that there would be no misunderstanding regarding rank and privilege. "The regular secretary is on maternity leave and..."

Celia could have asked when the regular secretary would return. What if she never returned? Why couldn't the company hire someone from one of those temporary agencies? Temporary. That was it. She was the temporary. They would throw so much stuff at her that she would be glad to quit.

She looked up from hands held tight in her lap. The meeting had concluded; the door was held open for her. She followed Sophie down carpeted corridors, past hushed anterooms, plush inner offices, and busy typing pools where the typing suddenly clattered to a halt.

She walked in the hard silence, listening to the echo of her footfalls, and stared straight ahead until the cramp in her neck began to radiate to her shoulders.

To hell with you all, she smiled to herself. Haven't you seen a black face before? Of course you have. Front-page pictures of rapists, muggers, and welfare queens. You've seen me before because if you've seen one, you've seen us all. Besides, you brought us over, remember? Remember? Well, here I am, she continued to smile, and to hell with you...

She knew the sales manager was from Texas as soon as he opened his mouth. "Ceelyuh," he said in a large voice. "Ceelyuh. Well!" He repeated her name as if to accustom himself to this new situation. Finally, he said, "Well. We gonna get 'long just fine. Just fine."

Mr. Wingate omitted her last name and stared hard at her haircut, but when he extended his hand, the handshake was firm and he did not withdraw his hand any quicker than anyone else.

Nevertheless, in the subway, on her way home, the nagging rage that had been building within her all day finally boiled over.

"So that's how they plan to do it. Southern exposure. More effective than radiation. Deus ex machina, circa 1963. Ten years ago, I would have gotten the mail room or stockroom treatment—break my nails, my back, then my spirit—and as a bonus, continue to hear a thousand Sophies say, "I don't understand why they'd rather be on welfare..."

The civil rights marchers could march until their feet swelled and dropped off. The sit-ins could sit until the seats wear out. What does it mean, this Law of the Land.

She thought, idly, of Newton's Third Law of Motion. *Philosphiae Naturalis. Principia mathematic:* To every action, there is always opposed an equal reaction, or the mutual actions of two bodies against each other are always equal and directed to contrary parts...

There will always be a reaction, resistance. They scheme while we sleep. Jonrobert was right when he said that we had a lot to learn, that we don't know how to "fuck over someone with finesse."

Now I see he was right, as usual. We don't know the art. In this game, we're beyond our depth, ignorant, innocent, and when the load gets too heavy, we react. Direct. We experience a spontaneous reaction. They see a riot. They see looters, predators, and thieves, and scream for the national guard...

The train jerked to a sudden halt in the tunnel, bringing her to her senses. The tight knot of people shifted restlessly, and in the break, Celia glimpsed a woman seated across from her. On the crowded train, she sat in casual isolation, oblivious of the yawning space on either side which no one wanted to share. Her clothing was an accumulation of castoffs, and her face spoke of events that had pulled pain to her, where it stuck like cold molasses.

Celia's rage intensified as her eyes searched the woman for a clue that would unlock the mystery of her sad condition. The layers of clothing could not hide her thinness, and her legs stuck out like two short ash-brown broomsticks beneath the large coat. A small shopping bag leaned near her feet, and her arms were loosely folded in her lap.

Celia had seen many in this condition but none with such a strange, sad, defeated look. Her eyes were so unfocused that she might have been asleep.

The woman's hands were swollen and her knuckles inflamed, and Celia's imagination immediately leaped to the crowded, noisy bowels of a nondescript clothing factory. She saw the woman bending over a power machine. Pick up a collar. Run it through. Put it down. Pick up another...ignoring the small tyranny of the floor girl and struggling to brush away the web of killing monotony. And one day, the woman had probably gathered up her thin sweater and small plastic pocketbook, gone to lunch, and never looked back—leaving in her wake the busy ripple of speculation that attends such defection. The next morning, new hands filled the void, the machine hummed once again, and the woman was forgotten in the continuing chaos.

Had it happened that way? Had she simply walked out...and kept walking, moving, moving, moving, to put as much distance as possible between her and the source of her pain? And now the sensation of perpetual motion has become a habit....She moves now with no place to go...

* * *

Celia passed her stop. At the next station, she decided to walk the ten blocks back home. She needed time to think, to plan strategy for the next day, and to lighten the mental load before facing her mother's sharp concern.

The third Monday, the silence still descended whenever Celia came into the ladies room. She had long ago abandoned the company cafeteria except to get Mr. Wingate's coffee, but the quiet gathered round now like a thick, deadly cloud and followed in her wake. By five o'clock, her head was hurting again. She joined the crowded streets and made her way to the subway, moving like an automaton, stiff from the habit of anger.

In the station, she thought of the Subway Lady and wondered again if she had walked away from a similar situation...walked away to keep from committing murder.

She did not remember climbing the stairs or walking down the hill from the subway. She did not remember passing Groovy Movers or wondering—if the truck was gone—where Al, Sam, and Dan might be.

She heard Frieda moving from the kitchen but did not see the expression on her face as she approached.

"Celia...?" Frieda's voice was tight with concern. "...another headache?"

She sat down, unable to respond. Finally, she said, "No one speaks. No one speaks to me, mother. No one. Except for Mr. Wingate, and Mr. Arnold in the mail room, no one says a word..."

She sat at the dining table and pushed the dish away. "I'm just so...tired...I'm tired..."

Frieda held the dish towel under the hot water, wrung it out, and pressed it against Celia's forehead. The pulse was strong through the damp fold of the cloth.

"I need some aspirin..."

Frieda heard these words as she had every night for the last two weeks.

Instead of going to the medicine cabinet, she stood over Celia, looking down at the stooped shoulders and the too-thin arms folded against the girl's chest as if to ward off some malevolent force.

She took a deep breath. "No...no, you don't," she said finally. "You been coming home every night for the last two weeks looking sick, and every night I've been wanting to tell you to quit if the job's that bad. Just quit. You'll find something else—but now you telling me what it is...that it's not the work, but the people at work...those people..."

She sat down at the table and pushed aside the place mats, teapot, and sugar bowl so that plates, cups, and silver were pressed in a jumble. She folded her arms and leaned her elbows in the cleared space.

When Frieda began to talk, she did not mention the Sophies of the world because experience had taught her that the nature of evil is constant. She concentrated instead on her own store of memories, describing Noel's strength and the calm he was able to find in the middle of the daily madness that some people called living. She recalled the determination in Noel's father's eyes when he lifted the shotgun off the wall and propped it against the window and waited. She spoke of finding her own strength to lift a pot of scalding water when she had to.

"...it's easy, once you get mad enough..."

Frieda listened, as she spoke, to the sound of her own voice and wondered why she was doing this, why she was at last releasing this information she knew would release her daughter. All she had wanted, after her illness, was to hold on, to protect Celia from harm, and by extension, to further protect herself from the galling pain which had become a part of most of her days.

She had labored to isolate her child, and she had failed. The madness had crept in. Now, the most she could do—and do it fast—was to try to immunize her, insulate her against the fine, genteel barbarism that Celia would have to take in along with breakfast, lunch, and dinner each day for the rest of her life.

As Frieda spoke, Celia remained quiet, studying her mother's changing expression. Her features softened, and she seemed to have gone back in time. Even her gestures were youthful and more fluid. She looked so beautiful that Celia wished her father could see her again, just this once. But her father was locked in the faded frame that was propped against the cold-cream jar on her dressing table.

And she tried, but could not imagine the face of her grandfather at all.

"Your grandfather was very strong," Frieda continued, as if she had anticipated Celia's question. "That's where Noel got his strength."

Then she raised her hands, and Celia noticed that the motion came slowly. "...but I can't help feelin' that it was their strength... that got them killed."

Celia inclined her head. "No. That's not...it wasn't their strength, mother, but someone else's weakness that killed them..."

"Even so," Frieda said, "what your father had, and his father, is still in the blood...your blood...you remember that..."

She leaned across the table and touched Celia's forehead. The pulse had slowed. It was time to see about dinner. "Even so," she said again, more to herself than to Celia, "there's many days, and nights, I had wished...I wished..."

Her expression changed as she smoothed the tablecloth and arranged the dishes once more into neat place settings. "I wish... life wasn't so...so..."

Celia leaned forward. "I know, mother...I know...it's hard. It's very hard...but I...I know it'll work out...I will make it work out..."

32

November 22, 1963

An assassin's bullet shattered the myth of Camelot. The mirage of the New Frontier, already shifty in the distant haze, disintegrated and disappeared beyond the red-rimmed horizon.

The heart of the republic faltered for a fraction of a beat while the illusion of power was transferred. Then the experts plunged into an orgy of analysis and accusation, leaving the mourning to those less qualified.

The turmoil was worldwide, a political *tsunami* that drew pools and seas and oceans of power into a single force of destruction eventually fated to turn back on itself. Below the turmoil, at a particular substratum of sufficient depth, the impact, though far from minimal, was absorbed just as a thousand other psychic insults had been.

Bad news comes in threes. So they waited, the denizens of this particular substratum, and watched as airports and expressways and launch pads and libraries underwent the change of name in elaborate ceremony. They waited, hoping that those in high places who saw to such things would have sufficient foresight to set aside a number of public structures for the next two occasions.

"Bad news comes in threes...you mark my words...," the Chock Full O'Nuts waitress said as she cleared the space in front of Celia. The personalized strip of plastic on her left lapel read Lu-Ann, though no customer dared get so personal. Other than a no-nonsense "order please," this was her first pronouncement to Celia, who had been coming there every day and sitting in the same seat for the last three months.

Tomorrow, Celia knew, would be like yesterday and the day before to this waitress, despite the anguish in high places. Lu-Ann would still place the spoon to the right of the bowl just as Celia would continue to indent the prerequisite five spaces.

Why, she wondered, had it taken the death of a president to open a line of communication between two black women struggling in foreign territory, dangerous waters where great white sharks circled in corporate murk to close in on one typographical error too many or one misplaced coffee cup.

"It's too bad," said Celia. "They didn't even give him a chance..."

"That's 'cause they didn't want to," Lu-Ann replied matter-of-factly. "They gettin' 'way with murder all the way 'round, but nobody can't say this ain't equal opportunity. Knockin' 'em off top and bottom."

She quickly added the bill and swept the money and check off the counter in a tight, practiced maneuver. "Can't wait 'til two-thirty...Jesus...got a corn that's killin' me..."

She waved as Celia went through the revolving door.

Celia crossed at the corner with the crowd and returned to the office to find Mr. Wingate exactly as she had left him—sprawled in his chair with his back to the desk and feet propped up on the windowsill. The half-opened door indicated that it was all right to enter. She saw the sealed container of yogurt on the desk where she had placed it earlier that morning. Only the coffee was gone.

"Can I get you some more coffee?"

"Naw. Thanks. Had two since you left." He lowered his feet and swung around. At six foot three, he lived in constant dread of his two hundred and forty pounds turning to fat, yet he indulged only in irregular, frantic bursts of exercise. Now, with his head sunk in despair against his chest, he appeared larger than ever.

"What I can't understand about the whole damn thing is—why Texas? Why Dallas? Dammit..."

He motioned her to come in and close the door behind her. The job really wasn't bad. Answer the phone in a pleasant voice, type his reports, ignore the silence of the other secretaries, and listen to him talk on and on about growing up poor in Texas.

"...you think all Texans are rich, well, let me tell you, it ain't all oil..."

He was proud of his football scholarship, proud of his alma mater, and proud of his home state. Now his humiliation extended far beyond his grief as he imagined the eyes of the world on his private place. "Why Dallas," he repeated. "Now everyone's going to think we're nothing but a bunch of trigger-happy hillbillies."

"But Mr. Wingate," Celia said, "there've been killings—assassinations—all over the world...Austria, France..."

She was trying, with her limited knowledge of history, to place the event within a global perspective for him. For several days now she had been a reluctant participant in this private wake, and she was wondering when he would put this behind him and return to the business at hand. Two weeks ago, she had given him some of her writing samples, and since that time, he had said nothing. Had he forgotten or had they been that bad?

Even if the samples were good, she knew it was too soon to expect anything, certainly not a promotion, but she wanted him to remember why she was hired.

Christmas and New Year's passed. She received a bonus of a week's salary, so she assumed he was satisfied with her performance. But some other part of her signaled something else: a vague restlessness, a dissatisfaction curling up from the edge which she struggled hard to keep under control.

In February 1964, the shock of Dallas began to recede as another Texan unveiled his blueprint for the Great Society. Mr. Wingate talked again of the good things of Texas. Celia only half listened because most of what he was saying she had heard before.

"...what's the matter, Celia?"

"...matter?"

"Yes. You've been looking very preoccupied lately..."

She had been preparing for this for weeks, and still he had caught her off guard.

"Well, I was wondering if your secretary was really coming back... and if there's going to be an opening in the copywriting department..."

She watched his face carefully as he spoke. She knew him well enough by now to detect any hint of evasion.

"Well. To answer both your questions, I can honestly say I don't know. My secretary may come back. Then again, she may not. You know how these new mothers are. But personnel would have notified me if she had called. Now, about the copywriting. I know you were hired for that, but you end up as my secretary—"

"—I understood that I was starting out as your secretary..."

She had told her mother, Al, Sam, and Dan, she had even written to Tessie, that she was going into copywriting, that it would only be a matter of time. But how was time measured? The Supreme Court mentioned "all deliberate speed." In terms of time, what did it mean? How much longer could she ignore the other secretaries, look through them the way they looked through her. "That's what I understood, Mr. Wingate..."

"I know. I know. But let's not kid ourselves..." He lowered his voice, "Besides Arnold in the mail room, you two are the only—what do you all want to be called nowadays—"

"—black."

"Hell...I can't keep up...every ten years, it's something new... you two are the only black employees in the company. And there's probably only about ten in the whole building. Just look in the elevator sometimes..."

Celia looked in the elevator all the time and knew the total better than he did.

"I don't want you to have any illusions about what you're up against," he said. "They told you that you'd 'make the rounds.' Even if they transferred you from my department, there's no guarantee that you'd end up in copy..."

He saw the expression on her face and continued quickly. "Tell you what, though. I looked over your samples and they weren't bad. With a little polishing up...anyway, what sort of articles... what area are you interested in?"

Celia could not believe her ears and did not trust herself to smile. "Any area. Anything. Travel, health, finance, food, homemaking, obituary, anything..."

He held up his hands. "Wait a minute. Hold it. Let's not go overboard...what are you particularly interested in. People write well when they write about what they know..."

"Well, I don't really know, Mr. Wingate, I..." She looked at her hands. "I just know that I want to write..."

"Well, you don't need to work here for that. If you're really serious about writing, you can work in a coal mine, a catfish factory, the post office....What I'm trying to say is—if it's in you, it's going to come out, no matter what..."

Celia shook her head. "I agree, but it might come out easier in the right atmosphere..."

"Touché. Old Hobson would be flattered if he were around to hear that...tell you what...vacation's coming up soon. Why don't you plan something around that...an article...

"...meanwhile, read some of the back issues from our library, familiarize yourself with our format. And tomorrow, I'll introduce you to the travel editor and the general assignment man...may as well get to know them...and if you bring back something on your own that's worthwhile, who knows...I'll shoot it past Sophie and... who knows..."

She stared at him, and his look told her all she needed to know about the politics of Hobson Publishing. It told her that Sophie had intimidated the other secretaries, frightening them into the silence that surrounded her; the look said that he and Sophie were equals, adversaries, and that she, Sophie, had recommended Celia to his department so he could have the onerous task of firing her for incompetence.

And the look also said that he was not about to be taken before the Fair Employment Practices Commission and that he was powerful enough within the structure to turn the tables and prove to Sophie and the rest of the company that this black girl had what it took.

The shock of recognition was such that Celia excused herself and walked quickly to the ladies room, hoping that no one met her along the way. In the booth, she adjusted her stockings and slip and smoothed her blouse. Then she adjusted her features and smoothed her expression.

By the time she emerged, the rage and dizziness had subsided and what she felt was the usual caution and anger. She had also made up her mind that whoever won this tennis match—Sophie or Mr. Wingate—she, Celia, was not going to be the ball thrown out of the game because of some perceived manufacturing defect.

33

Celia stopped by Groovy Movers to speak to Al before she went upstairs. She sat quietly as he concluded the sale of a maple chest of drawers with hammered brass handles on each of its six closures.

"...and I wanna find that brass on them drawers when you deliver it tomorrow," the buyer, a soft-spoken woman twice his size, warned.

"...what you seein' is what you'll be gittin'..." Al smiled, a trace of impatience creeping in.

"No harm meant," she replied. "It's just that it was that brass that 'tracted me to it in the first place. How somebody could give up somethin' as pretty as this, I'll never know...their loss is my luck, I suppose."

"Ma'am," Al answered soothingly, "it's more than luck. An eye for quality never closes..."

The woman beamed and blushed, and not wanting any further reverberations to disturb this rare good feeling, she whispered good night and left the shop on tiptoe, weaving her way like a tamed dancing bear around packing boxes, barrels, and odd pieces of discarded and forgotten furniture.

Al waited until the door closed; then he sighed, "Sometimes you gotta do that..." and he and Celia laughed.

"So." He turned to her. "How'd it go today...?" The question seemed to come from a general quietly concerned about progress and conditions on the front line. He listened as Celia talked excitedly about the assignment.

"...it's not an assignment in the real sense, where they pay a person to go to a certain location and do a story..."

"—you mean you gotta go on your own, bring back a story, and if they like it—"

"Yes. But that's what free-lancers do all the time—"

"But you ain't free-lancin'...you workin' for a company that—" He would have gone on but he saw her expression. "Okay. Try it. Play it their way for a while...just don't let 'a while' add up to more time than you care to tell....Anyway, the trip does sound nice...tie right in...you'll be seein' Tessie again...and my man, Willie..."

"I didn't know you knew Willie..."

"Everybody know Willie...used to pass him a couple a times on the block...see 'im in the Peacock...nuthin' too tough..."

He was talking too much, he knew, and so he defied his own "no smoking" sign and lit a cigarette.

A minute later he said, "What you think Frieda gonna say..."

"I don't know...that's kind of why I wanted to talk to you..."

"Well, I'll see what I can do," he replied.

In the span of five quick minutes, he had gone from general of strategic command to point man. He didn't mind. If he moved in the right place at the right time, he could avoid the mines and traps and perhaps be rewarded with his favorite dessert, his favorite, sweet, warm pudding—that's what Frieda's stomach reminded him of. Soft and warm and sweet.

He turned again to Celia, staring at her soberly, wanting to ask her the other question. How was she feeling? In particular, had she met anyone? Not on the job—he knew there were no black men there—but perhaps she had run into someone at lunch, on the bus or the subway, at the newsstand, waiting at the corner for the light to change, someone...something...somewhere...

He knew she still thought of Jonrobert, although neither of them mentioned it. He could see it in her eyes, the vacant preoccupation whenever conversation lagged.

She was still looking for him in the face of every man she saw, and no man had the strength, as he had had with Frieda, to move beyond the barrier and say, "I'm here. Look at me. I'm here."

Celia rose from the low packing box that doubled as a seat. "You can talk to mother. But I want to speak to her first. You know, every week for the last few months, I've been receiving an envelope with my name on it. I look at my name and the figures next to it. The figures don't amount to much, certainly not what some others, who were hired after me, are making. But my name on that envelope says...that I'm doing something..."

Al watched her as she moved slowly in a small circle among the cartons and touched the folded quilted packing covers.

"It says that I'm making my way. I don't know yet if it's the right way, but it's a way. Every Friday, when I see it, I think of Monday, Tuesday, Wednesday, and Thursday that came and went in complete silence except for my boss and the mail clerk. I think of seven and a half hours of typing alternating with 'heck with them...they'll come to their senses and start speaking tomorrow.' That envelope represents a milestone. It tells me that I made it another week. On my own.

"Some Fridays, I'd pass here and my head would be hurting so badly, I wouldn't even realize that I had an envelope until I was upstairs in my bedroom, looking in my bag for some aspirin.... But mother and I had a long talk one evening...and I know I can do the job. All I have to do is stick it out...this trip is part of the job..."

He watched her as she moved slowly around the boxes to the door. Her hand was on the knob when he said, "I'm glad you and Frieda had that talk, whatever it was about, I'm glad...she seem like she beginnin' to let up...but don't push her. Takin' a trip downtown is one thing. Outta the country is another thing altogether..."

"Depends on the destination," Celia said. "For some people, taking a trip out of the country may be less dangerous than taking the subway downtown. It depends on the destination..."

Al looked at her. "I see your point, and I ain't tryin' to discourage you. I'm just tryin' to tell you to be prepared..."

The door to the shop closed behind her, and she made her way to the apartment.

...be prepared. She sighed to herself....how can I prepare myself when all the time, they prepared to keep me right here...

The sewing had been put away and the table set for dinner. Celia paused in the doorway of the dining room and watched Frieda arrange the flatware and napkins.

In the busy arrangement of salt and pepper shakers, mustard jar, catsup bottle, sugar bowl, creamer, bread plate, butter dish, tea cups, and salad bowl, the two place settings appeared lost and alone waiting for the main onslaught of Frieda's effort, which was still in the oven.

"Smells like shrimp," said Celia.

Frieda moved to the kitchen, her voice trailing behind her, "You keep on smelling shrimp. It'll make that flounder much easier to swallow..."

She was in a good mood, Celia could tell, so there was no point in waiting until after dinner to convene in solemn council with her. Discuss the idea, the trip, over dinner. And wine. The way civilized people negotiated their lives and fortunes. Civilized.... why do we have to scream and cry and fight all the time...

"You look tired..." Frieda said as she placed the covered dishes on the table.

"I am," Celia replied, and she wished there had been an extra place set for Al. He had looked tired too. Then she said, "Thank God for the end of the week...I think we might have something to celebrate..."

"Really?" Frieda paused, her face closing as she spread her napkin on her lap. Had Jonrobert returned? Had Celia met someone new?

"What is it?" she asked quickly.

"I have an assignment..."

"An assignment...what's that...?"

"To do an article...when I go on vacation..."

"Vacation. Where—"

Celia rushed on, not pausing to look at her mother's face, which seemed now old and young at the same time.

When she did look at Frieda, Celia was suddenly furious with Al and with the limits of his love and imagination. Why hadn't he taken her mother to a Savoy dance, a Pelham Bay picnic, anywhere, instead of allowing himself to be circumscribed by her fear... allowing himself to be pulled into her small, tight little world where there was only the illusion of safety and comfort. Why hadn't he ever said to her, "It's going to be different, different from now on."

But then—had Jonrobert ever taken her to a dance, a movie, or a picnic? They had danced, moved, and picnicked in bed. They had a feast, not a picnic. Love had made her as weak and blind as Al.

...where does one get the strength to turn love around...to make it go the way you want it to go...

Frieda had put her fork down and was staring at her plate.

"A vacation. You're going away..."

"Mother," Celia said, rising from her seat, "listen, it's only for three weeks. I'll be back." She took her mother's hand. "Nothing's going to happen. I promise. Everything's going to be all right."

Frieda closed her eyes. She felt Celia's pressure but heard another voice intrude, at once soft and rough:...let it go, baby...it ain't gonna hurt...let it go...

The sound rose and mixed with the steady murmur of Celia's voice. "...everything's going to be all right, mother...everything."

The tears spread like a network down Frieda's face, coursing along fine lines near her mouth. Celia took a napkin and wiped her face. "Besides," she whispered, "Al promised me he'd take care of you. He—"

The doorbell sounded and Al came in. All three looked at each other in silence. Then Celia said, "Mama, he won't let anything happen while I'm gone..."

Celia waited until she had purchased the airline ticket before sending the cable to Tessie. "Arriving Flight 723, Sunday, 2 p.m."

A letter would have been too involved and would have had to be written at least a week in advance. In a week, anything could happen.

They came to see her off and stood, silenced by the unfamiliar chaos of the terminal. Frieda, still unreconciled to the turn of events, complained about the noise and powerful smell of the fuel. She was visibly unnerved, but the men said nothing. They hugged Celia and walked with her to the point where the sign said "passengers only" and hugged her again; then everyone spoke at once, wishing her a safe trip. Frieda appeared to be on the verge of tears, so goodbyes were brief. Celia hurried through the covered tarmac, passed under the radiant, reassuring smile of the flight attendant, and found her assigned seat.

The plane made a slow U-turn at the end of the runway, and Celia peered through the thick window, searching vainly among the shifting landscape for a glimpse of the terminal. She saw, instead, the trembling wing as the plane eased into position. Mysterious mechanisms near the jet engines were lowered, and the plane began to rumble along, gathering sudden, incredible speed.

The noise dissolved into a slight metallic groan as the plane left the ground, and cars and houses disappeared and streets became thin lines on a grid of green and gray.

She thought of Jonrobert and wondered if he had taken a plane when he left or if he had driven at awful speed to the sanctuary of the small Carolina town whose name she never knew. Or was he still in the city, remaining carefully out of reach.

"Good morning, ladies and gentlemen. Welcome aboard Flight 723."

The melodious voice blocked out the groaning of the craft, and eventually the minor shocks and trembling eased. She turned to the window again to watch the wing slide through amorphous formations of cotton candy suspended in a serene sea of white. She focused on this until tension closed in and she fell asleep. The dream was the same as always.

It was the shadow of a man with a wide-brimmed hat and incredibly soft leather shoes that enabled him to keep a finger's length in front of her. Her chest ached from effort and frustration. When she fell again, crying, the shadowy figure always stopped, turned, and, in the mysterious maneuvers of dreams, suddenly appeared behind her.

When he bent to help her up, she knew the wind would rise, screaming, to take his hat away, and she knew as she reached for him that he would have the face of the man in the brown-edged photograph on her dresser.

He was tall and thin, and his eyes were her eyes. But the shoes did not belong to him. She knew also that it would be Jonrobert's voice: "...how come you always fallin'...get up, get up."

His touch was as insubstantial as a ghost's, and by the time she rose, weeping and unsteady, he would be once more a finger's length away.

PART FOUR

34

May 1964

When the plane touched down, Tessie, Willie, and Marcus had been waiting for more than an hour. As Celia came through customs, Tessie approached, running.

"Ceeelyaaa...! Girl!"

Now that they had met, the months of silence and solitude each had experienced seemed more acute than ever, and they could not sum up in a word the accompanying relief. It was simpler to cry. Tessie and Celia and Willie all embraced and all started to talk at once.

"...Celia, you made it, you made it..."

"Tessie...you look great! And Willie! I can't believe it. You've gained weight. Maybe I ought to join you down here..."

"Why not, Celia. It's the good life—"

Willie had indeed changed. His tall, angular frame had rounded out, and though he still strolled in that soft, fluid way, the wraithlike quality was gone. He moved now with a solid, graceful precision.

It took several minutes for Celia to regard Tessie, and she did so with a profound mixture of love, fear, and envy. The scar was barely visible, but the laugh lines around the mouth were etched deeply.

Tessie was not yet twenty-five, and Celia wondered if time or circumstance had put the lines there. She knew that in the face of a contemporary, one can usually assess the development—or deterioration—of one's self. The method was more accurate than any conventional mirror and, depending on the damage, infinitely more painful.

She gazed at Tessie's face now and wondered what must be happening to her own. But Tessie's coloring had burned to copper and her eyes were startling. She was laughing, excited and happy, and Celia was happy for her.

"Come on, girl," Tessie said, "we can finish cryin' in the car..." She turned and threw up her hands helplessly. "Willie, where's your manners. Introduce Marcus..."

In the excitement, Celia had laughed and cried, and when she calmed down, she still had not noticed the man lounging quietly against the low fence. At the mention of his name, he pulled himself erect and strolled forward.

"This is Marcus," said Willie, somewhat unnecessarily.

Celia gazed steadily as he approached, but when he drew near, she stepped back awkwardly.

...is this Marcus? Is this the man Tessie had written about... taller than Willie and twice as big...never said a word about how good looking he is...not a word...only that he had a gold tooth which she hated...Tessie must be going blind in her old age....

She lowered her gaze and extended her hand. "I'm glad to meet you..."

When he touched her, his hand was soft—as if he'd never lifted anything heavier than paper money. "I'm glad to meet you too," he said slowly. "I hope you have a pleasant visit."

Marcus was smiling, but Celia did not see the gold tooth. She was marveling at his eyes and, later, at the way the muscles moved in his arms as he took her luggage and swung it lightly into the trunk of the car.

Willie slid in beside Marcus and Tessie and Celia sat in the back, Tessie chattering excitedly as they pulled away from the line of cars and standing taxis.

The road leading away from the airport wound through a narrow valley and then eased into a steep climb, bringing them through the same fern-covered forest that Willie and Tessie had each come through earlier. Celia was amazed at the profusion of color, the vitality and variety of bird sounds. She looked from one window to the other as Tessie described and pointed. As she did so, she saw Marcus's eyes in the mirror.

He watched her for an instant, then focused again on the road.

The house that Tessie and Willie lived in looked deceptively small on the outside, but inside Willie had designed and constructed a winding wood staircase that led to a balcony containing two private sleep lofts. Under it was a huge banquette strewn with pillows. There was no clear delineation between kitchen, dining area, and living room, but the design and placement of minor accessories seemed to meld the major pieces together in one harmonious flow. Clerestory windows and sliding glass walls allowed the maximum intake of light, which filtered through a profusion of plants and sprinkled a pattern of yellow across the straw matting.

In the evening, to celebrate Celia's arrival, they visited several nightclubs, speeding in Marcus's Jaguar along warm, dark roads that seemed to Celia to wind into eternity. Tessie still chattered nonstop, describing and explaining.

They returned after midnight, and Celia fell into bed, more exhausted than she had ever been. She fell asleep instantly, and for the first time in a long time, she did not dream.

The next morning, Celia and Tessie had breakfast on the small flagged patio hidden in an orderly growth of eucalyptus and lime. It was eight o'clock, and already the heat of the day was closing in like an invisible net, trapping those beneath in a steamy vacuity. Despite the heat, the two women lingered over coffee long after Willie had left for work.

Celia looked around her and sighed. "You're very lucky, Tessie, very lucky..."

Tessie shrugged. "Some who don't know might call it luck, but you know the real story. I got a million marks to show for my luck." She lit a cigarette and lowered her voice. "Some things never leave you. Even now, sometimes, in the middle of the night, I wake up, listenin' to the wind against the windows and imagine all kinda things.... I can't go out alone through those trees after it gets dark... 'cause I see, or think I see, somethin' that's not there. After the sun goes down, I gotta have the lights on.... If Willie's not here, I keep the radio blastin'...and the thing is... I have nobody to talk to about it.... I tried to get mama to come here, not just to talk to me but knowin' she'll have a better life, but she absolutely refuses. Girl, I'm so glad to see you..."

Celia was quiet for a moment; then she said, "...I know how you feel, but still, you have a lot to be thankful for. Willie loves you."

Tessie heard the familiar, peculiar rise in Celia's voice and said, "Nuthin's changed, has it?"

"You mean Jonrobert. No. I haven't heard a word. It's almost as if he disappeared from the face of the earth and left me to wonder why for the rest of my life."

"No. Not that long. Things'll change. Just give it a chance. You'll see. Besides...you must be holdin' up pretty good. You look all right..."

"If I do, it's because misery agrees with me..."

Tessie crushed her cigarette out and reached for Celia's hand. "Come on, girl....what we gettin' into...next week is carnival, and you here for a story. Marcus has to show you around and introduce you to people...we don't need none a this—"

"I don't want to impose on Marcus..."

"Impose? You're kiddin'..."

"No, I'm not..."

Tessie paused, looking steadily at Celia. "You really haven't forgotten Jonrobert..."

Celia moved her shoulder slightly, "The feeling comes and goes... I guess I'm not trying too hard..."

The truth was that seeing Tessie and Willie together sharpened the memory of her own loss. Against her will, the occasional dull pain which she had learned to ignore was fast becoming an intolerable ache. She looked away, hoping that Tessie would not probe too deeply. "The feeling comes and goes," she said again.

"That's okay," Tessie whispered, "but sometimes, we gotta open up and allow room for other things. A broken heart is like an old sore...if you keep pickin' at it, it ain't never gonna heal..."

Celia did not answer.

...an old sore...the heart is the hardest working muscle in the body. Never has a chance to rest...even when it's old and sore... it keeps on beating after taking a beating...hearts don't break... they endure the dull pain of disappointment, which sometimes can be worse than any physical damage...

"It hurts..." she murmured, facing away from the table.

"Healin' usually hurts," replied Tessie quietly. "I oughtta know..."

35

Marcus took Celia to dinner in a small open-air restaurant overlooking the ocean. They ate in the close, elegant silence of linen-covered tables wrapped in the muted glow of candlelight. Low palms gave off a rush of soft sound in the warm night air.

They watched a cruise ship in the distance, its lights ablaze against the black sky, head for the open sea. Marcus looked at her and then smiled. "Girl, you watchin' that ship hard."

"Was I?"

"Yes. Hard. Like you wishin' you was on it..."

"No...oh, no...I was wondering..."

"What..."

"Nothing. Crazy things. Like how many people on board have said goodbye to someone that they didn't want to leave. Or how many are watching just as we're doing, knowing that the one on board is never coming back, despite all the promises. I was wondering who was crying..."

"...and who was laughing," he finished.

She looked at him, then looked away

Marcus refilled her wine glass; then he said, "In the States, what kinda work you do, girl?"

"I work for a magazine..."

"You write..."

"Not yet...at least not for them...on my own, I do a few things..."

She began to feel uncomfortable by his questions. If writing was what she wanted to do, how come she wasn't doing it?

"Poetry...I bet you write poetry..." he said.

"No..."

"You should," he said softly. "You shoulda been a poet. I never hear somebody take every inch a life so serious and make sad things... sad thoughts...sound so sweet..."

They continued the meal in silence.

...he knows...she thought. He knows everything about me. I can see it in his face that Tessie didn't miss a syllable. He knows about Jonrobert. I see that in his eyes. Well. That's all right. Saves time. In fact, some enterprising person ought to develop the idea into a business—take the chance out of romance, the sting out of a fling. If you don't have the time, let us investigate your love of the moment. Fill you in with all the salient facts. History in a hurry. If you don't know who, at least know why...

She felt cheated.

I have nothing to tell...she thought. Even the things that were left unsaid were left unsaid by someone else...

She was surprised to feel his hand on hers.

"Tessie. She write you a lot?"

Celia did not answer immediately....what he really wants to know is how much I know, she thought. He wants to know how much he can trust Tessie.

She drained her glass before she spoke.

"Tessie writes quite often. I suppose she's lonely for the old neighborhood, though God only knows why..."

Marcus's gaze did not leave her face, and she began to feel more uncomfortable....he knows about me. Why shouldn't I know a little about him. After all, Tessie didn't tell me everything...

"Tessie mentioned that you're in construction and Willie's joined you as a partner," she said blandly. "You must have brought back a lot of money from the States..."

Marcus touched her under the chin, holding her face steady. "You no good a lyin', girl, no good at all, at all..."

Celia started to laugh, although she was not certain if she was laughing at his sweet, lyrical accent or laughing because of the mystery surrounding him that he assumed she was privy to.

And he laughed because she was laughing and he liked the way she looked when she laughed.

* * *

In the car, she sank back against the leather seat. "This is beautiful. It must have cost a lot to bring it into the country..."

"Too much," Marcus replied as he maneuvered the car effortlessly. "This P.M. we got here, they nicknamed him Jessie James. Whole government really a bunch a crooks, girl..."

"From what I've read," Celia said, "I was under the impression that things were changing..."

"From what you read..." Marcus laughed. "It look good to read. Like in the States, where everything look good on tee-vee, even dog food. Well here, everything look good on paper, especially the lies. Maybe some little thing change here and there, but big things? Never change. Never no change. Now me? I not a big thing. I see how this wind blow and I make up my mind I gotta change fast. So I change..."

"How?"

He glanced at her quickly, then said, "I know Tessie tell you a little about me, so I can talk straight...long as you promise you won't write what I sayin'..."

Celia hesitated, surprised, and then said, "I came to do a story on carnival, nothing else."

"Good. Now, when this P.M. start his campaignin', I listen close. What I hear not so hot. Not good at all. But long before the campaignin' start, I was thinkin' a changin' this operation 'cause a what was goin' down. My people take all a risks shippin' the stuff out, and the man no wanna pay cash. All a sudden is payment in guns. Can't eat guns. Can't use a gun to stick somebody else up, 'cause the next man ain' got nuthin' either. My shipments stop for 'bout a month after I cuff in a coupla heads. Then is money again. But now is to watch for counterfeit. And girl, mark me, if that happen, then is murder for them and penitentiary for me..."

She listened without saying a word. Tessie had written, hinting at something like this, but she had only hinted. Now here he was, talking to her as if he had known her all his life.

"But I livin' with luck," he continued. "I see the way this man campaignin', he scare plenty, plenty people. He only mean to make small changes, but he scare plenty big people in the process. Lot a rich ones run. Chinese, Syrians, Indians, plenty start runnin'. They git rid a property cheap, cheap, cheap, and I buy cheap, cheap. A hundred parcels I pick up besides what my mother leave..."

"And what are you doing with it…?"

"Ah. I see you didn' believe Tessie. I really in construction. I take you tonight, no not tonight, tomorrow, I take you, show you house on house we buildin'…right now, I feel to dance…."

They approached a curve and Marcus did not slow down. Celia closed her eyes. "I'm sorry," she whispered, "I don't dance…"

She felt the light touch of his fingers on her knee for a fraction of a second.

"I noticed that last night…you don't dance…tonight I show you…"

They hit an expanse of road and Marcus accelerated. Tiny insects flitted before the far reach of the car's high beam, then swept to either side, disappearing in the dark wake. Celia could see nothing, but she felt the steep rise of the mountain to her left and heard, to her right, the insistent wash of the sea above the power of the car's engine. Marcus, Celia thought, drove just like Jonrobert, except that there had been no mountains or oceans, just an occasional traffic light which Jonrobert ignored. It seemed that both men allowed nothing to slow them down.

The brass band was coming on as they walked into the pavilion. They moved onto the crowded floor, and Celia hesitated. Marcus's fingers were under her chin. "Look up…don't worry about the steps…you'll get it…"

"I never—"

"Don't worry about it. Look up. You'll get it as you feel it…"

The music did not stop, and they did not sit down. They were on their feet as one band dissolved into another without missing a beat. At one point, Marcus swung her around until he was behind her, his hands heavy on her hips. He pressed into her, moving with the rhythm of the band. He held her tightly and laughed as she tried to wriggle away.

"Look around you…don't worry so…"

And the rhythm enveloped her, surrounded and swept through her, filling her with an energy she did not know she had. She felt him moving behind her, pressing into her as his arms locked around her waist on the crowded floor.

The tempo increased and she felt giddy as the dancers, arms stretched to the hot night sky, began to jump, up, down, up, down…

On the bandstand, a low chant began. Celia and Marcus were side-by-side now, moving in a long, crooked line with other dancers. The crowd took up the chant. It became a wail, nearly drowning out the music. On stage, the timbale solo ended and the brass section leaped to its feet and began to jam. Trombones and trumpets, pointed skyward, joined piano and percussion and brought the dance to a shrieking, ear-shattering climax.

The crowd fanned out and away from the pavilion, moving in loose clusters. Marcus and Celia moved with them. He leaned down and whispered, "How you feelin?"

"Fine," she said, smiling up at him. In fact, she felt at once exhausted and exhilarated, and the feeling was confusing. They walked several blocks before she became aware that his hand had slid easily from her shoulder and rested lightly on her hip. Reflexively, she placed her hand on his and eased him away.

On the way home, she fell asleep, and when he woke her, they were parked outside the tall, dense hedge of bamboo that defined the perimeter of Willie's and Tessie's home. She sat up quickly and for a fleeting second did not know where she was. Her eyes, when she rubbed them, had a grainy feel. She heard the movements of the morning birds and insects creeping soft and hesitant on the new air and saw the not-quite-dawn sky more gray than pink with faint streaks of yellow to hint at the coming heat of day.

"...I'm sorry...I haven't been out this late in a long time..."

"...is all right," Marcus said.

Something in his voice told her that he had been watching her as she slept and he knew that she had never been out this late.

"...what you doin' today...later...?" he asked.

"Meeting the editor, remember...?" She was glad for something to say.

"Oh. Yes. I nearly forgot. Two o'clock..." He laughed a soft, private laugh and finally said, "Listen, that man is a friend of mine, but he the original windbag. Don't let 'im wear your ear out..."

"He won't..."

"I want you save some for me...I ain' begin talkin' yet..." His tone was light but insistent. Celia did not look at him, but said, "You mean there's more..."

"Always more..."

He walked with her to the door, and she was glad because she did not want him to watch her as she walked away. She fumbled with the latch and then turned to him.

"Good night, Marcus..."

"Good mornin'...I meet you at four..."

"Fine..."

He walked away, and she let herself into the darkened house and stood for a minute in the silence. She did not go upstairs because she thought the wood might creak and she did not want to disturb the close, perfect, privacy of the house. She lay down on the banquette and wondered if Willie had made love to Tessie while she was out.

The car's engine cut smoothly into the silence, and she wondered about Marcus. She had felt good dancing with him, feeling the strength and heaviness of his arms.

The quiet closed in, bringing with it the familiar loneliness. This time the intensity surprised her. Willie and Tessie were upstairs. Marcus had just left. Yet she felt cut off, disconnected from her surroundings. She pulled the light blanket over her head in an effort to push the feeling away. An hour passed before she was able to fall into a dreamless sleep.

36

Celia liked the motto of the newspaper: "Today's News Today." She also liked the assistant editor, who invited her to lunch in a high-ceilinged restaurant in the center of town, a busy place where huge, wood-bladed fans churned and mixed the vibrant hum of conversation in the heavy air.

They were seated on the second-floor veranda below which scores of workmen, wet-skinned in the noon heat, labored to install barricades of chicken wire, corrugated tin, and iron bars to the fronts of the surrounding stores.

The editor was a round, jovial man who, as Marcus had predicted, enjoyed talking.

"Those stores," he said, pointing below, "are preparing for the annual onslaught..."

"Is carnival that serious?"

"It is, but not the way you imagine. Carnival, you know, is more than an event. It's a sensation, a feeling...a rhythm in the air, something that affects the mind so that on *j'ouvert* morning, everyone who has a breath of life is caught up in the spirit..."

Celia listened as he spoke, and the sound of his voice was like a key turning a lock, the tumblers falling precisely into place—the hand lifting the shade—the sign at the corner that transported her to the small, red-lit dance halls jammed to the door, where people melted into each other under the pressure of heavy brass rhythms. She saw panyards filled with high-strung police horses pawing the damp earth, straining against the clash of tempered steel drums. She felt the shimmering heat of the savannah as revelers by the thousands swept across its wide expanse in costumes that made the sun look dull.

The sound of the hammering intruded again, rising in agitated waves from below, as the editor described the classic, bloody, steelband confrontations of years ago, when smoldering disappointments became hard scores to settle in the frantic confusion of "Ol' Mas'." Children disappeared, hospitals were overwhelmed, and unclaimed bodies swelled in the heat of makeshift morgues.

Her fingers ached, but she could not put her pen down. This was a world unheard of, and she continued to record it, not knowing what questions to ask.

He glanced at her and smiled, and his voice softened. "Since time began, you know that man has been preoccupied with—well, there's been this mutual preoccupation—Bacchus and man, and man with his various gods, but I don't want to go into all of that. You'll see it, come *j'ouvert*...you'll feel exactly what I'm trying to say..."

What was this spirit, Celia wondered, that crept in on the high sound of the drums, melodic and mischievous, insinuating itself in the quick glance between man and woman...spirit heard in a whisper...felt in the soft pressure of a moon ray on a secluded beach...

She looked up to find the editor gazing absently at the workmen and the crowd surrounding them.

Was the interview over already? The strange euphoria she had been feeling drained away like water from a basin. A space yawned.

The inane questions she had planned to ask, then rejected, came out, one after another, not because the space needed filling somehow but because she had felt a hint of that nameless spirit each time she looked at Marcus.

She left the restaurant later than she intended and hurried to the corner where Marcus waited. He was leaning against the car watching the crowd as it eddied around him, noisy and anonymous. She walked slowly now, needing time to study him.

He turned, narrowing his eyes against the white sun, and moved, smiling, in her direction. She watched him walk, slow and controlled, and thought of his dancing the night before. His movements had been loose and sensual and, at the same time, private and protective, as if he had danced for her enjoyment alone.

She watched him now and at once felt the stifling heat close in. When they hurried back to the car, she was grateful for the air-conditioning and the cool, moist feel of the leather against the underside of her knees.

"...how it go?" he asked as he moved through the slow traffic.

"Not bad. I have about ten pages of notes...your friend's very interesting..."

"He talk a lot...?"

"Yes."

"He talk you into goin' out with him...?"

"Of course not." She glanced at him, surprised by the question, and then asked, "Was he supposed to?"

"I dunno...fete soon start...everybody lookin' a somethin'."

"...oh...and what happens after carnival...?"

"...well. Some hold on, last...others...they come in playin' and go back to as before...like nuthin'...thing is..." he said, looking at her, "is not to plan next week before you know about tomorrow..."

...but who's making plans, she wondered. She shrugged and kept quiet. This was a strange place.

The ride into the country was slower this time. Marcus stopped at two sites, speaking to the foreman at one and going over some prints with Willie at another. He returned to her and looked at his watch. "Your next appointment is in twenty minutes..."

Celia closed her eyes, imagining the speed with which Marcus intended to get her there. "Is it in town?" she asked, dreading the answer.

"No. Short way away from here. Short way..."

The engine turned over, quiet and efficient in the heaviness of the late afternoon, and they wound their way up a steep road crowded with the traffic of cars, bicycles, and people on foot.

"...people lettin' off earlier, the closer we come to fete...everybody goin' home to change up and go back to town...plenty dance, dance, and more dance..."

They turned off the road into a narrow driveway and came to a stop before a low bungalow whose stucco reflected pink and yellow in the sun. From behind the house came the furious barking of a dog, but Marcus did not hesitate before opening the door and swinging his legs out onto the graveled walk.

As he did, the front door of the house opened and a tall, aproned woman stepped out shaking her head apologetically.

"...he only just called, Marcus, to excuse himself...another emergency...something about one of the bands...this thing, year after year...takin' the man's life blood..."

She waved to Celia and invited them in for an iced drink.

"...is all right," Marcus said. "Tell 'im I call in the mornin', maybe set somethin' else up..."

They made their way down the hill against the flow of traffic until they came to a left fork which branched onto a one-lane road. On either side, spears of sugar cane, ten feet high, waved pale green and purple in the slight breeze, splashing a dappled pattern of light against the windshield. "Well...your meetin' canceled, so how 'bout a swim...?" he said, his eyes shifting briefly from the road to glance at her. She had been quiet too long. Now he watched as she shook her head and smiled.

"Swimming? I don't own a suit. I don't know what I was thinking of, but it didn't occur to me to buy one..."

"No suit...well...is all right..."

Inwardly, he was aware that he was becoming more and more interested in her. A woman, a girl really, who did not swim, dance, or smoke. And he could tell by the way she handled a glass that she did very little drinking. How, he wondered, had she and Tessie ever maintained a friendship. They were as different as night and day, and she was certainly different from most of the women he knew.

He thought of them, especially the tourists who invaded the beaches and lay like dried sea moss, tucking too much flesh, dead white or ash brown, into too little bathing suit—hiding hungry eyes and mournful faces behind designer glasses. And all propelled by a fine, thin, desperate need to connect and establish a memory to take back home.

And the locals, two days from the country with the dust still in their hair and on their tongues, infected by the desperate sophistication of the foreigners.

He read them, all of them, as easily as a child's primer, and he closed the book as quickly as he had opened it.

They made a left turn into a long, paved driveway faced on either side by low palms. The house at the end spread out low and white with a sloping roof of Spanish tile.

"Is this your place?" Celia asked and, not waiting for a reply, said, "It's beautiful."

"...is okay," Marcus said, pleased that she liked it.

They pulled to a stop, and he led her into the house. They walked through the adjoining rooms and out, through the sliding doors, onto the patio. He watched her walk to the edge of the pool and turn back.

"It's beautiful," she said again.

She walked toward him, her face partly shadowed from the sun at her back, but he could make out her eyes, which seemed to him remarkably innocent. He wanted, suddenly, to tell her that she was like the sunset that framed her, beautiful and mysterious and steady and strong, but it would have come out wrong because it made little sense to him. He had never spoken to a woman that way.

Whenever he had brought one home, there had always been the feverish race to discard clothing, dive into the water, and dry off in a bed full of promises later obliterated by gin and reefers.

As he watched her, he thought of Tessie's warning: "If you can't be nice, leave her alone. You have a thousand other women." He had gotten angry, wanting to know what the hell made

Tessie's friend so different. But when he met her at the airport, he had watched the way she stepped back when he approached. She had avoided his gaze in the car. And she avoided touching him except when they had danced. It was fear mixed with something he did not understand, and the little that Tessie had told him only added to the puzzle. He could not imagine this girl being conned by a pimp, let alone being mixed up with one.

He listened now as she sat beside him, chattering excitedly about a job which she obviously disliked, and he made up his mind. There was no rush, no need to hit and run...

He hummed a tune, privately...first day, okay; second day, don't delay; third day, walk away...

And one year during carnival, he'd had fifteen different women and woke up angry because he had missed las' lap. The finale. Never again. It was time to go slow.

"Well," he said, interrupting her, "how 'bout a little something to wet your whistle?"

He rose and she trailed behind him to the small bar. "Please, Marcus, not too much. I have another appointment in the morning..."

"I know, I know..." He reached behind the counter and assembled the ingredients for a rum punch. She stood, watching every move with wide eyes.

"Listen," he said, smiling at her apprehension, "I never give you more than you can handle..."

The hammock near the pool was lower than she had imagined and she enjoyed the smooth feel of canvas against her back. The oppressive heat weighed in and did more to persuade her to try on the offered swimsuit than a whole year of talking would have done. Marcus had been smart too, saying nothing, simply handing her the suit and disappearing into the small cabana-like enclosure and emerging in swim trunks at which she tried hard not to stare.

The sun was setting fast, and the after-light spread a blanket the color of old brick over the surface of the pool. The surrounding hills lost their detail in a sandy haze; in the distance, lights winked on here and there. The dusk had a calming effect. In the gathering shadows, she felt serene and private. A second drink and the bathing suit slid on easily. Her legs seemed hardly noticeable.

Marcus rose from the chair beside the hammock and strolled to the edge of the pool. She watched him walk, watched the half-light pick up the smooth curve of his back, his hips, the moving muscles in his legs. He raised his arms and prepared to drive. She saw his shoulders and the angle of his neck and wanted suddenly to call out to him, call him back, but if he came back, she wondered what she would say.

So she remained silent and he completed his dive. He swam the length of the pool, paused for a minute, and swam back, his arms cutting slow and graceful through the water.

She had the towel waiting when he came out, but he took it and dropped it in the chair. "Not yet…come on…"

The water was frigid. Celia eased down the ladder a step at a time. When the water crept to her waist, she stopped, unable to go further. Marcus, however, dived in again without hesitation, showering everything with a luminous spray. He surfaced and swam toward her.

"You wet a'ready. Why so slow?"

She clung to the ladder, afraid that he would pull her in further and faster than she cared to go. "I didn't expect it to be this cold," she whispered.

"Water deceivin', like everything else. But look, you shakin' like a leaf in a wind…we try tomorrow, noon, sun hot, water hot…"

The water flaked from his arms as he wrapped the large towel around her and, despite his private promise, eased her to him. They studied each other for less than an instant in the silence. When he finally kissed her, she hesitated only slightly before reaching up and putting her arms around him.

Then she moved away and crouched on the hammock, drawing the towel around her shoulders as if to compensate for a sharp and sudden loss of body heat. She watched him walk toward her, and she felt suddenly alone. In a strange place with a stranger, in the middle of nowhere.

He eased onto a cushion beside her. "What's wrong?" he whispered. She couldn't answer but drew her shoulders in a helpless gesture and turned away, unable to give voice to her feelings.

How could she tell him that something had drawn her to him

the moment she saw him? She felt it when she watched him walk... smooth and fluid and soft and controlled all at the same time... the way Jonrobert had been when he moved...free and easy...

Watching Marcus made the old ache come alive again, sliding up from a deep and hidden recess. Now she felt his hand move around and away from her leg, his fingers weightless as a night bird.

"Come," he said. "Get dressed. You cold so..."

He rose and walked to the house, not waiting for her to follow, and by the time she reached the door, he had disappeared into one of the bedrooms.

Once she had gotten dressed, she felt better. Marcus had returned to the patio and was sitting at the small bar when she emerged. The beige slacks, white silk shirt, and open sandals made him look more handsome than ever. She hesitated in the doorway for an instant, watching him.

...I must be crazy...is Jonrobert, the thought of him, going to interfere for the rest of my life...

She eased onto the chair near him.

"You like one for the road?" he asked.

"No, thank you..." Then she remembered his driving. "Well... yes." She watched the quick movements of his hands as he fixed the rum punch, handed her the tall frosted glass, then refilled his own. He took his seat beside her again and suddenly she wanted to touch him, to enfold herself in the warm, dark, depth of him.

...this is crazy...why didn't I do it when I had the chance... I'll be gone in three weeks and I'll never see him again...

"—You quiet...quiet..." he whispered, "think long, think wrong..."

"I know, Marcus, I know..." She stirred her drink absently. "I was thinking that in three weeks, I'll be gone. I'll never see you again..."

He held up his hand. "Don't plan funeral without the body... " She laughed at this, though the meaning was not entirely clear.

"—what ah'm sayin' is, three weeks is a long way away. Let time in between take care of itself, okay?"

She nodded. Why not, a part of her wanted to say, while another part struggled to suppress an old memory. It would be nice to "let go" finally, once and for all, and have done with it. How long was she going to hang on to something that no longer existed for her? All she really had was the pain. Was she more comfortable with that? Was she afraid to forget? Her mouth went dry, and she raised her glass. She drank and hoped she wasn't drinking too quickly. Then she turned halfway in her seat to face him.

"Let time take care...that's what I've been trying to do for almost... almost..."

He could have let her talk. He knew that the more a woman talked, dredging up old hurts, the more susceptible she became to the balming oil of new promises. He did not want that. He put his finger to her mouth, removed it, then kissed her lightly.

"Come..." he whispered, "let's go...everything be all right..."

The second interview was more informative, but less interesting. Celia's mind wandered as her host, a member of the carnival committee, discussed the impact of tourism on the water supply and the balance of payments.

Her pen moved automatically, and she wondered why she told Marcus that she had needed at least two hours with this man. She could have gotten the same information from the local library. Her host was dry as paper, and she marveled at how Marcus could come to know such a person.

They were served tea and pilot crackers. She glanced at her watch as she reached for her glass and prayed for Marcus to call. She was fed more facts about the temperature—its highs and lows, its effect on band performance. They were discussing the extent of corporate involvement and the varying amounts of prize money when the phone rang. Her host nodded as he extended the phone, and she smiled politely, hoping that her relief did not show.

"All finish?" Marcus asked, sounding far away.

She held the phone close and wished she were with him, wherever he was.

"...I'm just about...what time will you be here?"

"What time you want?"

How could she say "now" without offending her host. She hesitated, then compromised on fifteen minutes, knowing that wherever he was, he would arrive on the dot. She replaced the phone and returned to the topic at hand. The voice droned on, and she continued to write until she heard the squeal of tires in the driveway.

"We don't see much of you these days," said Tessie over the phone, "or nights either. How the hell you doin'? I was worried about you..."

"I'm fine, Tessie. Really, I am. Marcus is wonderful..."

"How do you mean that?"

Celia hesitated. She had so much to tell her but not over the phone where the connection was bad and the line of people behind her impatient. So she laughed and said, "Not the way you're thinking. He's really nice. I mean it. I was calling to tell you not to worry..."

There was a short silence before she heard Tessie's voice again. "Enjoy yourself, but be careful..."

"Where have I heard that before..."

"I can't imagine. See you when you get in..."

Celia hung up and made her way back through the crowded restaurant to the table where Marcus sat nursing a rum punch. He looked up as she approached; then he rose to pull her chair out. "What happen? They think I kidnap you?"

She nodded and sat down, feeling vaguely irritated. Then she felt guilty. "I told her that I was in good hands..."

"...are you?"

Something in his voice made her look up, but in the mauve-soft dimness of the room, she could read very little in his expression. His question hung in the air as she raised her glass and put the straw to her mouth.

...is he annoyed...or worried because Tessie is worried...?

By coming to visit Tessie, she had hoped to escape her mother's sharp concern for at least a few weeks. Now here were three other persons who seemed more worried than her mother. She wondered what she had done to precipitate this. Had she packed an attitude and brought it along with her other baggage? What had she done or said?

"...care for another...?"

She heard his voice and looked up. Her glass was empty and

the straw drawn thin from the intake of air. She glanced quickly around the room. The restaurant, all at once, seemed crowded, too filled with people laughing and talking. She wanted very much to be alone in a quiet place with this man who was shaking his head in amusement.

"Marcus, can't we just leave...I'm not hungry anymore."

"Maybe you ain' hungry now," he replied, "but later you gonna need somethin' under them ribs. Tonight is big dance, and nobody go home after. We jam right into *j'ouvert,* nonstop..."

"Nonstop?"

"Nonstop 'til we drop."

"Well. I'll have to go home and change my shoes..."

"Good. Then Tessie can inspect and see you all right, still in one piece..."

She reached for the menu, ignoring his steady gaze.

37

A dim light shone in the living room as Celia opened the door, and she knew that Tessie and Willie were not at home. The note on the dining table read: "Meet us at St. James dance hall. Best band in the land playing tonight. If we don't see you, we'll catch up with you on the square at sunrise. Wear flat shoes. Love, T and W."

She turned to Marcus. "Where is St. James?"

"Not far. Everybody be there tonight..."

"Well...I'd better go and change—"

She moved away, but he reached for her arm. "Wait a minute. I wanna tell you somethin'."

He guided her back to the sofa and she sat, studying him in the dim light. He looked more handsome than ever, but beyond the handsomeness, she felt that there existed, at the center of him, a certain rare gentleness and patience.

...why can't I tell him...why can't I tell him what I feel? Would he think I'm crazy...people don't fall in love this fast.

Love. The word caught her off guard and she held her breath. Until this moment, she had not allowed the thought to take shape in her consciousness. Now it echoed and scattered in her inner core like the sound of a shot in a narrow corridor. She felt dizzy, and her chest ached with each indrawn breath. His image wavered before her and she reached out, not so much to touch him—she was still afraid to do that—but to confirm the fact of his presence.

"Marcus..."

But he held up his hand, placing a lone finger against her mouth. "Wait...lemme say somethin' first..."

The sound of him was warm and soft as the night air. "You ever hear a carnival fever?" he whispered.

She shook her head, wondering if it were another name for that strange spirit the editor had spoken of. Before she could ask, he said softly, "I tell you what it is..." He leaned forward slightly, the planes and angles of his dark face seeming to absorb the light rather than reflect it, and his eyes appeared to focus on something beneath her surface.

"Carnival fever...is when a man and woman meet. And they dance and laugh and dance some more...and then music get hot... drink get strong...and all of a sudden, everything fly up to they brain and the head and heart get confuse and they want more of everything, especially each other..."

He shifted in the dim light and went on. "...is too simple the way I sayin' it, but that's the idea..."

She watched him, wondering why he had to define what he felt.

"...anyway, what ah'm sayin', or tryin' to say, is this thing here ain' no fever ah'm feelin'. Why you think I talk so much to you when first we went out? I tell you things I ain' never tell nobody... I trust you and I wan' you trust me. You ain' no stranger to me, you know...you never was...even when first I see you..."

She listened to him and the pressure within her became so great that only by opening her arms wide and reaching out could she imagine any relief. She threaded her fingers around his neck and buried her face in his chest.

"Hold me, Marcus...hold me..."

His arms closed around her, lifting her up. She kept her head to his shoulder as he moved to the stairs, and she felt the rhythm of his breathing and the tight bands of his stomach rise and fall with each step.

In her darkened room, they sat side by side on the edge of the bed, saying nothing, breathing slowly in the silence.

She crossed her arms and hesitantly pulled her dress over her head. The unexpected warmth of his mouth against the small of her back startled her, causing her to shift forward, but he held her and his fingers pressed into her stomach in a slow, circular motion. She lay back on the bed and slowly reached for him, searching for his mouth. He leaned over her, on hands and knees, waiting for her to hold him, to guide him slowly into her.

After a minute, he whispered, "...listen, listen...lie still...a minute...don' move, love...you hear?...don' move." They lay still, holding to each other in the dark. She felt his thighs heavy on her legs and his hands pressing against her face. She felt the irregular pumping of his heart, and the beat played against the rhythm in her temples and she was overcome with the dizziness a starving person feels when suddenly confronted with a feast.

"Marcus...don't let go...oh...don't let go of me..."

"No, love, never...you ready for me finally..." He put his arms around and under her to pull her to him. "...ah know you ready for me now..."

He could feel her hold her breath, then expel it slowly as he entered her. She began to move and his mouth covered her ear. He whispered, "that's it, baby...that's it...raise your legs...little more...that's it...a little more...ah, love...that's it...oh...oh..."

Now he began to move, and she wanted to cry out with joy, to tell him that she knew from the moment she saw him that he would be capable of this...of making her feel this way...From the moment she saw him, she had wanted him and had wanted to tell him so. She wanted to tell him now, but the words kept getting mixed up. She could not concentrate. Everything was feeling and feeling was everything, especially when he changed from slow and easy to hard and fast. She felt herself coming apart, coming out of herself, and it made her laugh and cry and open her mouth wide to drink the moisture that had gathered in the pit of his arm.

38

On Amistad Street, all the stores were boarded up, and at four a.m. the night held the dense blackness sometimes seen one hour before dawn. The trees were still. There were no bird sounds, and the air was thick and sweet and charged with an element Celia could not define. She walked arm in arm with Marcus and joined the small knots of people, drifting, slow and silent, past cluttered, dimly lit stalls. They paused near one of the vendors.

"We could use some coffee," Marcus said, reaching unsteadily into his pocket. He seemed remote and distracted, as if the effort involved in the transaction was too much for him.

Celia watched his hands.

The long, almost exquisite fingers which had moved over her with such strength were trembling in the shadow of the kerosene lantern.

...he's shaking...his hands are shaking...

She looked down at her own hands, trying to steady the plastic cup....but we're not drunk...or hung over...what's wrong with me...with us...

It took some minutes to realize that they had not slept, that once they had started to make love there had been no thought of stopping until the tension that had torn at them had been eased.

She felt weak and exhausted and wanted nothing more than to go to sleep in his arms. Sleep, love, and sleep again.

She turned to him and whispered, "Marcus...why don't we go back...we're falling apart...we've had no sleep..."

There was more she wanted to say, but, suddenly, a cannon blast split through the night, shattering the silence. Her cup slipped through her shaking fingers and splashed to the ground, scalding her legs.

"Aahaa! Aahaa!" Marcus shouted. He was suddenly alive. A different person. So was everyone else who just a moment ago had been gliding down the street like so many somnambulists. He grabbed her wrist and pulled her along to catch up with a heavy truck, one in a long line of flatbeds decked out with palm leaves and paper streamers and loaded with drums, bass, brass, congas, reeds, and rum.

The musicians on board hugged their instruments and angled

for position. They sat with legs swinging over the sides, upper bodies tense, listening for the one sharp note that would set the beat and hold it in the air above the shouting crowd. When it came, it was a long, loud sound, cracking through the sweet thickness. It seemed to rock the ponderous truck with its rhythm and surged over the tight crowd snaking in its wake. Even the earth over which they moved seemed to tremble.

The note sailed through the air and connected, and three more bands struck up at once. They poured out of the side streets onto the avenue, followed, then engulfed, by wave after wave of shouting, singing dancers holding banners and torches and half-filled bottles.

Marcus and Celia were pressed into the crowd and his face was transformed with excitement. "Come on! Come on! This is it!" She was bewildered. Nothing the editor had said prepared her for this. Before she could assimilate what was happening, Marcus's hands went to her hips and she felt as if she had been touched by an electric current.

All around was the cry of the road march riding the beat of brass and drums and hundreds of steel pans.

"...for this we carnival...this we bacchanal...we gon' jam... we gon' jam...come shake your bam-a-lam..."

They melted into each other, moving in a slow, tight, gyrating motion, falling back, easing, twisting, and all the while, their feet making a sheesh-sheesh sound in the dust. The inky sky streaked gray as more bands joined the procession, which now snaked and crisscrossed through narrow, winding alleys. The beat pounded against them in heavy waves, as if a million musicians had struck the same chord at once. Arms waving half-filled bottles reached into the air as if to pull the fading stars into the dusty turbulence.

"...left, right, and center, come shake your bam-a-lam..."

Celia could feel the sweat start at the center of her scalp, forming a thin river and dividing at the outer edge of each eyebrow, pausing to burn her eyes, then reforming at the drop-off point under her chin. She had no handkerchief, no purse, watch, ring, nothing.

...leave everything home, Marcus had warned.

Now she blinked rapidly and the sting of the salt intensified, pushing the scrambled images further out of focus.

...leave this too...he had said...When he had unfastened her brassiere in the dim light of the bedroom, she was surprised.

"Is this what everyone does? Maybe we ought to stay home..." She had been exhausted but didn't know how to tell him. He smiled at the look on her face. "Nobody stay home today. And you only gonna be dancin' with me. I wan' you leave it off..."

So she had left it on the floor near the bed and had come out to dance and shake her bam-a-lam and God knows what else. Her eyes burned and she wished she had a handkerchief and she wished she had her brassiere on.

"...shake, shake, shake...we gon' jam, jam, jam..."

She was moving, caught up spoon fashion against the dancer in front of her, pressed into the back of him, feeling the wings of his shoulders delve into the very soft parts of her every time he threw up his arms. She tried to shrink back but Marcus, pushing from the rear, mistook her motion and pressed forward, holding her just under her breasts.

She held her eyes closed, concentrating on the sound of the bass and brass rolling up from the dusty street. It grabbed at her ankles, shaking her knees and her waist, forcing her to sing even though she knew not one word of the road march.

Each step sent a shock vibrating upward to settle in her chest. Suddenly there was a shout. "Look! Moko jumbies!! Look!" The cry was all around her and she opened her eyes to a troupe of stilt dancers swaying fourteen feet high, moving slow and graceful against a pink and yellow sky. They hopped, halted, and pranced, waving their arms languidly for balance, and then pranced some more, their skirts of dried palm leaves shimmying nervously with each giant step.

...shake your bam-a-lam.... A kaleidoscope of images. Arms, heads, masks, bottles, drums, trees, trombones. They came together, then fell apart, contracting and expanding to the beat. Faster and faster, bright, dim, sharp, fuzzy, round, round, round, until everything came together in a remarkably soft implosion. She no longer felt the vibration. The tremulous feeling in her legs gave way to no feeling at all, and she was disembodied, floating high, high above the crowd, marveling that she was able to view this and every parade that ever was in one fast flutter of an eyelid.

When she opened her eyes again, she lay on the sidewalk on her back with her head in Marcus's lap. The crowd danced wildly around her. A man and a woman, in blinding costumes, bent down, singing, "...you must jam, jam, jam, come shake your bam-a-lam..."

The man extended a bottle. "Girl had enough? Too much?"

She stared at them vacantly as they stepped over her and moved away into the whirling vortex. She closed her eyes again, feeling no pain, just light-headed, dizzy, silly, drunk without being drunk. She opened her eyes when she felt Marcus's hand on her face.

"...are you all right?"

"I don't know. What happened...?"

"Take it easy...just take it easy...you be all right..."

She squeezed her eyes shut again, imagining that the beat of the passing bands was coming from inside her own brain. Her fatigue was such that if her heart had stopped just then, she would have welcomed it.

"Marcus..." she whispered.

He lifted her to a sitting position. "What is it, love, what is it..."

"I...am so...tired..."

"I know...I know..." He touched her face again. It was covered with grime and sweat, and she could feel the grit under the light pressure of his fingers.

"I know..." he said again.

His hands slid from her face to her neck to her shoulders as if testing for the smallest of fractures. "You gonna be all right..."

They managed to retreat through the crushing crowd by crawling under the barricades and dodging the tight, practiced turns of the mounted policemen. In the car, on the way home, he whispered, "No lovin', we just sleep..."

But she had not heard him. Her eyes were closed and her head was deep into the backrest, shifting imperceptibly with the car's rhythm. He looked at her and whispered, "We got a long, long time..."

39

She woke with the sun streaming through the louvered windows and felt, in the stillness, a sudden disorientation. She lay quietly for a minute, then rolled over in the wide bed. The movement awakened the memory of the night before, and the sudden pain in her legs made her feel old. She wanted to close her eyes again but glanced at the small nightstand and saw the note folded against the lamp. She reached for it quickly. It bore no heading but simply read: "Return at four. I love you. M" She studied the words, then lay back and placed the paper over her face, breathing slowly, feeling the note rise and flutter slightly with each outtake of air.

...I love you...I love you...

She rolled over again to lay facedown on his pillow, inhaling deeply.

...I love you...

His essence was in the pillow, the sheet, and when she lifted her arms, it came out of her pores. She wanted to remain there with eyes closed, breathing slowly to hold him and the memory to her.

...who invented the bath...why must I wash all this away... this is wonderful...delicious...

An hour later, she could no longer ignore the pain in her legs and padded out of the room to reluctantly bathe in a round, marble tub filled with rainwater and eucalyptus.

The waiting was hard. She took off her watch so that she wouldn't keep checking the time; then she began a letter to Frieda but tore it up after the second line. She made a tour of the house, restlessly examining the silent rooms crowded with furniture on which no one, she was sure, had sat.

She strolled outside to the pool but felt the sun was too hot. Inside, the air-conditioning was too cold. Then she remembered her notes and settled in an old wicker chair midway between the bedroom and the patio to rewrite, but once seated, she simply stared at the scrambled handwriting and could not remember what she was supposed to be writing about. From time to time, she looked up and studied the position of the sun and the shadows it cast on the overhanging banyan leaves and tried to calculate the hour.

She wrote for an hour and then the ring of the phone shook her....let it be him...let it be...

She picked it up on the second ring, and Tessie's voice came on, loud and insistent.

"How you doin', girl? We missed you again last night. Everything all right?"

"Oh, Tessie! I'm all right..."

"Well, you sound a little tired to me...like *j'ouvert* got to you. You better rest up. I'll call you later. Maybe we'll stop in..." They said goodby and Celia returned to her notes. When she could stand it no longer, she picked up her watch from the nighttable. It said four-twenty.

...it can't be...Marcus, where are you...

She was about to leave the room to find another clock when she heard the sound of the car. She rushed to the mirror to check her makeup but saw eyes red and swollen and stared at the irregular-shaped dark-purple marks on her neck, shoulders, and breasts.

...my, my... what strong teeth you have...she smiled to the mirror. She felt suddenly animated. Alive. The mirror shook slightly as the front door slammed. She heard the quick, heavy, footsteps and rushed to meet him.

He was smiling broadly. "Hey girl, aye, girl...you not just walkin', but you runnin' too...and look...body hot like nine-day love..."

He lifted her and held her against him. She felt wild and dizzy and put her arms around his shoulders, not wanting to let go.

He hugged her and said, "Guess where I been?"

"I don't know...I woke up and you weren't here...I don't want to guess...tell me..."

"Okay, I talk while we go for a drive..."

Celia preferred to remain in the house where it was close and private. She was about to tell him this but saw his preoccupied expression and followed him out to the car without a word.

He drove slowly and kept his eye on the road. There was very little traffic, and the silence that crept in above the sound of the engine reminded Celia of the long, lazy Sundays she had tried hard to get through when the library was closed and she was forbidden to go to the movies. Marcus still had not spoken, and she felt a fine apprehension settling in.

The road curved in a wide, green spiral and ended at the top of one of the highest mountains on the island. He parked the car off the road, and together they walked through a thicket of grape trees and sat in the shadow of the broad leaves.

The town and harbor spread below in a wide panorama of activity. They watched in silence as a seaplane scudded along the water, trailing a foamy wake. Fishing boats bobbed, toylike, at their moorings and then settled once more into the serene rhythm of the bay.

"I sat here a long time the day my mother died," he said suddenly. "I come back every now and then when I need to think straight..."

Celia glanced at him, wondering what he was thinking now. "It's a nice place..." she said, waiting for him to speak.

He took a deep breath, then whispered, "You leavin' soon..." The tension in his voice surprised her. After a moment in which she tried not to think about it, she answered, "Soon, yes..."

"Well, what you do...gonna do...when you get home?"

"Return to work, I guess. See if they like the story..."

"...and if they don't?"

Her shoulders lifted slightly and she stared out across the harbor. "...the little that I showed you is only a rough draft. It needs a lot of work, but I can do it..."

"...I know you can, but you didn't answer my question."

"If they don't like it, well...I don't know. I hadn't thought of any alternative..." Her voice trailed off.

"You must always have a choice," Marcus said, filling the silence. "It make you feel better when you know the difference between beggin' and bargainin'...but look now, we gettin' off the track...I went in town to talk to my friend..."

"What friend?"

"The editor..."

"What about?"

"You. We had a long talk. Serious. He likes you...the questions you asked. Said he would hire you...train you...if you interested..."

She pressed her hand to her mouth and stared at him, unable to speak. From the time she had stepped off the plane, still giddy with the tension of her first flight, the vague expectation she felt had grown sharper by the second. All her senses seemed to expand from one minute to the next. From the beginning, she had felt something, a physical difference that she could not define, but she knew that the reasons transcended even the feeling she had for Marcus:

Sun-bright mornings which pulled her out of bed with a sense of expectancy. Expecting what? She did not know, but she felt more alive, alert, eager to get on with the business of the day, whose possibilities seemed limitless.

In town, it seemed natural to smile at perfect strangers. She spent hours watching the market women, slow moving, serene, with straight spines and high behinds, graceful as queens. She felt a closeness, a kinship, that she did not at first understand but came to accept after realizing that they were no different from the old newsstand woman back home near the subway who counted out change in fingerless gloves on frigid mornings.

Television: Newscasters analyzing events and children singing the praises of pepsident all looked like her. It was as if a dull film had been removed from a mirror, enabling her finally to see her reflection.

She marveled at the very politicians Marcus complained about. Had they laid aside the stiff suits, stiff smiles, and stiff glad hand, they might have come from her own neighborhood. The rhetoric was the same, but more raw and passionate. She had left home and come home all in one motion.

She turned to Marcus, knowing that she did not have to confirm what she was feeling. "You want me to stay..."

He did not hesitate. "Yes. I wan' you to stay." Then without stopping, he said, "I know we got together quick, quick, but sometimes it happen like that...and you know...when things happen quick..."

"You're not sure..."

"I'm sure as I'll ever be about anything...I just wan' you to feel the same. I seen too many a these things start out hot, hot and mash up cold. I ain' lookin' a that..."

She shrugged....I wasn't looking for that either, she thought. ...I was not looking for anything...I was still confused, waiting for Jonrobert to come back and tell me what went wrong...now it doesn't matter...it finally doesn't matter.

A warm breeze eddied up from the well of banyan trees and scrub brush. The scented air surrounded her and spread a light film of moisture on her face. She wanted to be near Marcus and feel his arms around her, but she did not move. She remained in her small pool of silence.

...here it is, she thought...a new beginning...I never thought it would happen again...

She felt the quick, squeezing, not unpleasant sensation in her chest which left her breathless and giddy.

"I love you, Marcus...I love you..."

She lay her head on his shoulder and gazed out over the harbor, watching as a second plane circled low before landing. They appeared to be coming and going at twenty-minute intervals. Where, she wondered, were all the people going. Why weren't they content to remain in one place, this wonderful place?

But something quietly surfaced from the back of consciousness, overwhelming her present euphoria, and suddenly she said, "Marcus, I have to go back...I can't leave there just like that... not home so much as that job...I have to go back."

Marcus leaned back, propping himself on his elbows, and stared at her. "...you kiddin'...you jokin'..."

"No..." she said, shaking her head slowly, "no, I'm not..."

"I thought you wanted to—"

"I do. I want to, but not like that. As bad as it is, it will only be worse for whoever comes after me if I quit just like that...that's just what they're expecting..."

"But those people givin' you hard time, you think they gonna change? Never no change..."

"I don't expect them to. I don't have any illusions. What I have to show them is that I'm leaving by choice, not from any pressure they put on me. I've withstood enough to know that I can stand some more. But if I walk away now, they will do this to the next one that comes in there..."

Marcus looked at her as she gazed out over the harbor. She was, he thought, stronger than he had imagined. He wanted to smile, remembering all the others who had cried and begged him to let them stay. Or at least let them come back. And all the unanswered letters and telegrams that he had thrown into the wastebasket. Life was not that strange, his mother once told him, when one understands that what goes around finally comes around...

Celia did not understand when he said, "...I'll be damned. I'll be damned...."

Still, he could not believe it as he lay back in the deep grass and reached for her. "Let's talk about it later," he whispered, drawing her to him. "Right now, you makin' it hard on me..."

40

"I don't believe it," Tessie said. "I just don't believe it. Lightnin' strikin' twice, and you can't see it. What's wrong with you??" She moved in quick steps around the mahogany dining table, watching Celia. Celia returned her gaze, wondering why Tessie was so upset.

"Tessie, please. Calm down. One thing has nothing to do with the other. I know how I feel about Marcus, but I have to go back. I have to—"

"All you have to do is go back and pack your clothes. You can't be responsible for the whole world. You gotta live your life and only yours."

Celia shook her head slowly. She was tired of explaining. "I know, I know. But I also know what I went through on that job, and it's not over, Tessie. If I let it go like this, it'll never be over for me and that's that."

Tessie gazed at her, knowing that she had lost the argument but afraid to let the conversation end. She lit another cigarette and looked around for an ashtray.

...suppose Celia went back and go caught up in...suppose her mother...suppose...

She crushed the cigarette out and walked to the small bar to mix a drink, needing time to absorb this new development. Celia had become her lifeline in a sea of silence, a familiar face in a strange land where the inhabitants stared at her own streaked hair and drew an invisible shade over smiling faces.

Before Celia came, all Tessie had was Willie, but in many ways he too was one of them. He was born here and better able to see through the drawn shades.

Sometimes, in the quiet of the night, she would wake up and cling to him, sweating, trying to absorb the essence of whatever she imagined she needed to neutralize her otherness. She lay on him, listening in the dark to the steady rhythm of his breathing, and knew that as close as she was, she would always remain outside, separate and apart.

Which, after a time, was all right because, after failing to penetrate the drawn shades, she had given up and decided that they could all go fuck themselves. But that annoyed her too because they were able to do so in the company of each other, whereas she had only Willie and her own close, screaming silence.

...Celia has to stay....I need the sound of someone from the old time to help me remember when my mother was beautiful and loved me...I need someone who remembers the Apollo...and who can describe the color of my baby's eyes...we could talk and listen to Lady Day the way we used to ...and peel back and compare all the layers of sorrow...and disappointment...

Celia cut in: "Tessie, it's not that bad. My goodness, you're making this seem like the end of the world. What's the matter with you?"

Tessie hesitated, considering the question for a moment. Then she said in a low voice, "Nothing...nothing...it's just that...I don't really have anyone to talk to...Willie's gone all day and...I guess I don't know what to do with myself..."

Celia looked at her, surprised. "—you don't know what to do with yourself...did you ever consider working?"

Tessie shook her head and laughed. "I considered it all right. Many times. But that was as far as I got...Willie wants me home."

"How come?"

"I don't know. He says that when a man earns enough to support a wife, that wife does not work. It would be insulting to her husband."

"What??" Celia had never heard of such a situation.

"A wife, he says, takes care of hearth and home in this part of the world, nothing else."

"But Willie's not from this part of the world. I mean, he lived in New York for years. You said so yourself. He met you there."

"—and I followed him here. And when in Rome, we—"

"But this is not Rome," replied Celia. "When I return, I intend to work at that newspaper."

Tessie lit another cigarette. Celia watched the smoke rise and waited, but when Tessie remained silent, she asked, "Tessie, are you happy?"

"I am happy, I didn't mean to upset you, I just wanted to let you know that things aren't always what they seem. I mean, I'm happy, generally speaking. I have a man who loves me, who works hard and enjoys his work, and God knows that livin' here in this house is a world away from the life I lived before. It's quiet and peaceful and I'm finally able to get my last nerve together, but..."

"But what? What else do you want? Certainly you don't miss that wild life at that bar. The most glamorous thing about that place was the neon bird. If you went back for just one day, you'd see that it wasn't the same. You're remembering that life as it was. But I'll bet even the crowd's different now."

Tessie shrugged. "You're probably right. Anyway, I wasn't exactly pinin' for the good old days. My problem is here. Right now. I'm uptight even though I'm happy, and I can't explain why. I can't go anywhere. Willie says he wants me home, but in the back of his mind, I think that he thinks somethin' will happen to me again...I have nuthin' to do outside this house. I mean, how much cleanin' can I do...what is there left to clean? And this is the way it's going to be...this is the way we live...I must stay home..."

"...and you think Marcus feels the same way...about women?"

Again Tessie did not answer; Celia rose from the chair and walked to the window. The sun streamed in at oblique angles through the half-drawn blinds and appeared to slice the room at intervals with strong, white light. She shaded her eyes and scanned the blue-green hills in the distance, trying to locate the winding rise that led to Marcus's favorite spot—his thinking tree, he called it.

In the blue haze, one bit of vegetation looked like all the rest.

She turned from the window and watched as Tessie busied herself mixing drinks.

"Anyway," Tessie said, "I'm not really trained to do anything, but you are. You have an education...some background...that might make a difference."

She handed Celia a glass. "...and Marcus might allow you to work on that paper—"

"Allow me?" Celia had raised the glass but put it down. "Allow me?"

"Well...maybe that isn't exactly the right word, but he'll be happy as long as you don't take the work seriously. As long as that paper doesn't pull you away from him..."

The room was silent and Celia could hear her own thoughts beat like the sharp wings of some small bird, whirring against another part of her.

"Listen," she said quietly, "I had one father who died the night I was born. Since then, it's been Al and Sam and Dan working with my mother, telling me what to do, where to go, and how to get there. I'm tired, I'm tired. I'm not going through any more restricted duty with anyone, I—"

"Celia, I didn't mean it. I didn't mean it that way..." Tessie said quickly. She did not, under any circumstance, want to discourage her.

Celia looked at Tessie and then looked away. She couldn't figure out who was becoming more upset. "Listen," she said, changing the subject, "did Marcus...did he ever talk to you about me?"

"He said you were different," Tessie smiled now, relieved.

"Different...in what way?"

"Well...you weren't lookin' for a man...you were lookin' for a story...he couldn't believe it..."

"Why not?"

"Past experience," Tessie said, sipping her drink. "A lot of these men are—"

She stopped and raised her glass to her mouth again.

...a lot of these men, she wanted to say, are like peacocks—either you function in their shadow or you don't function at all...

When she lowered her glass, Celia was still gazing at her, waiting.

"...what were you saying..."

"Nothing much...a lot of these men are...spoiled senseless..."

"By whom?"

"...the tourists..."

"I see."

The two women looked at each other in the silence, and Celia wondered what Tessie had really wanted to say. But they had argued enough. She felt tired. It occurred to her that Marcus never really said anything about their relationship beyond her returning and working at the paper. They were going to take it slow. One step at a time, he said.

She sighed. The sunlight had given her a headache, and she wanted to lie down.

...I should speak to him...get this whole thing, whatever it is, cleared up before I leave...but what can I ask him?

She started up the stairs, taking soft steps to avoid enlarging the steady pain across her brow. "I think," she said quietly, "that we're making a big thing out of nothing. He offered me a job, not marriage..."

"He loves you," Tessie said. "Don't kid yourself. That can be a full-time job."

41

The taxi moved quickly up the East River Drive under the shadow of the impenetrable luxury that at once enclosed and shut out the rest of the city. There were, however, infrequent breaches in the wall of money, and the grime managed to seep through at unsuspecting intervals. Celia looked at the gray facades and wondered what it was about returning home that made the houses seem so dull and the streets appear so narrow and crowded.

She turned from the window and looked down at her hands; then she held her right hand up and spread her fingers wide. The light caught the circle of jade and gold on her finger and she stared at the bright reflection, still surprised and fascinated.

"A present," Marcus had said, "...a reminder that you comin' back..."

At the airport she had hidden her face near his shoulder and cried so hard that Tessie and Willie turned away, embarrassed.

"Listen," Marcus said, "remember that night we watch that ship sail...and remember what we talked about then...about who was stayin' and who was leavin'...remember? Well, it happens to everyone, one time or another...is our turn now, that's all...is our turn... only difference is, you comin' back...you really comin' back..."

His arms had closed so tightly around her that she could barely breathe, but she did not want him to let go. When he finally did and she moved through the departure gate, she was still nearly breathless.

Tessie had given her an envelope to give to her mother, but she could not recall the message that was supposed to accompany it. She did not recall the meal served or the hours she was in the air.

As the plane circled, preparing for its final approach, she had become awake, anxious to reach home, not to see Frieda or Al or the twins, but to retreat to the small, closed cubicle of her room to wait for Marcus's phone call. She pressed her hands together and squeezed the metal against the flesh of her finger until it hurt.

The cab pulled into the block and she noticed that the plate-glass window of Groovy Movers needed washing. Across the avenue, the neon of the Peacock blinked dully against its shabby facade. She thought about this as Al and the twins rushed to welcome her.

"Why didn't you buzz? We coulda come and picked you up..."

"You lookin' good, kid. First time I ever seen a chocolate tan..."

"How was the trip? How was flyin—"

They crowded around her, voices vibrant with the rhythm of excitement heard only in their city and in their neighborhood. Even as they inquired of her adventure, their tone implied that anyone who left, even for a day, was certain to miss some event of enormous magnitude.

Celia listened to them, feeling a small moment of confusion. She was glad to see them but not glad to be home. Finally, she said, "I had a wonderful time...the trip was beautiful...how's mother...did everyone get my cards...?"

Al picked up the luggage and smiled. "You know your mama missed you, but everything's everything..."

The four entered the lobby, passing the wide-eyed, silent stoop watchers.

Once inside, Celia shook her head. "...nothing's changed..."

"What'd you expect?" Dan asked. "A welcome mat for doin' somethin' they only dreamed about?"

Upstairs, a door opened. Frieda had heard their voices. "You're back! You're back!"

Celia felt her mother's rapid heartbeat as they embraced. Then, stepping back, she saw that her mother looked different, slightly older. Small lines that Celia had not seen before appeared now like mahogany parentheses defining the boundaries of her smile. But her face seemed full and her eyes had not changed, and Celia was still fascinated by their depth and luminosity.

For a brief moment, she was able to regard her mother the way she would stare at a stranger, and at once she felt Al's dilemma: He loved Frieda, but he simply did not know what to do with her. Her mother, consciously or not, controlled him as well as Sam and Dan. They would have killed to keep her small world in place.

...and that's why they...we...are all still here, Celia thought.

She felt tired as they walked into the dining room.

"You the talk of the block," Sam said. "Ain't too many get to take a trip like this. How was it? Don't leave nuthin' out..."

She settled into a chair and talked for nearly an hour before Al noticed the ring.

"Don't tell us you went down there in all that confusion and eloped..."

Eyes darted from face to finger, and Celia felt, rather than saw, her mother flinch.

"...yes...that's a lovely ring, Celia...is it a souvenir?"

Celia shook her head, amazed at the ease with which some problems resolved themselves. Before Al had spoken, she had no idea how she would approach the subject. Now, seated around the familiar dining table, with its high-polished sheen, she found the solution.

"I met someone..." she said slowly, "who...asked me...uh, he asked me to marry him, and I said yes..."

She held her breath, trying to absorb this stroke of genius; then just as quickly, she felt fear. Why had she lied? Marcus had spoken of a job, not marriage. Perhaps not, but he loved her and one thing was sure to lead to another, so why not? Despite her fear, she felt exhilarated.

The reaction, predictable as it was, still unnerved her. Al and Frieda simply stared, while Sam and Dan moved casually toward the small liquor cabinet near the corner of the room.

It was useless trying to avoid Frieda's stare, and now Celia felt the strain and fatigue of having left Marcus begin to settle in. She tried to hold the feeling at bay, but it descended, like fog, damp and chilling.

The first words, as she had expected, came from Frieda.

"...what have you done..."

...I lied, she wanted to say. I lied...trying to find a way out... But instead, she remained silent and shifted her gaze to Al. His expression was confusing, and she was not certain if she read his signals correctly. His eyes had a 'can't-let-you-go-nowhere-without-you-acting-up' look, yet the thin smile that he tried to control seemed to say, "I knew you could do it..."

...but it's a lie...I'm not getting married...

She blinked away from him as five glasses and a decanter materialized through the swift skill of Sam and Dan, who still had not uttered a sound. Four glasses were filled. No ice. No chaser. Clearly, they were not toasting what should have been good news.

Above the clinking glasses, Frieda tried again, her tone implying a wire-thin control: "Celia, what did you do?"

The question floated in the air as Celia reached across the table for the unfilled glass. The four stared as she poured a drink and raised it to her mouth in a swift, neat motion that might have spoken of years of practice.

But the alcohol cut into her throat, forcing her to remain silent longer than she had intended. Finally, when her tongue regained some feeling, she said, "It's true. It's true."

...and nothing, not a syllable beyond that, would make it any clearer...what do they want...what do they expect...

She waited, watching her mother's eyes take on a flattened, faraway look. The luminosity faded, and she knew that Frieda had stopped listening.

The quiet around the table was like a suspension, at once light and fluid and solid and heavy. She imagined she could hear, in the silence, the sound of the ice cubes melting.

...let time melt...let an age pass...these changes that I'm waiting for...will never come...

She excused herself and left them. In her room, she lay across the bed, gazing around her. Nothing had been moved. Her books were still stacked on the shelves that Al had built; the place was dust-free and pretty, and it still reflected the condition of a very young girl. The ruffled curtains that Frieda had made still moved when the wind did, and on the dressing table, the young-old face of her father still smiled out at the world from its protective guilt frame.

The murmur in the dining room was low, as if in deference to the dead. Celia eased off the bed and closed the door. In the dark, the room no longer belonged to her, and the excitement of homecoming, the last heady remnants that one feels when returning to the familiar, finally vanished.

She touched the bed again, the palms of her hands fanning the sheets. They were cold and smooth to the touch, and she became aware of the new tension creeping in.

...Marcus...please call...call...you said you would...don't let me down...don't make this any worse...

Tears bit at the corners of her eyes.

She heard the ring and snapped awake. Her mouth tasted of the sour residue of alcohol, and her legs felt stiff because she had fallen asleep with her shoes on. She did not hear Frieda stir and guessed that she was alone in the house. The phone rang again as she rushed to pick it up.

"Celia...?"

Marcus's voice held the deep resonance of distance, and she strained to hear him, to catch every sound.

"Marcus! I'm here. What happened...what—"

"—I miss you, girl...I went and got drunk and I'm still drunk. I miss you...oh, girl..."

She held the phone so tightly that her fingers hurt. "Marcus, listen, I love...I love you. I miss you more than I know how to say—"

Loneliness brought her voice low. Her chest ached, and she finally started to cry.

"...don't, baby...don't cry," Marcus whispered. "Ever'thing be all right...go to sleep...I call tomorrow...when I'm straight...we talk longer...I love you..."

Before she could reply, the phone went dead and she sat listening to the hollow buzzing. Finally, she replaced the receiver and walked to the bathroom to brush the taste of alcohol from her mouth.

A tune, thin and sad, drifted in through the open window and she had to strain to make out its meaning. She gave up a minute later, deciding that another layer of someone else's sorrow was more than she could bear.

She leaned over the basin and pressed her head against the mirror, lightly, trying to absorb some relief from the cold surface and trying to figure out how she would go about embroidering the lie.

42

September 1964

It was generally assumed that the conditions that had persuaded the French to relinquish their interest in southeast Asia could be remedied with a fresh infusion of muscle and money, both of which America had.

Ten years earlier, the single geographical entity had had "north" and "south" appended by political legerdemain, and two new countries had come into being. The French, who had been there since the time of Napoleon III, took a breather, and America stepped in to pick up the slack. The planned devastation blew home on hot winds, drawing a new generation from the crowded street corners.

This time around, thoroughly disenchanted, the corner crowd went kicking and screaming. When "Uncle" Sam sent greetings, the recipients said, "hell no," contending that if they had to die, it made more sense to do it right at home, on their own turf, fighting the new war on poverty. The Washington march, fraught with drama and purpose, had raised consciousness, and consciousness now was raising hell.

Better to fight at home. The heat of earlier demonstrations still warmed the blood, and the skirmishes were consistent enough to cause alarm. In the uneven arithmetic of the opposition, two Afros plus one dashiki equaled one potential disturbance. The specter of riot was everywhere, but when the demonstrators chanted for jobs, industry balked: "Are you qualified?" business wanted to know, throwing the usual "stuff" in the game, always setting up obstacles.

"We always were and you know it!!" came the reply, in traditional call and response fashion.

Qualified! Corporate spines shivered. What had this country come to? Hadn't The Plan been accelerated: To expand dope, extinguish hope—and pack the prisons to wipe out the promise of future generations? What had gone wrong? Too many of the intended victims, like the old defiant ones of a century ago, had eluded the net, circumvented their circumstance, and by hook, crook, finesse, and fortitude had become qualified.

So Vietnam was timely. The wide net of mobilization pulled them in, qualifying the unqualified for the art of murder and mayhem, and in the end, mixed and fed them like so much fertilizer into the already blood-rich, foreign soil.

The aspect of the neighborhood changed again. The bar stools in the Peacock emptied, and small but definite voids appeared in the littered basketball court in the middle of the block as the postman delivered greetings by the dozen.

The women, made more nervous by the prospect of coping with yet another round of broken bodies, whispered in agitation: "Who's next?"

At Hobson's, the wind blew in lightly. The chairman had tried to buy a deferment for his son, but the last campaign contribution had not been significant. The boy was drafted and became an early, celebrated, casualty. Hobson's closed for the day, and Celia watched in silence as everyone else mourned.

She had been back three weeks, and with the exception of Mr. Arnold in the mail room and Mr. Wingate, who seemed glad to see her, everyone else pretended that she had never gone away (or had never come back).

But the impact of the silence was different. The anger that had drained her was gone, replaced with a quiet anticipation, since Mr. Wingate had given her article to the travel editor.

"He likes it. He's going to use it in the holiday issue, but keep quiet about it until you see it in print..."

Keep quiet! She wanted to dial her mother, Al, the twins, Marcus, Tessie, the whole world and tell them, but she hesitated to use the phone because she saw visions of Sophie lurking everywhere, eavesdropping.

She remained silent, but even so, in a matter of hours, the news was all over the office. The rage behind Sophie's smile when Celia encountered her warned that the woman still had the power and the will to sabotage her.

Celia watched her as she moved away, her hard, square heels digging into the soft pile of the carpet.

She's upset...really upset...that means the article's good, probably better than she expected...

Celia waited in silence for the elevator, walked through the crowded lobby, and, though she was not hungry, decided to see Lu-Ann.

The restaurant was filled with the thick, regimented, noontime chaos in which the chatter of waitresses competed with the clatter of the silverware and cash register.

She had almost forgotten what it was like to sit at a lunch counter. Someone vacated a seat and Celia, not quite back into the rhythm of things, was cut off by someone with a sharper palate and less time in which to satisfy it.

When Celia finally sat down, Lu-Ann paused longer than usual: "Welcome back. Somethin' down there sure musta agreed with you...you lookin' like new money."

Several diners within the wide sound of Lu-Ann's voice paused to inspect the currency. Celia stared at the menu until their curiosity was satisfied; then she ordered a bowl of soup and concentrated on its steaming contents.

What was it Lu-Ann saw? The thin red strip of wrist where her watchband had slipped? The bridge of her nose where the sunglasses had rested? Had she seen something beyond the "chocolate tan" that the twins teased her about? Or had she seen what Frieda had seen and refused to recognize.

...it doesn't matter...I'm going back...I know I'm going back...

The afternoon passed in the usual silence, and she knew without looking up exactly when five o'clock had arrived. The approaching footsteps of the other secretaries signaled the final phase of a daily ritual she had forgotten about: each, in turn, passed her desk, paused to say good night to Mr. Wingate, and moved on as if she were not sitting there.

She did not blink an eyelash.

...they think they're reacting now. Just wait until the article is in print...

The elevator closed, blanking out the faces of the last giggling group. Celia gathered her gloves and purse, said good night to Mr. Wingate, and left.

In the lobby, the revolving door cast the reflection of Mr. Arnold pushing gently on the partition behind her, signaling her to wait.

Outside, he touched two fingers to the brim of his plaid cap that hung at an angle over his brow. His sparse gray hair was covered, and he looked twenty years younger.

"Do you have time for a cup of tea?" he asked as he fell in step beside her.

A cup of tea. It was the sort of invitation she imagined her grandmother might have extended, had circumstances been different.

In the restaurant, Mr. Arnold removed his cap, restoring the lost twenty years. "That was a nice article..." he said.

Celia gazed at him, trying not to show surprise. "You read it?"

They both paused for the waitress to move away, and then he replied, "There's very little that I don't read in that place..."

The waitress returned, and he stirred the cup that was placed before him. He seemed to be waiting for Celia to respond.

But Celia raised her own cup and wondered...how could he... the envelope was sealed and given directly to the travel editor...it was sealed...

"You know," Mr. Arnold said quietly, when it became apparent that Celia was not going to say anything, "I've been with this company nearly thirty years. Met Hobson when he was a proofreader with another firm. I was working freight then. Times got hard; the place folded. Hobson had nothing to do but strike out for himself. Went into textbooks, medical books. Things picked up and he did all right for himself. This magazine is a spin-off, light, fun stuff. The serious business is on the eighth and ninth floors, where the texts are put together..."

"That's interesting, but what has that to do with me..."

"Who knows...you might get to the ninth floor. Too bad Hobson's gone. He would've liked you right off.... If he was here, there'd be no question about it. He'd like you..."

"Well, he died five years before I even knew I was coming here. He should have left something in his will instructing his employees to be kind to black folks..."

"Wouldn't have helped. We still gonna have people like Sophie no matter what...and that's what I want to talk to you about."

Celia replaced her cup carefully into the groove of the saucer and studied the imprint of her lipstick on the rim. The faint-mauve color contrasted with the busy, bright-red rose pattern of the cup, and she thought of Marcus. ...he likes this color...said it was quiet... like me...

She had bought ten tubes of the color when she returned home, and packed them, along with lingerie and other clothing, into a small trunk. She had made a list and comforted herself daily checking off small items.

She looked up from the imprinted cup and said, "What can Sophie do to me?"

"That's what we have to talk about..." He signaled the waitress for more tea, but Celia declined, feeling a sudden, peculiar fatigue. She wanted to get home, close herself in her room, and count lipsticks until the phone revived her.

I can't stand this...I can't stand it...

She felt her fingers close around the empty cup, which seemed as fragile as an eggshell. She pressed lightly, feeling the pressure of the ring against her finger.

"You know, Mr. Arnold, I plan to—"

She was going to tell him about Marcus, but he raised his hand. "Are you all right? I didn't upset you with this news, did I?"

"No, I...no..."

Should she tell him? She saw concern in his face, but could she trust him enough to let him know that she cared not one iota about Sophie's intrigues or any other petty plot hatching at Hobson.

She finally accepted the second cup of tea and tried to calculate his motives. How had he survived thirty years at Hobson? How could he guarantee anything?

She remembered his blank stare the day she had come to work and assumed it was part of the protective mask some black folks slipped on, signaling to all who looked for reassurance that he had nothing to do with the newcomer or her nappy haircut. Why, if it were left up to him, he'd have that red-hot straightening comb doing its duty restoring order in less time than it took to blink. He'd even straighten her eyebrows if that's what the boss wanted.

But the mask deceived. She remembered him staring as she walked in a sea of silence that day, and she had stared back, wanting to get away from him faster than she had wanted to run from Sophie. Then he spoke, the rolling bass of his voice shaking her, then easing, with a greeting that signaled unexpected and (at the time) incredible self-assurance.

Perhaps she should tell him.

Instead, she said, "Mr. Arnold, I appreciate what you're doing, but please, don't get in any trouble..."

"Trouble?"

"Because of me. With Sophie."

He tried to laugh but only managed a smile that was small and neat like the rest of him. "Won't be any. Let me tell you something. A little background. Hobson was a strange fellow. In the old days, he'd come in with a quiet 'good morning,' and you could see in his face that he had to be left alone that day, sometimes two or three days. Wife had been sick for years and he was devoted to her, but there were days when it took something out of him.

"Sometimes two, three in the morning, my phone would ring and it'd be him: 'Let's go fishing in the morning, Arnold, what do you say?'

"'Why not...'

"Except that his idea of morning was one hour from the time he called. He'd be out in front of the house, not leaning on the horn, but sort of hitting it in short beeps, trying to wake only me instead of the neighbors, and five a.m. we'd be sitting in a rowboat in the middle of a glass lake, nursing a quart of Scotch, watching the sun break over the trees. Here was a man could've bought a yacht and sailed around the world, but he preferred that little rowboat..."

"What did you talk about..."

"Nothing much. Sometimes company stuff, sometimes not. I ran mail and supply and knew just who was stealing what, but we didn't always talk. Most of the time it was just fishing. Quiet. Anyway, his wife died, and Sophie, who was his secretary at the time, thought she saw an opening. She was young then, and not too bad looking, but even at that age she had a hardness, a meanness of spirit that a blind man could feel. No makeup could hide it. Anyway, Hobson wasn't interested. Stopped her cold. Put her in charge of a department because she was very efficient, and he admired her for that, but otherwise he wasn't interested.

"So. Here she was, thirty-five, unmarried, and miserable as hell, but she wasn't about to give up."

"—what did she do? What could anyone do when someone's not interested in them?" Celia asked, thinking of Jonrobert and feeling a small sudden shock of recognition. She watched Mr. Arnold across the table. He played with the cup, tipping it over the saucer once or twice before answering.

"She tried to recruit me, thinking I could help her..."

"Recruit you? I'm surprised..."

"If anyone knew, they'd really be surprised. Sophie doesn't hate black folks in particular, she hates folks in general. Period. Hobson knew that. And how do you think she feels about those other secretaries...think she likes them any more than she likes you? No. The only difference is the other secretaries bend to kiss her behind. They bend all the time, by degrees, and since they're all the same color, you don't notice it. You see race in everything and don't bend at all..."

Celia wanted to tell him that the problem of race deprived her of a grandfather and a father, but she would mention it at another time, when she got to know him better. Instead, she said: "I'm sorry, but that's the way—"

"I know. I know. Eventually, you'll come to see that they're all not the same. They can't be. Anyway, she recruited me. Wanted me to explain her good qualities to Hobson, in case he'd overlooked something..."

"That must have taxed your power of imagination..."

"Well..." he coughed delicately. "I don't know how to say this, but that's not all she taxed..."

Celia put her cup down, wondering if she had heard him correctly and if she had, should she believe him.

"What do you mean...?"

"I mean that some things have a way of happening that no one can account for. I know I can't. She used to come to supply and sit and talk for hours after work. First about Hobson. Then mainly about herself.

"One night, she called, wanting me to bring some papers to her place. She had forgotten them, she said.

"I brought the papers, and she talked some more. Couldn't stop explaining herself, her 'qualities' as she called them. Talked so long and fast, I was beginning to get nervous. Then she stopped and started crying."

He shook his head and drew a deep breath. "You'd be surprised how things...just...have a way of happening," he whispered. "This went on for years. At first, we were scared to death that someone in the company would catch on. But after a while, we didn't care. Sometimes, I'd just be getting home and the phone'd ring and it'd be Hobson talking fishing. I'd snatch one hour's sleep and back out I'd go. Several times, I nearly fell out of the boat, I was so sleepy..."

Celia listened, amazed. Mr. Arnold's predicament must certainly have been funny at the time, but her mind was frozen at the point of his revelation of his involvement with Sophie.

Short, angular Sophie, with the big, heavy, square heels that dug into the carpet as if they were grinding underfoot all her real and imagined enemies.

It was difficult to imagine her in tears. Or in a negligee, sheer, shimmering, moving from bath to bed, where Mr. Arnold waited.

"Things just happened," Mr. Arnold said again. "And after a while she never mentioned Hobson to me. I'm telling you all this so you'll see that there's no threat to you." He lowered his voice and went on, "...and to make you see that there's a great difference between power, such as it is, and the appearance of power."

Celia did not understand but nodded her head anyway. Power was an abstraction that she could explore later. At the moment, she was interested only in Sophie's interest in Mr. Arnold. As he spoke, she gazed at him in a new light. His features were rather ordinary in a medium-brown face, and she wondered if he had always worn round, wire-rimmed glasses. He was about her height, and his frame was neat and compact.

She suppressed a smile, unable to understand what they had found in each other to hold them together all those years. When he spoke, his voice always had that self-assured quality, but what else, Celia wondered. What else?

She watched now as he played with the cup, his fingers elongated and exquisite. She suddenly remembered Marcus's hands and felt herself growing warm and uncomfortable.

...poor, lucky, wretched Sophie...

Celia wanted to know how and why the affair had ended. Instead, she whispered, "Did Hobson ever find out?"

Mr. Arnold smiled. "Yes and no. For one thing, I ended it because I had met someone else. A home girl I wanted to get serious with. That didn't work out either, but that's another story. Another thing was Hobson died. Left me a couple hundred shares, a job for as long as I wanted to work, and a letter I opened the minute I got back from the funeral and could lock the door.

"It read: 'Thanks for taking care of that problem with Sophie for me.'

"That one line. That's all he said. It shook me to my shoes that he knew all along. If it had been anyone else, I would've been fired or jailed. He could have thrown me overboard one of those mornings when I had fallen asleep. Instead, he left me that letter. If Sophie makes a move against you..."

He held his hands in a tight semicircle in the silence and then closed his exquisite fingers.

Celia had to tell him then. She spoke in a rush about the small trunk she had been filling and spoke of things she could not tell her mother. When she had finished, she was out of breath.

Mr. Arnold was quiet for several minutes; then he sighed.

"That's a real disappointment. Seems to me you're doing things in reverse. You know how many people are struggling to get from there to here? To leave where you're going in order to arrive at where you're leaving? Think about it. I'm not saying that Hobson's is any bed of roses. Far from it. You're going to have to fight every step of the way, because of the weaknesses in the people controlling the system that controls you. But you can do it. You're strong enough. And Wingate is a decent enough fellow. He can open doors. In fact, he's doing that for you now. And I can help in ways he never heard of..."

They looked at each other across the table until Celia finally looked away.

...stay and fight...be strong...but what about Marcus? being with him might be a fight too if I insist on working at the paper ...and if I stay here, I'm still going to have to fight mother's nervous concern every time I make a move...no matter which way I go...it will be a fight...

They walked to the subway, allowing the quiet between them to be filled by the sounds of fruit vendors and paperboys shouting and rushing to unload the remnants of the day's stock on the late commuters.

At the entrance, Mr. Arnold paused. "Why couldn't you have settled for a New York man. There're—"

"—it's not only the man, Mr. Arnold. It's the job. I'll be working with a newspaper..."

Mr. Arnold shrugged. "Maybe. Maybe not. You'll be working with a newspaper. Then what? Where do you go after you've outgrown it. And mark my words, you will outgrow it. Small islands, like small places everywhere, have very provincial attitudes. Now, it's true there's no easy way in the Big A, but this is where you are. Everything's happening right here, and you're easing out..."

"Mr. Arnold, believe me, I'm not easing out. If I thought like that, I wouldn't have returned at all..."

"Well," he continued quietly, "suppose Jackie Robinson had decided to take the easy way? What would have happened to baseball? And look what the Brown Bomber went through before he made it to the top."

"I'm not either one of them," Celia said. "I don't have—"

"You don't know what you have until you put it to the test. You just don't know. The first day you walked in there was a test. You should've seen your face. I wanted to jump up and down and clap and shout. You got the stuff. Now you should be looking in your mirror and saying to yourself, 'I see Hobson's first black executive editor.'"

Celia looked at him, shaking her head. "Please, Mr. Arnold... editor? I'm not even a good writer yet..."

"You will be," he said, expanding the dream for her, "once you sharpen your skill. There's that group uptown, Harlem Writer's Guild, I think it's called. Writer by the name of Killens runs it. Get in touch with them. See if they'll let you join. And just think... while you're working hard down here, moving toward your goal, a young man comes along—a New York man of course—just as ambitious and, well, you never know...think about it..."

They said good night, and she watched him make his way across the street to the bus stop. The idea of becoming editor she dismissed out of hand. That, she knew, was simply not going to happen. It was easier to concentrate on finding out about the guild and contemplating the prospects of finding a New York man.

A New York man. She entered the station, not knowing if she should laugh or cry. A New York man...she wanted to laugh...a New York man will tear the center out of your soul....She decided that she wanted to cry.

Normally she did not close her eyes when riding the subway, but the tight band that had circled around her brow when she remembered Jonrobert now seemed tighter.

Her eyes remained closed as she speculated on the various aspects of pain: generalized, particular, occasional, but lurking permanently in the recess of consciousness. At times, it refused to be confined and spread like a flame, scorching her. Sometimes it crackled along her spine, or snaked to her stomach and back again, causing her to fold like a fetus in the dark of her bedroom. Because of a New York man.

...why was I so surprised about Sophie...people do what they have to in order to make life livable...either we push pain as far away as we can, which often means pushing it onto someone else... or we shoulder it and gradually absorb it, being careful, very careful, to see that it doesn't absorb us...

She wanted to remain as she was, but the sound of wheel on rail brought her back. Iron screeched and ground in its monotonous rhythm. She opened her eyes and concentrated on the scarred walls and gum-blackened floors of the rumbling car and watched tired people find new energy to push through the doors and scatter like fleeing convicts away from the dreary station.

Moving among them, in slow deliberate counterpoint, was the Subway Lady. It had been months since she had seen her, but the sight of the slight, many-layered figure gliding within its usual ring of isolation brought Celia to her feet.

...there she is. ...there she is...

Impulsively, Celia slipped through the door just as it was closing. The lady by this time had gone through the turnstile and walked up the stairs.

Celia followed, bewildered by her impulsivity. The lady was a stranger. Why was she doing this?

She crossed the street and watched the lady enter the small corner restaurant. Through the window, she saw her move to the rear of the empty dining room and take the last stool at the end of the counter—as if it had been reserved for her. Then she saw the waitress, with hands flailing the air, move toward the lady.

Celia opened the door quickly and stepped inside. At the sight of another customer, the waitress softened her tirade.

"—you ruinin' my business. If I told you once, I told you a dozen times, I don't want you in here!"

"I'm payin' and you can't refuse..."

"You buy one cup a coffee and then warm that stool for three hours. Unh, unh. I can do without your dime. Take it on outta here!"

Celia moved down the aisle and slid easily onto the adjacent stool.

"Two cups of coffee, please."

The waitress and the lady both looked at her, and she felt the heat rise. Why was she doing this? The stranger meant nothing to her.

Celia gazed steadily at the waitress, who now stared as if she had two crazy persons to deal with.

"I said two cups of coffee," Celia repeated. Then she turned to the lady. "How do you like yours?"

"Black, miss, bless your heart."

The waitress sniffed and stomped to the front to make loud, clattering sounds at the coffee urn before returning with the two cups.

"Anything else?" she challenged.

"Let us have a menu."

"Menu! It's on the wall!"

Celia squinted at the brown, fly-specked chart while the lady quietly sipped her coffee.

"Would you like anything else?" Celia whispered.

"No. Not right now. I don't git hungry 'til real late. Then I come back here and bother her some more...we got a understandin'. She ain't as bad as she looks..."

"Oh." Celia opened her purse. "Then take this for later."

The lady reached for the money and the air around her moved, bathing Celia with the vague scent of lemon sachet. Celia watched the hands fold the bill with swollen fingers. The knuckles were misshapen and the lady could not make a full fist with her right hand.

She drained her cup and rose from the stool. "Thank you, but I gotta go. Don't wanna wear out my welcome." She paused and looked closely at Celia. "Listen," she said softly, "you a young girl, and I can see by the way you dressed, the way you talk, ain't nobody gonna take advantage. Keep it up. You doin' what I shoulda done. Don't let 'em wear you out, honey. You on that merry-go-round—we all on it—but don't let 'em knock you off..."

She did not wait for a reply but wrapped her worn coat around her and left.

The door closed behind her, leaving Celia alone with the waitress, who had been doing busy things behind the counter. She created noises which, if Celia closed her eyes, seemed to give the place an air of bustling activity. Then the waitress moved down the aisle, collected the empty cup, and wiped the space with a worn sponge.

"Listen," she said, leaning on the counter, "it ain't what you think. She's in here at least twice a week. Three in the winter, when she ain't riding the subway.... Sometimes, I even let her wash up in the bathroom in the back, but today...I don't know...I ain't feelin' so hot today..."

The door opened again, and the waitress moved in the narrow space back to the coffee urn as two men entered. "Be right with you. What you all havin', sweetie?"

"Chicken sandwiches, coffee, and some of that pie sweet as you..."

Her face lit up, and the clatter behind the counter increased. Celia waited patiently until the men were served and the waitress returned.

"What happened to that lady's hand?" Celia asked.

"Got it caught in the mangle at the wet wash where she used to work," the waitress said, glad now for conversation. "She worked there for ten years in all that heat and sweat, and the first accident, they let her go. Two weeks' pay and let her go."

"That's all they gave?"

"Didn't wanna give that 'til she threatened to sue..."

"Why didn't she? She had a right."

"Well, I heard she went to a couple of lawyers and they wanted so much up front, but she just didn't have it. Then she found one who took the case, won, and said she owed him for this expense and that expense, and after he added it all up, there was nuthin' left for her..."

The waitress left and returned with a fresh cup of coffee. "But you wanna hear the real sad part. The relief people say she ain't entitled to no welfare 'cause they got it on paper that she won this great big cash settlement. After that, she sorta give up, I guess. They wore her out, and she just plain give up...and been on the subway ever since..."

The waitress finished her coffee in silence, leaving Celia to think about the Subway Lady.

...she had not been pushed off the merry-go-round...she had been eased off. Finessed so smoothly that she found herself on the ground even before the music stopped.

...and in her helplessness, it has become her solemn duty to advertise the fact, the lesson of her defeat...

43

Seventh Avenue was crowded when Celia left the restaurant. The evening had turned cool and the street corners were dense with peddlers hawking the last of the season's cold crab and watermelon. Celia skirted the pushcarts and makeshift stands and fell in with the languid pace of the other strollers. She walked past Well's Restaurant and Connie's Inn and continued for several blocks before turning east.

The music from the Peacock sounded serene as she approached and she wondered if someone, a stranger to the neighborhood, had wandered in for a drink and then pressed the wrong selection on the jukebox. This was, after all, Monday, blues day, crying time in the city. How could the Peacock tolerate such a lapse?

The answer came at once on the breathy wail of Dinah Washington; her voice rising up and over the hum of traffic as it described the joy and anguish of her love. No greater love.

Celia remained at the corner, watching the traffic light change, and someone played the song again, and she knew that that was why she was waiting. She needed to absorb the sound and find its meaning before it drifted away on the evening air. She wanted to catch each sharp and flat and grace note and press them to her, crush them, until the answer was squeezed out.

When she finally moved, walking slowly to avoid disturbing the flow of melody surrounding her, she passed a woman who had stopped to gaze at her. "Well, I'll be! Hello! Hello, Celia!"

The women approached, running. She was as tall and thin as Celia, and her cotton print skirt swirled at her ankles as she moved. Celia recognized the quick steps from years ago.

"Shing a ling! Mary! What a surprise!"

They embraced and then held each other at arm's length.

"Look at you, Celia. I nearly didn't recognize you with your hair cut. But your eyes haven't changed. How are you?"

"Mary, I'm fine. I didn't know you were back in New York. What've you been doing? You look great."

Mary stepped back and executed a small dance step under the streetlight. "Remember that song 'Fine as Wine'? Well, that's how I am. Fine." She shook her head, and her hair, piled high in a thick round Afro, moved on the air as she laughed. Her wrists were heavy with large, gold bracelets, and a knitted shawl hung casually over her black sweater. "I was just coming from the library. Where are you headed?"

"Home, but I'm in no hurry."

"Good. We have a lot of talk to catch up on. Can we sit in the Peacock?"

They looked across the avenue at the neon bird and Celia shrugged. "Why not."

The long row of bar stools stood empty except for a solitary drinker near the end who was hunched over a bottle of beer. Another man leaned over the jukebox, which sounded extra loud in the empty space. He fed several coins into the machine and then returned to sit not far from the solitary man.

Mary sighed as she slid into the seat at one of the small tables. "Probably just lost the love of his life."

"How do you know..."

"I don't. But let's see what the oracle has to say..."

A second later, the deep pulse of a standup bass eased into the air, and the opening chords of Edmond Hall's quintet rumbled across the room.

"'Profoundly Blue,'" Mary smiled. "God, how I remember that song. Slow-dragged so many nights to it. That was Harlem's national anthem back then..."

The women watched the listener drum his fingers in time against the mahogany surface of the bar. Then he raised them to order a double gin.

"...and give the two ladies what they want," he said, turning toward them. His face held a permanent Monday look, but when he smiled, he was handsome in spite of his devastation.

"...didn't I tell you?" Mary whispered. Then she turned to the man and thanked him softly.

"I should have known," Celia murmured. "I pass this place every day..."

Mary turned from the man to look at her. "...still living at home?"

The waiter approached, and Mary ordered a gin and tonic.

"Rum and ginger ale for me," said Celia. "Yes, I'm still at home. But let's hear about you. What've you been doing since you last wrote?"

Mary sipped her drink and then closed her eyes. Celia thought she was concentrating on the music, but when she spoke, her eyes were still closed. "Let's see. I told you about the farm cooperatives, and SNCC, and the registration drives..."

She opened her eyes again to gaze steadily in the direction of the jukebox. "...I didn't say that I probably set some kind of record for time served in jail. If I live to be a hundred, I could never describe everything that went on down there..."

"When did you get back to the city?"

"Three days ago. By way of Mali..."

"Mali...??" Celia put her glass down. "You were in Africa??"

"Africa. Yes, I was," Mary said slowly. "And that is a story. While I was working at one of the cooperatives, I met this brother. Very serious, committed guy. It was almost as if events, bad as they were, had conspired to throw us together. Anyway, it didn't take long to realize how alike we were. We fell in love and learned to sustain each other pretty well through the craziness. But the remarkable part of the whole thing was his mother. I had never met anyone like her. I thought Andrew was made of steel, but this lady had been made of iron. She was right up front in the battle and never stumbled or grumbled. Not even in jail.

"Then she was arrested the last time, a month ago, on a Wednesday. We went to see her that night and left to pick up the bail money... the next morning, she was found dead.

"'Pneumonia,' the deputies said. 'Slept on that cold floor.' But we knew. You don't get purple marks from pneumonia.

"We wanted Andrew to call the FBI, the attorney general, and every other general we could think of, but he surprised all of us. I think he even surprised himself...I mean here was this really articulate, outspoken man suddenly become very, very quiet. Almost as if he'd crawled into a cave within himself. He said nothing for two days; then he called a meeting and made an announcement.

"'My mother fought the battle and lost,' he said. 'I will not bury her...in enemy territory.'

"Well, you never saw consternation. You should have heard the debate. 'Where you gonna take her? She fought and died for this place...she an American.'

"And he said if that was true, they wouldn't be sitting there arguing over her body...she'd still be alive and...and..."

Mary paused for a second, as if something had gotten caught in her throat. Then she closed her eyes and went on.

"He had her cremated. And we flew to Africa, to Mali, with the ashes..."

Her voice was quiet and easy, like a recitation, against the background of music. Now she raised her glass and took a deep swallow.

"Why Mali?" Celia asked in the silence. The question had nothing to do with what she was hearing, but she needed to counter the numbing sensation spreading through her with something that she could understand.

Mary lifted her shoulders; then she straightened the shawl. "At the time, I asked myself the same thing because Andrew was always so...rational, and...calm. I thought he might have been having a breakdown. He didn't know anyone there.... So finally, I found the nerve to ask him. And he said, 'Why not? Since we don't know which part we were taken from, the way I see it, this gives us the freedom to choose any part we like. I happen to like Mali. I'm taking her home there.'"

Celia looked at her glass again and held up two fingers to the bartender.

"Andrew didn't really cry," Mary whispered, "until we reached this small, deserted area near the Niger. He wanted to scatter the ashes alone.

"When he knelt down and felt what must have been her silver or gold fillings slipping through his fingers into that water, he knew she was gone.... She was gone."

Celia gazed at her friend in the dim light and a feeling, deep and profound, moved within her. A blinding rage and a numbing sadness that could not be articulated. She held her breath and tried once again to absorb the latest chapter in this bitter dream.

She thought of the Subway Lady, cheated, wandering without hope, and the tears she had been holding back suddenly stung her eyes.

She reached across the table to touch Mary's hand. "...we're born...and we have to fight...until we die, Mary. There doesn't seem to be anything beyond that. How do you keep going? Where do you find the strength?"

"Who knows. It comes when you need it." She was silent for a minute. Then she said, "That's not true. There were times I needed it and it didn't come. When he cried, I fell apart. I wanted to go on a rampage...and kill someone in the worst way. I wanted to... do anything *but* cry. When the tears finally came, I cried for days. When I stopped, he started again. It went on like that for three weeks. The people we were staying with were very understanding, thank God."

"Then I wanted to stay there—start a new life and forget everything that happened here. We talked for days...and...I don't know...maybe it was the distance...being so far from...the struggle when we were so used to being on the front lines...we'd be getting the news secondhand...not knowing if we were winning or losing..."

She shook her head. "No. We had to come back..."

Celia tried to imagine this girl, who had kept the boys on edge with her fancy dancing, who had lived for the slow drag; this girl, transformed, kneeling in silence in the mud of a river half a world away. Quiet, quiet, because the words hadn't been invented that could have comforted the man kneeling beside her.

"Mary...what are you going to do now?"

"We're heading back south as quickly as possible. Too much unfinished business. We've been gone too long as it is, and we don't want the folk to think we deserted them."

They were both silent for a few minutes and listened to the music from the jukebox. The record ended, and the man who had bought their drinks eased off his stool. "Y'all be cool now, you hear..."

He smiled and waved and was gone. Mary watched the door close behind him; then she brushed her hand through her hair and sighed. "I've talked enough. What about you? What're you doing now? Graduate work? Any plans for marriage?"

"Well," Celia said slowly. She paused, wondering if Mary were really interested in the little that was happening in her life. "I'm still at home...and working. Nothing much else has happened except that I visited one of the islands and was offered a news job there, but..."

"But what? That sounds exciting."

"Well, yes...it is, but...the job I have now also offers some... interesting possibilities..."

"...and you don't know what to do, is that it?"

"Something like that."

They ordered again, and Celia talked about Jonrobert and Marcus and the way the situation had developed at Hobson's. "It's a little more complicated than that, though not half as...involved as what you're doing."

Mary moved her shoulders again. "Who knows...we're all involved on one level or another whether we know it or not...Andrew and I came back because we felt we could do the most good here.... You have to think about the situation...if you go to work over there, you can't expect to write about our problems over here, you know. Civil rights?" She shook her head again. "Those politicians will hand your head to you just to keep that Yankee dollar flowing..."

She leaned across the small table and whispered although no one was within earshot and the music was so loud that no one could have heard her anyway.

"You know, Celia, this thing...is like a cancer. If it's not turned around, it will kill us all. We have to change things..."

She sighed again, leaned back, and took out a small notebook. "...Andrew's probably wondering what happened to me. Here's my phone number and my address. I still have yours, and this time, we'll really keep in touch. Old friends are too hard to come by."

They stood outside the Peacock for a minute, watching the strollers. Then Mary said, "Whatever you decide, it will be the right thing..."

Celia smiled. "I'll certainly let you know. I'll write soon."

Mary hurried away and Celia watched the swirling skirt and long shawl until she could no longer glimpse them. Then she turned to cross the street.

The time for slow-dragging was over indeed. The fancy footwork was a memory. The rhythm now was different and dangerous and only serious dancers were stepping out on the floor. She passed the darkened doorway of Groovy Movers and turned into the block.

She did not intend to speak to Al. She needed to speak to Marcus.

"I will fly down...to see him...this weekend..."

44

"You're what?"

Frieda's voice followed Celia to her room. "You just came back and you're going again. Why?"

Celia removed her sweater and hung it over the back of the chair. Then she removed her blouse, concentrating one by one on the small pearl buttons, trying in the silence to frame an answer.

She continued to undress as her mother approached.

"Didn't you hear me?" The voice had become soft and sad now, and Celia pulled at the belt of her bathrobe, tightening it, as if to keep her backbone firm and the sound of her heartbeat from spilling out. Finally, she said, "Yes, mother, I heard..."

She let the reply float in the air between them; then she continued, "I'm going Friday. I'll be back Sunday..."

She could have bitten her tongue. Here she was, tying herself to more schedules, more restrictions. Why not just go?

She wanted to sigh. No. She owed her mother at least that. Where she was going and when she would return. But the "why" of it. That was another thing.

They held each other's gaze in the mirror. Frieda leaning against the door frame, and Celia bent over the dressing table doing busy things with dabs of cold cream. She was surprised to see how tired her mother looked and was nearly tempted to change her mind, cancel this wild plan. She could write to Marcus, or call him, and make him see that the possibilities were all here. And that she wasn't going to miss a second chance.

She stopped dabbing and picked up the jar of cold cream to examine the label.

...no, she thought, no letter or phone call...I need to see him to explain this...

In the silence, she stared at her mother's reflection. The image in the glass wavered and then took on a shimmering quality as if it might come apart in a thousand fragments, each prism reflecting a small, perfect picture of her mother's bewilderment. Impulsively, she wanted to take her mother in her arms, if only to share the pain of her confusion.

Celia shook her head, crumpled a wad of tissues, and began to remove the light film of makeup from her face, methodically, in slow, wide strokes, aware that her mother was still watching her.

"It will be for the weekend," she said again. "I'll be back Sunday." She listened to the sound of her own voice, flat and uninteresting, and it reminded her of a stiffly rehearsed recording.

Frieda opened her mouth but then changed her mind, and without a word, she left the room.

"How 'bout some coffee?" Al said.

Frieda had been sitting at the tiny kitchen table for nearly ten minutes and had not spoken. It was as if she were alone in the room.

Al moved from the stove with two steaming cups and placed one before her. He filled the sugar dish and then sat down opposite her.

He was determined to wait until she spoke; even if it took all night, he would wait.

In the silence, he raised his cup and blew at the steam. The coffee was still too hot, so he held it near his face, inhaling the aroma, and glanced at Frieda over the rim.

...she ain't never been quiet this long...when she come in, it's usually "Celia this and Celia that" right away...now, not a peep...

He thought about—and quickly discarded—the idea of fixing a drink. That would surely loosen her up. But then, one would lead to another and another, and he had two heavy jobs scheduled in the morning. He'd be burned out by lunchtime. He made a mental note to speak with Sam and Dan about hiring an extra man, at least part time. The company could afford it...

He watched her hands move and close around her cup, cradling it as a cold person might, in order to press the warmth through the flowered ceramic and into her own skin. Finally, she lifted it, brought it close to her face, and gazed at the dark contents.

"...you know," she whispered, still looking into the cup, "...I was wondering...you know...about that fellow...the one that Celia brought to the house..."

It took Al a few seconds to answer, and he tried to keep his voice steady as he spoke. "...you mean that boy, Jonrobert...why you want—?"

He could not finish, could not mention the name without his stomach turning over. He felt the sweat begin to gather.

...why was she thinking about him all of a sudden...what had happened...

"That was over two years ago..." he added cautiously. "He long gone." Then, after a pause, he said, "...why'd you ask...?"

He watched her shrug her shoulders and remain silent.

Suddenly, he rose from the table and returned with a bottle of Scotch and two glasses.

Frieda looked up, surprised. "Thought you had a tight schedule tomorrow."

"I do...I do. This only gonna be a light taste."

Frieda watched him fill the glasses half full. Then she said, "You know, Celia's goin' away. For good."

Al put his glass down and gazed at her as she pressed the tips of her fingers against her forehead, rubbing in small circles. "She's leaving...going to that island...and I—"

"—and you want her to stay, right?"

"Well, I—"

Al watched as she shifted nervously in the chair. "You know," she whispered, "maybe Jonrobert wasn't..."

"'Maybe' don't cut nuthin', Frieda. That cat wasn't right. He was bad news..."

"But how do I know what she'll be getting herself into if she's a million miles away from—"

Al raised both hands and shook his head. "You don't know,

and you won't know. But what you ought to know is that when you left home, you was younger than Celia is now."

"That was different—"

He knew it was different but didn't dare acknowledge it. The first time he had seen her on the bus, she had been numb with fear and her eyes had reflected the same deathly shadow that he had last seen in Evie.

"Nuthin's different," he continued. "Nuthin's changed. Folks leave home for different reasons. Some 'cause they want to, some 'cause they got to. It don't matter. The point is they leave, and no matter what others say or do to try to hold 'em back, it ain't no use. It's like tryin' to hold back the tide."

He could sense her growing agitation but pressed on anyway. "She gonna be like water slippin' through your fingers, Frieda, no matter how tight you close your hands."

Frieda was on her feet, shaking. "I thought you were on *my* side?? Suppose something happens and I can't get there? Suppose she—"

Al reached across the table, took her hand, and eased her back into her chair. "Frieda, listen…it ain't a question a sides. You know that…"

"I don't know anything anymore, I'm so—"

She pushed the glass and cup aside, laid her head on her folded arms, and began to cry.

Al moved his chair around the table to sit near her. He noticed that there were scattered strands of silver in her thick hair.

Time, time, time was passing, flying by. He wished he could hold up the silvered strands and explain how fruitless her tears were. That things and people change and come and go, and she could cry herself a river and drown in her own tears and it would make no difference.

Well, no matter what, he would be right there with her.

He placed his hands on her shoulders and began to massage her gently. "Listen, baby, the old folks used to say that bad luck comes in cycles. Well, yours done come and gone. You had ten times your share. Now you gotta let go of the memory of it… 'cause that's all there is…memory…"

He lifted her face and looked at her, and the question that had lain for so long just on the underside of his tongue, like some soft, small candyball, took shape and rolled to the center. He opened his mouth, breathed a sigh, and pushed the sound out. "...we need memories of our own. Our own, you hear...?"

"What...?"

"You and me...we need to...why don't we get married...?"

She returned his gaze for a long moment and then said, "Why not?"

45

Celia lay wide awake in the darkened room, listening to the rain against the window and to the several answers that might have helped her earlier.

...could have said that the editor was sending me again...or that I wanted to do some more research on my own...

She listened to the water pour over the clogged drain on the far side of the courtyard. It had a turbulent sound, rushing with nowhere to go because the aperture at the bottom had been filled years ago with sand and sewage, yet the drain still clung stubbornly to the side of the building, swollen in sections and rusted in others, but clinging, mindlessly intent on performing its function. And in the morning after the rain had stopped, the super would curse through three feet of water because that was easier than repairing the drain.

...most of the time, the easy way turns out to be the hardest. Who had told her that...Al, Marcus, Mr. Arnold?

...there is no easy way. There never was. I missed a chance once and Mary took it.... Now...it's here again...

She finally fell asleep, but the running dream intruded and she was awake two hours later.

She sat up in the darkness, then eased out of the bed, and walked on tiptoe to Frieda's bedroom. She stood in front of the closed door and wondered why she was being so careful in the silence. Didn't she intend to wake her so that they could talk? But she eased the door open anyway, still unable to bring herself to disturb the quiet. She listened in the dark for her mother's breath sounds but heard nothing. A ripple of panic passed through her, and she fumbled for the lamp on the nightstand. The room came alive in a warm, pink glow, and Celia stared at the empty bed. She picked up the clock from the nightstand and blinked.

...it's almost five a.m....

She looked at the bed again. It was unmade, and she wondered if her mother had gotten up in the middle of the night and gone back up to Al's—because that was the only place she could be—or if the bed had been left unmade all day. She could not remember her mother ever leaving her bed unmade.

...it's almost five a.m. It doesn't take this long to tell him that I'm going away again...

The key turned in the door and Celia felt as if she had been caught in someone's secret place. Her first impulse was to slip back to her own room. She took a step but then stopped.

...I've got to talk to her. Even if I decide against Marcus, I can't stay here...I can't...

She sat down in the living room chair and listened as her mother moved down the hall and entered the bathroom. Minutes later, Frieda was making small sounds in the dining room, and Celia guessed that she was preparing a drink.

She left the chair and walked toward the dining room with no idea of what she intended to say.

She was not prepared for the sight of her mother. Frieda's hair was undone and fell about her shoulders in loose, ropelike coils. And she had a bathrobe on. A bathrobe.

Celia felt a moment of confusion, and she watched in silence as Frieda nervously tucked the lapels together.

"What are you doing still up?" Frieda whispered. She seemed tired and distracted.

"I...couldn't sleep..." Celia said. She moved cautiously into the dining room and sat down. "I want to talk to you..."

"What about...?"

"I don't know...I wanted to talk about my...going away..."

"You've made up your mind...?"

"I'm...not sure...I—"

Frieda closed her eyes, but Celia went on before she could interject.

"Mother, please...listen...I know this is hard, but listen... ever since I was a little girl, you have tried to shelter me and shape my life. You made my bed...made my food...and made my clothing... and I'm grateful to you for that. But then...more out of fear than love, you made my decisions about school and about my friends... I have no friends...really...Now I have to decide what I want to do. Even if I stay in New York, I want to be on my own..."

Celia watched as Frieda placed her elbows on the table and rested her head in the palms of her hands.

She noticed that her mother used the very same motions, lacing her fingers together in the same tight pattern, that she herself used when confronted with a threatening situation. Now the fingers remained intertwined, and Celia braced herself, watching.

It seemed that her mother was determined to bury herself in the shadow of memory and was equally determined to pull Celia in also, to keep her company among the fine, fearful cobwebs.

...I will die in there, she thought.... I will die...

She gazed beyond her mother to the window and saw dawn graying the bricks on the wall outside. She had had no sleep, and it surprised her to see that the night had ended. She was worn by fatigue and her thoughts spiraled as in a dream. Her mind seemed to dance and, in a split second of clarity, focused on her grandmothers, women she had never known.

It occurred to her that Frieda had spoken most of the time about the men in the family, who had been sacrificed to other people's fears. But the women, rarely mentioned, had been left to take vague and difficult shape in her imagination—which after a time enabled her, in vivid daydreams, to carve them into steel-willed women, able to take on, take down, and take over. Steel willed...

It was so simple that she wanted to cry.

Her mother was steel-willed, had been all her life. And it occurred to her that strength came in many guises. Frieda had used her insecurity like a velvet-covered crowbar to bend Al, Sam, and Dan and anyone else within her insular world.

Celia rose from her seat and moved around the table to the window. The rain had stopped and the sounds of the courtyard wafted in on the slight breeze. She listened to tired morning coughs, running bathwater, whistling teakettles: small and innocent echoes that signaled the start of another day.

She wondered about the Subway Lady. And Mary. And the desperate frustration that was so much a part of their twenty-four hours.

The fatigue she had been ignoring fell on her like a weight. A wave of dizziness passed over her, and she held tightly to the window frame. Another minute slipped by in silence before she turned, took in a sharp breath, and said quietly, "Mother, I'm going. Let's not...let's not..."

She wanted to say "Let's not fight, because there'll be no winners. I'm leaving no matter what...happens."

46

October 1964

Mr. Wingate's project to expand Hobson's market into parts of China and Africa shifted into high gear and negotiations with the company's legal and export departments were into the final phase. The sales office was inundated with projection reports, summaries, and revisions—work which kept Celia at her desk long after the office had closed. On Tuesday evening, Mr. Wingate left to attend another meeting, and Celia was alone with the sound of her typewriter clicking loudly in the silence.

She worked steadily and only paused when she heard the whirring sound of the elevator as it slowed to a stop. The doors opened, and she wondered if Mr. Wingate had returned. But the footfalls sounded soft and deliberate, and she knew it was Mr. Arnold even before he turned the corner.

"Thought I'd find you here," he said, "even though it's way past your bedtime."

Celia smiled and relaxed. "It's only seven and I think I can finish by eight. How are you? Haven't seen much of you lately."

"That's because you've been extra busy lately. Anyway I'm feeling pretty good for an old soul. Heard something on the vine today and thought I'd double back to fill you in."

Celia peered at him in the half-dark. Only the overhead lamp hanging low over her desk was on, and it was difficult to see beyond its small perimeter of light. Mr. Arnold took a seat on the other side of the desk, but his face was still pretty much shrouded in the surrounding gray. Celia heard her heart beat. What had Mr. Arnold heard? Was it more trouble from Sophie? They both waited in silence, and Celia felt her fingers tremble slightly on the typewriter keys. Mr. Arnold coughed gently; then he said, "In a couple of weeks or so, you're gonna be promoted."

Celia blinked and then leaned forward again to get a clearer look at him. "Are you serious? You mean I'm finally going into copy—"

"No. You're gonna go beyond copy. You're gonna remain right here, but your position'll be changed, upgraded, I think they call it. You're gonna be his assistant. New salary, too. Quite a bit over what you're getting now..."

"Well, I'll be...I'll be..." She leaned back and closed her eyes. "...I can't believe it."

"Well, it's true. Wingate pushed for it at that executive meeting. Played on the image angle and convinced them that it'd be good for the company. Naturally, the only one opposed was you-know-who..."

"Oh, God..."

"I spoke to her later, and all she could talk about was how unfair it was that some of the other secretaries had been with the company for years and here you were jumping ahead of them, getting special treatment because you're black."

Celia shook her head and laughed. "It's because of her that I've been getting special treatment all along. Real special."

"Don't worry about that now because there's more coming. I let her talk and talk, and then reminded her that the other secretaries didn't have a college degree. And just in case she forgot, you were not hired to be a secretary in the first place."

"What did she say to that...?"

Mr. Arnold leaned back in the chair, and Celia imagined she saw his small, neat smile.

"We had a nice long talk," he whispered, "kind of casual and quiet-like..."

Celia folded her arms across the machine and said again, "I can't...I don't believe it..."

"Believe it. And keep working as hard as you are now. They'll be watching you. And for heaven's sakes, remember to act surprised when he announces it. Folks love it when they can surprise you and love it even more when you're grateful for the surprise."

Celia looked at him carefully. "Mr. Arnold, where did you hear this? Did Sophie tell you? Maybe it's not true. Maybe it's a trap. Maybe—"

"No. It's true. I got it from the top floor. You see, somewhere down the line, a year or two, maybe sooner, they're going to need a black sales rep. The folks have some pretty long-range plans, and you walked in here—at the right place at the right time. Remember, they're not doing you any favors. The only thing they're interested in is their bottom line. They'd train a Martian to deliver their goods if they had to. Luckily, it hasn't come to that yet..."

Celia listened in silence as he spoke, absorbing the news. And the new title, rolling it around on her tongue until the sound of it fit. Then she laughed.

"You know, these reports have to be ready by Thursday. But I'm so excited, I can't even see straight..."

"Well, you better knock off. Tackle it tomorrow. You have time."

She pulled the cover over the machine and rose from the chair, grateful for the suggestion. "Mr. Arnold, I certainly appreciate what you're doing for me. I really mean it. I—"

He shrugged. "You don't have to thank me...there's a lot of reasons why people do things. Maybe I'm looking out for the daughter I never had. Maybe I'm doing it for the tribe. Yes. I think that's it. The tribe."

47

Friday arrived sooner than Celia expected and she had not packed. Her canvas weekend bag had lain near her dressing table, open and empty, and every evening she had come home, stared at it, and fallen into bed, bone tired. She had thought of postponing the trip, but the way things were developing, if she didn't go now, she never would.

Now she rushed home and pulled out a dress, slacks, and some lingerie, and tossed them into the bag. Her flight was not leaving for another three hours but she hurried, still propelled by the week's momentum.

In the lobby, she maneuvered through the stoop watchers, who saw that her bag was just large enough to leave them guessing.

She smiled and the watchers smiled back, but their eyes were hard and their teeth did not part.

The music from the Peacock was unusually quiet for a Friday night. It was so mellow that she changed her mind about taking a taxi and decided to walk to the subway, slowly, to keep the sound with her for at least another block.

She crossed the street and turned down the wide avenue. Every stoop was packed and the only available streetlamp was crowded with the usual card players. She moved near the tight group standing around the table and lingered on the edge—not to see the game but to remain with the music without actually having to go inside the bar.

Someone was playing Otis Redding now, pushing one selection after another, and she began to tap her foot, drawn into the rhythm with the rest of the crowd.

A half hour later, she glanced at her watch and knew it was time to leave.

Across the street, a tall man who had been walking in the opposite direction stopped abruptly and watched as she turned away from the gathering. Suddenly he made his way against the light and the line of cars. His gait was slow, and by the time he had threaded his way through the traffic, Celia was several steps away. He tried to move faster as the distance between them lengthened, but his body protested and he felt the shock of pain as he moved. Strollers out for the evening got in his way, and at one point he lost sight of her. But she appeared again, and he watched her legs intently until he was satisfied the woman was who he thought she was and not a mistake, a mirage, or another bad dream. At the next corner, she paused for the traffic light, and he was able to move up behind her just as she stepped from the curb.

"Hello...Celia!"

Celia turned and stared, speechless, at Jonrobert's tall figure, at his tired, still handsome face as it broke into an anxious smile.

"Where you goin'?" he asked quietly, as if he had just spoken to her yesterday.

She put her hand to her mouth and stepped back in confusion.

"Jonrobert!!"

Her voice was a whisper, lost in the evening noise, and she stood, immobilized, afraid to move. She knew that if she took one step, her legs would give way.

"...I don't believe it...I don't believe it..."

Without a word he took her arm and led her back down the block. In the Peacock, they found an empty table in the corner, and she was grateful to feel the seat under her.

A waiter approached, and Jonrobert asked, "What're you having?"

She stared at him, so he said, "...a Brown Lady for the lady, and for me Scotch straight up, please..."

She watched him closely as he ordered. Then they were alone again, facing each other.

She shook her head in disbelief. "Jonrobert, what happened to you...what happened..."

She could not finish, and he took the small napkin and held it lightly against her face. "Celia. Don't cry. don't cry. What I did wasn't right. That's why I came back. It's been a long time, but I had to come back...to straighten this thing out...if I didn't, my life would never be together and neither will yours...I love you. I never stopped. I never, ever stopped..."

The waiter returned and Celia reached for her glass with shaking fingers, but her throat had closed and the liquid remained under her tongue. Her mind was racing, trying to make sense of the reality of his presence. He was back. Sitting across from her. Talking. His voice was softer and his speech seemed slower. More precise. And there were lines at the corners of his mouth even when he wasn't smiling. But he was back.

Jonrobert drew a deep breath and looked beyond her.

"You know," he said, looking at her again, "I was coming to see you. I wasn't going to call, write, or do anything like that. I was coming straight to your house. If you weren't home, I was going to wait—just pitch camp and wait. But now..." He raised his hand and gestured. "...instead of me surprising you, it's the other way around....They say things happen for a reason, so maybe this isn't so bad after all...at least I won't have your uncles playing heavy like the last time—"

"What??" A wave of dizziness engulfed her. She leaned across the table, then rose halfway out of her chair.

He rose and held her by the shoulders, easing her back down.

"—wait, listen. It's not what you're thinking...it's a whole lot more than them not liking me 'cause I was in the life...I mean, that was a big part, but not all of it..."

He drew a breath and continued slowly. "I went away because of something they told me...but I came back because the something they said cheated me out of the one chance I had to be...to be a whole person..."

He hesitated again; then he said softly, "...you made me whole, Celia. And after what I just been through, I need to feel whole again."

She closed her eyes and repeated his words. "...to feel whole... again..."

The music in the bar seemed strange now. The softer it sounded, the heavier it seemed, and it pressed on her. Someone was singing about dreams, lost dreams.

The dizziness increased, and she felt a tight knot take shape in the center of her forehead. A huge, shapeless pressure rose within and she wanted to run, screaming, from the bar. She wanted to fly home on the wings of an old rage—and confront Al, Sam, Dan, and her mother—for surely her mother had everything to do with this: confront the protectors, the liars, the smiling, comforting thieves who had stolen the direction of her life.

Then the music slipped through the pressure, and she heard a voice grown old and wide and soft with time:

...open your eyes, girl...open 'em...don't let 'em knock you off that merry-go-round...

And the voice fell to a whisper and confronted the rage, checked it lightly, so that she was able to control the tremor, fold her arms tightly on the table, and hold her gaze to his.

"Jonrobert, tell me what happened..."

"I intend to," he whispered, "...after what I went through in 'Nam, there's nothing the real world can do to me anymore...

"I saw all kinds of strange stuff go down...and even as I'm talking to you, I still can't believe some of it happened..."

He wanted to tell her, to roll the unspeakable weight of it off his chest. But it was too soon.

He drew his breath and was silent a few seconds, waiting for the feeling to pass, while he struggled to contain himself. But he shifted in his seat and began to talk anyway: "You know, there was some pretty deep stuff goin' on over there, and I tried like hell to detach myself from everything around me. I made up my mind that I couldn't do anything about that scene 'cause that was Sam's shit. I didn't even know where 'Nam was until he invited me. All through it, I was trying to deal with my own nightmare... and you know...having two of them on your back is a heavy load. I made a promise that if I got out of one alive, I was coming back to straighten out the other one...

"You know what it was like? Imagine a ship sinking and everybody flounderin' and grabbin' on to anything that'll keep them afloat.... A lifeboat...a raft...maybe a piece of two-by-four. It's floating, so they grab it and hang on because that's all that's left.

"That's the way I hung on to you in my mind, in my memory. You and our music. I got hold of some of the old stuff we used to listen to, and I wrapped myself around those sounds...trying to stay afloat...and keep from cracking.... One time, I remember I came this close...we pulled a detail in the middle of the night, searching for this chopper that had gone down...couldn't wait 'til dawn because we had to get to the pilot before Charlie did... anyway, we walking through this paddy, up to our knees in water, about six of us, trying not to make a sound. It was about one o'clock in the morning...time was funny over there...it never seemed to get really dark.... Like in the countryside here, it gets pitch black, but over there, there's still a little pink left over from daytime...like the night never gets a chance to catch up...

"Anyway, in this half-light, we're walking and walking, and finally, we see the outline of the chopper blades in this clearing. Looked like some giant bird just sitting there in that tall grass. We closed in, silently, and all of a sudden, I hear this music, this piano, like Garner or Peterson—I forget which because I was so surprised—and the closer we got, the louder it sounded.

"I looked around me to see if any of the other guys had heard it, but nobody said anything. They just kept moving.... So finally I stood up in the waist-high grass to find out where it was coming from. And all hell broke loose. I mean the night lit up. Like Charlie must've showed the same time we did. Wasn't nothing to do then but rush the motherfu—I mean, rush the chopper, cut the guy out of it—and make a run. Me and two other guys were covering the rear. I was packing two pieces—twenty rounds to a clip—and I shot at everything. I raked grass, trees, leaves, and birds, loading as we ran. I was so uptight, I even shot at the moon. And all the while, this strange sound was still coming at me... I started to wonder if I was going crazy. I wanted to turn back and go find the player and shoot him because the sound had gotten so loud, it drowned out everything. But somebody grabbed me—I don't know who—and dragged me back. When we reached camp, and he dropped me, his arm was soaked and he thought he'd gotten hit...but then he looked, and everybody else looked at me...and there I was, laying on the ground with my side wide open. To this day, I don't know where that music came from..."

Celia leaned forward and put her hands to her head. This was too, too much to absorb all at once.

"...you could have died...died...and I never would've known..."

He lifted a small leather bag he had been carrying and placed it on the table.

"See this? Inside is nothing but letters. To you. If something had happened, someone would've brought them to you. I made it my business to put something on paper every chance I got, but I never sent them 'cause a letter can't tell the tale. Like the one I wrote when I left."

"...a lie?"

"No. No. It wasn't a lie," he whispered, "but it wasn't exactly the truth either because it didn't begin to explain everything that happened. It didn't explain a damn thing..."

He raised his glass again, drained it, and signaled for the waiter.

"When I left, I told you to go back to school. Well, I thought about it and figured maybe I should've been doing that myself. Because after my setback, I found I really didn't know the game.

"And I was determined to meet the man one on one and hold

my own doing it. I'm still determined. So I headed back home and back to school and was doing okay until Sam snatched me to do his duty.

"That experience taught me more about life than I cared to find out. It was the worst classroom imaginable…I saw brothers get done in for nothing…trapped, with Charlie giving it to us up front and we catchin' it from our own in the rear…some of them finally said 'fuck it' and went on over to the other side…lot of 'em still there…

"…I saw bombs, our bombs…fall short of position, doing us in…then the artillery…coming so hot and fast, it turned night into daylight.… Life was so cheap that you wound up caring about nothing, just to keep your sanity. If you're lucky enough to get back, then everything becomes important."

He fell silent as Celia reached into the bag and pulled out a stack of letters bound by a thick rubber band. She slipped one out and opened it quickly with her thumbnail. In the dim light, the familiar, left-slanted handwriting seemed to leap off the page.

> Dear Celia,
>
> Raining today and I miss you more than ever. Hospital food is still bad, but at least I can move my shoulder again. Only a matter of time before I'm stateside.…This arm has got to be perfect if I expect to hold you the way I used to…

The writing blurred from her tears, and she folded the letter slowly and slipped it back into the envelope.

"Listen," Jonrobert whispered, "I meant everything I wrote. Everything…"

He reached into the bag and piled more letters on the table. "…not because I was in a situation where I didn't know if I was ever going to see you again. I wrote what I felt. From my heart. My soul. What I feel…for you…is more important than anything in the world.

"Then tell me why you left," Celia said, "…tell me about my uncles. And my mother…" Her voice had gone tight and sank to a whisper. "Tell me…" she repeated.

"All right. I'll tell you everything that was told to me…everything. And maybe we can both make sense of what happened...I know your father was a hell of a dude. I saw him—"

Celia stared, not daring to believe her ears.

"You knew him?? You saw him??"

"I saw him a lot of times. We were friends. I can't remember exactly what he looked like, except he was tall and kind of good looking, with eyes...I guess his eyes were like yours...and the smile..."

She sat, stunned, not knowing what to make of what she was hearing.

"What else," she said slowly, "what else do you remember about him...?"

"Well...not much...I saw him that night...go up the fire escape, then the crowd...it sort of closed in, and I couldn't see him anymore."

Celia squeezed her eyes shut and saw her father struggling to bring the woman out. As Jonrobert spoke, she heard her mother screaming in the crowd.

"Your uncles were there too...but I don't think your mother really knew what happened. I mean, I don't think she ever knew about me...that's why your uncles said I had to leave...to keep her from finding out...and to keep you from knowing..."

Celia leaned back in her chair and took a deep breath. She wanted to close her eyes but was afraid that if she did, he would no longer be there when she opened them and this would be another dream that she would have to live with. So she stared at him, hard, until the image of him blurred.

...friends...they had been friends.... In the dream, I ran and ran and was always a finger's length away...and never understood what it all meant...I just kept running...

She thought of the figures in the dream. The wide hat, and the soft leather shoes...images mixing, merging...

She closed her eyes then and rested her head in her hands.

...all that time, and I never understood...

Mother must hear this story...if only to understand...what is happening in her own life...

She looked up and shook her head. "You know," she whispered, "you should have trusted me...or trusted something in our—"

"I know. I know," he said slowly. He gazed at her and then

looked away. "I think maybe I didn't trust myself. I just couldn't handle the idea that you might hate me for what happened..."

"...no...no...no." She reached for his hand. "Tell me again... about my father..."

The crowd in the bar ebbed and flowed with changing faces. The Otis Redding fan left and someone new programmed Wilson Pickett for the remainder of the night.

Beyond the noise and chatter, Celia re-stated questions to see if they fit old answers; and Jonrobert struggled to pull more detail from memory as they traced the warp and woof of a complex tapestry that seemed to bind them closer the more they unraveled it.

Finally, Celia looked at her watch and rose awkwardly from her seat. There was a nagging pain in her legs and her back felt stiff, but she remained standing as Jonrobert paid the bill. Then he turned to her.

"I know...I have no right to ask, especially after all that's happened, but...where are you headed?"

"To the airport...I have to see someone. A friend of mine..."

"...can't it wait?"

"No. It's important..."

There was a small silence in which each looked at the other and then looked away. Then Celia looked again and saw behind his painful smile a million questions biting at the tip of his tongue: Where was she going? Why was she going? Who was she going to see?

So she gathered her bag to her shoulder and prayed that he would not press for an answer.

With Marcus, she could be straightforward, explain her feelings in such a way that he would understand. But Jonrobert was different. He was always different.

She could feel him beside her as they walked through the bar and out into the crowded street. His presence overpowered everything, and her arms ached to touch him again.

A cab pulled to the curb and they climbed in. They rode several blocks before Jonrobert spoke again. His low voice was nearly lost in the noise of the traffic.

"Celia, it's been a long, long time...seems like I've been gone forever. I don't know how I'm gonna make this up to you. I—"

She reached over and her arms went to his shoulders and then around his neck. She touched his face and fanned her fingers over his mouth. "Don't say anything...not now...not now...I'll be back Sunday. We can talk then. We'll have plenty of time. Plenty of time..."

THE HARLEM WRITER'S GUILD PRESS ipsum dolor sit amet, consectetuer adipiscing elit, sed diam nonummy nibh euismod tincidunt ut laoreet dolore magna aliquam erat volutpat. Duis autem vel eum iriure dolor in hendrerit in vulputate velit esse molestie consequat, vel illum dolore eu feugiat nulla facilisis at vero eros et accumsan et iusto odio dignissim qui blandit praesent luptatum zzril delenit augue duis dolore te feugait nulla facilisi.

Lorem ipsum dolor sit amet, consectetuer adipiscing elit, sed diam nonummy nibh euismod tincidunt ut laoreet dolore magna aliquam erat volutpat. Ut wisi enim ad minim veniam, quis nostrud exerci tation ullamcorper suscipit lobortis nisl ut aliquip ex ea commodo consequat. Duis autem vel eum iriure dolor in hendrerit in vulputate velit esse molestie consequat, vel illum dolore eu feugiat nulla facilisis at vero eros et accumsan et iusto odio dignissim qui blandit praesent luptatum zzril delenit augue duis dolore te feugait nulla facilisi.

THE HARLEM WRITERS GUILD is Lorem ipsum dolor sit amet, consectetuer adipiscing elit, sed diam nonummy nibh euismod tincidunt ut laoreet dolore. Further information is available at

Please direct inquiries about the Harlem Writers Guild and Harlem Writers Guild Press to___.